Dale Peck

THE LAW OF ENCLOSURES

VINTAGE

Published by Vintage 1997

2 4 6 8 10 9 7 5 3 1

Copyright © Dale Peck 1996

The right of Dale Peck to be identified as the author of this work
has been asserted by him in accordance with the Copyright,
Designs and Patents Act, 1988

First published in Great Britain by
Chatto & Windus Ltd, 1996

Vintage
Random House, 20 Vauxhall Bridge Road,
London SW1V 2SA

Random House Australia (Pty) Limited
20 Alfred Street, Milsons Point, Sydney
New South Wales 2061, Australia

Random House New Zealand Limited
18 Poland Road, Glenfield,
Auckland 10, New Zealand

Random House South Africa (Pty) Limited
Endulini, 5A Jubilee Road, Parktown 2193,
South Africa

Random House UK Limited Reg. No. 954009

A CIP catalogue record for this book
is available from the British Library

ISBN 0 09 938961 4

Printed and bound in Great Britain by
Cox & Wyman, Reading, Berkshire

This book is for my stepmothers
ELISE, TERRY, and PAM
and for my father
DALE
φ
It is dedicated to the memory of my mother
EILEEN

Acknowledgments

For the many and various ways in which they've helped me and this book along, my thanks are due to the following people: Anne-Christine d'Adesky, Gordon Armstrong, Damien Boisvert, my editor in the U.K. Jonathan Burnham, Janet Burstein, Alex Chee, Michael Christie, Frances Coady, C. B. Cooke, Dennis Cooper, Michael Cunningham, Graham Dowey, Diane Ferrara, Steve Friedman, my editor in the U.S. John Glusman, John Goodman, LaTasha Harris, A. M. Homes, Dennis Hunter, Robert Jones, Judy Klein, Eric Latzky, Joy Linscheid, Ronnie Logallo, Will Luebking, Willem Melchior, Bruce Morrow, James Neil-Kennelly, Robbie Powell, David Rakoff, John Reed, Ivon Rosas, Roger Schulte, Alex Shapero, Choire Sicha, my agent Irene Skolnick, Malcolm Sutherland, Ida Veltri, Greg Vernice, John Warner, Edmund White, Scott Wilson, Linda Yablonsky, and my dentist Mike Young.

A special debt is owed to the staffs of Limbo café in New York City and First Out café in London, at whose tables most of this book was written for no more than the price of a cup of coffee.

I want, finally, to thank the John Simon Guggenheim Memorial Foundation for its support.

Spring 1990–Fall 1991

1

The Bough Breaks

The apparition of these faces in the crowd;
Petals on a wet, black bough.
Ezra Pound, 'In a station of the Métro'

1

Confection

The child Beatrice lived submerged in a world of emotion that swirled around everywhere but never touched her. Under water, in a wet suit, Beatrice felt the pressure of her parents' love for each other bearing against her own body: it lifted her up, it held her down, it tantalized her with its untouchable nearness. But she sensed that if she somehow managed to penetrate the thin membrane which separated her body from theirs, she would drown, and so she never poked too hard, just sat and watched, listened, silently. Watched and listened, and smelled and felt and even tasted: her parents' love was so palpable that it seemed to invade all her senses, and sometimes it was so strong that she floated to their bedroom on the current that filled the house whenever they were home, and in their small warm room the lid on emotions could never quite close. The heady air, the wrinkled bedspread, a discarded pair of underwear: all these things led Beatrice to believe that she was dangerously intoxicatingly close to their secret. Tucked into the pink plush of a chair, pretending that her attention was focused on the tiny black and white television, Beatrice witnessed again and again the contradiction of her mother's hair. Its gold plaits were as textured as the trail left behind a paintbrush; they made Beatrice think of running water gone suddenly cold, frozen. Hair swirled about her mother's head in a halo of long gentle rigid curls, each stuck in place by clouds of hair spray that fell on Beatrice's arms and clung to them like filaments from a spiderweb. 'Honey, please,' her mother would say if Beatrice dared touch the pointed tip of a curl,

'I'm trying to fix my hair.' Beatrice's father sat on their bed, and he too did a bad job of pretending to watch the television when his attention was really focused on his wife. Always, by the time her mother got to her hair, her father would be fully clothed, only shoeless, and on the quilted white satin bedspread his long legs in their dark pants floated like slivers of chocolate atop steamed milk. His hair was as short and wiry and dark as the brush her mother used, and his hands paced the length of his thighs. 'Pretty tonight,' he would say, every night, 'your hair.' In the corner chair Beatrice followed his gaze to its target, then looked at his eyes again, and then at the mantle of hair, and her mind filled with an image of candy-coated ice cream, soft underneath its outer shell. Her father's hands squeezed his legs lightly, his fingers ran through his hair, and the rippling brush played with light the way velvet does. And then her father would swing his legs in their black pants and black socks off the bed and slip them into black shoes, and then, together, her parents would be gone.

Later, it will come to seem prefigured: her mother had had to die before Beatrice could find herself, and her father had had to die before she could find Henry. There was an end to things, marked most clearly by her parents' death, and there was a new beginning, marked by her enrollment in college at the age of twenty-five—and then, as if in confirmation, there was Henry. Beatrice had lived exactly a quarter century: a third of her life, half her most productive years. Three-quarters of the age of Christ, she thought, and the whole of her youth was gone. She learned Christ's age through her literary criticism class, in which they were reading the Bible. The Bible fascinated Beatrice, but a stronger object of fascination was the young professor of the course. He was a man of about her own age who used his hands when he talked and who favored, on colder days, white and gray and black turtlenecks which made him seem quite skinny, in the way that Beatrice imagined scholars were skinny. Still, even Beatrice realized that scholars didn't teach at community colleges, but he *was* handsome, and Beatrice listened attentively when he spoke, though she couldn't imagine speaking to him. Instead, she took notes on everything he said so meticulously that on exams she was able to quote him verbatim.

But there was one thing she couldn't write down, and that was the moment when the professor stopped in the middle of a sentence at the same time as the door in the back of the classroom creaked open and creaked shut and then settled in the doorframe with a loud click. The professor was speechless for only a moment and then, a pained look on his face, he turned, made a mark in his roll book, and went on with the lecture. But the look on his face held Beatrice's attention for a while longer, long after, in fact, it had disappeared, until she realized that she'd never before seen anything animate the professor besides a book. She considered this carefully, not sure why it bothered her, until it occurred to her to wonder what had disturbed him. Beatrice remembered then the opening and closing creaks of the door, and the click as it latched. She turned around slowly, wondering how she'd be able to tell who'd come in late. The answer was simple: four rows back, three columns over, two weeks late for class, sat one boy who hadn't been there before, and, at the sight of him, Beatrice felt a spot of nothingness inside herself. She saw him: saw thin wrists and a thin neck poking from a sweater she'd have thought much too heavy for this weather, but then she supposed that if you were that thin you must get cold easily. Attached to his wrists were pale delicate hands with long fingers, and on top of his neck sat a head so perfectly spherical that it reminded her of a globe, an impression only heightened by the head's total lack of hair. He had neither eyebrows nor eyelashes, and his head wasn't darkened by even a shadow of stubble. She turned forward then, just as the young professor asked someone to explain what foreshadowing was. 'Foreshadowing,' the girl said, 'is predicting the future.' 'No-o,' the young professor said, his voice wobbling a little, 'that's prophecy.' Foreshadowing, Beatrice thought, and she turned around again, to

7

make sure that the boy really existed, and then she faced front for the rest of the class.

On the way out of class, a young black girl—they all seemed young to Beatrice, the girls there—tapped her on the shoulder, and when Beatrice turned at her touch she confronted an expression that was a mixture of confusion and determination and fear, and, seeing it, Beatrice took a step into the hallway to clear the door. Guardedly, she said 'Hello?' The girl blinked and looked down and said, 'Look, I don't know if I should say anything or not, it's just, well, I saw you turn when—' Just then the hairless boy came out of the classroom, and as he walked down the hallway Beatrice noticed again his slimness—no, thinness is the better word—the slender branch of a neck that poked from his sweater, his narrow shoulders, his flat ass, and she saw also a handkerchief dangling from the back pocket of his jeans. Then her eyes traveled back up his body and when she got to the hairless head her mouth dropped open in a silent O, for there, at the base of the boy's occipital bone, distending the globe of his skull like a polar distortion, protruded a lump the size of a robin's egg, and when Beatrice turned back to the girl she realized she'd been looking away too long, and when she saw the girl's expression, at once more confused and more determined, she knew that whatever she was going to say concerned the boy who was now walking out of the building. A flood of late-afternoon light cast a tenuous shadow behind him, and the door closed. 'His name is Henry,' the girl said then, and she laughed briefly, ruefully, and then she said, 'He's gay. He has AIDS. He—he's dying.' Her words hit Beatrice like barbed darts, and they hung from her skin painfully. 'Why are you telling me—' 'I saw the way you looked at him,' the girl cut in, and, as if she'd said something wrong, she blushed. 'Oh God,' she said. 'I'm sorry I had to be the one. It's just—you seem nice and all. You're Beatrice, right?' Beatrice nodded, and the girl stepped back from her. 'I've got to get to my next class. I'll, I'm Claire. I'll, um, I'll see you on Wednesday.'

She turned and ran down the hall, and Beatrice, dazed, watched her retreat, and as she watched she shuffled backward

8

out of the building. When she was outside she began to walk away from the building. She moved slowly at first, but the farther she went the faster she walked, and as she walked she pushed again and again at her hair, causing the sun to reflect off the silvery strands among the brown. The other students parted abruptly for her swiftly moving form, turned, looked back at her, and then turned away again, but Beatrice pushed on, almost running now. She made her way past a few more buildings, a few more people, she ran across a practice field at the edge of campus until she came to an oak tree, which she collapsed under and leaned against, and then she let her sobs free. She didn't know why she was crying. She only knew that she hadn't cried when her mother had died and she hadn't cried when her father had died, but now some dam had burst, and the stagnant water behind it was finally flowing away. Tears stung her eyes and steamed hot trails down her cheeks, rasping sobs burned her lungs the way pneumonia had burned them when she was a child. But when she finished crying she felt clean and empty, drained, but also full of energy. As she made her way to her car she thought of the boy called Henry. Before she had seen him, she realized, she had been waiting for something to happen. Now that she had seen him she knew he was what she'd been waiting for. Before, she had merely counted down the days, but now her mind was filled with an image of the white bulb of his hairless head, and she began to number her days from a new zero.

In the years following her mother's death, her father's intake of food had far surpassed his need for it, and his body had swelled like a balloon slowly but steadily and unceasingly filled with air, and by the time of the war Beatrice could only cook for him, and serve him, and stare at his bloated form as he watched the war on television. The flashing lights of night-time bombing raids sliced into his inflated white body and glinted off the silverware that moved without stopping from his plate to his mouth and back again, until, four weeks after the bombs had begun falling, they stopped. The enemy surrendered as winter surrenders to spring, and spring to summer, and in the rising heat Beatrice believed that she could smell the smoke of oil fires and burning homes and charred bodies, but then her nose cleared and she realized that all she smelled was her father's body, and her father's body smelled like death. He spilled out of his old chair in the living room and stared at the television, and on top of the television were five pictures of his wife, Beatrice's mother, and the images within all six frames— those holding his wife, and the television itself—were obscured by a settling film of dust and by the film that settled on his eyes, and in the days and weeks and months following the war he ate less and less of the food Beatrice brought to him until one day he asked her for a knife to cut his spaghetti instead of twirling it on his fork, and Beatrice knew that soon he would be rejoining his lost wife. And it was only when Beatrice thought of her father actually dying that she realized it had been seven years since her mother had been broadsided when she tried to access the Long Island Expressway from a newly completed on-ramp, and the sadness that had been the whole of her life since that day, the ache, the emptiness, the longing, the never-ending task of caring for her father, stepped away from Beatrice long enough for her to see that her own sadness, like her father's pictures, no longer resembled her mother, nor seemed, when it moved back inside her, to have anything to do with her mother at all. Her mother, she realized then, had always and only belonged to her father, and her father only to her mother.

It took a long time for Beatrice to accept the idea that her parents had never really loved her, but when she did accept it she accepted also that she had never really loved them, and this knowledge, like fire, eradicated everything that had been there before. Loveless, she felt capable only of hate, and on that day she called her father 'old man' and told him to cook his own meals. Before this small act of hostility she'd never disobeyed him, and what might seem like a delayed adolescent rebellion to some felt like civil war to her, and in its numbed aftermath she removed an application to the local community college from a drawer in the hutch, the seventh version of an application she'd filled out and never mailed every year since her mother's death, and this time she delivered it by hand to the campus. But by six o'clock her anger had dissipated, come unstuck like a traffic jam or a clogged artery: when she got home she made dinner for her father. She walked with his TV tray into the living room but he wasn't there. The television was on but the pictures of her mother weren't on the television; there were instead five outlines like footprints or shadows or ghosts in the dust on top of the console, and the shadowy footprints of a ghost-light form led down the hall, and Beatrice realized that her father had taken to his bed. That's how he came to live and that's how, four weeks later—a little more than three weeks before her college classes began and a little less than two months before she fell in love with another dying man—he died. He took with him, Beatrice felt, not just the remnants of his own life, but of his wife's, and her own. All he left behind were the dishes from his last meal, and these Beatrice washed and dried and returned to the cabinets and drawers from which she'd taken them, and there they waited, for whatever she might choose to cook next.

There were still grass stains on her skirt and tear tracks on her face when Beatrice lay down on her bed, and touched herself. She blushed when she thought of it in such old-fashioned terms, but she blushed even more when she thought of the word 'masturbating.' She closed her eyes and pulled her T-shirt above her breasts and pushed her panties around her ankles. She considered taking them off completely, but didn't, and then she made herself imagine the young professor. She imagined him naked. She knew the way his limbs would lock on to his torso with a minimum of fuss, and she guessed from the days before he started wearing turtlenecks, from the significant tuft of hair that poked through his unbuttoned collar, that he had hair all over his body, and it was the thought of that hair pressed against her own body that began to excite her, and then her

11

imagination took its usual turn as she was entered by a penis she couldn't really imagine since she'd never seen more than health class drawings of them—what did that word mean, she wondered, 'entered,' what did it feel like, did it feel like her finger?—and then she was reaching for her panties and pulling them up, but before she fell asleep she smelled her hand, and then she hid it under the pillow.

She sat in the back row of class after that. Before, she'd sat front row center, but now she found it impossible to sit so near a man she had imagined fucking, and she put herself all the way in back and it was only after the hairless boy came in a few days later that she remembered how for a couple of minutes she'd thought he could change, had changed her life, her new life, the one which had started with her father's death. And then she saw the black handkerchief hanging from his pocket and she remembered: he was gay, he had AIDS, he was dying. Some events should be scripted here, some record of Beatrice's thoughts for the next hour, but the next thing Beatrice knew class was over, and she sat up with a start. The other students filed out, but Beatrice remained behind, staring at the handkerchief that had caught in Henry's chair as he left. Then, slowly, making sure the last students leaving the classroom didn't see her, she grabbed it and pushed it deep in her pocket. It was her first theft and, like any first time, it placed an unexpected but very solid wall between what had come before and what came after. One of the things it fenced out was the young professor; one of the things it fenced in was Henry; and that night the thought of the professor produced not even a spark of passion. Beatrice sighed aloud, an old woman's sigh—an old maid's sigh, she thought as she heard it. A dull ache permeated her entire body. She thought this pain must be the frustrated ghost of the life she hadn't led, but she didn't succumb to its urgings and fake a feeling that didn't exist. Instead, she went to sleep. But in the morning, as she slipped on a shirt and put another in the hamper, pulled on pants and emptied the pockets of yesterday's, she found Henry's handkerchief. She stared at it blankly. Its white markings on their black background looked, to her unfocused eyes, like letters on a blackboard, and she

12

realized suddenly what the young professor had to do with her life. He wasn't the spark of a new story, he was what an already burning spark had set afire, burned, and consumed: the real flame was Henry. 'Henry.' She said his name aloud, and then she said, 'It's an old-fashioned name, but so is Beatrice, I guess. They're names you grow into,' and, at that, her voice fell off.

When Monday came she didn't go to class. She wasn't sure whom she couldn't bear to face, the young professor or Henry, but she stayed home and cleaned instead, and, as often happened, she came across a relic of her parents' existence. This time it was a silk scarf, long and thin and gold, the kind her mother had used to hold her hair back when every middle-class housewife was trying to dress like Jackie O. on a budget. Beatrice didn't remember this scarf, though, and as she held it in her hands she tried to imagine what it was: just a scarf she'd never seen, or perhaps a gift her father had planned to give his wife but never got the chance to. For a moment she allowed herself to think that it had been meant for her but, although her parents had given her things, she knew that neither of them would have given her this. It was the kind of thing they reserved for each other. Beatrice sat down with the scarf in her lap; she sighed, she snuffled, but she didn't cry. When her mother was alive, her parents' love for each other had overflowed its cup so much that she never understood it wasn't meant for her, and, despite herself, she missed that feeling. But there was nothing she could do about it now, and so she folded the scarf until it was a compact unidentifiable cube, she crammed all those memories into a tiny space and stuffed them in a drawer, and she went on cleaning. By the time she finished the day was gone; the windows of the empty house, clean and well lit, reflected only her own form as she passed from room to room. She shut the lights off then, but continued to walk aimlessly, her fingers trailing over objects as though she were a blind woman, and finally her fingers passed over Henry's, over the dying boy's handkerchief, and she picked that up and made a last slow circuit around her house, and then she went outside.

In the front yard she plopped herself onto the unmown damp grass. She felt her shirt and pants absorb the moisture, felt it immediately at the back of her neck, and on her wrists and ankles, and as she stared at the sky through the distant leaves and twigs and branches of a tree she felt that her entire self, her body and mind, was dissolving into the ground, that, come morning, all that would remain for the neighbors to find would be a thin scrim, the paste on a plate of food that's been eaten but now must be washed before the plate can be used again. And Henry's handkerchief—that would remain. She felt there was more substance, more real life in just this handkerchief than there was in her entire house, and that if some cataclysm should come along in her absence and destroy it—a fire, say, a nuclear explosion, a 'stray missile' like those which had wreaked so much havoc in last winter's war—there would be nothing for her to mourn, because there would be nothing that she could miss. She thought of the drama of Henry's life, for whatever else AIDS was, and she didn't want to think what else it was, it was different from the humdrum reality she lived and it bespoke a past that was already—well, exciting was the wrong word, but it was the right word too, or, at any rate, it was the only word she could think of—more exciting than any future she could envision for herself.

A car's lights passed over her then, and then another's and another's. A caravan of automobiles moved down her street and sent their headlights washing over Beatrice's body as she lay very still, afraid that she might be seen and thought foolish by people she didn't even know. But then, after several cars had gone by without noticing her, she remembered again her feeling of insignificance, and added to it now was invisibility as well, and she sat up, then stood up, and still the cars went by without stopping. Beatrice wanted to wave the handkerchief in her hand until a car pulled over, she wanted to climb into its warm unfamiliar interior and leave her life behind. But she didn't. She stood still as one after another the cars passed her until they were gone, and when they were gone she noticed that a wind was blowing, and that she was shivering, wet, and cold. And alone, she thought, as she turned to go into her empty house, and angry, and inside, on her parents' bed, she pulled up her skirt and spread her legs wide. How her face will burn with embarrassment when she remembers this; she felt embarrassed even as she did it but she did it anyway. She pushed Henry's handkerchief, wet now with sweat from her palms, into her pussy. It didn't matter that he was gay: the fact that he was dying overshadowed all that. And it didn't matter that she was invisible, insignificant: if her life was non-existent then she could do, would do anything, or at least this one thing. She would imagine Henry's body, lithe and slippery as an eel, coiling itself about her, touching her, loving her, entering her—fucking her, that was the word, fucking her—so that if, unlike her parents, she couldn't live for love, she could at least die from it.

ξ

His name was Henry. He wasn't gay, he didn't have AIDS, and he wasn't dying, though he thought he was. His name was Henry. He was straight, he had a brain tumor, and he thought the operation which could save his life would kill him. And he was beautiful, if only in the way that dying young men are beautiful. He was seventeen when he finally met Beatrice. Candy was bothering him that day—she'd been bothering him a lot lately—and he was hiding in the small conservatory on the edge of campus. He knew he should sit down before he fell down, but he didn't want to be discovered that way, so he kept walking. It seemed there were always people around him; he took every turn the paths offered even though he knew he was just retracing his steps, until finally there was only one woman who kept reappearing behind him like an apparition and it was no good anymore, he had to stop. He saw a boulder; he succeeded in not falling against it. He'd reached a point where even a bruise was intolerable, and the only pain he could take, a pain he almost relished, so long as it excluded all others, was his oldest, his dearest, his only friend, Candy. The stone he sat against was cold, almost wet, and his body was hot. By then the pain was migrating down from his head in waves and, to survive, he charted its course. Up in his head the pain was concentrated, solid, and yet there was a suggestion of fluidity

15

about it as well, like a sac filling with liquid. Suddenly it burst—that's when, when he was walking, his vision would blur—and his head burst into flame from the burning oil that spilled out. But almost immediately the pain dissipated, slipped down in a tight ache through his neck and into the rest of his body. It ran down his torso like lava and pooled for a second in his groin—there were times like these when he sat on the toilet, naked, so that if he had to, and he often had to, he could let the pain out of him that way—and then there were the tremors in his arms and legs as the pain moved through them and then, finally, he felt his fingers and toes do a little dance in the dirt as something that was not quite pain, something that was almost interesting, moved out of him and into the earth. After that he had a moment of peace. He couldn't gauge how long those moments lasted. Sometimes they seemed over before they started and other times they went on for so long that he thought the attack was over, but eventually the next sac would begin filling with its boiling liquid at the back of his skull. Or it wouldn't, and, slowly, he would open his eyes, always surprised to find that the ends of his fingers weren't open holes and that the ground around him wasn't muddy with whatever it was that had passed out of him. And this time, when he opened his eyes, she was there.

When he saw her he remembered the footsteps behind him, the one woman he couldn't shake. That was it, just a memory of sound; he still didn't feel ready for language. But she spoke: her mouth opened, sound came out. He glared at her and refused to answer, or even to understand, but she spoke again: 'Are you all right?' Fuck you, he thought, for asking such a stupid question. 'I'm fine.' 'You—you were asleep for a long time,' she said, and even as Henry realized she was lying he wondered, Why is she lying? But he only said, 'Is that all? Is there anything else you want to say?' At that, the woman looked ready to cry. She reached into her pocket and threw something at him. When she stood Henry saw that she was big, not fat, but tall and strong. 'This is yours,' she said. She brushed herself off then, and stood there. When Henry reached behind him to put the black bandanna in his pocket he found

16

a yellow one there already. He threw the black bandanna back at her. 'That's not mine,' he said. 'It is,' the woman insisted, 'you dropped it.' 'It's not,' he said, and he pulled his out. 'See?' he said. 'This one's mine.' 'It *is* yours,' she said again. She kicked it toward him. 'You left it in class the other day.' The bandanna splayed at Henry's feet as though it were a parachute tied to the body of a toy soldier, and as he looked at it he remembered that even though those parachutes never worked, the soldiers tied to them, plastic, invulnerable, always survived their falls. He still didn't pick it up; vaguely he remembered losing a bandanna a few weeks ago. When the woman spoke again it was in a whisper. 'I wanted to give it to you.' Henry looked up at her face, at her whisper. He looked at her until she was aware that he knew something was up, and then he looked away. The only things which could come out of his mouth would be unnecessarily cruel, and for the first time in years he didn't resort to that. Instead, he stood up. She was slightly taller than he was, and he looked up at her and, quietly, thanked her for returning his bandanna. When he bent to pick it up he was trembling a little; he tried to tell himself it was fatigue but he knew it wasn't, and he picked up the bandanna quickly, and without another word, walked away.

ξ

People give you presents when you're dying. Henry had sea-shells from Madagascar, red and white and blue gambling chips from Atlantic City, a doll made by gypsies somewhere in Eastern Europe. There was a marble chess set made in Mexico whose pieces were carved in the shape of long-dead Aztec gods, a gumball machine whose empty glass ball was the size of his head, and a Monopoly set in French—and another in German, and another in Spanish, and another in Japanese. These gifts had always infuriated him with their durability, their blatant boast that they would last longer than he would, and he hated too the way these objects planned out what little future he had left. Any repeated action is a way of measuring time, and to Henry these gifts were like notches on a stick, strikes against

17

the days he had known, and against those days he wouldn't. And now there was this woman's—his—bandanna. When he'd left her he'd carried it in his hand for a while but, having no other place to put it, he tied it on his head. It was something his mother insisted he do: wear a hat or tie a bandanna over his head whenever he left the house, as if it could conceal the fact that there was no hair under it. To appease her, he always left the house with his head covered, but as soon as he was out of sight he pulled the bandanna off and stuffed it in his back pocket. Usually he forgot to put it on before he came home but his mother never said anything: it was enough that he made it home. His mother spent her days cleaning the house, shopping for groceries, maintaining the yard, worrying always that the phone would ring and a strange voice would tell her that Henry was sick, that Henry was at the hospital, that this was it; and Henry knew she thought these things because she told him so, every day. She spoke to Henry in a feverish voice, told him she had to think this way, told him it heightened her appreciation of the time she had with him. She held his hand when she talked and looked fixedly at any part of the room that didn't contain him, and Henry sat there helplessly, joined with his mother in the task of waiting for his death.

But Henry didn't know what death was. He tried to imagine it sometimes: not death, but a pain so great he would wish for death. Though he'd lived so close to it for so long, the mystery of it was still that—a mystery, a word which meant nothing more than its definition. Sometimes he awoke in the morning thinking that while he'd slept he'd come close to an understanding, but by the time he opened his eyes his realization was just a fleeing figure in the distance. He'd been sick for so long that it seemed he'd never been well. He supposed he hadn't—Candy became visible just before he started kindergarten, but she'd probably always been there, waiting to appear. But still, there'd been a few years when everyone had believed everything was okay, that he, like any other child on the block, would live forever, and sometimes Henry tried to understand that too, or at least remember it. But even those memories fled from him, leaving him trapped and alone. This was all he knew: the dying

18

live somewhere between life and death, but he knew too that the living inhabit the same space. This dying boy lived in a roomful of curios which stared down at him with stone eyes, bone eyes, wooden eyes, plastic eyes, felt eyes, and even his bandanna seemed to stare at him, and command his attention.

Henry looked at it, but there wasn't much to see: paisleys, diamonds, other shapes that he supposed had names but which to him were just the things people pattern bandannas with. No, there was nothing to be gained by looking at it, or turning it over and over in his hands, and so he smelled it. He hadn't meant to. All he'd done was put it on his face the way gangsters in black-and-white movies do when they want to knock someone out with chloroform, and, when he thought of that, he breathed in as deeply as he could and pulled into his nostrils a scent not of chloroform—not of any poison—but of perfume and powder and sweat and body fluids that weren't his own: Henry smelled Beatrice, and he threw the bandanna into the air and filled the silence of his house with a shout. 'Fish!' He lay still then, laughing quietly, while his voice faded and the bandanna—ah, that parachute!—floated to the floor. He was still laughing when his mother knocked at the door. 'Henry?' she said without opening it. He managed a last chuckle. 'What?' 'Are you hungry?' 'No,' Henry said, and he resisted the urge to add, Go away. 'Oh. I thought I heard—' 'I'm fine,' he cut her off. 'I was only dreaming.' And he *was* only dreaming, to think that the woman who had followed him had somehow left that particular scent on the bandanna, and to think that she could have left it there for him. But he clung to that dream nevertheless, and it stayed with him until he fell asleep. While he slept, a hunter stumbled loudly through a thicket in upstate New York. Later, when he told his story to the media, the hunter would claim that he had found himself in the midst of hundreds of deer whose coats had been the deep murky red of arterial blood, and he stood among them, he said, so stunned that it never occurred to him to lift his gun to his shoulder. The deer eyed him and each other warily, pressed their noses into each other's flanks, and rubbed against oak trees as if as startled as the hunter to find themselves the color they were. But then, when the red didn't come off, they seemed to forget that they had ever been less wondrous than they'd become, and they bounded off in search of more important things, food, sleep, a mate, and they left the hunter alone. Henry saw him on a talk show the next morning: the hunter admitted he had no proof of what he had seen, and as he told his elaborate tale Henry thought of Beatrice, and he smiled. He had proof. He had their bandanna.

Prophecy is predicting the future, but fantasies about the future by a dying boy are just wishful thinking. Henry had thought he was beyond the reach of both. He didn't need a prophet to tell him what his future would be—he had doctors—and he believed he no longer had any wishes. Still, he went to his next literary criticism class on time. He'd left the bandanna at home but its smell was still with him, and he filled the empty space next to the woman's body with his own, and quickly, because he knew it was now or never, he leaned over and whispered, 'I'm Henry,' and after class they went to a diner. He *looked* like a fag, in black cap turned backward, in white V-neck T-shirt and ratty wool cardigan, in jeans that hung loosely from his body. Beatrice was lost in a dress. It was long and green and cotton and had no shoulders, but she'd worn a gray shirt under it which covered them, and too much of her hair, Henry thought, was trapped by a thin band of gold silk. She had incredible hair, thick, tightly curled, silvery brown, a mass that would have framed her face like a lion's mane. That face was exposed now, as was the neck that supported it, its small ears, the nearly invisible down that grew just in front of her ears. It was an amazing accumulation of details, and Henry wanted to trace each one of them, not just with his eyes, but with his fingers and tongue. Beatrice's eyes remained blank while Henry examined her until, blushing slightly, she looked down, and then she put her hand on Henry's, but Henry, afraid to do anything more than look, pulled his hand away. Literally: he used his right hand to move his left hand, which lay under hers, and then there was a bit of dead time between them while Beatrice fiddled with the mini-jukebox. Then they ate: Henry had a milk shake, and Beatrice had mashed potatoes and gravy; Henry had a slice of apple pie, and Beatrice drank a cup of coffee; Henry had pierogi—potato, boiled, sour cream on the side—and Beatrice nibbled at them, and, after their fourth or fifth round, Henry could see the waitress practically cringe as she approached their table.

They switched, finally, to beer, and that seemed the necessary catalyst. After two each, Beatrice said, 'You know, um, you know, at school they think you're gay.' Henry stared at her, and then he took a drink, and he said, '*What?*' Beatrice laughed. She shrugged her shoulders and she said, 'This black girl told me you were gay.' 'Why would she say a thing like that?' '*I* don't know,' Beatrice said, and she laughed again, and took a long drink. She sighed then. 'Your hair—I mean, your head.' She scratched her own head, and her fingers pulled a thick strand of hair free from her scarf, and Henry had to resist the urge to touch it. Instead, something about her face made Henry reach for his beer as she opened her mouth. 'They, um, they say you've got AIDS.' The beer in Henry's mouth spewed from it in a gold and white plume. It was laughter that had spewed it out, laughter that had erupted from a place he didn't know still existed within him. It was convulsive, and it proved contagious: his beer sprayed into Beatrice's face, and her eyes and mouth went wide in shock, and then she too was laughing, choking, snuffling. They slumped in their chairs, their knees knocked hard under the table, they laughed even harder. People stopped eating to stare at them and they stared back—a little crazily, Henry thought, they *were* crazy—and he stuck out his tongue at an old man, who averted his eyes and stabbed a french fry at his face so quickly that he missed his mouth and smeared ketchup all over his wrinkled cheek. When they had finally finished laughing Henry said, 'It's called alopecia universalis.' Beatrice sputtered, '*What* is?' 'My hair,' Henry laughed. 'My missing hair. I have a dis—a condition called alopecia universalis. It makes you lose all your hair.' Beatrice twittered, and then she was calm. 'It'll never grow back?' Henry made himself focus then; he kept his mind on his lie. 'Never,' he said, and then, slowly. Beatrice reached across the table and ran a finger under the rim of his cap. Henry concentrated all his energy on her finger, on just her finger. When she took it back from him she drew a circle in the residue of gravy on her plate and then she licked her finger clean. 'Well,' she said, 'I think it's sexy.'

Henry was nervous, because he knew he couldn't continue his charade, and he could see Beatrice pick up on his anxiety. As she looked at her menu at another restaurant a few days later, she pulled her hair into long silver and brown lines, and she twisted the ends into little knots between her fingertips. Henry imagined that it must hurt her when she combed them out; he imagined long strands littering the floor of her bathroom, her bedroom, outlined against her pillow, clogging her shower's drain. 'Quiet tonight,' Beatrice said eventually. 'Tonight?' Henry said, and Beatrice said, 'You. You're quiet.' He saw a conversation unfolding like a road map then, and he knew that it could only take one of two routes: either he would tell Beatrice he was dying or he would drive her away, but either way the final destination would be the same, and, to speed that end, he said, 'Are you in love with me?' Beatrice sat back. She nodded her head, then shook it, then nodded it again quickly, and then she surprised him. 'Do your parents love each other?' she said, and it was Henry's turn to sit back. 'I don't suppose it matters,' he said, 'they're married.' 'Mine did,' Beatrice said. 'They were like a story or something, a romance novel. They *burned*.' It was almost too easy to redirect the anger he felt at Candy against Beatrice: 'So,' he sneered, 'what?' Beatrice went on as though she hadn't heard. 'I can't remember how old I was when I first walked in on them. She was on top of him and the sheet was over them, but I could tell they were naked, and my mother's hair—my mother had this long hair she always wore glued into place, but that day it was all tangled around my father's face.' When Beatrice paused for breath,

22

Henry said, 'Are you trying to make me hard?' At his words Beatrice shut her mouth and stared at him so hard that Henry blushed. 'They were very mature about it,' she said. 'They said, Honey, come back later, and then they bought a lock for their door.' She bit her lip. 'I think they were too mature about it, actually.' Henry tried to cut in. 'Yeah, well, it's not that way for my parents—' But Beatrice spoke over him. 'They met when they were seniors. In high school. My father says they were never apart for a single day after that.' 'That's impossible,' Henry said, and Beatrice said, 'My parents were impossible. When you were around them you felt that the laws of nature and the laws of men just didn't apply. If they wanted to they could just fly away.'

Henry got lost in that for a moment. He imagined it, he wanted it, he wanted to fly away with Beatrice, but all he said was, 'My parents just dig at each other, all the time. They're digging each other's graves.' And then, for emphasis, he added, 'I'm sure I take after them.' They had their food, and Beatrice took a few bites before she said, 'It was all a lie of course. The truck that hit my mother spread her over the road like sausage on a pizza.' She stopped suddenly, as if her words had surprised her, but she didn't take them back, and she didn't apologize. Henry put his fork down with a loud bang. 'Well, I'm not trying—' 'Why do you keep assuming I'm talking about us?' She smiled then, and said, 'I mean, about *you*.' For a moment Henry thought he was being made a fool of, but then he realized he was a fool. 'Well, you are,' he said, 'aren't you?' 'I believe I was talking about my parents.' She continued to smile at Henry while he sat there confused and a little angry—or maybe he was angry and a little confused, he wasn't sure. He only knew that he'd been tricked somehow, and suddenly he was frantic. It was the way Beatrice spoke, her spine straight even as she leaned forward, her fingers flat-pressed on the table, the utter conviction of her tone: he felt her stealing his ability to resist. 'Look,' he said, 'I don't love you, okay? I can't.' Beatrice, still leaning close to him, smiled. 'Liar,' she said. And then it was over before he knew he was doing it. There was just Beatrice's turned face and the growing red mark on her

23

cheek and Henry's outstretched arm. There was a waiter at their table, then another, and then another. A fat hand gripped Henry's thin shoulder. 'What the *fuck* is going on here?' 'I'm sorry,' Henry said, 'I didn't mean to, I didn't know what I was doing, I, I'm sorry.' And then Beatrice's voice, again, stopped everything. 'It's okay,' she said, 'it's just that he loves me.' The waiters retreated, immediately satisfied, and in that moment Henry was glad he was dying because he knew that what Beatrice said was true, and he knew too that as long he lived he would never bring this woman anything but pain.

Later that evening Candy set upon him in a great explosion that knocked him off his feet. He awoke hours later in a bubbly puddle of saliva and tears and urine, and he mopped this up with shaky arms, seeing in the stewy liquid his future revealed as though he looked into a gazing pool, and he read there increasing debilitation and even incontinence—it was the kind of word he knew someone like him wouldn't normally use, but he'd been expecting it for a while. And he knew too that whether or not anything more happened between them he had to tell Beatrice he was dying, and the thought of that confrontation scared him more than the thought of dying itself, and so he drank. He pulled the whiskey straight from the bottle, three hot mouthfuls, and then, before he could change his mind, he climbed out his window and into his car. As he drove he felt the whiskey kick in, one, and his limbs loosened a little bit, two, and they loosened a little more and he took a hand off the wheel to roll down the window, three, and with a start he gripped the wheel tightly again and fixed his eyes on his destination: Beatrice, asleep in her canopied bed in a white lace nightgown, dreaming dreams that he could never know. And then he was there. He pushed her window open, sprawled into her bedroom in a drunken pile. In the light she turned on he saw her rubbing her eyes like a little girl, and he was surprised to see no mark on her cheek where he'd slapped her earlier. She slept in an old T-shirt rather than a nightgown, there was no canopy, and she said, 'The door wasn't locked.' Every part of her body was bigger than his, and beautiful, and he wanted to crawl inside. 'Beatrice!' he said, and he crossed the few feet to her bed and fell to his knees, his upper body splayed across the foot of her bed. Beatrice, in a calm voice, only said, 'Henry?' 'I'm dying,' he whispered, 'I'm as good as dead.' At his words, Beatrice turned out the light, but the room wasn't dark enough to hide her smile. Henry's voice was hoarse. 'Can you live without me?' he said, and Beatrice said, 'Yes,' quickly, and then she said, 'but I wouldn't want to.' He felt her fingertips on his head then, feeling the bumps there but avoiding, again, the one prominent lump, and then they were gone. 'Go now,' she said then, 'we both need sleep,' and he left and she fell asleep almost immediately, safe in the only truth she knew: that Henry loved her with a passion as great as any she read about in her literature class, a passion that meant the loss of his life and the gain of hers. She never once thought Henry was truly dying. I'm dead, he'd said. Her mother was *dead*, her father was *dead*: Henry clearly wasn't dead, and she decided he meant that he was lost, lost in love, lost to her. Later, after she learned that Henry really was dying, and after she learned that he would live, she thought that sometimes you walk right into language as though it's a chair out of place in a dark room: a word, an expression you live with all your life can become suddenly, completely unfamiliar. That night Beatrice stumbled over death, but it was dark, and she was tired, and she believed that she had stumbled across love.

2

The Window above Every Kitchen Sink in America

When they left it was midnight. By one the orange building-studded skyline of the city dominated the horizon, and by two they'd cleared it, enduring only minor delays on the Belt Parkway. Three o'clock found them racing through the dark hills of rural north Jersey, and by four they'd crossed the Delaware Water Gap into Pennsylvania. Around five they slipped into the lowlands of New York State, and sometime between six and seven, as the sun rose, they took the wrong exit that spun them off toward northeastern New York, toward Vermont, toward Canada for God's sake, but by then they were fighting and didn't notice their error until well past eight. The clock at the next tollbooth read nine exactly, and the clerk smirked in reply to Hank's request for directions. 'From the city?' he drawled, staring at Hank's bald head, at the stubble and brown spots and wrinkled skin collected there, and when Hank answered, 'The island,' the clerk winced exaggeratedly. 'The island, huh? Almost worse, the island.' Then he relented and pointed them toward Ithaca, and Bea fell asleep and dozed uneasily until around ten, pretending that her upset stomach was just carsickness. By eleven they were screaming again, but at noon Hank cut in with, 'We're nearly there,' and a little while later he said, 'Ten more minutes,' and they stopped fighting then, and Bea began to dread what awaited them. Roads dwindled rapidly in size as they approached their destination: the interstate dropped from eight lanes to six, the next highway had four, the road after that only two. 'This is it,' Hank said then, 'this is their road,' and Bea took a deep breath,

26

and sighed, and turned her attention out the window, and she had to stifle a gasp then because it was as if she'd fallen asleep again and awakened in a new world.

She found herself in mountains, surrounded by mountains, long low mountains dressed in the pale greens of spring, and here and there a hole cut into this fabric revealed a house, a horse pasture, the parallel lines of a cultivated field, and when the car slowed Bea thought Hank's attention, like her own, had been caught by a particularly beautiful lot. The wireless poles of a fence enclosed it, and it had been cleared and graded but remained undeveloped, and only dandelions grew on its flat surface. But they were the biggest dandelions Bea had ever seen, stems tall as wheat and blooms big as daisies, and they formed a mossy yellow carpet across acres of land. They were so big they reminded Bea of sunflowers; she'd seen a documentary on sunflowers ages ago, and what she remembered most were entire fields of flowers facing the rising sun each morning and imperceptibly turning their heads to follow it across the sky all day until, by nightfall, every flower faced west. The image, inexplicably, had struck Bea as oppressive as much as it was impressive, but then, when the object which demanded all her attention spoke next to her, she understood the sunflowers' plight. 'We're here,' Hank said, and then he said, 'And I'm glad. If I had to spend one more second with you I'd drive us over a cliff.'

Bea took a last look at the dandelions. They stood straight up or drooped to the ground in every direction, but no matter which way they faced their multitude infused them with a ragged beauty and made the skinny tin-sided trailer which housed Stan and Myra seem even shabbier by comparison. Long ago it too had been yellow, but the elements had aged it like overtanned skin, and its color was streaked now in softer and harder, but all faded, shades of dun. A small window was filled with the convex shadow of a cut-open plastic bag, fastened in place and criss-crossed by strips of duct tape which suggested opaque panes of glass, and the lattice of thin wooden slats which skirted the trailer was also painted yellow, and also faded, and punctured by a few dark jagged holes that reminded

Bea of the entrances to animals' lairs. 'Hank,' she said, and turned to him again. 'I don't think I can do this.' Hank turned the car off. 'Little late to back out now.' 'Hank,' Bea said, 'he's dying in there. Doesn't that—' She reached for a word but couldn't find it. 'Doesn't that affect you?' Hank just snorted. 'People can die anywhere, I guess. Even in a piece-of-shit trailer.' He stepped out of the car and stood up; he closed the door without waiting to hear what she said. Bea stepped out of the car then, looked around, and again she was struck by the fact that she had no idea where she was, nor how she'd gotten there. Sixty-seven years of history hung like a tattered cape from her neck. Every time she'd turned around to examine the cape it had turned with her and eluded her sight, and, by the time she stepped out of the car in Stan and Myra's driveway, she had stopped turning long ago. As she walked toward their trailer she looked neither left or right nor backward, only forward, only blindly forward.

Yesterday:

In the morning, after a night's reprieve, they plotted strategies of war. Sleep, Bea wondered, was that a reprieve? She supposed that it was, or that, in any case, after forty years of marriage it would have to do, and as the decades had passed she'd taken refuge in her bed more and more, using pills to knock her out when her body refused to sleep, and then using more pills to wake her in the morning. Now, groggy, groggily, she looked at her reflection in the toilet bowl. The toilet was light blue and its water was tinted a darker blue by the cleaner in the tank, and Bea kidded herself that she preferred the image offered her by the blue water to that in the mirror over the sink. No colors in this picture, she thought, save the blues of bowl and water: no gray hair or pallid lips or pale skin that a better reflecting surface might have brought out. Fewer wrinkles too, and it was harder to notice that her lips and eyes were losing their shape. For years Bea had taken secret pride in the fact that her lips and eyes were exactly the same shape, a long flat-on-top

28

curved-on-bottom oval. Only a few people had ever noticed that; Hank hadn't, and, Bea reflected, now he never would. Then she heard water plunging into the tub behind her and with the sound another wave of nausea rose from her stomach to her mouth and then, so painfully that it took all her effort not to cry out, her image in the water was splashed away. Not much came out; most of it had come out during the night. Bea wiped her mouth with a bit of toilet paper and flushed quickly, because she didn't want her face to reappear pocked with lesion-like chunks of vomit. She turned off the tub tap, pulled the plug. She knotted her robe tightly around her stomach, then loosened it, and then she made her way to the kitchen, where the Sunday paper waited, and coffee, and Hank.

The paper was on the table and the coffee in the pot and Hank at the sink, and he didn't turn from the window above it when she entered the room. His skinny old body was covered by pale blue pajamas and a dark blue robe, and the mottled skin and gray fuzz on his skull—he didn't shave it on weekends—caught the morning sun and glowed a little, whitely, and Bea could see that his hands cupped a big round-bodied cup of coffee, full and steaming and fogging the window with its steam. 'Hands bothering you?' she said in the most neutral voice she could muster, and poured herself coffee. Hank didn't answer her. 'It seems a waste of perfectly good coffee,' she went on, pulling the paper into sections, 'to pour yourself a cup just to warm the arthritis out of your hands.' Hank still didn't answer, but she saw him raise the cup to his lips and take a small sip, and grimace; she smiled. She fished a few bobby pins from the pocket of her robe and dropped them on the table, and as she skimmed a roundup story on the war she pinned her hair out of her eyes. A long time later she heard the quiet gurgle of Hank's coffee being poured down the drain, the click of his cup on the counter, the swirl of more coffee filling it; she got up and poured herself another cup as well, and looked at the brown film on the bottom of the sink. 'What a waste,' she said, and finally Hank spoke. 'My hands,' he said, 'are just fine,' and he drank from his cup again as if that proved it. At the table Bea's bobby pins caught her eye;

29

she hesitated only a moment and then she picked up a pin and tossed it at Hank's feet. 'Oh, Hank,' she said quietly, 'I dropped a bobby pin. It's right there, by your right foot. Could you get it for me?' Hank turned from the window, looked down at the floor and then up at her. His expression was unreadable, and she tried to keep her eyes steady against his but couldn't, and they dropped to the paper. From the corner of her eye she saw Hank bend slowly, and then he took a hand from his coffee cup and reached for the bobby pin. His fingers were calcified and stiff, his knuckles swollen and unbending, and his nails scratched at the linoleum with a sound that reminded Bea of the tick-tock the claws of a lobster had made last night as it ran across the floor, just before she'd picked it up and dropped it in boiling water. Hank made several attempts to pick up the pin but he simply couldn't. Finally he gave up. He stood up, and Bea heard his knees pop, and then, stiffly, silently, he walked to the door. The morning, Bea thought, is mine; but then Hank stopped.

'Won't your water be cold?'

Bea looked up, and there was her mortal enemy. He had summoned an expression of impassive hatred which, after a lifetime together, was as strange to her as the sight of her own face. 'Didn't I hear you running a bath earlier?' 'N-no,' Bea stammered, and then she said, 'I washed my face. Maybe that's what you heard.' Hank's eyes probed her dirty face and she had to turn away. 'Oh,' she heard finally, and heard clearly the triumph in his voice. 'I could've sworn I heard the tub filling up,' and then he was gone, but Bea continued turning pages for a long time, and her stomach, which had receded from her attention, started to churn again. It was a caption that saved her. 'Mystery Deer: Looks Normal, But Fur Is Red.' That was all she read; she looked at the black-and-white photograph of a deer, its splayed legs, the nubbins of antlers poking from its skull, its colorless fur, and from somewhere in her mind came a piece of trivia whose origin she didn't know. Bette Davis, she remembered, had appeared in a brilliant red gown in some movie whose title she couldn't remember, but what she did remember was that the gown had in reality been a rich chocolate brown, which for some reason appeared more red-like than any other color on black-and-white film. This deer's fur was just gray, and the photograph seemed to Bea particularly pointless. It was like so many of the photographs and television images of the war, just black rectangles with streaks of white in them which looked more like expressionist paintings than the night-time bombing raids which captions or voice-overs claimed they were; or the photographs they printed now, tank-tracked deserts and distant fires and pyramidal piles of rubble on which children climbed, as though playing king of the mountain. Bloodless: those photographs, and this photograph of the deer, were bloodless; the unseen and uncounted bodies of the dead hadn't even been plowed into their mass graves and already the papers were printing the sprouting springtime heads of deer. Of red deer, Bea scoffed, but before she turned the page she skimmed the short article which accompanied the photograph. It told her little: that there had been several sightings of these deer, and that most of them had been near the nuclear power plant that had just been completed up in Ithaca—that made her laugh.

And then time collapsed in on itself: she remembered Stan and Myra, old friends who'd moved to Ithaca when Stan took a job with the power plant. She hadn't thought about them in years, but later in the day, she called them. Myra answered; when Bea hung up Hank was looking at her and not at the television. 'What's wrong?' he said. Her first impulse was to lie: 'Nothing.' Then she sighed. 'It's Stan,' she said. 'He has cancer. He—' She stopped, looked at Hank, prayed he wouldn't start something. 'He's dying,' she said. 'Myra said it's just a matter of days.'

Myra's lawn was patchy, the patches of grass unmown, the patches of earth littered with cigarette butts. Bea found her feet landing in the bare patches, as though they were unwilling to hurt the struggling grass. She lifted her eyes then, to Hank's skinny legs in their stiff new pants, to his skinny back, to his

31

bare bald head and the faded X of a scar at the base of his skull, and she marveled that it had come to this. What had come to this, she wondered, what had it come to? She didn't know, didn't want to. Easier to understand were the porch steps that creaked under their feet and the X of tape over the doorbell; there were hinges for a screen door but nothing fastened to them. 'Jesus,' Hank muttered, and then he rapped loudly on the hollow wooden door. Myra pulled it open as Hank's hand was moving to strike it a third time and he nearly hit her in the face: Myra was short and, shoeless but in worn socks, at her minimum height. 'Sshh,' she said. There was a cigarette in her mouth and a stream of smoke flew out with the sound. She stepped outside quickly and closed the door. 'He's taking a nap. He had trouble sleeping last night, so I thought we'd let him rest.' She drew on her cigarette, threw it into the yard. She smiled. 'Look at you, baldy,' she said, and she gave Hank a quick hug and a smoky kiss, and turned to Bea. 'Looks like you still got all your hair,' she said. 'A little gray—' Bea began, but Myra was still talking. 'You always had the most beautiful head of hair I ever saw. Compared to mine—ugh!'

Her hands were busy shaking another cigarette from the pack, and Bea noticed they were trembling even as they shook. Myra tossed her head, as if for emphasis, and her thin brown hair, a little dirty, streaked randomly with gray, parted unevenly down the middle, obliged her by sending a few tangled strands into her face. She pushed them back with the hand that held the cigarette, now lit, but the strands separated like fraying rope and seemed stuck to the skin of her cheek. That skin was greasy but Bea tried not to notice because Myra seemed ready to collapse under the weight of negative adjectives. 'At least you got hair,' Bea heard Hank say then, and he pushed the hair out of Myra's face with his stiff fingers. Bea turned to look at him, and in a revelation that shook her with its clarity she knew how Hank must have won his mistresses during the early years of their marriage. Myra barked a laugh and ran her knuckles over the gray fuzz that covered Hank's temples. 'Guess it keeps my head warm, right?' she said brightly—too brightly. 'In winter, I mean.' 'Right,' Bea said, too quickly, too loudly. There was a long silence then, punctuated only by Myra's puffs on her cigarette, and then Myra said, 'Aw, I'm sorry.' Bea looked up at her. 'I know it's him who's suffering, but it's me, I mean, sometimes I feel like it's me who could just drop—I mean, fall down.' Bea was sure Myra had meant to say 'drop dead' before she caught herself. 'Myra,' Hank said, 'we know this is hard on you too. Nobody says it isn't hard on you too.' 'Oh, I don't know,' Myra said, 'sometimes I think there's no difference between being married to a dying man and a living one. Either way, you just gotta take care of him.' The three people on the porch stared at each other for a long time, and nobody mentioned the fourth person inside. Finally Hank said, 'Look, why don't we go in, have a cup of coffee, sit, calm down,' and Myra shook her head as if clearing it. 'Coffee,' she said. 'I live on coffee. And cigarettes.' She drew on her cigarette, threw it into the yard. 'Sshh,' she said again, in another puff of smoke, and she pushed open the door.

The door opened onto the kitchen, a small room divided into cramped cooking and eating areas by an awkwardly angled counter, and on the counter, Bea saw, were five clocks, four of which told the wrong time; she decided not to ask. The room was brightly lit by the window above the sink and by sliding glass doors which, incongruously, were blocked by a plastic-topped, metal-legged table and three vinyl-upholstered chairs. Threads of smoke—no, not threads, but ribbons, whole bolts of smoke—hung in the air, and the light passing through them would have been beautiful, Bea thought, if this scene had been in a movie. She and Hank walked purposefully to the table, and as the two of them walked past a doorway Bea caught a glimpse of a dark couch which held a white figure like a single egg in its nest. She and Hank took seats at opposite ends of the table while Myra poured coffee at the counter. An uncovered bowl of sugar and a carton of milk sat on the table; there was ash in the sugar and Bea suspected that if the warm air hadn't been clogged with smoke she'd have been able to smell the milk's rancidness. 'Oh, don't sit there,' Myra said to Bea when she came to the table, clutching three mismatched cups in her hand. 'I sit there so I can—' She nodded toward the door; she spoke loudly, but she didn't say Stan's name aloud, and Bea wondered why as she moved to the chair which faced the glass door. Bea knew the coffee would be bad even before she tasted it, but it was worse than she expected, sweet and thick, as though made with corn syrup instead of water, more than a little crunchy with grounds. Myra pushed the ashy sugar bowl toward Bea but Bea declined it. She noticed words written on her cup then: 'My sediments exactly' it read, and the caricature of the woman who was supposed to be saying them looked, remarkably, as tired and as crazy as Myra. It made Bea smile, a bright flash of teeth and emotion she hid by turning her face to her cup, and she saw them reflected on the brown surface of her coffee – her face, her smile, her teeth, and her emotion – until a tremor in her hand rippled it away, and she felt in that moment as if she were falling over a cliff. 'So, how've you been?' she heard Hank say somewhere far above her, and she was almost relieved to hear him back to his dense old self again. 'Good,' Myra said, as though the conversation they'd had ten minutes ago had never happened. Bea stared into her coffee without speaking, and Hank and Myra's words retreated from her like a thick dark shadow made thin and transparent by a suddenly shifted light. She heard Lucy's name, something about how she helped out with things. Lucy, Bea thought, she must be twenty, thirty – she was Susan's age. She looked up, thinking she should join the conversation, but her attention was caught by the back yard and the shock she felt when she saw it was the shock she'd felt earlier when she'd looked out the car window.

'Back yard' seemed inadequate to describe what she saw: a swath of green lawn running away from the house until some-where in the distance it dipped into a foliage-filled ravine of even denser green and then, in a grand spectacle of nature, rose into a perfectly smooth mound of mountain covered by trees which seemed practically forced into it in overabundance, like a clove-studded orange made by a child in elementary school. A pomander, Bea remembered, an orange with cloves pressed into it is called a pomander, and she whispered aloud, 'The pomander mountain. Mount Pomander.' Thoughts flitted

34

through her brain then, flickering and distant from each other like a swarm of fireflies in a field, and then they coalesced suddenly, as though the fireflies had been caught in a jar, and Bea realized that the past few minutes had been more emotional, more emotion-filled than the past forty years of her married life. But something had happened when she looked at the mountain. Something had cracked. For years, there had been an idea in her head—the idea of a clove-studded orange—and there had been a word, and suddenly, finally, they were joined. A clove-studded orange is a pomander: it was that simple, and it was that limited; nothing else came to her. There were other ideas, less clearly felt, and there were other words—'sadness,' 'money,' 'Henry,' 'death'—and these pairs were not joined but remained separated, remained waiting. Bea noted them. She felt them waiting, but she pushed them away from herself, just as for years she'd pushed away any thoughts save hatred for the person on her right. She was shielding herself and she knew it, in the past and in Myra's kitchen as well, but she let herself off the hook because she knew that soon the dying man would awaken, and to deal with that she would need all her strength.

Stan didn't awaken: he continued sleeping, a ghostly presence in the house, talked around but never talked about. Later, as the light faded, Myra hung a stained bedsheet across a rope that hung in the doorway to the living room, in which Stan had begun to snore. The snores relieved Bea, gave her something to focus on besides Hank and Myra; they assured her Stan wasn't dead. Myra, and Hank as well, had abandoned any effort at quietness, and at some point a whiskey bottle had appeared next to the milk and sugar. Bea added some to her coffee and watched the sun set behind the distant mountain. For a long time there was a beautiful pattern of orange light and purple shadow on top of it, and Bea mouthed the words 'the pomander mountain' again, and then, when the sun was completely gone, she saw only her own face reflected in the window. But she turned from this image as a young girl turns shyly from a mirror. 'Excuse me,' she said, 'I think I'm tired.' 'Oh, sure, the drive,' Myra said. 'Ain't it funny how you sit on your ass all day and then all you wanna do is sleep?' She laughed loudly, and Bea realized that she, Myra, was quite drunk. 'That's the story of Bea's life,' Hank said from her other side. 'She's lived like an old retired woman ever since we got Inez.' 'Well, we should all have a Mexican to clean up after us,' Myra said, and Bea turned back to her, feeling like a spectator—or the ball—at a tennis match. 'She's Dominican,' Bea murmured, and braced herself for one of Hank's 'bleeding heart' comments. But Myra was still talking and Bea wasn't sure they'd heard her. 'Hank, get your bags, we'll put Bea in the new addition.' She looked at Bea wildly. 'You trust me alone with your husband, don't you, honey?' Her husband rose unsteadily and wobbled out the door, and Bea suppressed a laugh. She hated that laugh and she hated more the impulse which produced it; she hated being drawn so quickly back to the immediate world of Myra, of Hank, of argument and rancor. 'Looks like somebody had a little much,' Myra said. She hiccuped, laughed, then said, 'Well, c'mon, let's tuck you in.'

The new addition turned out to be a shed-like structure that was literally bolted to the trailer. A hole had been roughly cut into the trailer wall; within the doorframe Bea could see insulation, wires, jagged tin. 'Stan hasn't had a chance to finish it,' Myra explained quietly, 'but it's fine for sleeping.' There was a door; when Bea closed it she saw that it was too small for its frame, and the bright border of light which encircled it made it float in space. Bea undressed; she used her shirt to soak up a little sweat under her arms and breasts; she pulled her nightgown over her head; she looked around for her purse and a pill and realized that she'd left it in the car, and she cursed silently and hoped she'd drunk enough whiskey to counteract all that coffee. The sofa-bed mattress was thin and the bars under it pressed against her feet and knees and hips, against her spine, elbows, neck, and head, but still she fell asleep quickly, and when she awakened Hank snored beside her. It was dark, the border of light around the door was gone, and, still half asleep, she imagined that the new addition had been hermetically sealed somehow, trapping her in the bed with Hank, in the dark, forever, and she shut her eyes against that thought. But when she opened them again she saw light coming through a window she hadn't noticed during the night. It was morning, and in the warmth of that naïve moment Bea rolled over slowly so she wouldn't wake Hank, and she let herself look at him. The country light was strong and clean on his body and in some places it made his skin seem as shiny as glass. Frosted glass, Bea thought, for as always Hank's skin seemed the beginning and end of him, as though there was nothing within and nothing it could call its own without. He lay on the bed beside her and he breathed. His skin covered him completely, sealed him off from her and the rest of the world. It seemed pulled tight across his body, but she knew that if she pressed a finger into him his skin would give a little, not a lot, but it would be soft before it was hard. There were suggestions of so much under that skin, the flat puddle of his stomach that sometimes quivered like a pudding, the lines of his ribs and the lines of his muscles and tendons and ligaments. If she put an ear to his chest she knew she would hear his heart beating, and if she put a hand under his nose she would feel air emerging from the wet caves of his lungs. If she shook him gently he would wake gently, until he saw who shook him. But she didn't shake him, didn't touch him, she *couldn't*, damn it, she just couldn't. She could only look at the bumps and ripples and valleys under his skin that assured her there was indeed something more to this man to whom she'd given her life, and who had taken it all and given nothing back except shouts and curses and the back of his hand, or just his back, turned on her like the wall of a fortress. But a wall is merely another kind of weapon, a weapon that doesn't move but in its immobility incites the enemy to smash against it again and again.

Bea realized then that she'd been alone with her thoughts for far too long and she left the bed. It was only a short journey to the kitchen. That room was quiet; the sheet was still drawn across the doorway to the living room; the hum of the clocks

37

was the only sound, but Bea didn't look at them. At the sink she stared vacantly out the window and ran warming water over her fingers. She decided to stay there a while, so she plugged the sink drain, added soap to the water, slipped in a few dishes—coffee cups mostly, a few plates littered with bread crumbs, butter knives and teaspoons but no forks. As she washed them she stared out the window. There was the front yard: their car, Stan and Myra's car, the road, beyond that another mountain. It wasn't as beautiful as the pomander mountain but it was still pretty goddamn gorgeous, and the foliage that covered it had caught a golden cast from the morning sun, and as Bea looked at it and washed dishes and dreaded Stan's awakening or Myra's or Hank's arrival in the room, she thought, There's a window above every kitchen sink in America. A mirror in the bathroom and a window in the kitchen—but how many of them look out on *this*? You could look at that mountain all day without reaching the end of it, Bea thought. You could think about that view forever, and never think about yourself.

ξ

The dying man, Stan, was duplicitous and hateful, and, worst of all, obvious; even Hank could see it. He had sacrificed his eye in a pact with the devil and the devil had reneged. Now he perched on his couch as though it were a throne and he a king, and his crown was the scar that ringed his head just above what remained of his hair and just below the black elastic band that held his eye patch in place. The scar and the bill for it—'the bills, Hank, the bills, the bills'—were all that remained of a failed operation when Stan's brain had been lifted from its skull and the cancer scraped from it like mold from bread. Now his back slumped but his head was unnaturally erect, and cocked so that he could see as much of the room as possible with his single remaining eye. 'They used a local,' he told Hank. 'That means they don't knock you out, just stick a needle under your cheek so your face falls asleep. Then they pluck it out and snip the muscles like they was cutting wires or something.' Stan shrugged, and for a moment Hank thought he had been referring to his brain. He smoked, and it made Hank sick to his stomach to see how hard it was for Stan to strike a match. His hands simply lacked strength, as did his whole body. He gestured sometimes, usually in anger, and Hank winced when he did, afraid that Stan's finger or hand or whole arm would fall off with the weight of his bones. He waved with the hand that held the cigarette and its ashes fell in a dark smear on the sheet that draped him. He was talking about the nuclear power plant he'd helped build.

'After all I gave those fuckers,' he said, 'breathing in their poisoned air the whole time, and they don't even want to pay my goddamn doctor bills. Well, we'll beat 'em on this.' Stan and Myra were suing the company. 'It'll be for Lucy,' Stan said. 'Myra and me are old, we don't need more than what we got. But Lucy's got a future, she needs this more than we do.' Hank looked at Myra, who sat next to Bea on the love seat. Myra smoked and stared so fixedly at her husband that Hank wondered if she saw him, and Bea stared at the coffee cup in her lap. 'Beautiful country up here,' Hank ventured, and Stan turned his eye on Hank so violently that he sat back. 'Shit, Hank, this is *nature*, of course it's beautiful.' He jerked his thumb toward the window, the window filled by the plastic bag. 'Ain't a exit on the whole L.I.E. that'll give you that.' Hank just nodded. 'But you wanna know the nicest thing about living up here?' Stan said. 'The nicest thing? Not a goddamn nigger or spic anywhere you look.' Hank saw Bea look up, braced himself. 'Ithaca—' she began, but Stan cut her off. 'I don't count Ithaca. Goddamn college town—they'll all go back where they came from.' Stan smiled then, a pointless malicious racist smile. 'Not *all* the way back,' he said, and he said, 'I wish they'd been there when we was dropping bombs on the towelheads.' He laughed loudly at himself, and by himself, and Hank knew Bea must be seething. 'I'm sure it makes things simpler,' he said, hoping to placate Stan and head off a confrontation. Stan wasn't placated. 'Simpler?' he yelled, his voice cracking. 'No crime, that's what it means. No crime, no niggers. You don't have to be a genius to put two and two together.

39

Myra,' he said, 'get me a coffee.' When she was out of the room Stan sat back against the couch. 'Yeah, it's a nice place to live around here. Pure. You don't have to guess what anyone means when they talk to you. We all use plain English up here.' He drank the coffee Myra brought him, smoked. He talked to Hank for a while longer. Eventually he sat up with a start and said he was tired, and he sent everyone from the room. Myra led them to the kitchen; she shook her head. 'Caffeine just don't seem to affect him.'

While Stan slept, Lucy led Bea and Hank to the mountain behind the trailer. Everything Hank saw reminded him of Stan. That dead tree with its gray sticks poking into the bright morning sky: he imagined that Stan's bones looked like that, gray and split open along their seams, gnarled at their ends. Hank looked at his own body as they walked. He dropped a few steps behind the women and held an arm out in front of him. They amazed him all the sudden, his fingers, their knuckles, their nails, the hairs that grew on them, the skin that wrapped everything up like a pastry. The way they curled when he willed them to, the way they opened up again—and the way they hurt.

'There's the stream,' Lucy said then. Hank looked up. He saw first a mud line: on this side the ground was damp, not muddy, but not quite dry, and on the other side it was silty smooth and dark with the water it held, and the plants were flat-pressed against it as if they missed having water to hold them up. The stream itself was wider than the room they'd slept in last night, wider than the trailer, but shallow, less than a foot deep. 'It's nice now,' Lucy said. 'If you'd come last month it would've been all brown with gunk from the mountain.' She knelt down and swished her finger around. 'Feel the water,' she said. 'You've never felt anything so cold in your life.' Hank was afraid to, but Bea put her hand right in and so he had to as well, and the totality of the cold surprised him. His hand went numb immediately, and he dropped his other hand in and left them there, and then he and Bea and Lucy crouched on rocks a few feet apart with their hands dangling between their legs and their fingers trailing in the water like vines, and Hank supposed he should have been thinking about Stan, dying while he slept on the couch, instead of about the ugly pain in his knees and the beautiful lack of it in his hands, and as he wondered which would give out first, his will or his knees, Lucy stood up. 'Do you want to walk up the mountain?' she said. Bea, standing quickly, said, 'I don't know, we're not as sturdy as we used to be.' Looking over at Hank, who had stood less quickly than she had, she added, 'And Hank has his arthritis.' Hank flung the water from his hands and shoved them in his pockets, turned to face the mountain. 'There's an easy trail up,' Lucy said, 'and the view's pretty,' and Hank said, 'Well, what're we waiting for?'

Lucy walked ahead of Bea and Hank on the gently sloped trail that ran up the mountain. The path was wide and clear like a hallway in the forest; it was impressed with shoeprints and a dog's pawprints and the gouges left behind by deer hooves. The posture of the trees impressed Hank. They grew straight up into the sky, not perpendicularly from the ground they were rooted in. Everything in nature grows toward the sun, Hank thought, even as he felt himself faltering, drooping, hurting, and Bea, he saw, was beginning to hang her head as well. Only Lucy looked up, and Hank wondered what she could have meant by an easy climb. They didn't seem to be even close to the top of the mountain, and his whole body hurt. But he kept quiet about it, the pain in his feet, knees, hips, spine, elbows, neck, head, and now his hands were hurting again too. He kept quiet because, though he might have been an old man, he wasn't a stubborn old man. He was instead will-less, and what Bea considered his unwillingness to change was really an inability to do so, and he wondered if he was going to faint before he reached the top. But then the ground changed underfoot, the soft dirt became hard yellow rock, and Lucy said, 'We're almost there,' and, thank God, she wasn't kidding this time. The trail seemed to dead-end in a sheer rockface, but then it made a sharp turn and there were ten steps carved into a narrow passageway in the rock. It seemed to go right into the sky, but it didn't: at the top of the stairs was a small plateau, slightly concave, shining like butter under the sun, and there were a few boulders scattered around that were clearly meant to be sat on. Hank was glad to see that Bea and Lucy were already sitting as he came onto the plateau, and he lowered his tired body carefully onto a rock, and then they sat there for a long time without speaking.

He got up eventually. It hurt but he didn't think it showed, and he walked to the edge of the bowl and was surprised to see that on this side the ground sloped away gently until the rock disappeared into the earth, and then the trees started. He'd expected to see a precipice but, as usual, nothing was as drastic as he expected. There was just the view: the view, what they'd come all this way for. Hank saw the trailer first, but he realized it was someone else's, and then he located Stan and Myra's trailer and a few other homes, and finally his eyes opened a little wider and he saw the world that held all these homes, and what he saw was a world that was a good place to build a home in. And then, behind him, he heard Bea say, 'What a good place to die.' He turned around suddenly and saw Lucy turning around suddenly, but Bea was turned away from them. 'Not down there,' she said, and she could have been talking to herself. 'Right here. On top of a mountain. On top of everything.' As she turned around, Lucy said, 'We should probably head back now,' and Hank said to Bea, 'What an insensitive thing to say.' But he was thinking, Oh, you're right, you're right, you're always right. This *is* a perfect place to die. And he was thinking too that this is what he'd come all the way to hear, and now it was time to leave.

He tried to shower slowly, but with sixty years of practice he was able to wash himself too quickly for his own good. Though he remained tired, the sweat and dirt of his long walk ran off his skin, and he felt foolish standing under the running water without doing anything. As he dried himself he saw in the mirror over the bathroom sink the fuzz of his remaining hair. It was patchy again, after all these years, and showed up on his skull like gray down. Bea was in the new addition when he returned. 'He's awake,' she said. 'He is?' Hank said, and then he said, 'He looks terrible, don't he?' He knew that he was giving her an opportunity for attack, and he almost wished she'd take it. Not as bad as you, she could say, or, At least he has an excuse. But she merely left the room, and the open door let in the sound of the television. As Hank entered the kitchen, Myra sang out, 'Soup's on.' She and Bea held plates piled high with BLTs and potato chips, and Hank followed them into the living room, where Stan's presence seemed somehow less substantial than the smell of bacon and the sound of the television. 'Turn that thing down,' Myra said, 'you can barely hear your heart beat with all that racket. Oops!' she added, and then she giggled, and then she led Bea and Hank to the table behind Stan, and Stan sat up slowly with his back against the arm of the couch and Myra handed him his food and came back to the table. Hank sat with his back under a painting— a reproduction of a painting, a country scene—and above it, just inches below the ceiling, hung a rifle, bearded with sooty, smoky dust, and he looked at the television between Bea and Myra and beyond Stan, and he did his best to ignore the conversation, concentrate on the television, his food, his coffee, his aches and pains, and when Myra pressed her finger into his forearm he was so startled he jerked his arm back and her nail cut him. 'I said,' she said, 'what time were you planning to head out?' She was smiling a dizzy crooked smile, all lipstick-smeared and tobacco-stained teeth, and there were too many smells on her breath to count. Hank looked at his wrist, realized he hadn't put his watch on after he'd showered. 'What time is it?' he said, and he saw Bea look at her watchless wrist, and then Myra looked around for a moment until her eyes settled on Stan, and Hank remembered the clocks in the other room. 'It's getting late,' he answered himself, and he too looked at the big white globe of Stan's head, fallen in sleep onto his chest, where his uneaten sandwich separated into its B's and

L's and T's and mixed with broken potato chips on his plate. 'I think we'll head out in the morning.'

They left him then, the women, his wife and Stan's, and he sat at the table with a fresh cup of coffee and an old stack of the local paper, and he read through them cover to cover. He'd almost finished when he heard Stan speak. 'I like that paper.' Hank looked up and saw Stan turned in his couch, and, guileless for a moment, he asked, 'Why?' 'Never anything you don't want to read in that paper,' Stan said. 'Never any bad news.' Hank glanced away from Stan for a moment but the women were nowhere around. He turned his eyes back to Stan's. 'How are you, Stan,' he said then, 'how do you feel?' On the couch Stan relaxed, and the effect was of shrinking. He said, 'I'm ready to go, Hank,' and Hank said, 'Tell me, Stan, tell me what it's like.' 'It's not like anything,' Stan said quickly. He wasn't looking at Hank when he spoke, he wasn't looking at anything. 'I can't imagine the future anymore,' he said, 'I don't know what "tomorrow" means. Every time I wake up I don't know what I am. If I'm dead or just dying.' Behind Stan someone was solving the puzzle on *Wheel of Fortune* but Hank refused to read it lest something cheap be revealed. He focused on Stan, and the skin of his head pulled so tightly in a squint that he could feel it all the way at the base of his skull. 'Do you need anything, Stan,' he asked, 'is there anything you need?' But he knew he had nothing to offer: he was asking for something, anything, and he hoped Stan knew this too. Stan blinked slowly, a willed blink, a test, and he said, 'You don't need anything, Hank. Dying's easy, it's simple, it's—' 'What, Stan, what is it?' Hank was gripping the edge of the table and he was sitting far forward in his seat, but he didn't notice this about himself; Stan did. He looked at nothing and his smile frightened Hank. 'It's not the dying that scares you, Hank. It's getting there and realizing you've wasted your life.' He turned away from Hank then and looked back at the television. He turned up the volume; a woman bought her dream vacation, and Hank thought that Stan's voice had been very calm for a person reading verdict on himself and finding the accused guilty. And then Hank saw that Stan's neck was creased by a

44

long fold of skin—he imagined the dry skin stretched too tightly when Stan's head had been turned—and the fold had cracked like old paper and now bled. The blood was red against Stan's white skin, Christmas red and winter white, and Hank turned from Stan to the paper he'd been looking at. He blinked several times, thinking he'd gone blind, but then he realized that the sun had gone behind the mountain, and he turned a light on and finished reading Stan's paper, the paper that didn't print bad news.

Bea had taken a small alarm clock from the kitchen and it woke him early; she wasn't in the room. He got out of bed stiffly, his joints complaining, and he dropped the alarm on the floor before he was able to turn it off and then, after he turned it off, he dropped it again because his spasming fingers wouldn't stay closed. It was all there in his fingers: his fingers could not hold anything. Bea entered the room then. 'What's keeping you?' she said. Hank saw her look at the alarm clock on the floor; she didn't pick it up, just looked at it for a moment, and then she pulled a bobby pin from her hair, smoothed it, her hair, and replaced the pin. 'Myra's waking Stan. Don't be late.' He wasn't. He stayed behind Bea in the dark living room, and Bea stood behind Myra, who leaned over Stan with her hair still matted at the back of her head from where she'd slept, and with the hand that held her cigarette she shook him. 'First one of the day,' she'd said to Hank when he'd come into the kitchen; not 'good morning,' but 'first one of the day.' Hank had surprised himself and hugged her, but now he stood far behind her as she shook Stan again, holding his breath against his fear and Myra's smoke. Stan emerged from sleep like a body dredged from a lake, and his eye, after he opened it, didn't focus for a long time, and after it had focused he refused to look at his audience, but lay curled under his blanket, slight, shivering. 'Are you going?' he asked the wall, and Hank called, 'Yeah, Stan, we're going. It's a long drive back.' Stan's nose wrinkled, and he said, 'Give me a cigarette,' and then he added,

'Myra,' as though he were just remembering her name. Myra used the cigarette she was smoking to light another, and she gave the first one of the day to Stan and kept the second one for herself. She'd put the cigarette right into Stan's mouth and he held it there without dragging on it and after a long time he said, 'Bye,' and he said, 'Thanks for coming up,' and then he took a long drag on the cigarette, but even though Hank stared at Stan for a long time he never saw the smoke leave his body.

Outside, Hank said, 'Myra,' but Myra waved her hand quickly. 'We'll be fine,' she said. Hank thought she meant herself and Stan, but then he saw her looking over his shoulder and he turned and saw Lucy standing, inexplicably, in the middle of the lawn, not doing anything, not close to anything, just standing and staring at the sun. He turned back to Myra. She drew on her cigarette, threw it into the yard. She breathed out the smoke in her lungs before she kissed Hank goodbye. 'Get home safe,' she said, and turned a little to include Bea in her farewell. Bea touched Myra on the shoulder and said good-bye, and then Hank and Bea got in the car, and Hank started the car and drove away, and he didn't look in the rearview mirror until he was sure the house was out of sight.

They fought, then stopped for breakfast, they got lost, then stopped for lunch, and then they lost the light late that day in a long curve of highway which put a mountain between them and the sun. 'Oh,' Bea said, when the sunlight disappeared, and then she unfastened her seat belt and turned around. After a moment she said, 'It's beautiful.' 'Turn around, Bea,' Hank said. 'Put your seat belt on before I get a ticket.' He wondered why he'd said that, when what he wanted to do was agree with her, when what he really wanted to do was stop the car and look at the sunset behind them. But he didn't answer his question and he didn't say anything else to Bea; he changed lanes instead, and passed a small car with a Cornell sticker in the window. There was only the sound of the road passing under the wheels and the soft wheeze of the heater. The rolling country around them, marked only occasionally with buildings, made the night seem bigger than the nights on Long Island,

and the bigness of the night made the silence in the car harder to bear, but Hank refused to break it after he'd made it so clear he didn't want to talk. He wasn't sure how much later it was that Bea said, 'Careful, Hank!' and Hank said, 'I'm driving, Bea,' even as he pulled the car quickly to the left to avoid a deer standing fearlessly, or perhaps just stupidly, on the edge of the road. 'Well, I didn't know if you'd seen it,' Bea said, and Hank said, 'That's why I look at the road, Bea,' though he hadn't seen it. And then Bea said, 'I never did ask Myra and Stan if they'd seen any of those red deer.' Hank scoffed. 'Nobody has time to look at red deer, Bea. Nobody has time to waste on something that don't exist.' Bea didn't say anything for a long time, but then she said, 'So you read the article too,' and Hank didn't answer her. She started to say something else but stopped, and she sighed loudly and then, quietly, urgently, she said, 'We almost missed him, Hank.' 'Missed him, Bea?' Hank said. 'Where's he going?' But Bea pressed on. 'What if he'd died before we got there, Hank? Wouldn't you have felt bad?' Hank wasn't thinking of his conversation with Stan when he answered her; he was thinking of himself. 'It don't matter, Bea,' he said. 'None of it matters after you're dead.'

Bea didn't say anything to that. She couldn't, because she'd always thought Hank knew more about dying than she did. Next to her she heard Hank move around uncomfortably but he didn't say anything. He never said anything. When, finally, Bea could speak, she put it all on the line. 'I never thought I would want anything besides you,' she said. Hank still didn't say anything. For a long time he just drove, but finally Bea heard him speak quietly but matter-of-factly, and when she turned she could see, faintly, the wet shine of his cheeks in the dashboard lights. 'That's your problem, Bea. Bea,' he said, 'you never did have ambition. You never set your sights high enough. You never had dreams.' And right about the time he said that, Stan died.

3

Life is but a Dream

He had been very young and very ill, and very hot, and his mother had put him in the bathtub to cool. When she set him in the tub she had already turned the water on but not plugged the drain, and only a sheen of liquid rippled over the cold cold cold surface of the tub, itself just a glaze of white enamel over bitter black cast iron. His ass and his heels burned for a moment and then were numb, and then gradually temperature and feeling rose again as his fever and his pain reasserted themselves. Drops of sweat coalesced on his skin and rolled together like rivulets; they slipped into the rising tide of the tub which, very slowly, very gently, more gently than even his beloved mother had ever touched him, took hold of his arms and started to lift them, and as his arms rose with the water level the leadenness of his body left him and he relaxed suddenly, too suddenly, and his back and the thing which he would come to name Candy slapped against the tub in a cold hard splash. His body retreated then. He felt incredibly solid and heavy, and yet impossibly light as well, like the filaments that glowed and floated in the air for a few brief moments after being spat by his Uncle Kenny's blowtorch, and he drifted in this daze for an unmeasurable length of time until he heard his father's voice tell his mother's shadow, 'Jesus, Candace, he's unconscious,' and then there was a feeling, a firmness under his back, an inevitable roughness, *hands*, and then there was just a blur that ended that time, and every time thereafter, in the hospital, where the cold hard instruments of medicine returned him to a state which could only be described as less sick, for it in no way resembled health. But he had kept hold of a memory from the tub, a feeling, a physical sensation, and it was that feeling he associated with his illness forever, and for a long time after he got out of the hospital he wanted only to be sick again, so that he could float again, and fly. This drifting was his only dream, his earliest desire; it was his desideratum. From that day on time moved remorselessly forward, toward the day of his death, and even in the blaze of fever Henry could not escape this. He could only forget about it for a while, and so forget his fear.

A B, capitalized, delicate, elegant, filigreed, almost gothic, entirely filled the sheet of stationery that came with the flowers. They came just a week after Henry had fallen in and out of Beatrice's window: a bevy of hothouse tulips whose egg-shaped egg-sized petals were the same color as the sheet of stationery that came with them, a creamy off-white just touched by red, and Beatrice had written her B with a bevel-tipped felt marker that gave her handwriting the look of old-fashioned calligraphy. But when Henry saw it, his heart, the organ he trusted much more than he did his brain, sank into his bowels in despair, because he realized that this was Beatrice's way of saying good-bye. There was no other interpretation possible, for he had told Beatrice of the gifts his relatives had sent him, and how he despised those gifts, and now Beatrice had sent him a gift. And sure enough, the phone didn't ring that day, didn't bring Beatrice's voice to him as it had every day since he'd fallen through her window, and the wheels of her car didn't roll into his driveway, bearing upon their axles her big clanking wreck and within that hull her precious body. They'd talked every day and met every night, and, on the night after their midnight rendezvous, he had driven them to the beach and parked on a bluff overlooking the ocean, and they had, for the first time, kissed. Beatrice had kept a hand on Henry's shoulder the whole time. He felt it wander up his neck occasionally, but never higher, never to the smooth magic marble of his head; and

Henry had kept a hand in Beatrice's hair, caught there in a woolen net so thick that his probing fingers never managed to find her skin. Beatrice kept her other hand on the door handle, and Henry, afraid of where he might put his other hand – afraid of where he might put it on her body, and afraid of where he might put it on his – kept a tight hold of some knob on the dashboard and they kissed and it wasn't until a boy Henry's age but with a full head of mussed hair and a tucked-in button-down shirt that was half-unbuttoned and half-untucked knocked on the window that Henry found out he'd been turning the light switch on and off for over an hour. 'What's up, dude,' the boy said, more L.A. than L.I., 'you know Morse code or something?' Henry was embarrassed, as was Beatrice, and they left that night but returned the next, and this time they held each other tightly, a little desperately even, and in the morning Henry found bruises on his upper arms where Beatrice had pressed her fingerprints into his skin. Henry looked at the bruises as if their pattern might reveal something to him, some mystery about life or love, but all they showed was his own fragility, his mortality, his impending death, and there was neither mystery nor revelation in that. He saw the same message in Beatrice's flowers, and it was summed up by the note which accompanied them, that solitary huge letter that said nothing, that said there was nothing to do except wait, as Henry had been waiting all his life, for him to die.

The flowers were still in full bloom when a note came from the post office: a package awaited him there. Henry dropped a few drops of black dye into the four water glasses that held the flowers; he tied a bandanna on his head; he drove to the post office, and there he was given a box which, like the flowers, lacked a return address. But he knew it had to be from her because that's how these things work, and as Henry picked up the big light cardboard cube he noticed that a corner was soaking wet and ripped open and leaking mushy newspaper. He pried at the box, at the seam and then at the wet hole, but the whole thing was sealed with a fanatical amount of packing tape and resisted his fingers. He used his keys then, cutting through layer after layer of tape, and then he scattered over a long counter wadded newspapers filled with alarming accounts of Iraqi tanks invading Kuwait, and then, at last, he held it in his hands, and it was a hat. A mauve hat, a fedora, old-fashioned and high-peaked and sharp-brimmed, and made of a felt as heavy and textured as the folded piece of paper that was tucked into the band along with the eye of a peacock feather. The paper was the same heavy cream that had come with the flowers, tinted this time a light orange, and the message this time was equally enigmatic but, to Henry, equally clear: 'It was my father's,' was all she'd written with her calligraphy marker, and below that the letter B, and this time she'd written in tiny letters so that the abbreviated sentence and affected signature floated in a peaches-and-cream sea in the middle of the page. Henry carried the hat on his balled fist as he went to his car. He felt a little fazed—his head was starting to ache—and at the car he found he was missing his keys, and he had to return inside and set the hat on the counter and search through the mess he'd made. While he searched Candy began to throb in earnest, and as soon as he found his key ring he shuffled back to his car, where he was almost undone by the gummy residue of packing tape that encrusted his keys, and when he made it into the car he stretched across the seat and let the attack bear him away from the world. When he'd closed his eyes the sun was high in the sky and when he opened them it was dark, and he closed his eyes again when he saw this. He went straight to bed when he got home, and it wasn't until he awoke sometime in the middle of the night and turned on the light to stare at the flowers, drooping now and bruised by black dye leaching into their petals, that he realized he'd left the hat at the post office. It had disappeared by the time he arrived in the morning. Nobody who worked there remembered seeing it although several people remembered the mess on their counter, and one gray-haired gentleman went so far as to say that this was life's little reward for being inconsiderate of the needs of others, and then he hollered, 'Next!'

The poem came next, a few sad wet days later. By then the tulips faced the dresser like narcissus blossoms, but they were the color of factory smoke and their petals had begun to fall off. By then Henry not only recognized the paper and pen but he knew, from a trip to the Hallmark store, that Beatrice had bought the Sunset Collection, a boxed stationery set that included sheets of paper in six out of the seven colors of the rainbow as well as a violet quill with which to write on them, and he was terrified, because she was only up to yellow. The poem was just long enough to fill the page completely, the smeared black ink of the marker obscuring the yellow in the paper's color in the same way that his dye darkened the tulip petals, and at the bottom of the page, squeezed a little tightly into a bubble created by the paper's simulated hand-ripped edges, was the letter B, familiar by now but strange as well, as the person who was represented by that signature retreated from his memory. He read the poem; it was a little sentimental, he thought, and a little sad as well, but mostly it was maddeningly vague, filled with falling tears and falling leaves and falling stars, and what it had to do with Beatrice, with himself, with the two of them, he had no idea. Poetry mystified him. He understood better real things: the lost hat, the dying flowers, the silent telephone. A wall of silence had built up and surrounded him by the time the last petal fell from the last stem. Henry had sat up watching, and he was almost surprised when the petal plopped to the dresser rather than wafting down, and he had to remind himself that they were not, after all, ink-stained pieces of paper, even though they resembled them. He swept the petals into the trash as soon as the last one fell, and then there were just twenty-four forlorn and brackish green stems poking into the air, their bare sex organs drooping like snail antennae. He threw them away too; he took the blackened water glasses to the kitchen and left them for his mother; he read the poem a few more times, but it remained a maze he couldn't navigate.

Before he could decide what to do next, Beatrice called. Her voice on the phone was nervous, apologetic, slightly crazed. She said, 'I love you,' and she said, 'Forgive me.' She said, 'Meet me at the beach tonight,' and there was nothing in her voice that told him why she'd called now, nor why she hadn't called yesterday, or the day before, or the day before that. Henry wanted to make love on the blanket she brought but it was October after all, the wind blowing off the ocean was freezing and wet, and so they only held each other, kissed and shivered and giggled, and as they lay there a memory opened in Henry's head, not like a box but like a pitfall, and he fell into its darkness. What he remembered was the faucet in the bathroom of the beach house his parents had rented in Cape May years ago: it had been plumbed in such a way that the four-year-old Henry, standing on a stool to brush his teeth, had been able to feel the hot water coming in the left side and the cold water coming in the right. He had stood there for ages sometimes, feeling the hot and cold stream pass over his hands, until all the hot water was gone and only cold water passed over both sides of his hands, and the seventeen-year-old Henry felt like that as he lay on the beach: the heat was inside him and the cold outside, and slowly, very slowly, the cold pushed into him, and as it did warmth, and consciousness, retreated, and the water that passed over his hands took him down with it, into the ground.

He closed his eyes on the ocean; he opened them on the focused glare of a hospital room; he saw Beatrice sitting by the side of his bed, and when he spoke it was to neither of them, Beatrice or the ocean. 'Mom,' he said, and then he said, 'I'm sorry.' He smiled at Beatrice for a long time as she looked at him with a confused expression on her face, and gradually he realized that she wasn't his mother and at length he took her hand; he pretended to have forgotten what he'd just said, and he said, 'Beatrice,' and he asked her how she was. Beatrice cried then. She blubbered and bubbled and babbled. 'Oh God,' she said, 'I didn't get it,' and Henry was confused because he thought she had got it, but Beatrice was still talking. 'I mean, I did get it. I mean, I didn't get it and then I did, but I didn't *really* get it until the other night. You got so quiet, I thought you were sleeping, but you weren't, you were, you—Henry,' she said, 'you were unconscious for *two days.*' And there was Henry: his legs disappeared beneath the hospital sheet and his arms, just as mysteriously, lay atop it, long thin blue-veined limbs that ended abruptly in the white crabs of his hands, which scuttled across the bed clutching at the railing, at the sheet, at his legs beneath the sheet, his left hand slower than his right because of the I.V. it dragged, until at last Beatrice did what he wanted her to do and took his hands in her own. 'Beatrice,' he began, but he stopped. He sensed that she was just starting to ponder something he had been pondering for years without success, and he wanted to tell her it was okay that she didn't get it because he didn't get it either—that, in fact, there was nothing to get, only to give up. But he didn't want to admit that, to her or to himself. He only said, 'It's okay,' and when Beatrice just stared at him fixedly, he said, 'It's okay,' again, and when Beatrice suddenly started and said, 'I'll take care of you no matter what,' he closed his eyes and said a third time, 'It's okay,' but his words carried the force of negation, and when he opened his eyes Beatrice was gone and his two hands held only each other, and he was looking at his mother.

He peered at her suspiciously, as though, again, she might prove to be something other than herself, but the body in the chair was defiantly solid and definitely hers, and behind it stood his father, and his father was looking at his watch. He looked at his watch and then he looked at the clock on the wall and then he made a minute adjustment to his watch. 'Dylan,' Henry's mother said, and then she said to Henry, 'I thought he should be here for this.' 'For what?' Henry said. 'Henry,' she said, and she reached out to touch him but he pulled away. 'They want to, they, they have to operate soon.' '*Oh God, no!*' his voice cracked, and in his panic he thrashed at his sheets and he even considered running for it, as if he could escape Candy that way. When, finally, he turned back to his mother he saw in her eyes a waiting patient triumph, and he realized then that she would not win this strange war between them but he would lose it, because he would die. If he hadn't hated her before he hated her then, and he shoveled that emotion over the rest of his feelings. 'I won't do it,' he spat, and his mother's voice was as cold as his when she answered. 'Then you'll die.' Her voice was so cold that his father actually put his hands on her shoulders and spoke. 'Candace,' he said, and Henry thought he even heard reproach in his voice. 'And if I do it,' Henry said, 'if I do it, then what? I'll die anyway.' 'We'll all die anyway,' his mother said, and she grabbed his hand before he could pull it away. 'Henry,' she said softly, though her hands on his were as rough as those of a cop on a criminal. 'Baby,' she said, and then she said, 'There's a chance,' and then her voice disappeared and she looked down, and Henry looked at all she offered him, and all she offered was the top of her head. Its hair was brown and parted in the middle, and tightly curled permed waves fell down either side of her face. The inch or so closest to her head was straight. It was more gray than the rest of her hair, and flecked with dandruff, and the scalp line of the part was tender and white. This was the woman whom Henry wanted to offer him a new life. It didn't occur to him that she had given him life a long time ago, and that it was neither her responsibility nor within her power to do it again, but as he stared at her skull shame filled him, then hopelessness, and then rage. He just wanted her to lie to him. He just wanted her to say, There's a chance you'll live, but he knew she wouldn't. She couldn't, not even if it was true, because his living wasn't a possibility that had been planned for in her mind, or in his father's. She cried all the time and his father stood in strangled silence, but really, they were only waiting, and for a moment he didn't blame them. What can you do with your dying son but wait? Even Beatrice was waiting, he realized then, and he was waiting too. They were all waiting for him to die, and when he realized he'd constructed his entire life around this event—the operation that had always been synonymous with his death—he laughed so loudly and so strangely that his mother winced and his father actually turned away. He refused to say anything more after that, and when his parents finally slunk from the room Henry thought they looked like rabbits seen through the telescopic lens of a rifle, and then, when he awoke in the morning, there was a doctor in the room, a young doctor but a good doctor, and it was time for Henry to choose the date of his death.

He chose, finally, the last day of the year. The good doctor tried to dissuade him of his choice, not because the date was too soon or too far away, but because he said he didn't want Henry to think of the operation in such all-or-nothing terms. Indeed, Henry realized, it wasn't all or nothing—it was something but it wasn't that. But, Henry reminded this doctor, as other doctors had reminded him in their sickeningly gentle terms, he wasn't expected to survive this operation, and he wasn't expecting to survive this operation. If he could have waited until May he would have, because it would have been neat to die on his eighteenth birthday, but he'd been led to believe that February was as late as he could possibly postpone this thing—that, come February, Candy would surely accomplish what surgery only probably would—and there were no interesting days to die on in January, so why not die on the last day of the year? The doctor, who wasn't so young that he hadn't heard this sort of talk before, nor so old that he'd found a way of responding to it, said brightly, 'Well, there's Christmas to look forward to,' and when he said that Henry tried to switch the day of the operation to Christmas Eve because he couldn't bear the thought of another surreal load of presents pouring in from his family. But when he suggested it the doctor shook his head. 'Even neurosurgeons have to spend some time with their families,' he said, and Henry said, 'Why don't they spend some time with *my* family?' The good doctor just laughed as though Henry had said something funny, and then he said, 'Well, I guess it's settled,' and Henry said that he guessed it was, and the doctor, who was sitting down, slapped the tops of his thighs with his hands and pushed at them. Not, Henry thought, as though he were pushing himself up, but as though he were pushing the top half of his body right off the bottom half, and Henry's only consolation that morning was the realization that he had made him do that. He had caused the good doctor that pain.

As he left Henry asked him to close the curtain that separated his bed from the other bed in the room and then, quickly but

56

smoothly, he pulled the I.V. out of his arm and watched the blood leak from his vein until his eyes closed. As a stunt, it cost him a few days, cost his parents a few dollars more, but it changed nothing. The date of his operation was pushed back to January second in the late evening. 'New Year's Eve,' the doctor said, by way of explanation. 'New Year's Eve?' Henry said. 'New Year's Eve,' the doctor repeated. 'We have to give your surgeon a little time to recover.' 'You mean he's going to have a hangover?' Henry said, and he waved his arm with the little bandaid on his wrist and tried to be dramatic. But it was hard for him to get worked up about it, and when he was offered the chance to choose another date he refused to answer. In the end he only stayed in the hospital for a week because, really, there was nothing wrong with him except a brain tumor. He got out before Halloween, and the only thought he allowed himself was that he had all of November and December to spend with Beatrice. Everything else he pushed away. It was as if choosing the day of his death had been his last tie to earth, and after he had severed it his feet never touched the ground: they hovered a few inches above it, suspended by the turning turning turning wheels of Beatrice's car, and by her love. For Henry was young; he was dying and he was in love, and these conditions, like lenses, aligned themselves before his eyes. What little energy remained in his body left it in a sharpened gaze that he focused on Beatrice like a laser beam. His love shone on the jewel he had made of her skin, was absorbed, reflected, refracted. It polished her until her brilliance was dazzling, almost hot, almost nourishing, and the last days of his life fed on that brilliance like a flock of greedy pigeons until, full to the point of bursting, they exploded into flight in every direction: up, down, forward, backward, north south east west, and then, as mysteriously as they had appeared, they were gone, and so was Beatrice—and so was Henry.

ξ

On a map Long Island's roads resemble a skein of yarn that's been had at by a cat: they're a tangle of bypasses, detours, alternate routes looping in and out and over and under each other so many times that it's impossible to know quite where you are, and yet impossible to lose yourself either, owing to the finite nature of an island's geography. In practice this meant that Beatrice could drive for hours without going anywhere, and this relieved her worry that something would happen to Henry and she wouldn't be able to get him home. What would happen, she wasn't sure, but in her imagination it took the shape of a fit, an epileptic seizure, convulsions and spasms and vomiting; and it was home she had to get him to, not a hospital, and why that was she also didn't know. It seemed, confronted by his illness, by Candy, that she didn't know anything anymore, and as she drove she asked him endless questions about being sick, questions that he answered reluctantly or not at all, until finally she took it on herself to explain it to him. She went to the college library, checked out books, looked through them; the next day she offered him the sum of her knowledge. 'Death,' she pronounced, 'is in all of us.' She looked down at him. Her lap held his head and his left hand; the rest of his body unfurled on the wide bench seat of her car. Even that brief glance seemed to convey the whole of his being to her, for in the past few weeks it seemed that something inside of Henry—some essence uniquely his, and yet almost universal, human—had leached outward, manifested itself on the surface of his skin, which seemed to glow in its translucence and hide fewer and fewer secrets beneath its drape.

Henry sat up. He looked out the window. The trees flashing by the road were scrub pine; it was daylight and exhaust-blackened needles were visible, and trash tangled around trunks in lieu of vines. He said, 'It is?' 'It *is*,' Beatrice insisted. 'I mean, we can all die. I mean, we all do die. We just forget about it for a while.' Henry didn't say anything for a moment, but then he turned to her. 'Oh, Beatrice,' he said, 'we don't forget about it. We just don't think about it. We deny it. We block it out,' he said, and that was that. After a pause, Beatrice touched his head. She touched it often: it was her right, a privilege accorded only to her. 'How's Candy?' she said. 'Candy's fine,' Henry said, in a voice so flat it made his former speeches seem sparkling. 'Candy's dandy.' 'Why,' Beatrice said, 'why do you call her, why do you call it Candy?' Henry just repeated himself. 'Can-Dy,' he said, breaking the word into syllables. 'It's just a combination of my parents' names, that's all. Candace and Dylan.' 'Can-Dy?' Beatrice said. 'Candy? Isn't Candy just short for Candace?' 'Oh, nobody ever calls her that,' Henry said. 'It's always Candace or it's nothing. She isn't exactly a Candy.' 'But Candy is short for Candace, right?' Henry nodded. 'And you knew that, right?' Henry nodded again. 'What *is* it about your parents?' Beatrice said then, and Henry said, 'Oh, you know. They only stay together for my sake.' 'A lot of parents do that,' Beatrice said, 'most parents do that.' 'It's different with my parents,' Henry said, 'with me. It's different.' Later, Beatrice realized that she should have figured it out, but the trees were gone and a town had replaced them; traffic was heavy, and she was distracted by the mechanics of changing lanes, accelerating, braking, checking the rearview mirror. 'Why,' she persisted, 'why's it so different?' Henry sighed. That always scared Beatrice: he had so little air to lose. His hands were still but Beatrice saw his shoulders hunch, his head droop. She was about to tell him to forget it when Henry said, 'They're just waiting for me to die,' and Beatrice gasped, as though sucking in the air Henry had exhaled, and then she was quiet. Henry was too. They were quiet until they had cleared the traffic and the lights and the town and were back on the open road, and then Beatrice said, 'I'm sorry.' 'It's okay,' Henry said, 'it's just, it's true,' he said, and he said again, 'It's okay.'

And it was okay, because it was the middle of November, and Henry was going to die a week after Christmas. In that context everything was okay. The roadside restaurants they ate in were okay, the lumpy mashed potatoes and leathery steaks and tepid coffee they served, and using his parents' credit cards to pay the bill: it was all okay. 'What're they going to do, sue me?' Henry told her when Beatrice said maybe they shouldn't. But Beatrice was really worrying about her own financial situation. Mail was invading her house, and she was beginning to understand that her father hadn't left everything in perfect order when he'd died. Letters were piling up on the coffee table and she was afraid to open them. Not just phone bills—and gas and water bills, and bills from plumbers and electricians and other repairmen who'd visited their house in the last seven years—but letters from the bank that were stamped 'Priority Mail' and 'Urgent—Reply Requested' and, most plainly, 'Mortgage Documents Enclosed.' At some point the letters were no longer addressed to her father but to Beatrice, and this frightened her even more: they knew who she was. They knew she was alone. But they didn't know about Henry, and Henry, she made sure, didn't know about them. November was slipping away: elm and oak and maple and sycamore trees stood naked among the pines along the highways; guttery ditches glittered with frost. The exhaust plumes from a line of jammed traffic waved like a salutatory colonnade of flags on the front of a hotel, and Beatrice thought that there was more than enough history in even these finite things to keep any mind busy. She would shelter Henry, she told herself, she would save him from everything else. She would save him for herself.

They drove to Great Adventure but decided for Candy's sake not to go on any of the rides. They drove to Lambertville, New Jersey, and New Hope, Pennysylvania, twinned towns joined by a few bridges and an endless number of antique, arts-and-craft, and pottery stores. They drove to Niagara Falls, sneaking out in the dark hours of the morning and getting there just in time to see the sun set over the water, and they left almost immediately, and Beatrice had to drink a half dozen cups of coffee to stay awake on the drive home. She felt like his sister on these trips. She felt like his nurse, his friend, a cousin, a companion, a stranger he'd grabbed off the street, but unless they were actually parked somewhere and making out she never felt like his girlfriend, or his lover. She wasn't his lover actually, not yet, but she felt Henry's hands growing more insistent as the days passed, and she felt she was becoming less resistant, though she wasn't sure if that was because she wanted to, finally, or if she just wanted Henry to get his wish. His hands pushed at her now, pressed frankly against her crotch and unbuttoned the buttons of her shirt. Her hands would trail after his, fixing her pants, buttoning her shirt. She took to wearing long skirts and when Henry pulled them up they sat in a huge pile of fabric in her lap and his fumbling hands clearly didn't know what to do about that. But finally he surprised her one night: he simply asked. 'Beatrice,' he said.

She had driven them to Rhode Island. She had found a hill overlooking Long Island Sound and parked there. Outside the car a long hedge rippled in a breeze like a stroked patch of velvet, and in the distance a slight haze might have been Long Island. She had driven a long time to get to that spot, but as she looked at the haze across the water she felt acutely the futility of trying to cross a frontier that didn't exist anymore, and it was into this that Henry had interjected her name. 'Yes,' she said eventually, 'what is it?' Her words, her voice, her mind was distant; she concentrated on things outside the car. 'Beatrice,' Henry said again, 'I want to be inside you,' and Beatrice, still preoccupied, only said, 'Why?' Henry was earnest and awkward. 'I guess, I don't know, I just feel like we've come so far, grown so close, that we should, you know, we should *complete* it, I guess, get as close as two people can get.' Beatrice continued to look out of the car, though she was aware that Henry faced her. 'It's not that simple, Henry, there are other things we have to think about.' Henry's sigh was exasperated. 'Oh, Beatrice, don't worry about me—' 'I'm not worried about you, Henry.' She turned and looked at him. She wanted him to realize she wasn't being selfish. 'I'm worried about me.' Henry sat back a little. 'You?' he said quietly. 'I have to think about these things, Henry.' 'You mean a baby?' Beatrice nodded, though that wasn't what she was thinking about. 'A baby!' Henry sounded incredulous; he leaned forward eagerly. 'Do you want a baby, Beatrice?' 'No, Henry, I don't.' Henry sat back again. 'Oh,' he said, and then he said, 'For a moment I forgot. I mean, I thought about having a son, a daughter, and I forgot who I was.' He turned to her again and grabbed her hands. 'But that's not why I want to make love to you,

Beatrice. I want to make love to you, not to someone else, not *for* someone else. Not for some baby.' Beatrice looked at Henry then. He had a hat on, and he looked for the first time since she had known him like what he was: a college freshman. A teenaged boy who, under different circumstances, would soon become a man. She said, 'Henry, I love you,' but it sounded like a diagnosis, not a declaration, so she said, 'But what will I do when you're gone?' 'When I'm gone?' Henry echoed. 'When you're gone, Henry. When you're gone, I'll still be here, and what do I do then? What do I do with everything that making love to you is going to give to me?' Henry didn't say anything, and, beside him, Beatrice still heard her words, 'I love you,' and as she heard them it occurred to her that the terms of her affair with Henry were words and only words, and while this made sense to her it also seemed wrong, for at the root of her words for Henry were, she thought, real things, feelings, and she decided in that moment to give him what he wanted. But she could think of no other way to say it, and so she only said, 'New Year's Day.' 'New Year's Day?' Henry said, and Beatrice said, 'We'll do it New Year's Day.' 'Why,' Henry asked, 'why wait?' 'Because I only want to do it once, Henry. That's all I can bear.' Then Henry whispered, 'I have to go in the hospital a day early, for tests,' and it was almost enough to destroy Beatrice. 'Then we'll do it the day before,' she said, starting the car and ending the conversation. 'The night before. New Year's Eve.' She laughed at that odd coincidence—she didn't know that Henry had set it up that way—and then she repeated, 'New Year's Eve.'

He looked like an angel when she opened the door. He wore khaki pants cut for a person several inches bigger around than he was, and he wore a blousy white shirt that was moving in the wind, and his head was bare and gleaming in the porch light. The only things that held him down were a few brown spots on his collar: blood, Beatrice wondered, or gravy, or dirt? He had his hands pushed deep into the pockets of his pants and he just stood there for several seconds after Beatrice opened the door, staring into her eyes. She thought he was having a blackout at first, but then she saw Henry's mother back the car from the driveway and as soon as it had disappeared Henry leaned far forward on his toes and he kissed Beatrice on the lips, very slowly: he leaned slowly, he kissed slowly, but he never opened his mouth, never put his hands on her, and it was several minutes before he leaned back. Beatrice just stood there, smiling, stunned by love, and then Henry pulled his right hand from his pocket and in it there was a jeweler's box. Henry said, 'Beatrice, I love you,' and the ring said it too, *Beatrice I love you*, engraved on the inside, and Beatrice just said, 'Henry,' which the ring, an engagement ring, a thin gold band with a diamond fleck lost in its setting, also said: *Beatrice I love you Henry*, in a tight little circle that held Beatrice's eyes for a long time: *Beatrice I love you Henry Beatrice I love you Henry Beatrice I love you Henry Beatrice*. Then he put the engagement ring on her finger and they kissed again, more passionately this time, and then Beatrice blushed and invited him in with mock formality. The house smelled like apples, not just from the pie in the oven, but from dozens of scented votive candles that burned in the living room and dining room and kitchen and bathroom, in coffee cups and water glasses and cereal bowls, and the shadows that they cast were yellow and wavered across the walls like water.

They ate at the dining room table. There were six daisies in a green glass vase, and Henry plucked a flower and played she-loves-me, she-loves-me-not with it, and he won. He urged Beatrice to but she was superstitious, and so Henry did it with every flower and with every flower he won, and by the time dinner was done the black lacquered top of the dining room table looked like a shattered chessboard because of the white daisy petals strewn all over it. After they had eaten they went in the living room and turned on the television and laughed at the out-of-focus black-and-white footage of the red deer everybody was talking about, and Beatrice was just about to suggest that they go see them when she realized that they couldn't, and then, immediately, there was a report on the possibility of war in January, and Beatrice, to her surprise, began to cry, and to her surprise Henry joined her, and though she knew that their tears had little to do with the news on the television it would be far too simple to claim that she knew why they were crying. All Beatrice knew was that the hand she put out to comfort Henry landed on his breast and the little comforting kiss she gave him ended up drinking his tears and then she just took him on the couch, his pants open but not even pushed down, her dress around her waist, her panties pulled to the side. They just sat there for a few moments, she atop him, he with his head thrown over the back of the couch, and then Beatrice felt Henry twitch violently, and a shudder moved up and down the length of his body and he let out a long slow grumbly moan and then, almost as if someone had whispered it in her ear, Beatrice realized that she was even more wet inside than she'd been a moment ago and she understood that Henry had just come inside her, and just like that her orgasm took her over and she finally felt Henry's dick in her, really felt it, as her vaginal walls squeezed tight against it, let go, squeezed tight again, and she threw back her head and let her moan out, and she was so surprised when it turned out to be a scream that she nearly threw herself off Henry, but she grabbed his shoulders and held on while Henry, beneath her, writhed around desperately as if he wanted to escape her— and then, abruptly, it was over. Beatrice lay still, and she felt her still body sway gently up and down on Henry's like a tethered rowboat. Her head fell next to Henry's, and she heard his breath in her ear like the breath of a conch, whispering its message of eternal departure, eternal return.

They bathed together. Beatrice noticed how easily their clothes came off: three buttons and her dress slipped off her shoulders, two buttons for Henry's pants, just one for his shirt, and it billowed over his head like an unfettered sail, and then they stood in front of each other, naked. While the bath filled they looked at the parts of each other's bodies that before they'd only touched, until Henry's cheeks turned red and he turned away, but Beatrice saw him peeking out of the corner of his eye and she blushed and looked away, but tucked her hair behind her ear so she could continue to see him. Henry, she realized, would've been a big man had he not been always ill, not tall but broad and strong. Instead he was the empty frame of a big man. He was bone, and he was muscle, not a lot of it, and he was some other things that she didn't know about, and he was all wrapped up in skin. 'You're bleeding,' Henry said then, the first words either of them had spoken since . . . She searched, but couldn't find a word. Since. Beatrice smiled, but didn't speak; they were both smiling. Henry didn't seem alarmed and she didn't feel alarmed. She looked down below her belly, saw the matted thatch of her pubic hair and a few drops of blood. There was a little silent negotiation in the tub, and finally Beatrice lay down first and then Henry, his arms between her legs and his back between her arms, and Beatrice moved quickly to press his head against her left shoulder because otherwise Candy would have been staring her right in the face. When Henry turned once the sharp bone of his hip grazed her vagina and she felt a sudden push of water into and out of her. 'Ssth,' she said then, and Henry steadied himself, and he said, 'Does it hurt? Like they say it hurts?' Beatrice was reminded of their first meeting, when she'd asked him if he was okay. She said, 'It hurts,' and then she said, 'How do they say it hurts?' and when Henry didn't answer her she said, 'It doesn't hurt too much,' and it didn't, though she sensed that it would hurt more tomorrow. Then they just lay in the tub. She kissed him occasionally on the top or side of his head, and she was aware that he slept at some point, or had a blackout, from the sound of his breathing. They never did wash, and when they left the tub they left the water in it and they dried each other and then Beatrice led Henry by the hand to her parents' bed.

The white satin spread had not been turned back since her father's death; Beatrice had fluffed it to keep dust from settling on it but that's all, and underneath the bedspread were the same sheets her father had almost died on, and underneath the sheets was the mattress on which she had been conceived. Henry lay down on this bed and the spread billowed around his outstretched limbs like a cloud. His body sank so far into it that Beatrice thought he would continue sinking until he disappeared. But he didn't, he only said in a voice muffled by a pillow, 'Beatrice,' and then he said, 'I want to again, but I don't know if I can, again,' and Beatrice, who wanted to again and again, also didn't know if she could, again, so soon. She burned now. But she only lay down beside him and pulled him close to her, his thin hot white body, her mind a mixture of tenderness and sadness. She whispered his name as she held him, 'Oh, Henry,' she whispered, and then a long time later she whispered again, 'Henry,' and then she whispered it again and before long she was whispering it over and over again and it was futile because his body lay in hers like a straw doll's, unmoving except when she moved it, unfeeling except when she felt it. His breath was hot and shallow on her face, and when she sat up to look at him she saw bright red flushes stain and then fade on his white skin, irregularly shaped patches that seemed to rise and fall like continents, first rising and then falling back into the sea.

He came back eventually, and when he did his hands flailed about like a blind man's until he had hold of her and he pulled her to him and he said, 'I'm so scared,' and he twisted and turned on the bed, curled up his limbs and straightened them, opened and closed his eyes. 'I would give anything not to die,' he said, 'but I would never give you up.' Beatrice pulled him closer, felt him shivering in her embrace, and she folded the bedspread over him. 'Henry,' she said, 'if never seeing you again meant that you'd live, I'd do it, I'd do it in a minute.' And then they were quiet for a while, and Beatrice thought it was somehow an indictment of their love that she knew, and she knew that Henry knew, that they were lying. Then, eventually, she felt him stand up between her legs, and all at once he pushed her over with the insistent strength that men get at moments like these, and after a couple of false stabs, one too far to the left, one too far to the right, he shoved into her, and in just a few strokes he was finished. And Beatrice was glad, pinned beneath him and biting her lip to keep from crying out, because, though she hated herself for not wanting it to happen, she hadn't wanted it to happen. Not like that. When he pulled out of her she sucked in her breath in pain, but she pulled his body down on hers and pushed his face past hers until she could regain her composure. Until her loins stopped throbbing with pain and her blood stopped boiling with the strange rage she felt at him for hurting her. Her anger went, and then the shame that followed it, and then Beatrice still held Henry atop her, his light body holding hers lightly, his snores indicating that he was safely asleep. Everything left her then, everything except Henry, who would be hers as long as this moment lasted, and so she waited for time to stop, or her heart, or Henry's. She closed her eyes, the better to forget what had just happened, and to remember everything that had happened before it, and in the morning, before Henry got out of her car to go into his house, he pulled another ring from his pocket. This one was a wedding ring, and as he slipped it on her hand he said, 'I stole it,' and he dashed from the car and into his house, leaving Beatrice stuck in his driveway, because she didn't have enough strength to lift her hand to turn the key, weighted down as it was with the rings and the stolen life they represented, the life that she would never live.

There is no name for that ceremony. There are marriages, christenings, birthdays, graduations, anniversaries, and, finally, funerals, but of her first sex Beatrice had only a bedspread, once clean, now dirty, and candles, once fully formed, now shapeless blobs. Little drops of green wax splattered walls, shelves, books, knick-knacks, photographs, the television even. The dining room table was sticky with spilled food and drink and mushy daisy petals fast turning brown, and the kitchen was crowded with food and the remains of food and dirty dishes. She ached. There was a heavy smell in every room of the house. In the front rooms it was the smell of food, in the bedroom sex, but as the day progressed they began to smell the same, stale, sweet gone sour. She really ached. She wished some kind of device existed that could push her inner thighs apart when she walked because she felt like someone had taken sandpaper and rubbed her raw. Still, she concentrated on her physical pain and did nothing to alleviate it, because it was easier to deal with, easier to understand, than her other pain. She cleaned: the dining room, the kitchen, the bathroom with last night's water still in the tub, the bedroom. When the entire house was clean, every last drop of wax scraped off every surface, Beatrice realized she had made a mistake because, without a name to remember last night, and without Henry, she'd had nothing but those other things to keep the experience fresh in her mind: stains, smells, spilled food. Now, without them, she had nothing. She had been defeated; she had defeated herself. She turned on the television then, plopped on the couch and immediately she saw an ugly red-brown stain on her parents' white crushed-velvet sofa, and she wondered if this, whatever it was, had leaked from her body, or from Henry's, or from Henry's body into hers, and then, finally, she started to cry. She gave it up quickly because she knew it wouldn't change things, and because she sensed that the time for tears was over now, for her. She looked at her father's recliner. It sat there empty, her father's soft black chair next to her mother's soft white chair, also empty, and she believed she understood her parents in that moment, and she begrudged them nothing, none of the touches or hugs or kisses they'd given each other rather than her. And then she slid onto her knees in front of the sofa, and she used her tongue and she used her saliva, and she removed the final stain and the final reminder of last night, and of Henry.

In the hospital, Henry was scared and didn't say much, and his parents never left the room, so Beatrice didn't stay long that first day. She came early the second day and she had an hour with him before his mother and father showed up. Henry's father read a newspaper and Henry's mother watched soap operas and Beatrice held Henry's hand, and though they managed to speak occasionally they were in general silent, and Henry stared at the wall below the television. Beatrice stared at Henry's face and only toward the end of the day did she realize that the top of Henry's head and his chin and his cheeks were all stained by the slightest hint of hair. He'd stopped chemo a few weeks ago, but his hair hadn't come back. She looked now at Henry's mother—brown and permed, but probably straight—and Henry's father—a darker brown, almost chestnut, with a slight curl at its longish ends—and then she looked back at Henry. 'Henry,' she said, and then, rather than saying anything else, she took the hand she was holding and she put it on top of his head. He didn't seem to understand at first. He put his hand on Candy, larger than a robin's egg now, and he felt that, and then he passed his hand over his entire head several times, and then the skin where his eyebrows would have been—there were dark spots there too—raised, and he looked at Beatrice and smiled. He looked at his hand then, and at his arm, he unbuttoned the top buttons of his pajamas and everywhere there were the same dark spots, and when Beatrice put her hand on Henry's hand again, on his arm, when she touched, tentatively, his head, and, surreptitiously, his chest, she could feel the stubble faintly. 'Your hair,' she said, 'what color is your hair?' He blinked, and Beatrice imagined long pale eyelashes lowering themselves over his eyes. 'It was brown,' he said, 'like hers. But it used to go blond in the summers.' 'Brown,' Beatrice said, 'blond,' and the words excited her, reverberated in her mind and evoked for the only time in their entire relationship the notion of time, of real time beyond the few months they'd spent together. She felt suddenly full of hope. 'It's a sign, Henry, I know it is, it's a sign.' Henry smiled at her when she said that, and then he let his smile fade. 'Ah, Beatrice,' he said gently, like an old man to a young girl. 'Don't you know your hair keeps growing after you die?'

A nurse poked her head in the door then, and then she left, and then another wheeled a covered cart into the room a few minutes later, and left, and then a third came, and she stayed. Henry's father folded his paper and stood up, and then he unfolded it and refolded it in a different way and then he just looked at his shoes, and Beatrice wondered if this man could eat, if he could even chew, because she had never seen a face so rigid in her life. Henry's mother threw herself on Henry, and her lamentations were loud and terrible and embarrassing. 'My baby boy,' she said, and she ran wet hands down either

69

side of Henry's face and made it look as though he were crying too, which he wasn't. Then, in the waiting room, Candace suggested that Bea—Candace called her Bea—should get a breath of air, should get some real food, should get some sleep, and finally she just said that she and Dylan needed to be alone at this particular moment in time, and Beatrice left. It wasn't Candace's words that drove her away. It was an aversion to waiting in a smoke-clouded room drinking stale coffee and looking at *True Story*. She felt she'd end up doing something stupid, like going to the chapel and praying.

Outside it was cold, really cold, and Beatrice, sure that her car wouldn't start, didn't even try. She walked instead, and a long time later came to a diner. Inside it was overheated and the air was heavy with the grease of french fries and light with the vapor of boiled potatoes, and the booths were shit-brown vinyl, but sparkly. The waitress behind the counter looked up from her Harlequin romance only to say, 'Anywhere you want, honey.' Beatrice looked at the huge laminated rectangle of a menu. She wasn't hungry but she felt bad about taking up space without paying for it, so she ordered a coffee, and when that was gone she ordered a plate of fries, and when that was gone she had more coffee, and then she nibbled at a saccharin slice of pie. When, somehow, the pie was gone and Beatrice looked up at the waitress again, the waitress was already looking at her. 'Honey,' she said, 'if you just want to sit here it's fine by me.' There was a long moment while Beatrice and the waitress looked at each other and Beatrice's stomach churned on the heavy food and the desire to tell another woman everything, and then, quite suddenly, she did. 'My fiancé's in the hospital,' she said, and the waitress said, 'Oh my God,' and put her book down and came over with the coffeepot and her fuchsia lips and cracked nails and thick Italian hair kept artificially black with a shoe-polishy dye, and she was as familiar and comforting as an old blanket at the top of the closet. By the time her shift was over the sun was up and she and Beatrice had cried a lot of tears. Beatrice's hot puffy cheeks had cooled and returned to normal, and the waitress, muddy swaths of dried makeup on her cheeks, looked worse than

Beatrice did, and she drove Beatrice back to the hospital. When they got there she took Beatrice's head in her hands and looked at her face for a long time, and then she said, 'Do you know, your eyes and mouth have exactly the same shape,' and at these words, which took place so far from anything else they'd said, Beatrice wanted to kiss her deeply, passionately. But then the waitress said, 'I don't know what I'd do if something like this happened to me. I think I'd kill myself.' Beatrice sat back suddenly, because that thought had never occurred to her, and it felt like a mark against her that it hadn't. The waitress seemed to sense that she'd said something wrong, and she stuttered for a moment and then she just said, 'You come by, okay? You tell me how everything turns out,' and Beatrice said quickly, loudly, falsely, 'I will,' and then she left the car.

Inside the hospital, Candace and Dylan held each other on the couch. Candace looked bad, back bowed, face greasy, hair a mess, but Dylan looked worse. He looked broken, like a toy. His face looked almost normal but rounder than usual, blown up—like a balloon, and like a bomb—and at the sight of him Beatrice thought, He's dead, and her breath caught in her throat like a solid thing and she sat down before she fell down. 'He's alive,' Henry's mother said then. 'They think he's going to be all right.' 'But—' Beatrice began, but Henry's father's voice cut her off. It was stale, guttural, and twisted, she realized, by hatred. 'No more buts, Bea, no more. He's alive.' He was alive, but he didn't wake up until the next day, late. He lay there so long that Beatrice was convinced that he wasn't going to wake up after all, that he would go on lying there with his slowly moving chest and closed eyes, with his hair growing under the bandage that covered his head, but then, just when the sun entering his room had reached a deep shade of orange, Henry opened his eyes, and Beatrice looked into them. They all looked into them. There was something different there, Beatrice knew, but she didn't know what was different because she couldn't quite remember what had been there before. There was something moving there, spinning around and falling down, and after a very long time Henry blinked and Beatrice knew that he had willed it, that this blink was the test

71

he had set for himself, but she didn't know if he had passed or failed, and neither did Henry. His vision, which had been focused like the narrow beam of a flashlight, expanded so suddenly that images crashed on his eyes like a falling television. They all seemed to be falling on him, his mother, his father, his Beatrice, and he closed his eyes before they hit him. When he opened them they wore different clothes but they were still there, and the pain at the back of his head was some new feeling, not threatening but mundane, merely painful. Something had changed. Everything had changed. Beatrice and his mother spoke to each other over his head, they yelled at each other and he didn't understand any of it, but eventually his parents left the room and Beatrice brought her face so close to his that she seemed to be on the wrong side of a fishbowl. She said something, but it might have been air bubbles escaping her mouth. She said it again but still it made no sense. She said it again and again and then again; she said it until finally the question sat on his chest like regurgitated food.

'Do you still love me?' Beatrice asked him, and Henry, when he finally understood her, squeezed her hand in reply, and he smiled, and he said, 'Of course I love you.' He heard their words and was frightened by them: it was his *of course* combined with her *still* that made him afraid.

4

Sixty Seconds of Peace and Security

Stan died on the answering machine, between a message from the receptionist at Hank's company wondering if he was coming in that day, and another message from the receptionist wondering if he was going to be in the next day. And it wasn't like Stan was Hank's first friend to die or anything: there were no first times anymore. No, Stan was merely the latest in a long line of people Hank had known who were dead now, but his death was the first in a long time that had made Hank think of his own. Hank had looked into Stan's face and seen the one expression he couldn't bear to see, regret, and even though he tried to get out of bed the next morning like it was just another day, he knew that something had changed. He warmed the pain out of his hands with two cups of coffee, had it out with Bea, sat it out behind his desk for eight hours, and then, before he went home, he reached out to Myra. It seemed like she'd been awaiting his call. 'Oh, Hank,' she said, 'you don't know the state I'm in.' There was enough distance between Hank and Myra that he felt consoling, generous even. 'Tell me,' he said, 'Myra, what's wrong?' 'The bills, Hank, every day there's another one. One doctor bills you for cutting him open and another one bills you for sewing him shut. And the funeral expenses. I'm telling you, Hank, it costs more to die nowadays than it does to stay alive.' 'Myra,' Hank found himself saying, 'we want to help.' Myra seemed as surprised as Hank at his words; her voice, when it came, was suspicious. 'You want to help?' They talked for a long time. Hank offered to pay Stan's medical and funeral bills, and then he offered

Myra money, and then he offered to buy Myra's plot of land, and the one north of it as well; Myra would go on living in her trailer, and he and Bea would build a new house on the adjoining plot. After he hung up he sat in his office for a few minutes; he had sat in this small dirty white room for almost twenty years, and as he studied its familiar dimensions he couldn't believe what he'd just done. But he had done it, and before he could call Myra back he went home. It took him another day or two to get up the nerve to tell Bea, but she surprised him by not taking it badly. She didn't take it well either. She just took it. 'It's your house,' she said. 'It's your business. It's your *money*.' She left him then, and they avoided each other until they moved.

Then everything vanished with frightening simplicity. A yard sale, a real estate broker, a lawyer to handle the sale of the business: Hank was surprised at how much it was worth, but he was more surprised by how quickly it went. For one moment it was all there, brightly illuminated, and then it was gone, and it seemed that his life with Bea had never existed. He found himself in front of Myra's trailer, stepping out of his brand new Jeep; the Jeep was still spotless, as though it had materialized there. He shut his door, Bea shut her door, the alarm beeped in the dark. Bea looked at him disparagingly. 'An alarm, Hank? I thought we were moving *away* from crime.' 'Standard feature,' Hank lied. 'Came with the Jeep.' Behind Bea, Myra stood in her doorway; Hank could see the glow of a cigarette in one hand, the glint of a glass in the other, and her voice staggered across the lawn: 'Now it's time for the party!' She gestured with the drink in her hand, spilling some on the carpet as Bea and Hank squeezed by her in the door, and then, as if for balance, she gestured with her cigarette and dropped ashes on the wet patch. 'I got lonely here all by myself,' she said, 'so I kind of started the party a little early, a little.' Bea looked past Myra. 'Where's Lucy?' she said. 'You mean my daughter, Lucy?' Myra said, and she giggled at herself, and then she attempted a straight face. 'Lucy, you know, Lucy's got her own life to live, she . . . Oh hell, Bea, she was just waiting for Stan to go. She's gone now.' Neither Hank nor Bea spoke for a moment, and then Bea said, 'I think I'll take this to our room,' and she disappeared with her bag, leaving Hank alone with Myra. They waited several minutes but Bea didn't reappear, and Hank realized that she wouldn't. 'Pour me a drink,' he said then. 'You said this was a party, right?' 'A party, right!' Myra repeated, and when she smiled her teeth were as slick and shiny as her forehead. 'Whiskey and soda,' she said, 'or just whiskey?' 'Just soda,' Hank said, 'Coke, if you got any,' but when he smelled his drink he could tell that Myra had ignored him, and he was glad. He took a long drink, and then he took another, and then he said, 'Myra,' in one of those opening-of-discussion tones. But Myra said, 'Hank,' in a closing-of-discussion tone, and he looked at her eyes and saw that beyond the haze of alcohol she looked a lot more focused than he felt, and he was surprised when she said, 'Hank,' again, this time borrowing the tone he'd used when he said her name. She sat back in her chair in the way that only old friends can, and she waited. Hank took a few more drinks from his glass, and then it was empty and he got up to refill it, and as he poured he rediscovered the clocks on Myra's counter. They all told different stories, but, though they were all starting from different places, they all proceeded at the same pace, and four minutes had passed—or sixteen, depending on your point of view—before he sat down again and started talking.

'It was time,' he said. 'We've been in that house fifteen, nearly twenty years. We've been on the island our whole lives. South Shore, Suffolk County, Sunrise Highway to and from work every day for forty-something years now.' 'Forty years,' Myra said. 'You know what I mean, Myra. You and Stan did it, what, ten years ago?' 'Closer to twenty,' Myra said. 'It wasn't too long after you and Bea moved into the new house.' 'The new house.' Hank laughed. 'That house hasn't been new for a long time, Myra.' He paused, drank. 'You know, every summer Bea had something done to it, the swimming pool, the rock garden. She wanted me to put a greenhouse up this year. I said to her, Bea, you had trouble with a rock garden, how're you gonna cope with plants? But I'd've done it. Because I understand, you know, Myra, I knew what she was trying to do.' Myra said, 'Hmmm?' quietly, sleepily, and Hank looked up at her. Her hands were folded in her lap, her head was bent forward and her eyes were closed. A faint smile lingered on her lips. Hank took a deep breath. 'It's no secret that Bea and me ain't been getting on too good lately. I won't pretend that's a secret. But I've always understood her. I've always understood my wife. A man should understand his wife, should know what she wants.' 'Are you trying to convince me or her, or just yourself?' Hank looked up, startled. Myra had opened her eyes and looked at him; the smile had left her face. 'Convince you,' Hank said, 'of what?' 'That this move was mutual, Hank. That Bea wanted it as much as you do.' 'That's what I'm trying to tell you, Myra. Bea never told me she wanted to move, but I could tell she needed it, Myra, she needed it just as much as I did.' 'Needed what, Hank?' 'A change, Myra. Something different.' Myra leaned across the table and took Hank's hand in her own. 'Listen here, Hank,' she said. 'I know what you mean about needing a change.' 'You do, Myra?' Her words gave him hope. He wanted to hear someone say that it was okay, it was the right thing to do. 'Look, you wanted a change, that's fine, Hank. You got a change. But now it's over. Now you have to do something.' 'Do something?' Hank said, and Myra said, 'Make a decision, Hank, make a few choices. It's one thing to retire, but you can't sit at home reading the Sunday paper every day of the week.' Hank was confused. 'I don't understand,' he said, and Myra said, 'What I'm telling you, Hank, is that there's two parts to every move—before, and after. And you're in the after part now, Hank, you're in the do-something-new part. So what's next, Hank? What's next?' Myra shut up suddenly, but she kept her eyes focused on Hank's. Hank looked at Myra for a long time after she finished speaking. He knew he was supposed to say something and he could tell from the way Myra was looking at him that it wasn't supposed to be about himself, or merely himself. It occurred to him then that you give other people the advice you yourself need to hear, and he said, 'You are too, Myra.' Myra blinked, but she didn't say anything. 'You've got to do something new too,' Hank said again. Myra blinked again, and turned away.

Hank spoke one more time. 'Stan's *dead*,' he said, and Myra stood up abruptly. 'Well, I'm not!' she said, and she walked toward the door. She turned before she got there. 'And neither are you,' she said, and then she turned again, and left.

After a while he went outside, found an old picnic chair in the back yard, turned it upright and sat down. He'd only worn his socks outside, and in the dozen steps he'd taken through the grass his feet had become wet with the night-time dew, and he curled his toes up against the cold. There was a little sharp twinge of pain when he did that, and when it was gone it left an ache, a soft almost pleasant ache, the kind of ache that reminded Hank his feet hadn't fallen off since the last time he'd checked. There were some guys at work, he thought, who could use that kind of ache in their balls. He put his hands in his pockets because he didn't want them to get cold and start hurting as well, but they were cramped in there, so he untucked his shirt and put them flat up against his stomach, which felt warm and full from the whiskey. He sat for a while, listened to the night sounds, but the only thing he could hear was a persistent hum coming from somewhere in or around the trailer. When it shut off with a click after a few minutes he really could hear nothing, and the next sound he heard was only a memory. 'It's beautiful,' he heard, and the words were whispered and the words were Bea's, but he pretended not to know that, and he whispered himself, 'It's beautiful.' But then he remembered more of Bea's words. 'What are we going to do about your father?' She had asked him this when he told her they were going to move; it was the only thing she had asked him. What they were going to do about his father was put him away. The old man had looked his ninetieth birthday in the face a few years ago, and at the sight of it he had backed down, and as the days advanced the years receded, from his memory anyway, from his mind, and by the time he felt the two hands on his shoulders, his son's on his left and his daughter-in-law's on his right, he was ninety-four going on five. Just five. He held a newspaper in his hands because he had held a newspaper in his hands every evening for nearly three-quarters of a century, but only every once in a while did it seem like he even remembered that he had forgotten how to read. He looked at Bea's face and then he looked at Hank's, and the smile his father gave him was something Hank knew would be held over his head come Judgment Day.

It was hard, after that, to return to simpler things, but Hank wiped his face with his hands and distracted himself by thinking about the animals that were probably all around him, an owl in the sky, a rabbit or two in the grass, a raccoon in the trash. Who knows, maybe there were a few of those red deer everyone had been talking about. Maybe he would go look for them, not now, but in the morning. He would take Stan's rifle, the one hanging in the living room above the framed country scene, and he would bring home a trophy for his new house. Other men were taking their rifles, other men were bringing home trophies. He wasn't sure how long he'd been outside when he realized that he was just waiting for a sign—waiting for an answer, really, to Myra's question. He shook himself then and tried to think of something real, something immediate, something that needed attending to. He looked at the lot next door, his property. It was marked out by the vertical shadows of wireless fence posts, and he thought at first that it was covered with fog. But then he realized that the fog was really a layer of dandelion balls catching the moonlight and glowing a little, silvery gray, and suddenly his house sprang from this carpet, and he knew exactly what it would look like: it would be long and lean, all one level, like those California-style A-frame ranch houses that were popular in the early eighties. The ceilings would be high and vaulted, the windows tall and uncovered so he could see as much of his new home as possible, although as he imagined it he wasn't quite sure if he was meant to be looking in or out of those tall bare windows: he wasn't sure if his new home was the house he was going to build, or the land he was going to build it on. When his hands began to emit little warning tingles and the ache in his feet had increased substantially, he went in. He went back around front first so he could see how his new truck had survived its first long trek. As soon as he looked at it—spotless, he noticed again, and solid as a rock—he was reminded of the four slips of paper that were supposed to be in the glove compartment. The papers represented all the other things, mostly furniture, that they'd decided to keep but had left in storage until the new house was completed. Hank wasn't sure if he'd left them in the glove compartment, or if he'd put them in his wallet, which was in the new addition, or if he'd done something else with them.

He remembered giving money to the man behind the storage warehouse's counter—was it really only yesterday afternoon?—and receiving in return the four pink receipts. The long list of entries, in faint carbon-copied purplish letters, had seemed, without his reading glasses, unreadable, and he'd wondered for just a moment if it was the key to someone else's possessions he might be holding in his hands. He'd watched two men pack all of his and Bea's furniture into a room that was much smaller than their old house. He wanted a larger room: he wanted there to be enough space so that he could sit on one of the wing-backed chairs if he wanted to, put his feet up on the coffee table and read the paper before dinner. Instead, two end tables, upside down, lay one on each chair with their legs poking the air. How small the whole pile of it looked, how puny each individual piece, how marked by time with little nicks and cuts that showed up like age spots on pale fabric and bleached wood. That long sewn-up rip in the love seat was where Bea had shoved a pair of knitting needles, that stain on the bottom of a rolled-up rug must be the other side of the time Hank had dumped an entire bottle of red wine on the carpet. There was the gouge in the hutch where the ashtray had hit; Hank didn't remember who'd thrown it, and if it had been thrown at the hutch or at a person. Bea really loved that hutch. Once, when he thought he saw the men exchange wry smiles across the length of a long couch upholstered in a floral feminine print, Hank coughed and said, 'My wife picked that out, that, that cloth.' The men looked at each other without speaking and Hank said again, 'The cloth. The fabric. The, the'—and then he found the right word—'the upholstery.' At that one of the men said to the ground, 'That's nice,' and Hank thought he saw the other cover a smirk with his hand. He sat down then on a dining room chair. He felt vaguely humiliated, but he wasn't sure if they'd humiliated him or if he'd managed to do it himself, or if, somehow, he could blame Bea for what he felt. But he had to get up immediately when the older of the two men came for the chair he sat on. The man, Hank noticed, was his age. He set the chair on top of the quilt-covered kitchen table as though it were an odd-shaped plate of food, and then he closed the garage door that led to the room, padlocked it, and handed Hank the key. 'Don't lose it,' he joked, 'it's the only one we got.' Hank looked down at the bit of brass in his hand, but it was suddenly plucked away by foreign fingers. 'Just kidding,' the young one said. 'We keep the key. You get a receipt.' But Hank was suddenly terrified that he'd made the one wrong decision that couldn't be undone, and he couldn't let go of the idea that he'd lost the key, the key to everything he owned and everything that had any meaning for him: it was all sealed away like bones in a tomb and separated from him forever by a sheet of dull gray accordioned steel.

His feet were cold and he couldn't remember where he'd put the receipts. He thought of going to the truck but his feet were killing him and his hands were starting to throb, and he decided the receipts had to be in his wallet then, and he limped inside to check. He went into the new addition. The receipts weren't there, but Bea was, in bed, sleeping. Snoring. Sprawled out almost as though she'd fallen, though she'd managed to change into her nightgown and pull back the covers before she fell. They're in the glove compartment, he told himself, and he undressed quickly before he could go back outside and get his aching feet wet again. He found and slipped into a pair of pajamas in the dark, but when he got in bed Bea moved away from him with movements that let him know she'd awakened. It was a relief to have her distract him from the thought of the missing receipts, but it was hard too, and he pushed his legs under the covers reluctantly, laid his arms atop them. Next to him Bea was all straightened out as well, and he thought they must look like two corpses side by side and stiff as boards. His left hand felt her right hand squeeze the blanket over and over, squeeze it and release it, and because she was doing it and because his hand hurt he resisted the urge to do it himself. He kept his eyes closed even though it was an effort to do so, and he thought, How stupid this is, yet he knew that he didn't have the strength to do anything about it, that he would lie there until morning came or hell froze over or he, at last, fell asleep, but he wouldn't move until she did, and damn it all, he still wasn't sure if those receipts were in the glove compartment. He lay there, frozen, because that was the game they were playing, the war they were fighting, and though the only thing one got for winning was the chance to play, to fight again, he realized that it was never a game fought to be won, only not to be lost.

And then, without quite realizing it, he was up, muttering to himself, and he wasn't sure if the sound behind him was the bed complaining or Bea, he was going to see once and for all if those receipts were in the glove compartment. The metal grill of the porch was merciless on his feet, cold as only wet steel can be cold, and the grass completed the job, bathing him up to his ankles in dew that he would have sworn was frost. 'Fuck, fuck, fuck, fuck,' he said aloud as he minced his way to the truck, and then he had the passenger door open and he sat on the leather of the seat and breathed in new-car smell for a moment. There was a light in the cab, and there was another in the glove box, and with the aid of both he could almost read the writing on the four pink slips that lay on top of the truck's registration. They were there; there they were. He shut the glove box with a satisfying snap, the car door with a rewarding thump, and he limped back to the trailer. 'Knew they were there all the time,' he told himself. His feet hurt but it didn't matter: beyond Myra's dinky trailer he could see the space that his own house would occupy, a strong solid structure that *he* would hold the key to. And as Hank looked at that mirage his sixty seconds of peace and security ran out, as his new truck's new alarm sounded its note for the first and final time. The alarm rang for as long as Hank's previous minute of safety, and the car's lights flashed on and off like a beacon, and when it was over Bea and Myra were at the door looking at him. 'Don't ask me,' Hank said, and he pushed past them as he made his way into Myra's trailer. 'Because I don't know.'

But he did know. The shriek of the alarm had skinned him like an onion, layer by layer, and in that naked minute he couldn't deny it. He hadn't lost the key: he had lost his life. He had squandered it, and now it was gone.

ξ

The grocery store was an ugly brick building perched vertiginously on top of a hill, and Bea's stomach pitched as she looked down at Ithaca: everything in this town either crowned a hill or was crammed into a valley. She'd nearly lost it twice during the drive here, and when Myra's car left the parking lot she pulled a pill bottle from her purse and shook a couple of yellow circles into her hand. Yellow, she wondered, Halcion? She popped them in her mouth, and then she straightened her shirt in a window, grabbed a cart off the sidewalk, and went inside. She steered toward the nearest aisle, aisle three, 'pasta-sauce-salsa-chips-party-favors,' and the next thing she knew she'd gone all the way through aisle four and was almost out of aisle five, her cart was still empty, and she realized with a start that it wasn't Halcion she'd taken. She grabbed a half dozen eggs then, and then she began grabbing things randomly from shelves, cans of vegetables and boxes of dehydrated foods which stared at her with funny expressions on their square faces. She moved through the store's seven aisles in a daze: she found herself in the dairy aisle and grabbed a gallon jug of milk, and then she had her hands around crackers, saltines, and then she went looking for soup to dunk them in, chicken noodle soup, and she went through the store this way and that, filling her cart, overfilling it, replacing some items with others. She hid a frozen pack of broccoli deep in the ice under the fresh broccoli, fluffed a bin of paper flowers around an eight-stick foil-wrapped package of butter. She grabbed a pound of coffee beans, and she grabbed food she'd never tried before, crumpets, pickled beets, baloney stuffed with olives and pimentos. What *are* pimentos? she wondered, and grabbed nine cans of them, clutching them precariously in all ten of her fingers; they fell on the pile in her cart like sprinkles on ice

82

cream. She continued like this until she found her path blocked by a big man in a white apron with bloodstains on it, or ketchup, a big man who put a hand on her cart and pulled it up short. Bea looked at him, and when she turned away from him she saw Myra, and Myra's face was confused and a little frightened, but mostly it was embarrassed. She looked at the floor and saw eggs leaking around her shoes. She looked at the man and decided that the stains were definitely blood. And then she looked at Myra. 'Stan and I used to eat like this when he came over,' she confessed. 'When he came over,' she said again. 'After we were finished.'

In the finite space of the trailer it was almost possible to start at one end and clean your way to the other, and Myra did, or Myra tried to. Myra was clean now, and cleaning, and between her industry and Hank's, Bea felt even worse. Still, there was something nice about the way Myra worked, Bea had to admit. The first thing she cleaned was the rifle. Bea watched her take it from wall hooks and run a soapy sponge over its metal and wood and then hang it, still damp, back on the wall. She sat at the kitchen table drinking coffee. The curtain in the doorway had been removed, so Bea could see Myra clearly. Myra held a cigarette with her lips and a scrub brush with her hands, and she worked the brush so vigorously over the walls that her hair and her shirt became soaked with splashed water and sweat, and her wet hair and wet breasts flopped in sync with her moving arms. 'Goddamn,' she'd say sometimes, 'I can*not* believe we lived in this pigsty.' She spoke to the walls when she talked, which made Bea glad, because there were often tears rolling down her face. She wasn't sobbing; she wasn't really crying. The tears seemed divorced from the rest of her body: her shoulders didn't heave, her breath was only slightly affected, but all the same she felt that if she didn't let those tears flow from her eyes then she would explode in a flash flood of untapped emotions. 'Look at this, Bea,' Myra would say. 'Are you looking at this, Bea?' Under Myra's brush a layer of soot was rolling off the walls in black oily water, and paneling that Bea had thought was dark brown was revealed to be light brown, bleached in places by a sun that hadn't touched it in years. It ought to be that easy, Bea thought, as easy as the hopeful tone in Myra's voice. Bea thought she ought to be able to climb into the tub and sit there under running water until a layer eroded off her and some older but tenderer self emerged. Her tears should be as black as the water rolling off Myra's walls. 'Damn, Bea,' Myra called from the other room, 'you can see your face in these walls.' And then, in a changed voice, she called out, 'I knew, Bea. Stan told me a long time ago. He told me before he got sick.' Myra was silent for a moment, only scrubbing, and Bea sat thinking about what Myra knew, and then Myra said again, 'I knew. Or I'd've smacked your face off for saying something like that to me.' And then, almost to herself, she said again, 'You can see yourself in these walls.' No, Bea thought, as she sat at the kitchen table with a cup of Myra's bad coffee. You can see yourself, but I can't see myself anywhere. And you can't see me either.

As the days passed, only one part of them had any meaning to Bea: the evenings, when Hank and Myra sat down with a grimy pot of coffee and Bea took a pill, or two or three pills, and went to bed. Bea hated every pill she took and she had to force herself to take them, but she hated even more the way the world looked when she didn't take them: the way she looked in the mirror, the way Hank looked chattering on the phone with builders and carpenters and electricians, the way Myra looked as her sweat and ashes mixed with soapy water on the linoleum in the kitchen, and the way that body-dented couch looked. No one sat on that couch anymore; the dents were from Stan's body, and Bea turned away from them. She turned away from Hank and Myra, and she took a pill, and she went to bed. She didn't think about Hank then, or Myra, or even about herself. She thought about Stan. Stan used to come over after work; that's how it had started. Hank was there in the beginning—he and Stan came to the house together—but then he and Bea had another fight and Stan came over by himself. Bea found out later that Hank ate at a diner and then went drinking, and by the time he got home Stan would have gone and Bea would be asleep. The basement was where they always drank—Bea and Hank—because they were ashamed to get drunk in front of their children, and for their part Susan and John avoided it like a haunted place; the basement was where Bea took Stan. It was still unfinished, the basement, like so many rooms in Bea's life, just a cement box and a skeleton of wooden studs and the thin horizontal slits of windows. All of the windows were dirty, and one was broken and boarded up, and another was blocked by the flues from the washer and dryer that Hank's father had given them for their tenth anniversary. The washer and dryer hadn't been new when they'd arrived, and by the time Bea and Stan had their affair they were on their last legs, and what Bea remembered most, from her bed in Myra's new addition, were the sounds of the machines at the far end of the basement making war on the clothes inside them, and the softer sounds of Stan's head under her dress. There was the cold hard neck of a bottle in her right hand and the warmer softer shape of Stan's thick curly hair under her left; there was the abrasiveness of the cement under her ass and the fleeting, flickering but always soft touch of Stan's hands on each of her thighs, or on her breasts if she wasn't wearing a dress fitted at the waist. And the boxes. She remembered the boxes, which had come from her attic and from Henry's, boxes which had been filled and sealed once and never opened again.

Sometimes they had sex with their clothes on and lying on the bare cement floor, and sometimes they had sex with their clothes on and leaning against a rough wooden pillar, and sometimes they had sex until one or both of them began crying, and then they stuffed their mouths like starving dogs. They were usually drunk, and they didn't love each other, and they were miserable, but they were always nice to each other, Bea remembered, even after it became mechanical. Then Bea faked her orgasm a few times, and Stan started losing his erection in the middle of things, and right about that time Hank announced that he was tired of diner food and so it all ended too easily: one evening Stan came over as he always came over, and he found Hank there, and after a few beers he left. Things were never strained between Bea and Stan after that, which surprised her until she realized how little it had meant to her—until she realized that the main reason she had sex with Stan was to be discovered by Hank. And it was right around that time that Hank told her the Old Man was retiring, and because he was no longer married and no longer had children, and because Hank was his nephew, he was leaving him the company. Bea remembers finances still being tight for many years after that, but they were tight on a bigger budget, and somewhere during that time Stan and Myra moved away. Though most of her affair with Stan was a blur—or perhaps because of that—Bea always associated him with their change of fortune. He had filled a space Henry left empty, and when he moved away the Old Man's money had rushed in behind him, as though filling a vacuum.

The stack of plans she found one evening had been rendered on child's graph paper in pencil. They showed a long lean cold structure set against the shakily sketched outline of a mountain. It looked like a lowercase *t*, or a cross with a very short crossbar, and she hated it. She looked through the several perspectives and she hated it from every angle. She felt bad for hating it. She knew, as she looked at Hank's house, that she should've looked at the plans weeks ago, but hell, that was water under the bridge and this was the rest of her life. She turned to a clean sheet of paper and grabbed a pencil, and then she grabbed an eraser, and then she was stuck for a moment and so, like Hank, she drew the mountain first. The pomander mountain, she remembered, and then she began drawing and erasing and drawing in new lines until long past the time she normally took a pill and went to bed. It seemed that a house just flowed from her mind onto the page, and she didn't stop until she heard gravel crunching under the truck tires outside. She did take a pill then. She pulled her drawings from the pad and she put everything back the way it had been and she went to the new addition. The first couple of bottles she found were empty and the next several had only one or two pills in each of them. She took one then, from one of the bottles that only had one pill, and then she went through her purse and her suitcases and her drawers and her clothes, and then, when she'd found every bottle, she lined them up on the dresser. The bottles stood at attention like a double row of chess pieces. This long, she told herself, this long and no longer.

Then the bulldozer arrived, and their houses were built. The field that had once been yellow with dandelions was green now, the blooms having all turned to puffballs and blown away, and then it turned brown as the bulldozer went to work. It wasn't just the bulldozer: it was a caravan of tractors and tractor-trailers, and trucks full of soft-bellied rough-voiced young men with tattoos on their forearms and biceps and deltoids. Bea watched them sometimes, the men and the machines, their movements as graceful and incomprehensible as ballet. Once she saw the backhoe operator bring his shovel down on the naked shoulder of a blond boy with a thin defiant mustache. Bea caught her breath, expecting the boy's arm to be ripped off, but the shovel only tapped him and lifted away, and the boy swatted his shoulder as though a fly had landed on it. The shovel tapped him again, and this time the boy turned, and then he fell backward when he saw what had tapped him, landing on his ass in a soft pile of sand. Bea found it hard to talk to men who could do that to each other. When she tried—when she came too close to the 'site'—they talked to her instead. They talked at her. They called her ma'am, they asked her to wear a hard hat but couldn't find a spare, they told her that everything was going along smoothly, and they suggested, with their strong hands pushing just slightly on her back, that a construction site was no place for a woman, and Bea had to be short with them. 'My husband and I have conferred,' she would say. She hated that she had to phrase it that way, but it got results. 'You're to follow these plans now.' 'But, ma'am, these plans call for a house fifty feet shorter than the foundation we've dug.' Bea just waved her hand and started to walk away. 'We'll have a nice big patio then, won't we?' she said, and she heard someone say, 'Swimming pool's more like it,' but she also heard the foreman say, 'Okay, guys, let's switch gears.'

Her plans were for a house that would be simple and a little old-fashioned, a little deeper than Hank's and a lot shorter, so that if you sat in the living room you could call into the kitchen without raising your voice. Bea stumbled for a moment on that thought: who would sit in the living room, alone, who would stand alone in the kitchen, who would call out to whom and would the other answer? But if she couldn't have a perfect life then she would have a perfect place to live, a home, with large and simply proportioned rooms and a single sensible central hallway running down the middle of each floor. There would be three floors. The first would have the living room, den, kitchen, and dining room, a half bath, and a good number of closets. Upstairs there would be bedrooms, four big ones, with closets large enough that you could get dressed in them, one main bathroom, another for the master bedroom. Above that would be a third floor, an attic, a cavernous room with sloped ceilings and dormer windows. Bea liked the possibility an attic offered, the idea that if one day they needed more space it would be there. She liked to imagine Susan or John—well, Susan, really—taking over the house and expanding into the attic. Perhaps Susan would have grandchildren of her own and they might be a little closer than she and Susan were, perhaps one day there might be an extended family living here, all under one roof.

But first that roof had to be built, and Hank made it as difficult as possible. Bea feared going inside the trailer for more than a few moments, because Hank would be out there immediately, changing things, heightening ceilings, enlarging windows that he wanted to fill with single sheets of glass that couldn't be opened, and if she let her attention slip then what had been three cozy rooms on Wednesday would, by Friday, have become a single narrow tunnel. Bea and Hank never spoke to each other about the war they fought but, like rival generals, used their soldiers to communicate for them. Only, Bea thought, they shared the same army, and when she realized this she spoke more frankly than she'd spoken before to the foreman, whom she thought a little more sympathetic to her house than Hank's. She brought her checkbook with her, and she only spoke for a few minutes before he began nodding his head blankly, and then she shut up and wrote a check. She paid him off irregularly after that, whenever he managed to translate some part of her plan to the actual house. She had her triumphs: when the third floor was definitively up and running, she looked at Hank smugly over her coffee. She'd run out of amphetamines by then, so she drank Myra's coffee. It made her jittery and exacerbated her nausea, but it kept her awake too, and vigilant, and so she forced herself to drink cup after bitter cup. But one morning she awoke early and went into the kitchen. It was dark there, and cool, and the last of the night air licked at her ankles, and she made a pot of coffee. She didn't even think about what she'd done until she drank it, nose scrunched up against an awful taste that never came. It amazed her a little bit. She'd been in the trailer for months now, and in all that time it had never occurred to her that she could make her own coffee, even though the pound of coffee she'd picked up on that first wild shopping spree had sat in the freezer for months. Myra came out a few minutes later, Myra with her old lady's gray hair, her adolescent's lacy nightgown, and her child's shuffling steps, and Bea poured her a cup, which Myra accepted unconsciously, as though Bea always made the coffee. She drank half of it, half-asleep, before looking up at Bea. 'Damn, Bea,' Myra said after another swallow, and then, after another, 'That's good coffee.' Bea blushed as if she'd just made something spectacular, a banquet dinner, a multi-tiered wedding cake, an airy soufflé; she sipped at her own cup in lieu of speaking. Then Hank's heavy steps came down the hall and Bea poured him a cup. He took it from her casually but took only one sip from it, and then he looked up at her with wondering eyes. But he said nothing, and Bea didn't either. She just looked at him and felt the small grin on her face freeze into a caricature of itself. 'I've gotta say,' Myra said to Hank, 'Bea makes a better pot of coffee than I ever have.' But Hank didn't answer her. He looked into his cup and didn't drink from it; he only held it in both hands as he'd done on Long Island, warming them. The image confused Bea in a way it hadn't on the island, because it suddenly occurred to her that Hank was using something she had made, and if it wasn't exactly bringing him pleasure, it was, at least, lessening his pain.

As their houses continued to take shape, Bea was reminded of a scene from *The Wizard of Oz*: the scene that came to her mind was the one in which Dorothy Gale's house falls on the Wicked Witch of the East. In this case the Wicked Witch was Hank's house, and it was Bea's homey white farmhouse that had fallen on it, leaving only two wings sticking out on either side. But most of the clashes were inside. Outside, the house was an eccentric amalgamation; inside, it looked like two jigsaw puzzles forced together. The big problems were where Hank's high ceilings met her shorter ones, so that some rooms were several feet taller at one end than the other, and upstairs this was reversed in some rooms, which had floors on two levels. 'Stairs,' was Bea's one-word solution, and so there were stairs in one of the bathrooms—there were five bathrooms in the end, not two, five full bathrooms—and stairs in Bea's master bedroom, and Bea realized that if she put a heart-shaped bed on the platform, her room would look like a honeymoon suite. There were other ticks: the end of one of Hank's long narrow rooms grew wider by half where it leaked into Bea's house, but this lip was barely two feet wide. 'That's a nook, that's what that is,' Bea heard him tell the workers, and someone behind her said, 'No, it ain't. It's a cranny.' As the second floor interior walls were going up she realized the rooms she'd planned were simply too big, and at the last minute she subdivided them, and she had to add a few angles to her single straight sensible central hallway to accommodate her changes. It remained the single and more or less central hallway, but it was neither straight nor sensible, as it varied in width by several feet and went up and down stairs and even double-backed on itself once, though neither she nor her foreman knew quite how that had happened. Hank's only comment was, 'It's a house, Bea, not a warren,' but he'd also said that anything

90

above the first floor had nothing to do with him, and that was all he said.

But in the end—or close to the end, there was still the permanent staircase to install—in the end it was Myra who said, 'It's kind of weird, but it's kind of wonderful too,' and Bea overheard one of the workmen say, 'All it needs now is wings, and it could just fly away.' In fact, it had wings: what else could you call the two extensions of Hank's house that stuck out from either side of Bea's? She wandered through every room—there were so many more than either she or Hank had foreseen. From one step to the next the house seemed perfectly normal, until after twenty steps you realized that the paneling had changed three times, the ceiling had dropped four feet, and you'd just climbed a short flight of stairs that ended in a wall. And then the main staircase arrived, the grand one that connected the first and second floors. It had been made somewhere else and arrived in one huge piece on the back of a flatbed trailer like a piece of absurdist sculpture, and its fit into the house was absurd as well, because it had been measured against Hank's walls but was destined for Bea's. Bea and Hank watched as it was laid against the wall and bolted into place, and Bea was immediately aware that it was much too big. The staircase stuck into the entranceway so far that she was afraid the front door wouldn't open. A worker must have had the same thought because he swung it back and forth several times as the staircase was fastened in place; the door cleared the bottom step by a few inches, and Bea sighed with relief. Then a worker called from above, and Bea's breath stopped like a knotted balloon. 'Uh, we got a problem up here,' he called, and then he added, 'I think,' in a tentative voice, because who could say what was a problem in this house? Neither Bea nor Hank spoke; instead, after a pause, they mounted the steps together slowly, and someone called out, 'Hey, Hank, shouldn't you be carrying her?' Everyone laughed except Bea and Hank. At the top of the stairs they paused and looked down at the worker who'd suggested there might be a problem. They looked down because the staircase was several feet higher than the second floor. Its elegantly carved banister

91

ended in a delicately spiraling line of newel posts that floated in the air like a strand of RNA. Bea and Hank looked at the workman for a moment, and then they turned to each other for a longer moment, and then, suddenly, Hank laughed. His laugh, Bea noticed at once, was without malice: he was laughing at her but he was also laughing at himself, and Bea knew that she should join in and laugh with him. But she didn't, because, though the gulf she had to cross was shallow—no deeper, really, than the drop to the second floor—she was afraid that if Hank, or someone, didn't catch her, then she would fall to her death.

Night forced itself under Bea's eyelids, and then the wedge of darkness pried her eyes open. Immediately there was information: the clock told her that it was nearly four in the morning, the little dot in the lower right corner indicated the alarm was set. It was October, she realized then. It had become October, and she slipped out of bed and out of Myra's trailer and went to see her new house. She could think of it now as one house, not two. It sat on a huge plot of level mud, and she remembered the beautiful field of sunflowers, no, dandelions, they'd been dandelions, the field of dandelions they had sacrificed in order to build their house. She braced herself for it: she told herself to look at it in bits and pieces before looking at the whole thing, but as soon as she looked up she saw that it was only bits and pieces, her rectangular peach shutters, his round windows. 'Portholes,' he'd called them, and of course they didn't open. Nothing opened in Hank's house. She'd asked him if it was supposed to be difficult to get into or difficult to get out of, and Hank had responded that everything opened in Bea's house, that if she'd had her way they would have mounted the roof on hinges like a dollhouse, and he'd asked her if it was supposed to be easy to break into her house, or easy to break out of, and neither of them answered the other's question.

Now, alone, at night, just days before she was to move in,

Bea could admit it: she didn't want to go into that building, and if she did go in she didn't want to be trapped. There'd been jokes from the workmen, from Myra, that this was a newlywed's house: everyone had said that this was the house they would spend the rest of their lives in, and it was, but it was also the house where they would die. And there it was: she would die here, and she would die soon, and she'd never thought she would die in a place like this. She'd always thought she'd die in an old folks' home somewhere, like Hank's father, alone. She'd thought that she would have done everything she wanted to do by then, and she wanted to be in a place that expected nothing of her, that encouraged her to look backward rather than forward. All this striving, tugging, pulling, fixing, re-arranging, changing, all this *doing*—she didn't consider it a defeat to give up all that, she considered it life's due for having survived. She'd imagined herself knitting scarves for people more helpless than herself, infants, the senile, and dying in her sleep. But now she knew it wouldn't happen. It never happened—except, probably, to people who didn't want it. Bea knew that she would spend the rest of her life trying to make this place habitable, and just before she finished, just when the end was in sight, she'd die. She was in front of the door by then, and she went up to it quickly. She'd get started now, and maybe, just maybe—The door was locked. It was locked. She knew then why none of Hank's windows opened, why all the doors had burglar alarms. She knew who the burglar was. She knew what was going to be stolen.

She walked around the house once, not to try the other doors, just to walk around it. It was a long walk, and with each step her feet grew heavier with clotting mud and the strands of wild vine that had sprung up here and there. What was it Myra had called it? Itch ivy, aitch ivy? She wasn't sure, but as she tried to shake the mud and vines from her feet she remembered something else Myra had confided to her. 'I scattered Stan's ashes here,' she'd told Bea. 'I thought you were buying the other lot. I never could tell my east from my west.' And Bea had thought, North. Our house is north of yours. As she walked she let herself remember a few things about Stan, a few good things: his chest full of hair, and his laugh that made children run to him, and his hands that could hold a beer in one hand and her in the other and use both effectively. And a few bad things: Stan, driving his car over a fire hydrant in a drunken spree and literally floating out the window; Stan, calling his wife a cunt and her husband a faggot while he fucked her so well that she cried; and Myra, sleeping on Bea's couch, or faking sleep, her eyes swelled closed by bruises. She only allowed herself a few memories because she didn't have any more pills and she was *not* going to get more, but she savored those few things, the good and the bad, she savored the memory of Stan. He had been a real man, with a real man's passion and a real man's flaws, and in the end he'd probably treated her better than he'd treated his wife, and if that little coin of information had two sides to it, well, so did everything.

Their furniture arrived the next day, and it was early evening by the time the delivery workers left Hank alone; he hadn't seen Bea all day. The building ached with the haste of its construction, and the rough edges poked through everywhere, but it was sturdy. He found himself in the attic eventually, among his parents' furniture, and in the attic he found with a push here and a shove there that he could reconstruct his old house exactly, everything in place except for the walls, and though he knew it was a silly thing to do he did it anyway, and when he finished he looked at it all from the vantage point of his old room. With two turns of his head he took in the whole thing. He saw how small it was, how the first third of his life floated in the vast empty space of this attic, and then, through a window, he saw Bea. She was emerging from the trees, stumbling a little, pieces of vine were stuck in her hair and clothes, and Hank stumbled to the window and called to her. 'Bea!' he called. 'Bea! Bea!' He knew he should say something else, something that would tell her why he was calling, but he didn't know why he was calling, and so he only called again: 'Beatrice!' He called her into their new house, their retirement home, their mausoleum. 'Beatrice!' he called in his wavering old tones, and he saw his voice pull her toward him and toward that house, just a few dragging steps. 'Beatrice!'

he called. 'Beatrice! Beatrice!' And then Bea opened her mouth. 'Henry!' she called. 'Henry! Henry!' But she didn't take another step, and Hank continued calling 'Beatrice!' but he couldn't say anything else and he couldn't come down from her high window. 'Beatrice!' 'Henry!' 'Beatrice!' 'Henry!' And then Hank watched as Bea clutched her stomach, and fell to the ground, and when her mouth opened again it wasn't words that came out of her but vomit and bile and blood. And then her mouth closed, and she was still.

5

Telescope

I can't tell you how much I love you, was the first and last line of the letter Beatrice pulled from her mailbox, the letter that was supposed to arrive sometime after Henry died but arrived instead two days after he lived. I can tell you I love you—and he wrote it three times, I love you, I love you, I love you—but I can't tell you how much I love you. All I can do is repeat myself. I can write it four times—I love you, I love you, I love you, I love you—and I can write it five—I love you, I love you, I love you, I love you, I love you—but I can never, no matter how hard I try, tell you how much I love you.

Everything was confusing then. It was easier to lose things than to keep them. Everything was in motion: there was a month of daily visits to the hospital, and there were two more months of Henry convalescing in his parents' house, and then there was the wedding: 'Quick,' Henry whispered, 'give me the ring,' and then he gave it back to her formally. There were three weeks in the house that had belonged to Beatrice's parents, and then a man from the bank came with a man from the sheriff's office. 'I thought they only had sheriffs out West,' Beatrice said as they changed the lock on her front door and posted a notice of an auction to be held some months hence, and after the sheriff left there were four nights in a hotel while they looked for and found a house to live in. 'A dump,' Henry called it, and Beatrice said, 'But *our* dump.' But it was Henry's dump actually, and Henry's parents', who co-signed the loan from the same bank which had just turned Beatrice and Henry out of her house. Their dump had five rooms and five rooms only:

living-kitchen-dining room, bathroom, and bedroom; there were no closets at all. Upstairs was an attic with a steeply pitched roof, and the nails that held the asphalt shingles to the outside of the roof poked a sixth of an inch into the room, studding the ceiling like an iron maiden. Downstairs was the basement. At some point somebody had attempted to divide it into a warren of small rooms: there were studs up, partitioning it into seven tiny spaces, but whoever had erected the studs had run out of money or, Beatrice liked to think, come into money, and moved to a better house. Spring was well under way when they moved in, the Gulf War had been started and the Gulf War had been ended. A hundred thousand souls were hastily taking their leave of this planet, but Henry, Beatrice reminded herself every day, was not among them. Henry was still here, and measured against that, their dump—no front yard to speak of, but a back yard with a lovely view of the Long Island Railroad's Montauk line—didn't seem intolerable.

There were other things to distract them: Henry's hair had come back, for one thing. It was inky black now—not brown, not blond in the summers—and it was patchy, so he kept it extremely short. Once a week Beatrice stood him, shirtless, sometimes naked, in the middle of the kitchen floor, and she ran the clippers over his head, and then she wiped the loose hair from his body with a warm damp cloth and dried him with a towel, and after she finished, Henry, embarrassed by his mottled skull—it looked, Beatrice teased him, like the hide of a dairy cow—immediately covered his head with a baseball cap. His wasn't the only hair to change color: his mother's had gone completely gray in the months between his operation and their wedding. Beatrice carried daisies at the wedding, and when the ceremony was over she kept them because there was no one to throw them to. Her old car broke down on the Southern State Parkway, and she knowingly wrote the first hot check of her life to the towing company, and then the second, to the garage. Henry took a job as a bookkeeper with a rapidly growing plumbing company run by his mother's brother, who was referred to ominously as the Old Man, and who referred to Henry as Hank. Beatrice planted daisies along the short length of the driveway, but she planted them too early in the season and before they bloomed a late frost came, and they died. Henry dropped out of school. When Beatrice asked him about it he said he'd wait a semester or two, he'd go back in September, or next February. Beatrice went back to school, and she also took a job in a King Kullen as a checkout girl, and she clipped coupons and recipes from *Newsday*. She clipped another article about the red deer as well, an article illustrated with yet another black and white photograph, and she stuck it to the refrigerator door, where it was soon effaced by still more coupons and recipes.

Henry's relatives came through as they always had: they hadn't come to the wedding; they had instead sent dozens of gifts. The appliances were the only things Henry unpacked; the others he put in boxes, and he put the boxes in the basement with other boxes from her house and his. They had a king-sized bed and a set of silk sheets, and a set of cotton sheets, and a set of polyester sheets, and they had a couch that didn't fold out into a bed. From his job Henry brought home a water cooler, whose hum filled up the front room and whose cold water filled out Beatrice's whiskey glasses, and he brought home a pair of faux Louis Quatorze fixtures for the bathroom sink, which ended up in a box in the basement because Henry didn't know how to install them. They didn't have a dining table inside, but outside, in the back yard, they had a round picnic table with an umbrella that covered it. The bed and the table they'd bought themselves, and they had also the things they bought each other. For their wedding Henry bought Beatrice a pair of tortoiseshell combs to show off her hair, and Beatrice bought Henry a fob to go with a pocket watch he'd had for years but never carried, and later she bought him a vest to wear them on. Beatrice told Henry the silk scarf story, and Henry bought her one, and then another. Beatrice bought Henry an abacus for his office desk, and Henry bought Beatrice flowers every week, and Beatrice bought Henry a hair dryer as a joke, and used it herself. They went through a his 'n' hers phase—shirts, sweaters, jackets, towels, coffee mugs, underwear even, and Henry also had an X etched permanently into the base of his skull, and that was his alone.

Neither Beatrice nor he thought of it as a possession and, whenever possible, they didn't think of it at all, though for the next several years Henry had monthly, and then semi-annual, and then annual visits to the doctor to make sure he remained in remission. This was the only thing Henry's parents still paid for, and one month before the fall semester he told Beatrice that they were two months behind on their rent: they were only three months in the new house and four months married, and so Beatrice dropped out as well, and went full-time at King Kullen's, where they paid her less than five dollars an hour and called her Bea. Almost every evening after they got off work—Henry got off at six, Beatrice at seven—Henry cooked something outside on the little hibachi his relatives had given them, and they ate at the picnic table and shared a bench and a case of Coors. It was Coors because it seemed everyone at Henry's job was named after some beer or other—Bud Abruzzo and Pauly and his girlfriend, Ann Heiser, and the Miller father and son—and Henry refused to drink a beer named after any of them. Some nights Beatrice surprised him with a bottle of wine, and some nights they made love on the living room carpet. Other nights they made love on their couch or on their bed, and sometimes they did both—made love on the couch, and made love on the bed. At least three months went by before they missed making love during the night, and at least two months went by before they missed making love during the day, but only one month went by before Beatrice missed her period, and it was when they decided not to have the baby that they fell behind in their rent.

The checkout girls Beatrice worked with were all women actually, but at King Kullen they were all girls, and they were all named after flowers: Rose the Italian and Daisy the WASP and Violet the yuppie wannabe and Pansy, who was anything but that. There was a Lily who worked part time, and the two

99

black girls, Hyacinth and Orchid, who always sat next to each other when they went for coffee, and there was one little old lady called Flora. It was Violet who grabbed her one day. On Saturday and Sunday Violet was the weekend manager but Monday through Friday she was just another checkout girl, and she said, 'C'mon, we're gonna have coffee and bitch about men.'

Rose's husband Rocco was trying to make it into the carpenters' union or the Mafia but he wasn't related to the right people for either one, and he'd already failed the test for the police academy, so now he sat at home drinking up her salary. 'I don't know what he's waiting for,' Rose said, 'his long-lost uncle Salvatore Genovese ain't gonna come knocking on the door anytime soon.' Daisy said that Rose should knock her husband on the head or get her brothers to throw him out. Daisy was artificially blonde and artificially skinny—it seemed she took a Dexatrim and four Sweet'n Lows with every cup of coffee, and no one ever saw her eat anything else—but she was pregnant in a very real way. She had two boyfriends and two engagement rings; one was always on her finger and the other always in her pocket, depending on whom she was expecting to see next, and she was hoping for twins because she didn't know what she was going to do otherwise. Flora had been married for thirty-seven years. She said she'd slept with her husband exactly six times and she had three children to prove it: 'Three times for the first girl,' she said, 'two times for the second girl, and just once for Sam Jr. The only thing that improved about him was his aim.' Pansy was Irish and single and very good at pointing out why: she was fat, she had frizzy orange hair and freckles, and her teeth were brown with nicotine and coffee stains. But after a half hour of the other girls' talk she said she was glad to be single, and to prove it she ordered a second slice of cheesecake. 'Is that all there is?' she said, ''Cause if so, I'll just remain pure and chaste, thank you.'

'Pansy honey,' Daisy said then, eyeing her slice of cheesecake, 'what's the point in being *chaste*, if you ain't being *chased*?' Someone laughed; it was Orchid. 'Now, *I* don't want another husband, or kids,' Orchid's voice sang out from the end of the table opposite Daisy, 'but the only thing better than a man nosing along your trail is when you let him catch you!' 'Oh!' Rose groaned a little loudly, and squeezed Orchid's hand in hers. 'I do know why I stay with my Rocco. I do.' After that, the conversation grew more bawdy than Beatrice was used to, and, like Hyacinth and Flora, she blushed and looked down at her lap, but a hand on hers brought her attention back to the table. Violet had her hand on Beatrice's engagement ring, and she flicked it with a long polished plastic nail. 'And you, Bea,' Violet said, 'what about your man? He certainly ain't rich.' Beatrice put her hand in her lap but kept her cool. 'If he were rich, I wouldn't be working here.' 'Ooh, touché, baby,' Orchid said, 'but you ain't getting off that easy.' Beatrice sat quietly for a moment, and then she said, 'Well, Henry, my husband, Henry, he don't make that much money right now but he will someday, and then he'll get me a bigger ring.' 'Yeah,' Rose said, 'and my Rocco says he's thinking about investing in real estate down in Atlantic City, but I don't see no key to the Taj Mahal.' 'It don't matter if he makes money or not,' Bea insisted, and then she said, 'I love him,' and she sat back when she said it because she realized it was the first time she'd said it to anyone besides Henry. Daisy just laughed. 'Love is a four-letter word.' Violet said, 'Wait'll you have your first kid.' Violet had two, and a third on the way, and she was twenty-three. Beatrice blushed then, and thought of her abortion, and then she said, 'Look, after everything I went through with Henry, I could never turn my back on him.' 'Except when he snores,' snorted Pansy, but it was the quiet black girl, Hyacinth, who asked her what she'd gone through. Hyacinth had a way of speaking that made Beatrice feel alone at the table with her, and when she said, 'Well, for starters, Henry was supposed to die,' she was shocked, both by the fact that she'd said it and by the sudden silence of the other girls. 'What do you mean, "supposed to die"?' Rose said. Beatrice said quickly, 'I mean, he *almost* died, I mean, I mean . . .' But nothing she could think of meant what she meant. Suddenly, she remembered Henry's love letter. One of the things Henry had written was that the more he tried to

101

talk about his feelings for her, the more he limited them, and as she sat in the diner she realized how true this was of so many things. But there were some things she did want to talk about with Henry—his illness was one of them, and his recovery, and the promises they'd made each other before his operation, and how hard it was to keep them after—but Henry refused to talk about those things or those times.

'Bea, honey? Buzz, buzz, Bea? You there?' It was Orchid who'd spoken, and suddenly Beatrice was back among the bouquet of checkout girls, and they made it hard not to talk. 'Henry had cancer,' she said quietly. 'Henry has cancer. With cancer you don't ever say "had." ' 'Oh my God,' Violet said, and then her hand was back on Beatrice's, only this time it held it consolingly. When Beatrice looked into her eyes it seemed as though Violet had been bewitched, and she heard herself saying, 'When I met him he had a lump back here the size of a bird's egg.' Someone gasped violently and Daisy put her hands on her breast. Beatrice felt full of power, and she went on with her story, embellishing details sometimes—'his mother used to tell him that she wished he'd hurry up and die'—and erasing others—'making love to him the first time was the most beautiful experience of my life.' By the time she finished and they had to return to work she felt as though she were drunk. 'Girl, you should write that down,' Orchid said. 'Wasn't this the movie of the week last week?' Rose laughed, but her makeup was streaked like mud. 'Oh, it's nothing special,' Beatrice said, and Daisy said, 'No, *my* life is nothing special. You, yours—that's something. That's special.' Everyone had something to say except Hyacinth, who only spoke after someone asked what she thought. 'I don't know what to say,' she said, which made everyone laugh uncomfortably. Still, they went on talking as if they could chatter their lives back into perspective, and they all had comments to make, comparisons with other stories they'd heard, suggestions. But Beatrice only remembered something Orchid said, Orchid, who was fifty-two and five times married. 'Honey,' she said, 'men are like dogs. They only do tricks when they're hungry.'

Beatrice wrote the words 'Free Time' on their calendar in thick red marker. She wrote the word 'Free' over the word 'Saturday' and she wrote the word 'Time' over the word 'Sunday,' and in this way weekends became their free time. It became a game to see how literally they could live up to that expression: to see how little money they could spend on Saturday and Sunday, both immediately, on things like eating out, and over time, on things like water and gas and electricity. They didn't turn the lights on during the weekends. They didn't bathe either, or use the phone, and for a long time they only ate sandwiches that Beatrice had lifted from work. They didn't watch television; they did read the Sunday paper, but, like bums, only when they found one on a bench or in a trash can. It was Beatrice who unplugged all the clocks one weekend, though when she did it she was thinking of the second word, not the first. When they went out, they walked: to the beach during the summer and to the park during the fall, and sometimes they went to the movies; they only went to matinees at the revival house, which was a long walk but was easy to sneak into, and, as well, the tampon machine in the women's bathroom was broken: one good slap, and a couple of white cylinders always fell into Beatrice's hand. For a while poverty itself made Beatrice happy. The sight of Henry's ghostly form running from the bedroom through the front room to the bathroom filled her entirely. There was the candle in his hands, there was the shadow of his one pair of pajamas dancing crazily on the wall, there were his cold feet pressed against her warm ones: what more could she want?

The smallest breach in their rules became a luxury. Once, at the beach, Beatrice slipped a quarter into a pay-per-view telescope before Henry could stop her, and the smiles they gave each other even as the timer buzzed audibly were full of guilty pleasure. She let him look first, but then, when he swung the telescope around to Beatrice, its sharp metal corner smacked her on the cheek, hard enough to cut her. He was beside her in an instant, first a finger on her cut and then his mouth, and he licked the blood from her cheek like an animal. 'Ow,' she said, and laughed a little, and Henry said. 'The guys at work say I let you get away with too much, gotta keep you in line.' He pulled her close again, and he licked the blood from Beatrice's cheek again, and his tongue, she had to admit, felt warm and soft and good. 'I'm sorry,' he said between licks, 'you know,' he said, 'I'd never,' he said, 'hurt you,' he said. 'I was watching this TV show,' Beatrice said as he licked. 'It was about the AIDS,' she said, 'and I don't know, you weren't home, I got to thinking about, you know, those rumors at school, and then I got to thinking about those operations you had—' When Henry pulled off her the wind was cold on her cheek. 'Beatrice,' he said, 'none of that has anything to do with us. We're married now. We're man and wife.' A click sounded within the telescope's apparatus as her quarter ran out, and Beatrice knew that if she'd been looking through it everything would have gone black as the click sounded. 'I know,' she said, 'I know,' but she didn't just then; she didn't understand what she was feeling except for Henry's one hand, and his other hand, and his lips on her cheek again. 'I feel a little dizzy,' she said, 'I think I need to sit down.' Henry led her by the arm to a bench like a Scout helping an old lady across the street. 'Maybe we should go home,' Henry said after a long moment. 'I hate that house,' Beatrice said quickly, vehemently, and then, to soften her words, she changed the subject. 'I hate this whole fucking island,' she said, and Henry said, 'The whole thing? Isn't there anything redeeming about it?' Beatrice laughed. She said, 'The people.' She paused. 'The good thing about Long Island is the people, and the bad thing about Long Island is that there are too many of 'em,' and then she laughed again, and Henry did too, and when he said, 'It is an ugly piece of shit, isn't it?' Beatrice knew he was talking about the house. 'It is the ugliest piece of shit I've ever seen,' she said. 'The question,' Henry said, 'is not who picked out carpeting in that particular shade of green—' 'Lime green—' Beatrice said. 'Lima bean green—' Henry said. '*Boiled* lima bean green,' Beatrice said, and Henry said, 'The question isn't who picked it out, but why a factory ever bothered to make it in the first place.' They made fun of their house for a while longer, and each time Beatrice felt Henry's tongue on her cheek she closed her eyes

104

and smiled. 'You know,' she said, 'I'd let you hit me more often, if you're gonna be like this afterward.'

ξ

In the past year his body had caved in on itself and filled out again, like a bellows. In the weeks after the operation he'd dropped to a hundred pounds and now he was up to one-fifty, and for the first time in his life if he tried real hard he could pinch his stomach and pull out something more than two flaps of skin, and sometimes after he came home but before she came home he took off his clothes and stood naked in front of the full-length mirror, and he pinched himself, pulled and pushed and prodded his body all over, and he could now say, proudly, that he didn't look like a walking skeleton. He was merely skinny now, and he would always be skinny—unless Beatrice's cooking made him fat, in which case he would be a skinny man with a spare tire. But he would never be big. He would never be Bud Abruzzo, who was, the Old Man said, almost too big to do repair work because he had a hard time fitting his shoulders under a bathroom sink. He would never be Pauly, who did have a spare tire, but who also had a back as broad as a tow truck to hold it up, and he would never be the Miller boy, who was only seventeen and who would, just to impress his father, peel off his shirt if it wasn't already off and do ten or twenty chin-ups on the pipe rack at the end of a full day's work. The Miller boy was as dumb as a fence post but he was going to be big as a tree one day, and though Henry suspected the Miller boy disliked him even more than the other men at work did, he also spoke to him more because Henry was getting some, and the Miller boy, despite his pretty girl-friend, Becky, was not.

Sometimes when the Miller boy talked about women he held his arms in the air in front of him, and the sleeve of his T-shirt, if he had a shirt on, stopped in the dip between his deltoid and his biceps, and as Henry stood in front of the mirror he knew his own shirt would never fit him like that. On his thin frame his penis looked out of place, grafted on; if he turned sideways then the front of his body from his neck down to his ankles was virtually a straight line, interrupted only by that lump of flesh and fuzz at his middle. Fuzz: hair. Hair: he had too much of it now. Now, at eighteen, he had a hairy crotch and a short thick growth of dark hair that fanned across the base of his stomach and narrowed into a line up the center of his torso like the bottom half of an hourglass. There was a little patch of down just above his ass that Beatrice loved: she always rested her hand there, and she pulled at it, and sometimes she rested her face there, and Henry would threaten to fart if she lingered too long. And he had hair on his head at last, a thick mossy growth that had finally become uniform. He wanted to grow it out so it would cover his scar, but the Old Man said he didn't need any hippies in his accounting department. The Old Man let Henry wear a hat, though. He never said anything about Henry's hat.

The Old Man was Henry's mother's brother, and that was how Henry had got his job, for, though he could add and subtract tolerably well, he had no experience at all in bookkeeping. Once the Old Man had been married, and he'd had two boys, and he'd lost all three members of his family. One boy had been shot in Vietnam and the other had, as far as anyone could tell, drunk an entire bottle of Jack Daniel's on a dare and then climbed into his car and drove it into Long Island Sound. The Old Man's wife had, in her forties, left him to shack up with a used-car salesman with prospects, and the Old Man, after negotiating an alimony of, he said, less than two dollars a day, had turned his first profitable year in over a quarter century of business and never gone into the red since. He had an office that looked onto Henry's back through a large window set roughly into the sheetrock, but he was almost never in there. He was, instead, when any of the men were in the shop, with them, and from his office Henry could see through his door the Old Man and a group of his employees— the ones, he said, who made him money, as opposed to the ones who cost him money. The men always stood just a little apart from the Old Man, and they always treated him with respect and the tiniest bit of awe. Henry had been told at various times and by various men that the Old Man could outdrink, outcurse, outfight, outfuck, and, above all, outplumb any of the men who worked for him, and Henry watched him, and watched them, longingly.

But at the end of Henry's third month the Old Man had pronounced Henry's books flawless, or as flawless as books that the Old Man hadn't done himself could be expected to be. Hank, he announced, couldn't plunge a toilet to save his life, but he was good at what he could do, and after that Henry was allowed to join the other men for a beer. Usually he stood silently, listening to the Old Man's stories of plumbing in the days before machines did all the work, and sometimes the Miller boy would pull Henry back a little, and he would tell him that he'd felt Becky's tits then, and he would describe what they felt like, hands in the air, imaginary breasts in his hands— Becky, it seemed, had small breasts. He would ask Henry if Beatrice's breasts felt like Becky's, and Henry would describe Beatrice's breasts or any other part of Beatrice's anatomy that he was called on to describe. One time the Miller boy just talked about how Becky's body was soft all over and how that scared him because it meant that he was supposed to be gentle with it. 'Hell, Hank, I ain't never been gentle with anyone in my whole life, I'm used to other guys.' He was drunk when he spoke, and he burped then, and he laughed at himself, and then he said, 'I'm afraid, Hank, I'm afraid that if I try something I'll hurt her. But, shit, if I don't screw something soon my balls're gonna blow up.' The hand holding the beer snaked down to his balls then, and tugged them just once, and he put his other hand on Henry's shoulder, a strong hand connected to a strong arm, which landed heavily on Henry's shoulder but sat there lightly, and he asked him then, one guy to another, what he should do. 'I don't know,' Henry said. The Miller boy squeezed his shoulder once, his whole drunken body lurching with the squeeze, and he waited, and then he squeezed again, and lurched, and waited again, and then he said, 'C'mon, Hank, don't let me down.' 'I don't know,' Henry said again, though by now he wasn't sure what he didn't know. The Miller boy's hand slipped off his shoulder and flopped to his side like a thick

107

rope of pasta, and Henry left then. He went home and examined himself in the mirror, contrasted every defect in his body against every perfect part of the Miller boy's anatomy. Sometimes when he looked at himself in front of the mirror like that he played with himself, though he never actually masturbated, and he didn't actually masturbate that time, and sometimes Beatrice would get home before he was dressed and then he would play with her, and it was only when that happened that he didn't care what he looked like because he was looking at Beatrice, and when he saw Beatrice looking at him there was never anything in her gaze that made him feel inadequate.

Something happened at King Kullen, Beatrice wouldn't say what exactly, but she was cut back to three days a week. 'We'll make do,' Henry said. Beatrice was dry-eyed but red-faced with anger. He wanted to comfort her, kiss her, tell her he loved her, and make love to her, but his mother called; 'You never call me,' was the first thing she said, and Henry said, 'That's because you always call me,' and as Beatrice left the room his mother said, 'You never come see me,' and Henry said, 'That's because you always call me,' again, and Beatrice closed the bedroom door behind her. When his mother asked him if he knew how much she loved him, he said that he didn't know how much she loved him, but if the number of times she called him was any indication of how much she loved him, then she loved him far too much, and then he hung up.

When he found Beatrice a few beers later she was in bed. Henry undressed slowly, lay down beside her, atop the sheet, on his back. He pulled the blanket over them and took Beatrice's hand beneath the blanket and held it through the thin layer of silk. 'Beatrice,' he said, 'how did your parents die?' 'You know how,' she said. 'My mother died in a car accident.' Henry waited for a moment. 'How did your dad die?' 'He died right before I went back to school.' 'Beatrice—' 'Oh, Henry.' Beatrice's eyes, voice, suddenly dropped. 'Why are you so curious?' Henry rolled over onto his side and his narrow chest

108

bunched up, seamed down the middle; a few defiant chest hairs poked from the thin chasm like grass from a river. He put a hand on her side, and she pulled a hand from beneath the sheet and put it over his. 'Oh,' he said, 'I was just thinking about my parents.' 'Your mother?' Beatrice said. 'My mother,' Henry admitted, and laughed a little. Beatrice started to say something, then closed her mouth and her eyes. They seemed connected that night, her mouth and her eyes. Henry watched her face relax, watched the lines framing her eyes and bracketing her mouth slowly disappear. 'My dad blew up,' she said slowly, 'and then he blew away.' She opened her eyes. 'He spent the seven years after my mother died growing enormously fat, and then in about six weeks he wasted away to skin and bones. He spent five days in the hospital, insisting he was dying even though the doctors couldn't diagnose anything, and then he died. I had his body on display for four days before I realized nobody was going to come see him. Only three people ever did: the undertaker, his sister, and me. It took two hours to bury him, and I've visited his grave exactly once.' She spoke quickly but quietly; there was no urgency in her voice, just an earnestness that sounded like resignation. She ticked her fingers down one by one as she spoke, and she finished almost before Henry had noticed she'd started. 'Henry,' she said, 'parents die just like anyone else.'

'Did you love him?' Henry said then, and Beatrice smiled wryly, as though humoring a child. 'I didn't not love him,' she said. 'I took care of him.' 'Do you miss him?' 'I took care of him,' Beatrice said again. 'He made himself helpless. Men,' she said softly, and she tapped Henry on the chest, 'make themselves helpless.' She stopped, sighed. She said, 'He had to have a woman to take care of him. I'd watched my mother do it all my life, so there was no way I could avoid it.' She paused. 'I don't miss taking care of him, but I remember it in the way you remember anything that takes up a big chunk of your life. I don't use pepper when I cook because he didn't like pepper. I put an ice cube in your coffee because he liked his coffee warm, not hot. I don't use fabric softener because he was allergic to it. But I couldn't tell you his shoe size. I couldn't tell you the color of his eyes.' She stopped talking. Her sigh was wet, her eyes moist. She closed them and she leaned forward to kiss Henry softly, squarely, on the mouth, and then she lay back down. Henry propped himself on his elbow and looked at her for a long time; he remembered his mother's phone call distantly now; he remembered that Beatrice had had a problem at work even more distantly. He thought she'd fallen asleep but then she said, 'That's a lie.' She smiled, and Henry thought how odd a smile looks when the smiler's eyes are closed. She said, 'Eight and a half.' She said, 'Blue,' and then she put her hands over Henry's eyes. 'Hazel,' she said. 'And my shoe—' Henry began, and Beatrice said, 'Nine.'

Just after Thanksgiving they bought a small tree, and they hung it with a bit of tinsel and garland and crowned it with a single star, and for the first time in his life Henry was looking forward to what his relatives might send him for Christmas. The lights were off when Henry walked into the house; it was late, a Friday, and he could see that Beatrice had prepared the house for the weekend. He walked with his boots on toward the bedroom but in the doorway he saw Beatrice on the bed, asleep, and he bent over slowly, a little afraid that he'd tip over, and he unlaced his work boots, the same tan suede work boots that the plumbers wore—Christ, they'd cost a fortune—and he stepped out of them quietly. Then he tiptoed to the bed in his socks, and as he approached he saw that Beatrice had put the silk sheets on the bed. They were all that covered her body. A strand of hair was in her mouth and the silver in it shone in the candlelight; there was a candle on the bedside table, and an empty glass, and the same novel Beatrice had been reading since they'd gotten married. He sat down quietly on the bed next to her, the very sight of her sobering him, and she stirred a little, put out her left hand and found his leg, but didn't awaken. Slowly, he pulled the sheet down. It was warm in the house, heat was one thing they didn't scrimp on, and Beatrice ran her right hand up her abdomen and over her breast, let its fingers weave into her hair, but she still didn't wake, and Henry just looked at her for a while. Her skin was white, so white, her mother had been a redhead, Beatrice had told Henry, and she'd told Henry that she, Beatrice, had never sunbathed in her entire life. Here and there was a faint blue trace of a vein, on her breast, on her neck, though in the dim flickering light they might've just been shadows. Her nipples were flat and dark, her lower ribs just showing under her skin, her belly smooth and skinny and filling and emptying with long slow movements as she slept. He kissed her then, he couldn't resist, but it was a light dry kiss: he placed it on her stomach between her navel and her sternum, and his touch was so light that when she exhaled and her stomach shrank it moved away from his lips, and when she inhaled and her stomach filled it rose to meet his lips again.

He sat up then and Beatrice's left hand moved slowly up his leg and across the side of his ass to her stomach, and she scratched herself lightly and left her hand there, its fingers spanning the distance from her navel to the top of her vagina. He sat quietly until he was sure she was still again, and then he pulled the sheet down to her knees. There were her hips, her pelvis; the bones flared to accept her upper body and their lines pointed straight to her vagina. Her pubic hair was thick, curly, long, the same coarse texture as the hair on her head but light in color, nearly blond—amber, he'd called it once, but Beatrice had said that Amber was a name yuppies gave their children and light brown would do just fine for what grew between her legs. He put a hand there suddenly, softly, flat at first, but then he let his index finger trace the hot dry line of her labial lips, once lightly, then twice, but on the third time he started low, at a point invisible to himself between her legs and he drew it up slowly, lightly at first but a little more heavily with each fraction of an inch his finger moved, so that by the time he reached her clitoris his fingertip was firmly between her lips and when his finger passed over her clitoris Beatrice sucked in her breath sharply and her right leg rose, bent at the knee, but Henry let his finger keep going, out of her bush, up the soft hill of her solar plexus and down into her belly button, and there he spun his finger around like a corkscrew, twisting it just a little into her body, and when he pulled it out Beatrice sighed and was quiet again, but her eyes were open. He looked into her eyes for a long time, his hand flat on her crotch and feeling the heat of her body as she woke up. She blinked and then her eyes focused on his. 'Henry,' she said in a lazy voice heavy with sleep and touched by drink, and full of love, and Henry, inexplicably close to tears, said, 'Beatrice, my beautiful Beatrice,' and Beatrice smiled and closed her eyes and said, 'Kiss me, Henry.'

He only took the time to take off his shirt before he lay atop her. He tasted the whiskey on her breath and he imagined that she tasted the beer on his and they kissed for a long time until he was sure it was her mouth that he was tasting, and then he dragged his stubbly chin down her neck, between her breasts, down her stomach, and he felt the stubble on his chin catch like Velcro on her pubic hair before it was through and when his nose was right above her clitoris he stopped and then his mouth opened and his tongue came out and he buried his face in her. He used just his tongue at first, left his hands on her breasts, but when he felt one of her hands on top of his head he brought his hands down to pull her pussy open and his tongue burrowed even deeper into the pink and red and purple and soft and wet parts of her, his teeth nibbled at her full clit now, his tongue dug like a shovel. If he pulled back for breath Beatrice's hands pushed him down again, and her hips rose off the bed to meet him and when she came, she held him by the ears with both hands and she beat his face into her crotch, covering his cheeks with thick sticky juices. In the quiet panting moments after she'd finished coming, he licked them from his face and from her matted hair, and when his tongue pushed a little too far she twitched and gasped, and after a while he stopped licking and just rolled his face from side to side on her vagina, and after a while he moved his head up a few inches and laid it on her stomach, and Beatrice rested a hand on his head, and his head rode up and down on her breath. Beyond his closed eyes and under his head he felt Beatrice stretch a little, and blow, and then the room was dark and he smelled the smoke of the extinguished candle.

'Maybe I'll wait another week before I refill my prescription,' Beatrice whispered, and Henry giggled quietly and whispered, 'Don't you dare,' and Beatrice whispered, 'No, no,' and then she whispered, 'I get paid on Wednesday, I'll go in then.' And then she whispered, 'Next weekend,' and Henry lifted his head off her shoulders and looked at her and whispered, 'Next weekend what?' Beatrice smiled and licked her lips and whispered, 'Next weekend you can fuck me.' 'Why are we whispering?' Henry whispered then, and then he yelled, 'I'll fuck you right now!' and he pushed his body up and on hers, kissed her and ground his penis inside his pants against her, and when occasionally Beatrice pulled her mouth free of his it was only to call out 'Henry!' and once, after he'd gotten his pants open and his dick out, she said, 'No!' but then, when Henry started to stop, she said, 'Yes!' and she spat twice in her hand, reached down to his dick and guided it in her, and when he was all the way in she held him pressed still against her with her hands firm on his flat ass. His legs were entwined in her legs, his crotch meshed with hers, but he held his torso up with his arms so that he could look down and see where he and Beatrice were joined. Then, when he looked at her face, she said, 'If you come in me I'll cut it off,' and he nipped at her jawbone and said, 'No, no, I won't, I won't,' and then her hands grabbed his ass and pulled and pushed, starting him off like a Model T, and then they fucked and that time he didn't come in her, or not really, because he'd had too much at the bar.

It wasn't the first time they'd run out of money just when her prescription was due to be refilled. It was, in fact, the third time. It was pretty obvious by then that they both wanted a kid; there were other bills they could've skipped, but they never did. Christmas came and went: Henry's relatives weren't as generous as they'd been in years past and they only sent cards and cash, and not very much of the latter. They didn't have a phone in January, and in February Beatrice told Henry she was pregnant again. 'Oh, Henry,' Beatrice said, 'I can't manage anything. I fuck up at work all the time, I lost the house, I, I, I'—she stuttered breathlessly, hysterically—'I can't even take care of my body.' Henry pulled her closer to him, said, 'I guess you do as well as anybody. You do a lot better than most. Look at that Daisy girl.' That Daisy girl had starved herself into her eighth month and then gone into labor. Both she and the baby had survived, barely, but neither of her relationships had. 'I don't give a shit about Daisy,' Beatrice said loudly. 'Me, Henry. I can't take care of me. This is twice in one year.' 'Hey,' Henry said, 'it's partly my fault. You didn't get pregnant by yourself.' 'Oh, Henry,' Beatrice said, quiet again. 'One of the few things my mother taught me is that it's always the woman's fault. Men don't get pregnant. Men don't get it, period.' 'Beatrice—' 'No, Henry, I mean it.' She softened her voice. 'I could never blame you.' 'Beatrice,' Henry said, and he kissed her. 'This isn't about blame. We're married now. We don't have to blame each other.' Even as he said it he realized it didn't make any sense: they were married, they weren't infallible. But he'd always thought they were. What they did to each other could never be wrong because they loved each other, and they loved each other so much that they'd put it down on paper and made it official and made it forever, and it didn't make any sense to him, the idea that they could wrong each other. They talked for a long time, they held each other, Beatrice cried sometimes, and eventually, because it was the only thing they knew how to do, they made love.

When they were finished Beatrice said, 'I'll scrape up the money somewhere and make an appointment at the clinic next week.' She lay in his arms, her back to his chest. Henry was stroking her cheek, her breast, her stomach, and he spoke without thinking. 'Why don't we wait a few months,' he said, 'we can save some money on your pills.' Beatrice's temperature dropped under his hands, her body stiffened. He wished then that he could retrieve his words, but language, like time, only runs forward, and he lay there silently, cursing himself. He couldn't even apologize. After a long time, Beatrice said, 'All right,' and Henry said, 'Aw, Bea, I wasn't serious,' but Beatrice cut him off loudly. 'I said all right. I said *we'll* wait.' For the first time since he'd known her Henry was frightened of her, and he didn't say anything more.

It was Friday, one of those early spring Fridays that still felt like late winter, when everyone had worked outside in frozen mud and drunk more than a few to take the edge off their tempers, and Henry found himself in the Old Man's old Caddy with the Old Man, who was driving, and Bud Abruzzo and Pauly, who were drunk, and the Miller boy, who was also drunk and who would have gone home with his father except his father had called in sick. It was dark and it was snowing, and the snow glittered in the streetlamps and clicked audibly against the windows. Henry was sandwiched in the hot car between the hotter bodies of Pauly and the Miller boy, and he, like the others, held a can of beer between his legs. By some unspoken arrangement only one man drank at a time, and when sometimes they passed a car on the road everyone left their hands and their beers in their laps and composed their faces into poses of competent sobriety. The Old Man, who was drunk but not as drunk as his employees, drove with the too steady slowness of an experienced drunk driver, and Henry knew that if a careless child ran in front of the car the Old Man would run it down with the same too steady slowness.

From the front seat the Old Man called, 'Hey, Pauly, how come that Ann Heiser don't come in to visit me no more? You keep her chained to the bed or something?' The Miller boy laughed loudly at that, and Pauly did too, but he said, 'The only thing that girl is chained to is the TV. I swear she quit her job and moved in with me just so she could watch her soaps on my big screen.' 'That's too bad, Pauly,' Bud Abruzzo said, 'since this is the closest thing to a honeymoon you and Ann Heiser are ever gonna get.' 'And what is *that* supposed to mean?' 'Well, shit, Pauly,' Bud Abruzzo said, 'everyone knows that if you let a woman move in with you she'll never be stupid

115

enough to marry you. She's already got what she wants, so why should she give up her freedom? Besides,' he said, nudging the Old Man's arm with his elbow. 'Everyone knows she's gonna leave you for the Old Man anyway.' Everyone laughed except Henry, who was made nervous by the fact that the whole car moved when Bud Abruzzo touched the Old Man's arm, and Pauly put one of his big hands on one of Bud Abruzzo's big shoulders and gave it a squeeze. 'Bud,' he said, 'if you wasn't so advanced in years I might just ask you to step out of the car.' 'Well, you can go on and step out if you want to,' Bud Abruzzo said. 'However, given as we're moving along at about'—he looked at the speedometer—'forty-three miles per hour, I think I'll let you step out by yourself.' Everyone laughed at Pauly again, including Pauly, but he didn't say anything back to Bud Abruzzo. 'Looks like you better find someone else to pick on, Bud,' the Old Man said.

Then the Old Man said, 'Hey, Miller boy, you awake back there?' The Miller boy, who'd been sitting next to Henry with a slightly stupefied smile on his face, roused himself enough to say, 'Yeah, yeah, I'm awake.' 'Well, how's that pretty little girlfriend of yours? Ain't seen her in a while either.' 'Oh, she's fine, she's fine,' the Miller boy said, and then he added, 'Becky's fine.' 'She a cheerleader?' Bud Abruzzo asked. The Miller boy said, 'No, no, not no more. She was, though. She graduated two years ago.' 'Oh, ho, an older woman,' Bud Abruzzo said. The Miller boy would've graduated last year, if he'd graduated. The Old Man said, 'I seem to recall that your old man liked older women too.' The Miller boy blushed and looked down into his beer. 'Married one, actually,' he said. 'So, Miller boy,' Pauly said, 'is Becky as tight as she looks?' He laughed loudly at himself, and, on the other side of Henry, the Miller boy crunched his beer can between his thighs. Up front the Old Man, who had also laughed at Pauly's joke, said, 'Pauly, you got no business talking about another man's woman when you're not even married to the one you're shacking up with.' 'Aw, I was just having some fun.' 'Yeah,' the Old Man said sternly, and in the same voice he said, 'well, I'm sure that's

116

what the Miller boy and Becky are having too,' and then everyone laughed except the Miller boy.

Then Pauly said, 'Hey, Hank, you been pretty quiet.' Henry said, 'Ain't got much to say,' but Pauly said, 'I mean in general, in general you don't say much. My ma always said it was the quiet ones who always turn out to be serial killers or queers or something.' The Old Man said, 'Well, he ain't queer, I'll say that much,' and Pauly said, 'And how do *you* know?' ''Cause I've met his wife,' the Old Man said, and then he said, 'and she's pregnant.' 'What?' Henry said. 'How do you know?' 'Whoa, Hank, you sound like you're surprised.' Henry said, 'I am. I mean, I am to hear someone else say it. I didn't know she said anything.' 'She don't have to say nothing,' the Old Man said. 'You just have to look at her.' There was a pause, and then Pauly said, 'Well, hey, Hank, congratulations.' But when Henry said thanks his voice was so unconvincing that Bud Abruzzo said, 'Shit, Hank, you don't sound so excited.' Everyone waited for Henry to speak, and finally he said, 'Well, to be honest, we're not so sure we can keep it.' 'Don't you think you should have thought of that before?' the Old Man said, and Pauly added, 'There ain't too much you can do about it now, is there?' 'Yeah, there's something we can do about it—' 'Stop right there, Hank,' Pauly said, and put a hand up as though he were fending off a blow. 'That shit is fucked up, and I don't want to hear about it.' Ignoring him, Henry said to the Old Man, 'We did, you know, we did think about it, but, you know, sometimes accidents happen.' The car seemed very quiet now. Henry felt as though he were on stage. 'Shit happens,' the Old Man said. 'That what you're saying, Hank? Yeah, I know about shit happening.' But, despite his words, or perhaps because of them, Henry knew that shit didn't just happen, neither to him nor to the Old Man.

The Old Man was quiet for a moment and then he said, 'Her name's Bea, right?' 'Yeah, Beatrice. But yeah, everyone's starting to call her Bea.' 'Well, she's a pretty girl, Hank.' Henry said, 'Yeah, she is.' 'What's she look like?' Bud Abruzzo said. Henry just wanted to say that she was beautiful, but he also wanted to say something beautiful about her. He looked out

117

at the snow and said suddenly, 'A summer's day ain't got nothing on her. I mean, she's beautiful. She's got this snow white skin all over, and every part of her is round, you know, and you can hold on to any part of her, and she's got this hair, this huge head of hair, and sometimes I sleep with my face in it, it tickles my nose a little but it smells like a field or something, like sleeping in a meadow.' There was a brief silence, and then Pauly said, 'Well, excuse me, Mr. Poetry.' From the other side of Henry the Miller boy said, 'Well, Pauly, maybe if you said half as much to Ann Heiser she'd do for you what Bea does for Hank.' Henry wasn't sure if the Miller boy was defending him or setting him up. 'And what is that supposed to mean?' Pauly said, leaning forward to look around Henry. 'Shit, Pauly, I ain't the one to give away Hank's secrets. Why don't you ask him?' Pauly looked at Hank. 'I'm asking,' he said. Up front the Old Man said, 'I think Hank's business is Hank's business,' and then he chuckled. 'Not that I wouldn't mind knowing just what the Miller boy was referring to.' There was a long silence in the car, and suddenly Henry realized that everyone was waiting for him to speak, waiting to hear what he had to say: he was the center of attention. He thought about it for a moment. He wasn't ashamed of anything he and Beatrice did, but he knew that the men would never really talk about their wives, their girlfriends, in the way that they were asking him to talk about Beatrice. Someone coughed, Bud Abruzzo lit a cigarette and cracked his window. Henry felt their attention being sucked out of the car with the smoke. Quickly then, before he could think too hard, he said, 'Well, you know, Bea's an animal in bed.'

There was a pause, and then someone laughed, and then the Old Man said, 'What kind of animal, Hank?' and then Henry was off, and if everything he said exposed something about himself it didn't matter, because everything he said, he said about Beatrice: 'Bea likes going down on me,' he said, and 'Bea likes to do it doggy style,' and 'Bea likes to scream, she's a bona fide screamer,' and as he spoke the men laughed, or they said, 'Shit,' and as Bud Abruzzo left the car he said, 'I been married nearly fifteen years and I ain't never done *that*'. As

118

Henry continued to speak he felt like the only person on a seesaw: one side of him was sinking as he sold Beatrice to the men like a pornographer, and the other side of him was floating as he felt the men communing with him, recognizing him, paying attention to him. Even Pauly said, 'Well, who'd'a thought Hank here was Don Juan Casanova?' and later, when the Miller boy was getting out of the car, he gave Henry's leg a hard squeeze, and Henry jumped and pulled violently away, because the Miller boy's hand had squeezed Henry's erection along with his leg.

'Hello?'
  'Henry.'
  'Mom.'
  'Henry.'
  'Mom . . .'
  'Henry—'
  'Mom!'
  'Henry!'
  'Mom?'
  'Henry . . .'
  'Mom—'
Henry had had enough then, and he hung up on her.

Henry watched Beatrice cautiously over the next few weeks: she developed voracious appetites, he saw, for eating, for drinking, for sleeping, for fucking and cleaning the house. She attacked a task like a warrior, killed her food with her fork and knife, emptied a room of furniture as though she were clearing a plot of land before she vacuumed. Pencil leads snapped when she wrote, a couch leg splintered off when she threw herself down to rest. House plants died right and left. Sometimes when she picked him up from work Henry would see that hundreds of miles had been added to the odometer, and

119

more than a few times Henry just caught rides home with one of the men at work, and one night he walked into the house and it was empty. He looked out the window: the car was there, and immediately he was worried. He drank one beer, and then another; he'd drunk an entire six-pack by the time the phone rang. 'Hello!' When Beatrice heard his voice, so nervous, so vulnerable, she sighed. Why was it Henry, always Henry, who needed tending to? She was in the hospital, she told him then. It had been simple, she said, a light fever, tightness in her chest, abdominal cramps, wetness, a clear fluid, then blood. There had been something else, but she didn't tell him about that. She told him instead that it had happened on the toilet. She'd called an ambulance, just in case, and they wanted her to spend the night in the hospital, just in case. It was their first night apart in a year. Henry picked her up in the morning, drove her home; later, when the bill came, the Old Man paid it. But that night he only cried into the phone, 'Oh, Beatrice, oh my God, Beatrice,' and Beatrice said, 'Henry, stop,' but Henry went on. 'Beatrice, oh honey,' he said, and she said again, 'Stop,' and when he still didn't she yelled into the phone, 'Stop!' There was distance between them, just a few miles, but on the small plain of their marriage it seemed wider than the Grand Canyon. Beatrice forced herself to speak. 'I lost our baby, Henry.' She said, 'I lost our child, and it doesn't mean anything, because we didn't want it. We couldn't *afford* it.' She knew that she should be saying this to him in person, but she knew that if he were there he wouldn't let her say anything. He would only put his hands on her body, as though he could make it better that way.

2

Lamentations

As the dinner is eaten, my father tells of his plans for the future, and my mother shows with expressive face how interested she is, and how impressed. My father becomes exultant. He is lifted up by the waltz that is being played, and his own future begins to intoxicate him. My father tells my mother that he is going to expand his business, for there is a great deal of money to be made. He wants to settle down. After all, he is twenty-nine, he has lived by himself since he was thirteen, he is making more and more money, and he is envious of his married friends when he visits them in the cozy security of their homes, surrounded, it seems, by the calm domestic pleasures, and by delightful children, and then, as the waltz reaches the moment when all the dancers swing madly, then, then with awful daring, then he asks my mother to marry him, although awkwardly enough and puzzled, even in his excitement, at how he had arrived at the proposal, and she, to make the whole business worse, begins to cry, and my father looks nervously about, not knowing at all what to do now, and my mother says: 'It's all I've wanted from the moment I saw you,' sobbing, and he finds all of this very difficult, scarcely to his taste, scarcely as he had thought it would be on his long walks over Brooklyn Bridge in the revery of a fine cigar, and it was then that I stood up in the theater and shouted: 'Don't do it. It's not too late to change your minds, both of you. Nothing good will come of it, only remorse, hatred, scandal, and two children whose characters are monstrous.'

Delmore Schwartz, 'In Dreams Begin Responsibilities'

6

My Mother's Body

Dedication: June 4, 1971

This is for you, Francine Hannett of Huntington Station, originally of Glen Head. Dear wife of James. Beloved sister of Stanley, Anthony, Chester, and Edward Nosel, Anna Kopian, Valerie Gosden, and Patricia Nosel. This is for you, Rosa La Torre of Bedford, Mass., formerly of Westbury, L. I. Beloved wife of the late Emanuel. Devoted mother of Richard R., Vincent T., and Michael, who loves in Anaheim now. I'm sorry I missed you at the Thomas F. Dalton Funeral Home, 47 Jerusalem Ave. (corner of W. Marie St.), Hicksville, but I was busy with you, Eileen Peck, of Spur Drive, Bay Shore, formerly of Seneca Castle. You were the beloved wife of Dale. You were the devoted mother of Dale Jr. and Dalene. You were the loving daughter of William and Dorothy Eaton. You were the dear sister of Dorothy Staplin, Veronica Logallo, and Diane Ferrara. Now you are just a name on a page. James A. Weaver, this is for you. Beloved husband of Gail E. (née Fraser). Dear father of Christine and Deborah. Son of Katherine and Harold. Only brother of Patricia, Barbara, Margaret, Deborah, and the late Joann. You too are just a name, but that's enough for me to mourn you. Arthur L. Woodard of Lynbrook, this is for you. This is for your beloved wife Rita. This is for your loving children Rita Popple, Jane Woodard, John G., and Arthur L. Woodard, Jr. This is for your dear sister Lucy Hohenberger, and this is for the two unnamed grandchildren who also survived you. I will visit you, Arthur L. Woodard, when I visit Eileen Peck in the Long Island National Cemetery in Farmingdale, N. Y. My grieving will be orderly and neat: I will come between 2 and 5 p.m. or 7 and 10 p.m., and I will find your name in the endless list of the names of the dead, and I will take the map given to me on which your approximate location will be indicated in red pencil, and after visiting Grave 4103 in Section 2X I will make my way through the grid of identical white crosses until I find the one that marks your final resting place. I will not litter the grounds, cut, break, or injure trees, shrubs, or plants; or otherwise conduct myself in a manner not in keeping with the dignity and the sacredness of the cemetery. I will call Hengstenberg Theo and Sons at (516) 741–0810 and have them deliver cut flowers, or artificial flowers if I visit during the period of October 10 through April 15, and I will lay them on your graves aware that they will be removed as soon as they become faded and unsightly. I will eulogize you in abbreviated sentences that are only as long as the number of relatives you had. The language is not ours, mine or theirs, but borrowed from someone else, paid for line by line; still, it is all we can do for you now, you who were all beloved, devoted, loving, and dear.

My mother was. Her hair was long and straight and brown and you'd have never known it because she was always cutting and curling and dyeing it; it was fine, as one says of thin hair, and offered no resistance to the combs and brushes and fingers that passed through it; and I imagine that it would have been soft as my hair is soft if she hadn't always been dousing it with chemicals. In the one picture of her that I've kept her hair is hidden by something which looks like a blond beehive or a cone of cotton candy; her head disappears into this wig like a finger shoved into a lump of cold clay; her head disappears like the fruit of a banana poking from folded peels; her head disappears, and the wig hides the shape of her face, and her ears are completely covered. In one of the few memories of her that I've kept she is bent over the bathroom sink and her hair hangs from her inverted head in a single thatch.

It is long, wet, lumpy, matted, thick. I ask her what she is doing and she says she is dyeing it. I think she is dyeing it red.

Sometimes I want to be recaptured by the absolute physical sense of her. I want to swim again in the warm wet darkness of her womb; I want to grow and feel her skin expand around me; I want to know the squeeze of the birth canal, its awful pressure on my head, the pain my head must have caused her; I want, finally, to be stretched between the two pulls, the one out, the other back in. Another's hands touched me before hers did but this doesn't matter. It is her hands I know. These hands have held a newborn once before; they aren't shocked this time by the slime of blood, mucus, amniotic fluid; they aren't afraid of the harsh red and brown wrinkled skin wrapped around me like soiled butcher paper. These hands hold me; they bring me to her face and she kisses me; we are both crying. They bring me to her breast; there is a hospital gown between us but she will remove it soon. Someone has gone for my father but he's not here yet. Perhaps she already knows that when he comes she will be forced to surrender his son to him, but in this moment, in this moment only, I am hers alone.

How did she lie beneath him as he fucked her? On her back or on her stomach? I think she must have lain on her back because I think he would have liked to touch her breasts while he was inside her: one hand on a breast, the other on the bed to steady himself, the bulk of him bearing down on his center and into her center. She would have enjoyed this if she was like my father and my sister and myself; everyone in my family enjoys fucking. The naked expanse of her skin would be uniformly white except for her pink lips and red nipples and whatever marks my father might have left on her body. Her breasts would be full, her waist high and thin. A suggestion of extra flesh clung to her upper arms; it might have turned to flab if

125

she'd lived, but it's really only her hips and thighs which were, as she would have said, heavy, not fat; her hips, thighs, her ass too, they were all round mounds made lumpy by cellulite, and they shook like pudding when she moved, offered handholds for children and lovers. Then there was a sudden tapering into knees which were merely functional and calves which were still firm, and then came the ankles, which were thin, too thin, just like her wrists. They look to me like bones easily broken, and I must wonder now if she ever thought this, and wonder, also, if my father did.

The bruise appeared in the soft flesh of her upper thigh; it looked like the petal of a dying purple iris; time begins here, but it runs both forward and back. The bruise spread like ripples in water until it seemed like a black continent floating in a white sea; but where did it come from, how did it get here? When she could no longer walk my father carried her to the hospital, and his hand pushed a pencil over forms he didn't understand; inside her uterus a seven-month-old fetus competed for her life with the embolism now wandering her veins. My father pulled helplessly at his hair; soon both the baby in her womb and the clot that had found its way to her lungs were still, and as her lungs filled with blood the doctors punched a hole in her throat, stealing her voice forever. It wasn't supposed to happen, my father told me years later, it was a freak accident; the clot shouldn't have gone to her lungs, it should have dissolved under medication, it shouldn't have broken free from her thigh, *the bruise shouldn't have been there in the first place.* Nine days before my mother died her baby abandoned her body like a sailor flees a sinking ship; the sun rose and set on his body only one time and then a vein burst in his brain and his lungs fluttered briefly, filled with blood, and he died. Late on the morning of June 4 my mother wrote 'yes' on a sheet of paper when her aunt and uncle asked her if she'd like to stay with them when she left the hospital. My mother's sister had been in and gone already that morning; left behind were the notes 'are you ok?' and 'did he hurt you?' My mother wrote 'double' when they asked her what size bed she wanted them to set up, and then she crossed it out and wrote 'single.' Her aunt and uncle and their daughter went to lunch then, and when they returned she was dead. I don't know where my father was. The doctors had cut a chunk from her leg at some point, and there was the hole in her throat, and who knows what sort of mess the birth had made of her stomach. I don't know if my father ever held his son. I don't know when he last touched his wife. The baby was named Keith Rodney. I don't know if this was something they'd agreed on, or if, like the others, my father made this decision on his own.

My mother's unmarried sister is coming to see her in the hospital, and she will stay with my father. My sister and I have been sent away. My father is wondering what he can do with his body now. It is the pedestal that supports the bust of his head, and he's worked hard for it: it's still almost perfect. But even he must realize that this single unit has become somehow discontinuous, like a chain. Some links are strong, others weak, and the weak and strong seem to exist next to each other without affecting their individual tensility, only that of the unit as a whole. Forearms thick and short and knotted like summer squash; biceps big, round, hard as softballs; shoulders that join these arms to his body and cap them like plates of armor. Chest and upper back have the girth of an oil drum, but his waist has the same thickness: his lower back is underdeveloped and often aches now, and his stomach has filled out during his married life with the imperceptible growth of a rising loaf of bread. He has no butt to speak of—he's probably proud of this—and his legs are still solid, if disproportionately thin when compared to his arms. There are his feet, his ugliest extremity: they're wrinkled and callused from years hidden in tightly laced leather work boots, and they end in long finger-like toes capped by jaundiced toenails as sharply cambered as rural highways. And then there are his hands: when they're

127

open—when he's reaching for a baby, or a wrench, or a piece of furniture—his fingers appear long and thick and slightly flat like cigars carried around in a back pocket all day; when they're closed, his fists are cylindrical but blocky, like two swollen beer cans, dropped, shaken, waiting to explode. On one hand there is a letter tattooed in the hasp of thumb and forefinger. It's either a lowercase *d* or a lowercase *p*; it represents an aborted attempt at having his own name permanently written on his skin. On one finger the wedding band that will later be given to me gleams dully like a single brass knuckle. And what can he do with this body now? What can he do with its colors, the single green letter, the yellow toenails, the blue-veined marble whiteness of his legs, the red sunburn on his chest, the brown patina of freckles spread across his shoulders and back like a mantle? What can he do with its odor of beer, sweat, corrosive glues, dirt, other people's shit? What can he do about his needs? How can he feed his body the steak and pork chops, the baked and mashed potatoes, the broccoli and corn and string beans it needs to survive? What can he do with the things his body has brought him? How will he raise his children? What can he do in his bed now? Who will answer these questions for him?

I lacked memory as a child. I don't mean that I couldn't remember things: I mean that I was unable to make any connections between my memories, as though each of the things that had happened to me had happened to a different person. Every six months the house we lived in would become unfamiliar to me, and I'd wander through it like a prospective tenant. This had something to do with the fact that we moved a dozen times in as many years, but there were other reasons too. Sometimes it wasn't the house that was unfamiliar but the things in it. What was in that drawer, that cabinet, that closet? When my father and whoever he was married to were out I went through boxes like the neighborhood snoop: I read letters, scanned court documents, examined canceled checks. One time I came across my mother's glasses. They were in the bottom of our big scarred pine hutch. They were packed with some of her other things but I only remember the glasses; I only remember them because I didn't realize, or remember, that she'd worn glasses, and if they hadn't been packed with her other things I'd have passed over them without interest. Instead I held them in my hand. They were cat's-eyes, black, plastic, heavy, with simple silver pins at the joints; they were ugly, or at any rate unfashionable by the standards of my time. I held them folded in my hands and through their thick lenses I saw only their two arms and the skin of my hand. They seemed too small for an adult head; I thought they might fit me but some superstition kept me from trying them on, and I put them back quickly, and forgot about them. Years later I found them again. They were in the same house—our brown and white trailer—but the house had moved two hundred and fifty miles across Kansas, and the glasses had moved as well. I'd been rifling through the two dressers in my father and third stepmother's room, hers long and low, his tall and thin. They both wore the same things mostly, stained T-shirts, faded work jeans, but her underwear was more interesting than his: nylon bras and panties in transparent blues and oranges, lace-edged things, G-strings that didn't have nearly enough fabric to hold me. They looked old, all of them, most of the panties were stained with menstrual blood, and I was sure she'd bought them before marrying my father. The glasses weren't in her dresser, though, they were in his, in the bottom drawer, in a little box, by themselves. I held them gingerly again, still didn't try them on. I stared at them for a long time and tried to remember the face that should have been behind them. It occurred to me that the last time I'd seriously thought about that face was the last time I'd held these glasses in my hand. I put them back then; I forgot about them again. But in a few years I went looking for them purposely—I don't remember what the purpose was—and they were gone. Not in my father's dresser or his night table, not in my stepmother's dresser or night table, not in the hutch, not anywhere in the house. We'd built a barn by then, had boxes out there; that's probably where they were but I didn't think of that then. I simply thought they were gone. At the time it didn't occur to me to think that my mother was gone as well. I hadn't gone looking for her, after all. I'd gone looking for her glasses.

I've seen my mother die a hundred times, a thousand, more. Every time she dies differently. She's fallen from a great height, she's fallen under blows from my father, she's been mauled by a giant dog, or mauled by the doctors who attempted to cut a baby out of her dying body, or she's died attempting to force the baby from her body herself. There is the bruise on her thigh, always the bruise. It's like a black hole grafted to her leg: it sucks the light and life out of her. I was three when she died, my older sister six; I don't know if it was my father's decision or the hospital's but we never visited her during the two weeks she spent there, and we weren't allowed to see her body, or attend her funeral. I don't remember being told that she was ill or injured, or even that she was dead. I only know that when I search for traces of her there is a time when memory stops, and when it resumes, perhaps a month, perhaps a year later, she is not there. Each time I search for truth now I really search for her body, yet I've never let this exactitude limit my thinking about my mother herself: every year I've told a different story of how she died. Those stories don't culminate in this one; this story is merely a point on a line that will go on for as long as I do. There was the dog first, I thought it must have been a St. Bernard; and then there was the real fact of the embolism which lodged in her lungs, though I thought it had formed in her knee, and I didn't know what had caused it; when I was sixteen my sister told me that our father had beaten her and this is where the bruise came from; then, when I was twenty-one and my sister had become a Christian and forgiven our father, she denied ever telling me this; when I was twenty-five, finally, my father told me that she'd fallen while cleaning a window, and it wasn't her knee she'd injured but the back of her thigh. He told me how the bruise had festered when it shouldn't have, and grown, and he told me how a clot had formed and then broken free rather than dissolving naturally, or in response to medication, and he told me how in the hospital she'd grown whiter and weaker and thinner—every part of her except her womb—and he told me how the clot had come to rest in her lungs and the doctors had been forced to perform a tracheotomy so she could breathe, and then, crying, he told me how she'd slipped away from him, muted, eyes full of fear and pain. What details did I add as he spoke? Drops of sweat rolling off her skin? The wig perched on her head? I put her in a single room, but she could have been in a ward for all I know. My father cried when he told me his story, he said he hadn't thought about these things for twenty years; at times he too lost the ability to speak. He cried, but I didn't. 'Sadness' isn't the right name for the emotion his words produced in me; I don't know what that name is. Long before, these accounts of my mother's death had become fables to me, and I'm not sure, now, that they could ever be anything else. I'm not sure that I want to know what really happened; I'm not even sure I want to know if he was in any way responsible. By which I mean that sometimes I do want to know, and at other times I don't, and that these two impulses exist in me on either ends of a rapidly moving seesaw. One fact rises above all the others: my mother is dead now. And one fantasy rises even higher than that, made no less powerful by the fact that its strength is wholly dependent on the force with which it is asserted: my mother, I tell myself, is an angel now.

Souls don't exist. They don't, at any rate, exist in corporeal form, and, dead, my mother's soul seems no farther from mine than when she was alive. Though I have had twenty-two more years to judge him, I know my father no better than I know her. No, only her body was taken from me, and it's only her body I want to recover, and the things it produced. What was her voice? What odor lingered after she walked through a room? What sound did her feet make on shag carpeting, on floorboards, on linoleum, on bathroom tiles, on the cold cement floor of the basement? And *how* did she move: was she

131

graceful, was she clumsy, did she move with an awareness of herself and of others' eyes on her? When she was tired how did she rest? Yes, if I could I would kiss her. To know her better I would lick her skin. I would put my nose into her hair, under her arms, between her legs, at the soles of her feet. I would push my fingers into her skin and find out which parts of her were soft and which, if any, were hard. I say all this because I am three years old and I don't know any better. I say it because she is dead and there is no chance she will ever read this. But I will say it about my father too, and I say it about you: I can come no closer to you than your body. Everything else I will never touch. Everything important is hidden from me.

It's a little hard to see through the mist that shrouds everything, and the sheen reflecting off the pearly gates and the streets of gold beyond them doesn't help. The gates are a little overdone, but impeccable, as though an Art Nouveau architect had been at them, and they're taller and wider than they need to be, as if the dead might arrive in truckloads. At any rate, there are no walls on either side of them, and I'm surprised no one's there to meet me, no questions to answer, no tests to pass. I push the gates lightly, expecting them to be locked, but they open smoothly and silently, as you'd expect of Heaven's machinery, and I walk through and close them behind me politely. I wander slowly, still tired from the hard work of my dying, and a little spooked by the deserted streets and the ever-present fog, which swirls up like startled ghosts every time I take a step. Another surprise: Heaven's a simple place, familiar and comforting. It's just a bunch of one- and two-story buildings covered in the same mother-of-pearl that sheathed the gates, and though the buildings are all about the same size, each has its own design, so there isn't that housing-development feel. The ones I've passed so far have seemed empty, and it occurs to me that they might be destined for future inhabitants. That's a little eerie, but the most disconcerting thing, besides the fog, is the lack of a sun. There's light in Heaven, perhaps even a bit too much, but it seems to be sourceless, and it doesn't cast shadows. Eventually a figure appears in the distance. Instantly, I'm nervous. Is this ... But as we approach each other I see the outline of wings, which the figure seems to be trying to hide unsuccessfully behind its back. I sigh, relieved: just an angel, a female one, judging from her silhouette. When we're closer to each other I notice that one of her legs glows a little, and in a few more steps I notice a little glow at her throat, and a faint light even seems to penetrate her simple white gown at her stomach. Then I see the wig: it fits in here, white and softly styled, no harsh edges to it. I hang back when I realize it's her, ashamed of my own ravaged body, my ragged earthly clothes, my baldness, but my mother comes up to me without hesitating. I wave a little, to stop her. 'Hi,' I say. My mother mimics me: ' "Hi"?' she says. 'Don't I get a hug after all these years?' I point to my hospital gown and its fresh palette of blood and other body fluids, at the sores and gashes in my skin, which don't hurt any more but which are open and oozing nonetheless, and then I point out her own immaculate appearance. 'I don't want to get your dress dirty,' I say. 'Oh, we can take care of that,' my mother says. She touches my shoulder, and my hospital gown is transformed into a masculine version of the one she wears—toga is a better word than gown, I guess—and then she lets her hands pass lightly over my arms and legs, my torso, my head finally, and almost before she's finished the flesh has returned to my body, taut, filled out, uninterrupted by sores or scars. I notice that my skin glows a little, like hers, and I notice also that I lack wings, but I don't ask about this little discrepancy. Then a lock of hair falls into my eyes, and when I push it away my fingers pass through hair longer than I ever had during my lifetime. My mother is smiling sheepishly. 'I never liked that crew cut you had,' she says. I just nod, and then I say, 'Your wig...' 'Oh, this,' she says. 'I thought it would help you recognize me.' She pulls it off and lets it drop into the knee-deep fog, which swallows it neatly. Crowning my mother's head now is a short, multilayered, permed shag in her natural brown, with blonde highlights. It was 1971 when she died, I remember. 'We always appear in a form that won't shock newcomers,' she tells me, but when I start to question her she stops me. 'I want my hug,' she says. I nod but don't move toward her. The implications of her last statement disturb me. Is Heaven completely subjective? Does everyone see it differently? How do I know this is even my mother? At the root of my disturbance lies the simple fact that I'm afraid this is just a dream, that at any moment I'll wake up and find myself merely alive, and alone. But my mother doesn't wait for me, she takes me in arms made strong by grace and, if I understand her, by my own expectation that they will be strong, and I throw my arms low around her back, so that I won't break any of her feathers. After a long time she steps back a little, kisses me on the forehead, lets her hands slip to my waist. The tears in my eyes make everything in Heaven even more hazy, but through them I notice for the first time that she isn't wearing glasses. 'Your glasses,' I say, and my mother only says, 'Look,' and points to her eyes, and I see that, like her leg and neck and stomach, like my own body, they glow slightly, and as I continue to look into them I wonder, suddenly, how much they've seen. We've only been reunited for five minutes but already I want her approval; I wonder if we'll be forced to pick up where things left off, when I was three. 'Mom,' I say, the old unfamiliar word falling slowly from my mouth. 'There's something I have to tell you.' She hushes me: 'I know,' she says. She comforts me: 'It's okay,' she says, and then she says, 'We'll have time to talk later.' She takes me by the hand. 'Come,' she says, 'there's someone I want you to meet.' There's something commanding about the liquid solidity of my mother's hand in mine, and I follow her meekly. 'Really, Dale,' she says as we walk. 'Those gates were a bit much, don't you think?'

My mother's body is dumped in a field. I am the farmer who works that field. It's early in the morning when I find her, the air still and cool, the sky clear but not yet light enough to be blue. The silence is broken by a few crows who caw and fly away heavily as I approach. I recognize her, I won't deny that: though her throat is ripped open, her stomach shredded, and one leg only a blackened stick, her face could never be unfamiliar to me. The field she lies in is tilled but still unseeded because virtually nothing will grow in it any more; I look at it, and at the stunted trees that ring it, and at the cloudless sky, devoid of the possibility of rain, and then I go to my truck for some tools. There is a shovel there, a rake. They will do. I use the shovel like an ax: I bring it down on my mother's head, on her chest, on her arms and her legs, on what's left of her. I hack at her until she is in pieces, and then I chop the pieces into bits, and then I mash the bits until they are a chunky pulp, and I use the rake to spread her over the field. The field is big and as I work in the rising heat of the day it seems to grow, but so does my mother, and there is more than enough of her to fertilize every acre of it. The work is tiring, seems neverending; the heat brings out the stink of rotting flesh, and I'm forced to chase away the scavengers who compete with me for my mother's remains. But as I work I think of my hungry children at home, and I spread her flesh evenly through the furrows; when I'm done I plant my crops, and over the next months I use the rest of my mother's body to fertilize them and keep them growing, and by the fall my husbandry has yielded enough food to last the winter. My children are overjoyed at first, and eat greedily, but when they are sated they become suspicious and question me. Where did it come from? they ask me. How did it get here? I hide nothing from them, and when they hear my story they are aghast and refuse to eat again. Eat, I tell them. Eat, I show them, and eat myself. Eat, I force them; if I didn't make them eat then they would die too. I didn't kill her, I tell them. I didn't put her in that field. I only found her there. I only did what I had to do.

This time I do swim. This time I'm alone, and this time is even darker than the last time. The sky, I think, must be overcast, but if I look up all I see is a featureless black plain only slightly lighter than the land at the horizon. I wonder, briefly, if the sky might not be full of clouds, but empty of everything; I think this, and then I wade through a thick low growth of abridged trees, tangled shrubs, long damp grass that coils around my ankles. The vegetation ends suddenly and sharp rocks abrade my feet without actually cutting them, and then gradually the rocks thin out until there is only coarse sand underfoot. In this darkness I can almost believe that it's my steps which have ground the rock into sand. Then there's the water: in the distance it's white with the reflected light of an unseen source but up close it's as black and impenetrable as the sky; it could be three inches deep, or three fathoms, or three leagues, but I know it's shallow here because of the quiet sucking noise it makes where it laps at the shore. This time I swim: I take a deep breath, and I look around as though I might see someone through the darkness, and then I pull off my T-shirt and shorts and drop them on the beach. When I'm naked I feel a cold breeze I hadn't noticed before. I shiver, and cross my arms over my chest; I feel goose pimples stud my skin, feel, even, the perceptible shift of my testicles as they retreat into my body. My first surprise is the water's temperature. It's warm, not cold. I suppose the heat comes from the sunshine the water must absorb every day, but this notion seems fantastic to me, because I only come here at night: it's so dark now, here, and cold, that it's hard to imagine it could ever be light, or hot. Still, I let the warmth of the water pull me in. I'm wading, then treading water, then swimming and I swim with my eyes closed. I swim until the sluggishness leaves my body and I'm full of energy, and then I swim until I'm tired again, exhausted, and then I swim until I can't swim any more. When I stop I open my eyes; the slightest movement of my arms and legs pains me, but it's also enough to keep me afloat, and the sound of my hot panting is the only thing I hear. I wait then: for my tired limbs to give out; for a current, any current, even a weak current will do, to take hold of me like a hand around my ankle and pull me down; for everything to stop. I wait for everything to stop. But I wait and nothing happens. I look around me and I'm not surprised that I see nothing in the darkness, nothing that my eyes can recognize, my mind give a name to. I feel the water moving, and moving around me, and moving me as well. I'm not frightened but I'm impatient, and as I continue to wait for whatever the water will do—what can it do, after all, but pull me under or wash me ashore?—I feel time passing within my body. My lungs cool, my breath slows, strength returns to my limbs. Time passes outside of my body as well: the water cools a little, the breeze slows, and then, eventually, I realize that the darkness isn't as complete as it once was. The sun is rising. I can't see it but I see its effects: I see land. It isn't far away, I could swim to it. I wonder if this is how far I swam in the first place, or if the water has pushed me toward the shore. I suppose I have to swim to it. So I do. I had wanted to make the one choice that would have saved me from ever making another, but I didn't. This time I swam: I swam because I'd wanted to be one of those persons carried along helplessly by their destiny, but I'm not. And then, as I take my first stroke toward land, something grabs me from behind and from above. It lifts me out of the water and into the sky, and it carries me far, far away.

My mother disappeared from my life even as my conscious mind emerged into it, and thus she exists always and only just below the surface of my consciousness, and emerges vividly in my thoughts only right before or right after sleep. In everything I write, there is water. It appears and reappears obsessively. Like any obsession, it seems to lack all meaning beyond the fact of its existence. Whitman called the sea his mother but the sea, like my mother, was taken from me when I was very young and we moved from Long Island. All water is my mother: she is the leaky faucet in my stories, she is the Kansas drought, she is the aquifer that exists, invisible, far below the surface of the land and nourishes everything that grows on it, and nothing as simple, as discrete, as the body of another woman can take her place. It is not homage I pay to her when

I tell you this, or when I write a story. It's just something that happens. It's beyond my control. I feel like I owe her an apology for this—for something which is less than transubstantiation but which, I hope, is more than mere transformation—but I don't actually know that it would offend her. In the end words are only a shroud. They are bandages that take on her shape as she takes on theirs. They press her hair against her skull, bind her arms and legs together, flatten her breasts and stomach and hips in their tight coils. They protect her against the boring worm and the gnawing termite and they seal in what little air remains in her lungs, so that when she is awakened and freed at last the first breath she takes will be her own. They are an imperfect armor, I know. I can't protect her with as many layers as I wish because I know that every new word, every additional inch of cloth I wrap around her obscures her just a little more. How can this rough, white, smudged surface reveal the color and texture and smell of her body, how can it move as she moved, how can it speak with her voice? How can these violent elisions reveal the gentle person that everyone tells me she was? So I stop before she becomes completely unrecognizable, knowing that air will seep in, that worms and termites will find her. Her flesh will be eaten slowly, her bones crumbled to dust. What will remain is this shroud, an empty shell, an imperfect likeness, something that becomes more and more itself the less of her there is in it. It's just a matter of time until it becomes its own thing, while she—and I—become nothing at all, and I don't know if the knowledge that this too shall be erased by time is a cause for further grief, or if it is in fact my only consolation. But only when she is forgotten, and I am forgotten, and everyone who has ever read this is forgotten, only then will the wound of her loss be closed and the world be, once again, whole.

7

Elisions

I remember her marriage to my father as a catalogue of petty
injustices she perpetrated against my sister and myself, but I
know almost nothing of her life with him, or before him or
after him. She was seventeen. She had dark hair and fair skin.
She had been my father's sister Lois' friend, and it was Lois
and another of my father's sisters, Edie, who discovered her
sponging blood from my face, and I always think of them as
the people who made her go away, not my father. Had he come
home before Lois and Edie, he'd have beaten her but I don't
think he'd have sent her away. Yes, she hit us. She yelled at us
constantly and she dressed us in diapers after we started wetting
the bed again, and the end came when she lifted me above her
head and threw me face first onto a wooden floor, ripping my
lip open and becoming, I now realize, the first person ever to
commit a violent act against me. But her only real crime against
us was that she didn't seem to make any effort to understand
why we—myself, my sister, and my father—did the things we
did to her. She committed another crime, though: she lied about
her age, and it was on this basis that my father was able to
have the marriage legally annulled. He'd married her, I think,
less than three months after my mother's death, and in less
than that time she was gone. I heard, years later, that her
boyfriend or husband had been arrested as part of a thirty
million dollar drug bust and that the mob was protecting her
from the police. I didn't question the story; there's probably
something interesting in there somewhere, but I didn't look for
it. I'll say this for her: she was sexy enough that when my

father ran into her sometime in the year after their annulment and before his third marriage—he dropped by Lois' house, and Elise was in the shower—he jumped in and they had sex one last time. If her name weren't so odd I'd probably have forgotten it by now. Elise, as though Lisa had been reversed. Elise, a lease, as opposed to a permanent sale. Elise, short for elision. She was neither a replacement for my father's first wife or his children's mother, nor a new individual who could create her own role: she was merely a diversion, a stopgap, someone whose place in our lives would be omitted later, skipped over if not actually forgotten. She probably made a difference in someone's life, maybe in the lives of several people—who knows, maybe she made a difference in my father's life—but he never mentions her now, and, though I feel callous writing it down, I know she didn't make a difference in mine.

8

Original Sin

This is based on an excuse my father offered me:

Who is he, this man, what is he doing in her father's house? His dragging footsteps seem to be unheard by her parents: he plods past their door, stops at hers, and then he steals her in the dark just days before her wedding. His heavy hands hold her still—still enough—and silence her. They are heavy with meaning, but the words he whispers defy her to make sense of anything. What has she done to deserve either his love or his hatred? She's been a good girl, as quiet as her mother; she's kept every one of her father's secrets. She thinks of her mother often that night, a small plump Italian housewife stained sometimes with tomato sauce, other times with blood and bruises, an unconscious figure on the kitchen floor or draped across the couch in the living room. When this man finishes with her she thinks of the words her mother used every time her children found her—'I fell'—and she thinks of the baby she is pregnant with as he leaves her behind. He has punctured her and crushed her, his bulk has forced all the air from her body. Later the air will return to her lungs; later, beneath my father, she will surprise him and struggle and scream, but tonight she is as speechless as her mother. She is flattened and pliant, a pennant hung from one man's pole and then another's. She is twenty-three and she is pregnant with my father's baby, and because of these two facts she will become my second stepmother in a few days' time. The creature creeping from her room is her uncle, and I only hope that, like her father, he is dead now.

She lay on her stomach, a tiny almost flat figure with its face hidden in crossed arms. I crouched on my father's side of the bed. My face bent over Terry's body, my fingers combed her hair. Her hair marked her apart from us: we were a family of thin plain browns, but her hair was luxuriously black and thick, nearly as thick as her body and thicker than my fingers were long. It reached well past her tiny waist, and as she lay without moving my hand traveled its mysterious length. My fingertips just grazed her shirt through its dark mass and the strap of her bra was an invisible unexplained bump on an otherwise smooth surface. The morning was warm: sunlight came through the closed windows and my father was at work; my tough sister was out playing with her friends and Terry and I had the house to ourselves. The bedroom carpet was red plush, the walls stained blue, the ceiling white stucco: her black hair and my fingers walking up and down it were the road that might have led us up up up and out of there but we never took that path, and she cut it off years later, after she divorced my father. Hair so beautiful doesn't end up in the trash: it ends up as a wig, it ends up on somebody else's head. The face it frames now is unknown to me, as are the fingers that run through it. I wonder what brings those other people together: love? physical proximity? a legal document? Maybe it's just my imagination. I don't know—so, in some ways, nothing has changed.

It was always dark when we left for vacation. I close my eyes now, and imagine myself in darkness and silence and dreams. Then there is a hand on my shoulder that slowly shakes me awake, and I am five or six again, and half asleep. Terry dresses me. She pulls shorts over my underwear and a shirt over my chest. The cold line of the zipper against my skin is the first thing I feel, its *zip* the first thing I hear, and then we're in the car. My sister and I sleep in the back seat; my father drives; my stepmother fills what would otherwise be an empty space next to my father. When I awaken the world has changed. The land unfurls with an expansive generosity not found on Long

Island, yielding scattered hills, ancient trees, boulders that seem as large as houses. There are picnic tables and barbecue pits and a light blue sky dotted with tiny clouds. A dark calm lake provides a focal point to our play. The pictures of that day are just memories now, like the trip itself, but in them I remember my father is always with my Uncle Pete and they always have beers in their hands. Aunt Lois is there, and Cathy and Sissy and my sister and me, and Terry is there as well. She wears a dark blue short-sleeved shirt and her black hair resists all of the sun's efforts to lighten it. My brown hair, though, is almost blond, but my shirt is blue like Terry's, and, like Terry, I am not smiling in any of the pictures. When I remember that shirt I remember the word 'elastic,' because that's what Terry called the shirt's fabric: it could be stretched out and then, magically it seemed, it would return to its former size and shape. I miss those childhood discoveries, when a mere hundred miles could expand the limits of the possible. On that trip I saw volleyball for the first time, and on that trip I took my first ride in a rowboat. It was just my stepmother and me; I don't know if that's what actually happened but that's what I remember. I remember a boat that was small but heavy, wooden, unpainted, mossy—I could smell the moss—and Terry's narrow shoulders and tiny arms tugging at the oars; there is some concern that the oars, which aren't fastened to the boat, will slip into the water, leaving us stranded, and I am just frightened enough to be excited. At some point I lie down. The life jacket I'm wearing cushions me, and all my eyes can see is sky. I close them then, and am left with the sound of creaking oars and the movement of water: not a splash, not even a plash, certainly not a lash, unless it's an eyelash. An ash? No: it is a *sh* of water. *Shhh, shhh.* You can add as many idealized elements as you'd like to such a pastoral, but the one thing this scene can't support is the idea of evil. This leads me to question whether nature is actually good, or if it is, instead, a respite, from both the pollution and chaos of the modern world as well as from the necessity to make moral judgments. If that's true, then the philosophical value of nature—as distinct from its usefulness as a place to go on vacation or build a summer home—isn't threatened by strip malls or acid rain, but rather by the anthro-pomorphic tendency to place moral value on things which are amoral; this, I think, is the true consequence of what some people call original sin. The environment's ability to resist these encroachments is great but, like the elastic of a shirt I outgrew long ago, not infinite, and even a lake that big and that calm and that far away from 218 Spur Drive South couldn't save her, couldn't save us, from this: on another night my father dragged my sister and me from bed; he dragged us into his bedroom; he had one of his guns; he had a shotgun, and he used the business end to awaken my stepmother. Then, as we watched, he put the gun to Terry's head and made her beg for mercy; then he put the gun to his own head and made her beg for mercy; whether the price was her life or his, the sin was the same, and it was a woman's, and it was a woman's responsi-bility to atone for it. The only thing that links these two scenes—the boat and the bed—is the body in both of them, and my eyes. I never know where to go from here. White ceiling and blue sky. Red carpet and black water. Doorways, and sunlight glinting through the trees. I find myself yet again with a woman's body in my arms and a man standing over me, and I'm faced yet again with the probability that I can save neither of them. White ceiling and blue sky. Red carpet and black water. Blue walls, and the brown trunks of trees. Sometimes I wonder why he didn't just kill us all, but that blood refuses to flow. White ceiling and red carpet and blue walls: I testify that bad things happened. Blue sky and black water and the brown trunks of trees: better we should take our vacations in unlighted caves, that neither we nor the caves should see the atrocities we do. But it's under the sunlight we play, so that everyone may join in our games.

Her daughter, my age, was named Erica, but I don't remember the name of the woman who was our next-door neighbor; her husband was a cop. Years after she divorced my father, Terry told me that the woman had been having an affair with a hit man. Her husband worked days, so that's when the hit man would go over, but her husband's beat was also in the area, and some afternoons suspicion or love or laziness drove him home. I remember the husband's cruiser in the driveway, but I don't remember the hit man, who used to hop the back fence and leave through our house. This happened often enough that he began stopping for coffee with Terry, and the presence of two coffee cups and extra cigarettes on the table led my father to believe that it was Terry who was having the affair, and that she was having it with Jackie Miller, the son of our neighbor on the other side. I don't know whose divorce ended the afternoon coffee sessions—Terry's, or Erica's mother's—but the last time the hit man came to our house he thanked Terry for the hospitality she had shown him over the past few months and, like a good Italian boy, offered her a favor in return. He offered her a free hit. The man to be killed was my father. Now I imagine Terry considering his offer, cigarette in one hand, coffee cup in another—that's almost the only way I can imagine Terry—her eyes glazing over as they do when she has a blackout. Her blackouts are caused by epilepsy; what caused her epilepsy is a chicken-or-the-egg dilemma. Did my father come home, drunk, climb into bed beside her and throw her from it, smashing her temple on the corner of the night table and sending her into her first grand mal seizure; or did my father come home, drunk, and climb into bed beside her, only to have her go into her first grand mal seizure and buck from the bed beside him, smashing her temple on the corner of the night table? It remains, like so much else, a mystery. But there are other things she can remember as she sits before the angel who has offered her God's revenge: a dozen meals thrown into the back yard, all her clothes, a chair once, which went through the window above the kitchen sink. Everything flew in our house: her body, eight and half months pregnant, over a chair—that was the morning she gave birth to her son—and her son's body, across the dozen feet of the room we shared. He missed death by inches, landing instead in his crib, landing flat, rather than on the still-soft plates of his skull. It was a house of almost-dead people we lived in. Our souls were always poking

145

at us from the inside, eager to be freed, and in this my father was undoubtedly the most tormented of us all. I remember him standing over the open pit of the Millers' cesspool one day. 'Don't let me fall in, Dale,' he said, ''cause I'll just sink to the bottom like a stone,' and I remember imagining that, my father, his strong limbs unable to move his body through years and gallons of shit and piss. How many car accidents didn't kill him, how many men—uncles, fathers, brothers, beer buddies, hit men—how many women? That last is the only question I can answer: when Terry declined the hit man's offer, she became the second woman not to kill my father, the second to give him life. The first was his mother.

The line of words I am forbidden to write spins around my body in an endless spiral, a dust devil that continually threatens to grow into a tornado. Words have been whispered in my ear, spoken above my head, screamed in other rooms, or they have been hinted at only, covered by other words in the same way a sheet covers a dead body, and God only knows how many of those words were lies. When I was fifteen years old I sat in the back of Terry's car, and the words she cast back to me on that occasion could have put at least two men in prison for life. But the windows were open and the words, like Terry's smoke, like dust, were sucked out and blown away: people's names, their actions, entire histories have been dispersed in that way. Dispersed, but not disappeared: because I can't refer to the things that happened by their true names I will call them something else instead. I will call them eggs, potential lives destroyed and left to rot, a shell of silence formed by Terry's closed mouth—or mine, or my sister's, or even my father's—springing up around it and hiding the mess. These eggs are like paving stones on the path of history, and even those of us who aren't covered in their slime are forced to breathe in their stink. But now I say this: Remember that you are an animal. You have a soul, but it is housed in a body, and one of your body's tasks is to protect that soul. Remember your body's eyes and

146

ears, remember your nose. Look for danger, hea
recognize its smell and recognize what lies beneat
the scent of fear. Remember your teeth. Curl yo
and expose them, snarl, bite at the air. Rememb
Eat lots of calcium to keep them hard, and kee
and sharp as well. Practice scratching. Your fingers were claws
once, remember that, and remember that they can be claws
again, and fists too. Hit things. Hit what you have to, when
you have to, but don't forget about your legs. Kick like a mule
or run like a horse, but remember, your legs are there to defend
you. Remember that a threatened animal makes itself look
bigger, and remember that the thing which threatens you is
also an animal. Learn from its example: remember that it can
be hurt. It has been hurt before, it is hurting now, it will hurt
you if it can. Remember this, and remember the capabilities
of both your bodies; remember their mission. Remember the
possibilities to which their different parts can be put. Remember, and let those memories find expression in your body. Speak
them, or they will be taken from you again.

9

Prairie Woman

Does she recognize the shrunken giant she nurses? His skin is jaundiced, mustard-colored, his hazel eyes are piss-colored and shot through with blood like spoiled eggs. The muscles in his arms and legs, once taut, hang now in slack ropy piles. His chest is empty, his stomach swollen only by gases, his hair uncut, uncombed, unwashed for months, and staining the pillow a greasy yellow. They met last fall in the town's only pool hall; now it is winter and they are meeting in the town's only hospital, which he plumbed last year. There's not much you can do for hepatitis besides feed the sufferer, and she makes sure he eats every day. Still, he shrinks as he eats: months of fever burn off the gluttony of three failed marriages, and of course he can't drink. On quiet nights they talk, the nurse in her white uniform, the patient in his white gown. He tells her of the months he languished on his couch, sure he was dying; perhaps he mentions the death of his first wife, maybe he even mentions his second and third marriages, but he fails to talk about his children just as he failed to take care of them while he was ill. She grows as he shrinks: she is pregnant, unmarried, but this doesn't seem to bother him; it may even be the point that tipped the scales in his favor. By the time he leaves the hospital in late spring he is as handsome as he ever was and his smile, his jocularity, and his engagement prove that illness has made him humble enough for yet another woman to love him. They wait until she has the baby and her wisdom teeth are pulled; sometime between these two events his children show up at her house, surprising her with their

148

arrival—and, they think, with their existence. He meets her parents for the first time shortly before the wedding; she will wait seventeen years to meet his mother; his father is long dead. In the tiny Methodist church in her hometown his son is one of the ushers. The groom tells the boy to disregard guests' requests for 'bride's side' and 'groom's side,' else one half of the church will be empty. Behind an accordion door, cake and champagne await: are cut, opened, eaten, drunk, discarded. Then the departure for their honeymoon is delayed for nearly an hour as the groom sifts through bags of mown grass in one of which his keys have been hidden, and then he wipes off the smear of shaving cream that covers the keyhole, opens the door to his crimson '76 Monte Carlo, brand new, and drives west with his bride toward the ski slopes of Colorado. Neither of them is as new as the car: they have been married in brown, and it is just a few seconds before they become invisible in the haze of dust spit by the car's harried wheels. It lingers in a cloud behind them, like their souls, and then it disappears into the ground.

> *Me and you*
> *You and me*
> *That's the way*
> *It'll always be*

She has accumulated a lot in her twenty-six years, but most of it isn't very big. Dozens of small cardboard boxes overwhelm her new husband's trailer house; unpacking them has taken weeks because there simply isn't room for everything, and after she puts something away her stepdaughter hides it in an effort to maintain some level of control; her stepson just watches, silently. She is unsure how to act around them because her husband has told them to call her Pam, but she has learned that they called his other wives Mom. The children, eleven and nine, have no chores, no responsibilities, a state foreign to her. Their beloved dog, which has outlasted three marriages, is half starved when she moves in because it is fed so irregularly. In time she will impose farm-bred order on suburban laziness—

dishes will be washed after every meal, the house cleaned weekly, the yards mowed and raked, the goddamn dog fed—but this morning she is alone with her stepson. Her husband is at work, her stepdaughter out playing, her infant daughter asleep. 'How would you like pancakes for breakfast?' she says. He smiles, says, 'Thank you.' She cooks for him, serves him, but sits a long way across the wooden table while they eat. He eats hungrily, leaves his plate empty, but when he leaves the table they still have not touched each other. This is his father's fourth wife in five years, and there was also Maureen, the housekeeper who shared his father's bed for three months in Colorado; the boy is wondering when this woman, like the others, will disappear. She does the dishes after her stepson leaves, but as she does them she is thinking that he should be doing them—at least should have offered—and she is trying to decide if she won't wash them next time, or if she just won't cook him pancakes again.

On the cupboard door in the kitchen hangs a small plastic message board, its non-permanent marker dangling from it by a string. The board covers a hole in the cupboard where my stepmother had aimed my baseball bat at my father's head, and missed. There are other souvenirs of that night, most notably the shattered trim outside their bedroom door, which he'd barricaded against her. Onĕ leg of the dining room table wobbles from when he threw it against the wall, and the window in that room is conspicuously framed in wood. All the other windows have metal frames, but her head, propelled by his hand, had bent the dining room window out of shape just after the table leg was broken. Mostly they just hit each other, though, when they hit each other, and the other things they destroyed in their rages, cups mostly, other dishes, a truck once, are gone now. The majority of the wreckage in the house, broken mirrors, rotting floors, bubbles in the ceiling, are due to the inevitable decay of the cheap materials used to build trailer houses. Kitchen cabinets sank into the floor until their doors wouldn't open, and they had to gut the entire room, start over; new carpet covers the uneven floors; wooden siding conceals sheets of sun-warped tin which originally covered the house like a cracked eggshell. They even added a wing, a single huge bedroom that continually threatens to float away because it is so truly empty. Clothes censor nakedness; carpet, paint, wood, furniture, cheap framed pictures, and old sayings rendered in needlepoint do the same thing to their trailer; the question no one dares ask is why they don't just build another house. Nothing more substantial than 'milk' or 'potatoes' or 'heat casserole @ 350° for 1 hr' is ever written on that board, but behind it is a hole that my stepmother sometimes wishes was in her husband's skull. The board isn't a bandage, because beneath bandages healing occurs. It's some kind of camouflage: those who don't know the hole exists never suspect it's there, but those who do are reminded of it every time they buy food, or cook it, or sit down to eat a meal.

She prefers to sit and let the blond bowl fill her lap. She curves her back and bends her head forward, folds her long hair behind her ears, first the right, then the left, and then she presses her fingers against the silver strings. The calluses on her hands are years older than the guitar: they come from a childhood spent on the farm, from plowing and planting and harvesting, and they serve her well when she sits down to play. Beneath her fret-playing left hand she feels the satisfying vibration of the strings, and with her right hand she picks out songs, strums with her fingertips, uses her short nails to produce crisper notes. She plays carefully, without fault or flair, and when she sings her voice is a steady alto, nothing special, but everyone who listens is aware that she has the courage to do what they'd like to do, and, as well, that she means it, and when she finishes and buckets her broad-brimmed brown suede hat it returns with enough money to feed her and pay her few bills. For a long time she lived simply, the successful by-product of an era, but as that era drew to a close she went back to

151

school and only had time to take the guitar out on weekends, and then she graduated and began nursing, and the guitar came out even more rarely, on nights when she felt lonely or nostalgic, or when she had someone over she particularly liked. Then Erin came, and then my father, my sister, and I, and a few years into these additional responsibilities someone sold her a dented saxophone for forty dollars. My father told me, 'You will learn how to play at school, and then you'll teach Pam.' Not even Pam had the stomach for these lessons, and for the next year the saxophone was merely an easily justified method of tormenting me. 'An hour a day,' she said, 'before you go out to play.' She begrudged me even the few dollars it cost to buy reeds, and I splintered my lips on old cracked ones as I squeaked my way through 'Twinkle, Twinkle, Little Star' and 'When the Saints Come Marching In,' and I don't think it was coincidence that she waited to vacuum until I got home from school. The school year ended, and I put the saxophone away; when classes began again it wasn't mentioned. Then we moved: from the town where we'd lived for one year in two rented houses to the country, where they still live. The saxophone in its case was just another box, one with a handle, green, a trapezoid rather than a rectangle, and in the next months it moved from closet to closet as our things settled into place in that house like silt in still water. It landed, finally, on the top shelf of my sisters' closet, and sat there with the reproachful silence inherent in unwanted musical instruments. The guitar case was another box, beige, leather-trimmed, scuffed and aged and with a shape that recalled a woman's body, and silent. For years she kept it behind her bedside table, on which a gradually growing pile of old magazines, clothes, jarred coins, and unwanted but unreturnable items slowly hid the guitar from view. I suppose she put it there because she thought she'd pull it out and open it and take the guitar from its funereal velvet bed and play it sometimes, though maybe she put it there because there was nowhere else to put it. At any rate, I've never heard her play it. Maybe she played when I wasn't home, when no one was home, but I think she never got past thinking about it at first, and then, as the case became lost behind further accumulated debris, she didn't think about it at all.

She was born to inherit a small farm of long skeletal barns covered in skins of corrugated tin, a few leaning wooden structures, a farmhouse whose bathroom is only slightly older than she is, and a scattered network of wheat fields and pastures. She grew up piloting tractors, driving cattle, collecting the eggs of twenty thousand chickens on a daily basis. She walked through blizzards to get to school, she raced hailstorms to get the wheat in on time: she is the daughter of everything I esteem, a child of the silent hidden harsh strength of the prairie. A second daughter followed hard on her heels, and then a third, but they were never a threat to her. On her farm she developed the muscles of a man beneath the curves of a woman, a jaw that could take a punch—and took, she said, many from her father—and a fist that ached to return it. That the sixties happened to her is probably a testament to the power of television more than anything else: how else to explain the arrival of drug culture in a town that had fewer people than there are days in the year, high school classes in the single digits, only one branch of one religion. But they did happen, and when they passed they left her with more than a few fried circuits and the foggy memory of a pregnancy and a child, a son, surrendered for adoption. But that decade produced another adoption, another son: her parents brought their fourth child into the family before my stepmother became pregnant, but it's hard not to imagine some sort of connection between the boys, the one found, the other lost. My sister told me Pam had her first baby when she was nineteen, my father told me, later, that she had it when she was eighteen, and, still later, my stepmother told me that she'd had the baby when she was seventeen and that she hoped I could take his place; that last part is, I think, just more of the bullshit we were lobbing at each other by that point in our relationship, but at any rate James, her brother by adoption, is fifteen years younger than she is. Other things

153

are more difficult to date, but of them all I'm most fascinated by her will, her anger. Like the Kansas winter it simply, bitterly is, manifesting itself only occasionally but then ostentatiously in a blizzard of punches and curses and self-pity. But everything *was* taken from her: her son and her farm, intended first for James, who didn't want it, and then surrendered to Linda, the middle daughter, most probably because her parents didn't like my father. She gave up nothing after that: she clings to a marriage that stinks like curdled milk, but every year she cuts off a little more of the long hair my father demanded of all his wives. At its longest it was a mare's mane that slipped out of whatever pins she used to hold it off her neck and fell in a hot sticky mass to her waist. Now it bristles just above her shoulders; in a few more years she could be bald. But I suspect that she will scalp herself before she loses anything more. She has given birth to two other children. The summer before Erin started kindergarten I overheard Pam tell her that she wanted them to spend more time together, because after Erin began going to school she would no longer belong to Pam; as I write this, Erin has just given birth to a daughter, Vanessa Diane Wenzel. Of her third child, born a decade after Erin, who was born a decade after that first boy, I will only tell you that the one time Pam threatened to kill me was while she was nursing Amanda, and she lurched toward me, fist raised, with the baby at her breast. Her hair was parted into two soft feathers then, their beating wings just touched her shoulders. The feathers are gone now, just down remains, and there's no hair left on the land we both love either: the cultivated plains may be the breadbasket of the world, but they are no longer the long-grass prairies. Small changes are crucial; here, an entire ecosystem was destroyed. The possibility of disaster is contained in every sunrise: species disappear, millions of tons of topsoil blow or flow away, and the aquifer recedes deeper and deeper into the ground. I don't think there's much left of the woman my father married, but I don't know what's left of Pam. Whether it's her heritage or if it's just because she doesn't trust me, she's the only person in my family smart enough to hide her true feelings from me. When she speaks to me now it's with a gaiety that's not quite disingenuous, but which is based upon distance and absence, and which decreases as I come closer to her, and to her husband, my father. I've tried to find some detail of her life that isn't overshadowed by hopelessness; I know my search is hampered because the strongest emotions I feel for her are pity and distaste; but the best I can come up with is this: she is nobody's fool but her own. The only journey her body has ever offered me is a trip down the raised red river that runs from her neck to her navel. Once that plain was bare and white and once it was not a plain but a chasm, when doctors pulled her open and redirected her blood so that it would travel out of her torso properly and feed her arms and legs, her hands, her feet. Now it is closed, stilled. Sewn up in her flesh is an endless future of total immobility, of oxygen-starved limbs that would have atrophied and left her like an old woman in a rocking chair before she was thirty-five. Medicine has rendered that story an empty threat: she can work as hard as ever now, she can fight, she can do the things she likes to do. The mottled flesh will never embarrass her. It's ugly but it doesn't make her ugly because she is thankful for it, for what it represents. She was breaking, but now she is fixed; she will continue moving, but the river will never travel further than the length of its eighteen inches, and over the years it will recede into her skin, as if embarrassed to testify that in her, as in everyone else, there once existed the possibility of weakness.

10

Rolling Back the Stone

Now I enter my father. The skin which has served as his fortress all his life and protected him against me offers no resistance, and I crawl through all the holes left open to me. I am in his mouth and I am in his ears. I slip into his eye sockets and I slither up his nose. I leave his head for his groin: I am in his urethra, I am in his anus. From every orifice I take something out with me. From his mouth I pull his tongue and every word it has ever spoken, every curse, every endearment, every gasp of confusion or pain. From his ears I pull the words he has heard, the dirty jokes, the secrets, the pleas. I see what he has seen and I smell what he has smelled. I flow out of him like the heavy stream of a morning-after piss. I drop from him with clumps of shit. Then, with a hooked finger, I reach into his navel and pull out his organs in one long connected string: coils of intestine, half-inflated balloons of stomach and liver and kidneys, lungs which resemble bunches of grapes that have been stepped on. His heart bounces on the floor like gelatin spilled from its mold. I have entered my father. I have left him. I have turned him inside out and exposed him to anyone who cares to look, and, in doing so, I have created the story of his life—not biography, which is a kind of cannibalism, but biography's opposite: not consumption, but regurgitation. In pulling my father out of himself I have pulled him out of me, and I look at the mess I've made in the same way I would look at my vomit: here is something which, if it had stayed down, would have been digested, would have, eventually, turned into me.

At four, I stole a drink from my father's beer. I took one sip and spat into the air. As the mist cleared, I waited to be punished. But my father said, 'I'm proud of you,' and drank until he finished. He said, 'Go get me another,' and I went to find my mother. In the kitchen I grabbed a bottle. It was cold, like a wet gun. Quietly, I called out, 'Where are you? Where are you, Mom?' As if in answer, my father's voice pushed into my ears. 'Hurry up,' he yelled, cutting off my search, like shears. His hazel eyes were beer-colored, and I saw that they were dead. 'Don't ever drink,' he commanded, 'don't be like your dad.' He just filled his chair then, as a lamp fills its shade, and I became the child who was always afraid.

There was always a smell in my father's truck, and the smell was always dusty and cold, and underlain by smoke. The trash on the floor told of a limited array of choices: beer bottles and the cardboard cases they had been taken from, or beer cans and the plastic rings that held them together; coffee cups made from ceramic or plastic or styrofoam or paper; crumpled napkins stained with mustard and ketchup, wadded bags stained with grease. There were rags crusty with plumber's glues—purple and black especially—and dirt, and perhaps an old T-shirt lay there, and a cap or two. The bench seat held three comfortably, if two of the three were children, and at night there were only a few small contained lights: the dashboard, the cigarette lighter, the end of my father's lit cigarette glowing far above me. In the dark, in Kansas, the truck moved like a submarine along the ocean's bottom. I could feel the swells and dips in my stomach, saw wheat swaying like seaweed, saw dark thick torsos of cattle floating over the seaweed like foraging fish. I saw all this from eyes that barely cleared the dashboard, but I kept those eyes open and I kept them peeled: as long as my eyes stayed open my father's eyes would stay open, and we would not stop. His head would nod sometimes, but never fall, and the truck swayed gently across the road like an empty swing rocked by a breeze, but it never slipped into the ditch and my eyes never closed. We never talked—my sister and I were afraid to talk—and usually the radio was off, and the only sounds besides the straining aging engine were the sounds of smoking and drinking. Click, puff puff, sigh; snap, glug glug, sigh; but we never stopped. In the years before the drunk-driving campaigns it was stopping I feared, not wrecking. I feared the strange sea that was the combination of endless prairie and empty sky, and I feared being lost in a world whose single boundary was the horizon's radius, whose only pole was my father.

The ottoman measured one foot by two feet, and from its green plaid polyester surface I pushed my father's feet and dumped his hoard of quarters from a gallon jar, and I counted them under his eye while he drank a before-dinner beer. The uncounted mound of quarters swelled from the ottoman like an overstuffed stomach, and I pulled coins from this mound and stacked them in neat piles of four: one dollar, two dollars, three dollars, four. As the dollar piles grew by rows and columns the mound shrank, but not quickly enough, and to accommodate the spreading grid I pushed handfuls of quarters to the floor. I kneeled, counted; a host of founding fathers gazed into the distance with serene indifference; with his toe my father nudged a stray quarter toward me. By some miracle there were exactly enough quarters to cover the ottoman completely. A little adjustment here, some air in the lines there, and a silver net concealed the green and captured my attention. What had been a messy suggestion of opulence had been rendered a declaration: I'd never seen so much money in my life. Many years later I learned to play a drinking game called quarters. Players attempted to bounce a quarter off the bar and into a glass. When you lost you drank; when you won everyone else drank; in either case you played until everyone lost. Over the past year my father had bounced hundreds of quarters into a glass jar and now I had spread his shining silver net over the ugly green footstool. I was drunk with the effort, drunk with his wealth, and with his power, and his victory over me.

Billy Graham was my father's beer buddy for a few years. We always called him that: Billy Graham. He was a skinny malnourished thing, with long greasy brown hair, a wispy beard, a wife and two sons I don't remember. He lived in a run-down two-bedroom house in the southern part of town, which is to say the white trash part of town, and one night when I was eleven or twelve my father brought me over there. It was just fathers and sons that night; the fathers sat in the kitchen drinking and the sons stared at the television. At some point Billy Graham's voice made itself heard above the TV. 'Dale,' he called. 'Hey, hey, Dale, can you c'mere a sec?' I looked at him. His gangly shadow awkwardly filled the kitchen doorway. The light and my father were behind him, and one of Billy Graham's hands held a beer, and the beer rested against his crotch. I moved toward him slowly, and as I drew closer bits and pieces of him jumped out at me: the dirt on his red T-shirt and his jeans, the odd expression that twisted his face. He held his beer can directly in front of his crotch, and through a crook in his elbow I could see my father, and the stupid grin on his face as he hunched over his own beer. Billy Graham said, 'Can you help me?' He said it quietly. He said, 'I've got a problem with my, um, my, I've got a problem, I—my zipper,' he finished then, and he moved his beer can. He moved it to his lips. A red thing poked from his pants. It was maybe five inches long and an inch and a half thick, and hard, and it tapered to a blunt tip. The fly of his underwear gripped it like lips gone white from sucking, and Billy Graham nudged it with his free hand. 'Can you give me a hand?' he said. 'I, um, I can't get it back in.' I moved a step toward him, a step away, I tried not to stare at the red thing but it was all I could look at. I took another step toward him, my hand reached out. But before I touched it I looked up at Billy Graham's face and that broke the spell. Billy Graham started laughing when my eyes met his, and he pulled the red thing from his pants and tossed it at me. It took me a long time to realize that the thing in my hands was a radish. It took less time to realize that my laughing father was in on the joke. We slept there that night because my father was drunk. I shared a bed with the two boys. The older one was a year or two younger than me. He was blond and small and snotty; he stripped down to his underwear and strutted through the room, and I was embarrassed by what was visibly different between us. In bed he took up as much space as he could between his brother and me, pushing against me often, fidgeting, falling asleep finally with his drooling pink pout turned toward me and his butt poking into the air. I never once thought of Billy Graham's radish that night, although now I try to imagine what passed between him and my father. 'Hey, Dale, I've got an idea. Why don't I let this radish hang out of my zipper and pretend it's my dick?' 'I've got a better idea, Billy Graham. Why don't you see if you can get Dale in there to put it back in your jeans for you?' But I didn't think of that then; I thought instead, and all night long, of the blond boy's beautiful butt. There are a few questions I'd like someone to answer for me now. First of all, why didn't I fuck that little boy? And second, why didn't my father just fuck me? If he was truly trying to teach me that desire and contempt are manifestations of the same impulse, and if he was trying to express contempt for a desire that was already manifest in me, wouldn't that have been the most effective way? And, finally, where did my father sleep that night? That's a cheap shot, I know, with potentially serious implications. *I know.*

This was my heterosexual moment: I had a big red '76 Monte Carlo with five hundred horses under the hood, and I had a full-time job at Sirloin Stockade. I had money in my pocket and gas in my tank, and the snout of my car jutted north on 30th Street like a dog straining at its leash. I had pride and I had power—and then he floated past. The boxy white egg of his van was heading east, heading toward the highway and home, and the sign magneted to its door—*Dale's Plumbing Service*—was an unnecessary reminder that I bear his name. Here's what I wanted to do: I wanted to blow him off the road. My foot would drop to the floor, the gas needle would dip into the red as those twelve big cylinders sucked up fuel, the engine would growl for a moment in warning, and then *bam!* I would be behind him, beside him, then past him, feeding him my dust. That's what I wanted to do. But instead I followed him. It was midnight, and the Monte Carlo, faded red during the day, was brown at that time of night, and in my work uniform I was brown inside of it, and invisible. I turned onto 30th Street and followed my father, who took the back way home: Lorraine to 56th, 56th to Tobacco Road, Tobacco to 69th and the little jog over to Cottontail Lane, and then the bumpy gravelly mile to our driveway. He took the back way because he was coming from the bar and he was drunk. I knew he was drunk because he drove with telltale overcaution: thirty miles per hour when the speed limit was forty-five, signaling a half mile before he reached a turn, and as I followed him I hated him for the transparency of his gestures. I tried not to ride his ass, but I stayed close behind him, and I knew that he wasn't aware it was me who followed him: he would have given me a sign if he knew it was me. It was on the long stretch of Tobacco Road that he surprised me. By then he was driving barely twenty miles per hour and I had to ride the brake to keep the MC behind him. As he inched toward home his van slipped slowly from the right side of the road to the left, its progress slow, steady, inexorable, like the movement of a needle in the groove of a record, but then, before the song should have ended, my father's van slipped into the ditch that bordered the left side of the road. I screamed as the perpendicular sail of the van's rear end tilted crazily. I screamed, 'Daddy!' because I thought it was going to roll over. The rear end of the van fishtailed left and right as my father jerked the wheel toward the road, and then, as simply as he'd slipped into the ditch, he slipped out of it, and continued his journey as though nothing had happened. But for that brief tottering moment I knew only one thing—that my father would die—and I felt only one emotion: grief. My brown and white plaid polyester uniform was saturated with the grease of a deep-fat fryer and the fingers which gripped the steering wheel of my father's hand-me-down car were singed from turning over dozens and dozens of pieces of buttered toast on a flat steel grill: that was my job. I was his son. When we got home my father laughed when he saw it was me; I'd scared him, he said, he'd thought I was a cop. But I was furious, because he'd scared me even more. He'd made me ask myself why I'd followed him, and he made me realize that the answer was, in part, because I wanted to protect him. He made me realize that I still loved him, and that's why I was furious.

He stopped the same way that I imagine he started: when no one was watching. The impulses were the same too: at fourteen, fifteen, he'd already shouldered the responsibilities of a man for years—just ask his sisters—and now he wanted its privileges. Forty years later, he finally realized that those privileges were, in fact, responsibilities, and one evening during the spring semester of my junior year at college he called me. 'Dale,' he said, 'I haven't had a drink for two, three weeks now.' I was suspicious. I said, 'And . . .?' and he said, 'And I don't think I'm going to have another.' Fifteen hundred miles separated us, and it had been two years since I'd last seen him. Other things also filled that space: his youngest daughter was two, and his oldest had emerged from an A A detox center and now was getting married; I'd taken my second drink a little over a year earlier. The second of my mother's three sisters had died, this one of cancer, and I came out a month after that. I remembered, without acknowledging it—in the same way I hadn't acknowledged it at the time—the feeling of excitement I'd felt when my father came home drunk. Now something will *happen*, I'd thought, and it made me a little sad to realize that now nothing more would happen. I still don't know why I stood by him during the next year, but I did. I called him every few weeks to check his progress, offer him encouragement, thanks even,

162

and love. He will probably remember that as the last time I stood by him. The only other time he tried to quit drinking he'd lasted one month. Then, on Christmas Eve, a house he'd worked on burned down—it was later proved that he wasn't to blame—and the owners threatened to sue him. In the darkness of Christmas morning, Erin awakened me, and we opened presents in the living room while my father watched us from a chair. He was nearly immobile with alcohol, a snowman whose hard head was sinking into the melting ball of his stomachy torso; he managed only to slide from the chair to his knees, and then he made us join hands as a family and pray, and thank God for what we had received. That was the Christmas I got the typewriter on which I typed a speech about wife beating which won me gold medal after gold medal in state speech tournaments. Middle-aged women with hair permed to the texture of curly straw would clutch vinyl purses to their chests and cry when I gave that speech, and I would shift my gaze from their leaking eyes to the magic spot on their foreheads, the place where priests aim their thumbs and executioners their bullets, lest I too exchange a real sorrow for the one I was manufacturing with my words.

This is the first story my father told me when I told him I was going to write about him: 'I almost didn't graduate high school, Dale,' he told me. 'Never was a good student but that's not why. Nope, one time my senior year I borrowed the teacher's pointer and I flipped up the dress of the prettiest girl in school so I could see her underpants. Her panties. Just a joke, just a little flip, she giggled, she and me was friends, no harm done. But this asshole teacher turned around and he said, Dale Peck, go to the principal's office right now! and he sent this little brownnoser with me with a note. As soon as we hit the hall I said, Give me that note, and this kid said, Aw, Dale, I can't do that, and I said, Give me that note or I'll kick your goddamn ass. Well, this note said that I was being sent to the principal's office because I poked so-and-so in the *anus*. In the *anus*. As

163

soon as I read that I marched back into the classroom and started yelling, You asshole! I did *not* poke this girl in the *anus*! I did not—but he cut me off and told me to get to the principal's office, and I went, but the minute I got there I just started yelling again. Fuck you! Fuck your school! You're supposed to be teaching us honesty but you're all a bunch of fucking hypocrites! Well, Dale, to make a long story short they wanted to suspend me for three days for poking this girl in the *anus*, even though she told 'em I didn't do it, and I just told them they could take their school and shove it up their ass, and I walked out. So. I got a job, something, I don't know, whatever it was I'm sure it didn't pay much. Started eating at this diner. Didn't really want to be home much, with Ma there. There was this other fella who ate there a lot too, and over time we struck up an acquaintance. Turns out he was a history teacher at my high school, and I told him all about what happened, you know, about how they'd called me a liar, and one day he says, You really want to go back to school, don't you, Dale? and I said, Aw, man, I'd give anything to get my diploma, I don't want to end up a bum like my old man. You never met my dad, Dale, but he was a real bum, a true no-good drunk. You may think I was bad but you kids got off easy with me, compared to him. Anyway, this history teacher got me back in school, and he made sure I graduated. He even had me over to his house to study. He lived with this other man, and I figured out pretty quick that they was, you know, they was ... The other one was a florist. My teacher, he quit teaching later on and they ran the flower shop together, but I didn't know them any more by then. One night, we'd stayed up late studying, I ended up sleeping there and they only had the one bed. Well, I woke up in the middle of the night. And the other one, the one who ran the flower shop, he was playing with me. Through my underwear. Well, I played it cool, just rolled over and pretended I was asleep, but I never saw them again after that. I kind of wish I had. They were real good to me, both of them, they were decent men. But I was young, you know, that sort of thing freaks you out when you're young.' He paused then. He was fifty, and I was twenty-five, and in so many ways I knew

I was half the man he was. And then he brought it home: 'Well, I guess it doesn't freak you out,' he said, 'but it freaked me out. I never did see them again.'

I remember many night-time drives but I only remember stopping once. No accident: there was a storm coming, and my father was tired, and he decided to sleep it out and sleep it off. He parked the truck on the side of the road, and when he shut it off what little light had existed disappeared, and so did my perspective. My father and sister folded away from me, each leaning against a door, and I sat upright between them like a caterpillar between butterfly wings, my vigilant eyes still open, my ears straining for something in the silence. Oh, that sky: it's why I still dream of Kansas. The stars crowded against each other like pebbles in a streambed, and as the clouds advanced they interposed their blackness between me and the stars like a muffling blanket. Lightning leaked from them. Distant harmless flickers moved closer, gained size, clarity, power, single trunks of lightning and big oval clusters that were as branched as tumbleweeds, and then thunder, the kind of thunder that scares little children. When the rain came it surprised me; I'd thought the sky was spending its all on light and noise, but no, it had strength for more. Then I was truly under water. The rain was solid as a curtain, and through it the lightning was blurred and diffuse, the thunder muffled, and I wondered that my father and sister were not shaken awake. I twitched and fidgeted; I peered out all the windows. I think I thought of running away but I knew better than to wake my father. They say that as soon as you think about the weather in Kansas it will change, and it did. I'd thought of the rain as a curtain, and the curtain simply lifted. When it was gone I saw that the thunder and lightning were on the other side of us now, and it was the first time I realized that the weather doesn't actually change: it moves. The clouds peeled back slowly, and slowly the stars reappeared. My father was a snoring wreck to my left, and the archaeology of his life lay in ruins beneath my feet. I suppose

I loved him most in that moment after the rain, and I quivered next to him, protecting him somehow, and I remained awake until he awakened and drove us the rest of the way home. What I miss now, when I miss my childhood, are those twinned, those entwined lies: that it's the world that's out to get you, and that, when it doesn't, it's because you've somehow managed to overcome it yourself. But strength is just an illusion that some people perpetuate and other people believe in. I always was a believer.

My grandmother sings a lullaby to my five-year-old father:

> Baby boy, baby boy,
> what have you done?
> Baby boy, baby boy,
> where have you run?
>
> Baby boy, baby boy,
> why won't you come?
> Baby boy, baby boy,
> are you still my son?
>
> Run the bath water;
> you know how it's done.
> Only turn the cold on,
> and listen to it run.
>
> Take off all your clothes.
> I'll pierce you with my eyes.
> Why do you always disobey me?
> Now you've earned your prize.
>
> I'll drop you in the water
> I'll hold you by your nose.
> I'll hold you 'til you turn blue,
> and lose the feeling in your toes.

166

Listen through your ice baths,
and remember what I say:
You can never please your mother,
and you can never run away.

I'll tail you like a shadow;
I'm the night to all your days.
I'm the puzzle that you can't solve;
you're lost within my maze.

A mother's love is sourceless,
but her hatred never ends.
There's nothing that can change this,
no way to make amends.

Baby boy, baby boy,
do you know what you've done?
Baby boy, baby boy,
do you know you can't run?

Baby boy, baby boy,
your sin is an old one.
Baby boy, baby boy,
you were born my son.

There are no mysteries inside the body of a man. Any man knows this; this is why he uses his hands so much. There is nothing inside a man's body that he can't see represented in a car's mechanics, or the plumbing in his house. There is food. He puts it in his mouth and chews it up, just like the garbage disposal under his sink. It slides down the pipe of his esophagus into the bellows of his stomach and sits there for a while, is softened, decomposed. Put a potato in a pot of water on the stove and the same thing happens. Eventually the stomach's done all it can; the food slides down again, more pipes, the small intestine, the large intestine. Nutrients are leached out, along with color and a bit of mass. If you squeeze the soapy water from a sponge you can see this too. What's left is com-

167

l, stored, then passed out in brown bricks in which bits
l are still recognizable, as is garbage in a trash compactor.
it. When a man looks in the mirror he knows that all
he sees is all there is. His piss is a shower, his cum, what? Air
in the pipes. Sweat: a beer bottle can sweat. You wonder at his
hopelessness, you wonder at his rage? You ask me why men
kill? Ask a man what comes from his body and he will look
at his hands and say, Nothing. Nothing that he didn't put in it
first.

Before my father will let them bury his mother he has the body
brought to him. My father recognizes the ability of experts; he
is a good carpenter and a better plumber, and he knows his
way around under the hood of a car, but this is a body after
all, and he has hired a vivisectionist. 'Every pipe,' my father
says, 'every tube. Every part of her that she could get to, I
want to get to.' The man with the knives starts at the throat
and works down. He works slowly, slitting with his knife and
folding back flaps of skin with his rubber-gloved fingers. My
father waves away most of the important organs as they are
identified to him, the heart, the lungs, the liver, the kidneys. 'I
want to see what was in her stomach,' he says. 'I want to know
what she ate.' The liquids that come from her are blue and
brown and black, but my father doesn't notice them as they
drain off the stainless steel table and flow thickly toward the
drain at the bottom of a hollow in the floor. He notices instead
that the drain cover has been drilled with holes in too narrow
a gauge for the fluids that are supposed to pass through it, and
as a result a pool is forming on the floor; he thinks of how
much he would charge to fix that drain. When the vivisectionist
has gutted and opened all of my father's mother's alimentary
canal, working first from the front and then flipping her over
to go in from the back, he looks at my father to see if he is
satisfied. He's not. 'Up there,' my father says, 'up there.' The
vivisectionist sighs but he doesn't speak; he is, like a plumber,
paid by the hour. With a little cutting, a little snipping of

threads, things come out more easily than my father would have thought. The strung-together body parts, vagina, birth canal, uterus, fallopian tubes, ovaries, resemble an animal made from twisted-together tubular balloons which have slowly lost their air. The vivisectionist opens them quickly, easily. 'There,' he says, 'there's nothing.' But my father, whose job relies on his ability to spot an object where it doesn't belong, says, 'What's that?' It's a little piece of plastic, the size and shape of a credit card, almost covered in body stuff. My father wipes it off with his bare hands, sees then that it's a piece of laminated cardboard. The first side he looks at is blank, but the other side has a message, and to make sure that there's no mistake his mother has written it in her own hand. The expression on my father's face as he reads is not inscrutable, but instead indescribable, and, after a moment, he tosses the card into the opened carcass, to be sewn up inside it. When he leaves the room the vivisectionist picks up the card and reads it: 'I knew you would look here for answers.' The vivisectionist shrugs his shoulders. He has buried sons in their mother's clothing before, and mothers in their son's; he has seen more than one son entombed in a year's salary's worth of stone, and he has prepared many a matriarch for permanent display in a glass coffin. Hunters call this stuffing, and they call what is stuffed a trophy; sons call it love. Like any man, the vivisectionist just calls it the work he does. He tries not to think about it while he does it, and he immediately forgets about it when he's done.

Every boy discovers the world through the nearness and then the withdrawal of his mother's body; and every boy learns to rely on himself by emulating the distant pillar of his father's strength. But these are gifts the foolish copulators who produced you never offered and so, out of all the things in this world, you have chosen to take comfort in those which you can hold in your hands. Anything solid, anything that has a shape, anything that you can pick up and put down and handle.

If you could touch it you believed you could know it; you believed that everything you touched was everything that could be known, and this knowledge was your small defense against an inhospitable world. Do you remember the fruit you stole as a hungry child, the food your brothers and sisters stole in turn from your sleeping body? Do you remember the cars that you rebuilt and drove to pieces in a night? Do you remember your first baseball, your first football, the first dumbbell you ever clutched and curled? Who threw the ball farthest, who built the biggest strongest muscles? You did, because you knew why those objects existed: they existed to save you. Do you remember your first cigarette, your first beer? Think of the power you felt as you pulled the smoke into your lungs and the alcohol into your blood. The rush knocked you out of the world's orbit and for the first time in your short unhappy life you thought you could see yourself clearly, be yourself, be only you. In the years that followed you held every beer you ever drank tightly in your hand; you never set them down but if your hand grew tired you let the cold bottom of the bottle rest against your groin. Do you remember your first hammer? Driving a nail through one piece of wood and into another, thrilling as you fixed an object in place for all time, proof against the inconstancy of man and Mother Nature. Do you remember your first wrench? The flex and growth of your forearm and biceps as you fitted its mouth over a pipe, pulling nipple from joint, clearing the clog, resealing the works with a smear of pipe dope, a deft adjustment of the wrench's bite with your thumb and just the right amount of pressure. You never squander your strength when you work; there's no need; when you hold a wrench you know where you are and what your purpose is. Do you remember the first person you hit? A brother, perhaps, or someone who threatened one of your sisters; perhaps it was a rival, for food, for work, for a woman. Do you still remember the difference between someone who is standing and someone you have knocked to the ground? Do you remember your first gun? What was the first thing you killed? That pheasant that has hung, stuffed, in the living room of all your houses? Remember your first house now: the first time you turned your

170

own doorknob, raised your own window, flushed your own toilet; she wouldn't disturb you there. Now let your hands run again over the body of the first woman you made love to. I won't ask you who she was; I know she wasn't my mother. You were eighteen, you once said; you said she raped you. Though you didn't know it, this is when your plan first betrayed you, for you made the mistake of believing that this woman was no more than the length and breadth of the body you touched, you stroked into passion, you fucked to orgasm. Who can blame you for this oversight? Your hands had never failed you before, and they haven't failed you since. Your *hands* have never failed you. You have never left a woman unsatisfied. You have never lost a fight. You have never faced a plumbing problem you couldn't fix. In your own way, or, at least, on your own turf, you are invincible. Certainly I would never challenge you; believe me when I tell you I'm not challenging you now. Nothing you have ever confronted has beaten you, not even, at long last, your mother. With one hand on her shoulder you led her into the family room. Ma, you said, this is my wife, Pam. That's Dalene, that's Dale, that's Erin, and this is Amanda. Ma, you said, this is my house. Only then did you take your hand off her body, safe in your belief that without your touch your mother's old and arthritic limbs had as much motility as a dropped wrench. But, my father, but. Everything you refuse to confront will take you down in the end. Unseen shapes and formless forces gather around you. You have pushed through them all your life as through water, as though against a head wind, pretending that they didn't exist because you couldn't touch them. But every day the things which have comforted you seem a little less steady in your hands, and every day you retreat from them a little more; every day your fear grows. Do you remember the last cigarette you smoked? The last beer you drank? When was the last time you woke without pain, when did you last make love? How long has it been since you took any pleasure in hurting another person? The weak shortsighted people who surround you say you have mellowed with age. They don't see the general whose entire army has been wiped out. Now you dread the day when the wheel of your truck slithers out of your hands like a snake, when your wrench is no more useful in your arthritic fingers than a breath of air. Now the only thing you let yourself touch is your youngest daughter. Lightly, laughingly, lovingly: hers is the only body you have ever touched and never hurt, and in this knowledge, in this touch, in this body you are most secure. But even she is growing away from you, and there will come a day when she will be gone and then the ground under your feet will be revealed as a layer of dust over a bottomless pit, and you will fall. There will be nothing for you to grab, nothing solid for you to purchase. You will be completely alone, in darkness, in sadness, in a place with no name. Because you never trusted language, never once relied on words, they were all you left for me, and if you call me then, trembling and full of fear, I will come. Your gifts are fists and curses, your punishments kisses and caresses, and I have grown bitter with your love and sweet with your hatred. You are my god, my father, but I am your bible: I turn your flesh into words, and words have always outlasted the gods who fathered them. I have built you up and I have torn you down, and I can do either again, or neither, or both. Words are my wrenches, words my hammer and nails. Words are my fists, my liquor, my food, and words are my women. With my words I will protect you. I will save you as you have saved me. I save you forever, and for everyone, and for eternity. Dear father, I am saving you now.

3

Red Deer

Oh bury me not
on the lone prairie.
These words came low
and mournfully
from the pallid lips
of a youth who lay
on his dying bed
at the close of day.

Oh bury me not
and his voice failed there.
But we took no heed
to his dying prayer.
In a shallow grave
just six by three
we buried him there
on the lone prairie.

11

Coffee and Other Rituals

The dawn sun pierced the clouds with rays that were long and thin and limb-like, and it ran toward the east side of the mountain that cast shade over Beatrice and Henry's house every morning. The clouds filtered the sun, and the trees, still clinging to brown leaves, filtered it still more, but even so the sun ran on silently, and it trampled lightly on everything it touched. By the time it reached the top of the mountain it was galloping, and it crashed through the mountain's crest of trees in a burst of flameless fire, and that was when the mountain's shadow made its daily appearance. Before, there had just been darkness, but now the darkness had a shape, a boundary. Far longer than the mountain itself, the shadow engulfed Beatrice and Henry's house in an oval patch of darkness and then, as the morning continued to advance, the shadow retreated; it shrank; it measured its regress in blades of grass lost to light, in stones, in branches and then whole trees slowly uncovered. The shadow was a skin, and the skin was being pulled back, and as the sun ran over the earth's body dew began to steam like sudden breaths. The grass quivered and the trees stirred and creaked into painful life, and in his house, in his bedroom, in his chair sitting and watching his sleeping wife, Beatrice, Henry saw none of this. He was aware of none of this. The pupils of his eyes contracted slightly; the faint colors of his body emerged. To Henry, there had been light and there had been darkness, and that was all. It seemed to Henry that there always is. There is always light, and there is always darkness, and Henry felt trapped in that darkness. Outside it was light now,

175

it was morning, but to Henry the darkness remained, inside him, inside his house, and all around Beatrice it was especially dark. She lay like a shade on their bed, still sometimes, fitful other times, cool to his touch or sweating profusely, quiet, or occasionally making a noise that was louder than a sigh but not quite a moan. This sound, and her sweating and her twisting and turning, frightened Henry, but he was more frightened by her stiff silent coldness. When she lay like that she seemed like a corpse to Henry, and he was sure that she would never awaken. For the doctors had told him: his wife was ill. Beatrice was ill, dying perhaps; they could say no more.

He felt himself tugged to the top of the stairs and then down the extra steps to the second floor, tugged along the long crooked hallway, tugged toward Beatrice. A heavy food-laden tray hurt his hands, but as he walked he paused to look into each empty room, and he wondered if any of them would ever have a purpose, if they would house a person, a television, a sewing machine, or if they would remain empty for as long as the house remained. He had called Susan to tell her that Beatrice was sick, and he knew that they would never house her, not even for a night. John wouldn't even give them his phone number. At the door of the room he shared with Beatrice he stopped. He had considered building separate master bedrooms when he was drawing up his plans; he'd considered putting them at opposite ends of his house. He hadn't abandoned this idea exactly, merely forgotten it in the battle to build the house, and now he stood outside the door to their room and listened, heard only his own breath. He waited a moment, attempting and failing to calm himself, and then in a single abrupt step that splashed coffee out of both cups he was in the room. He sighed, relieved: Beatrice's eyes were still closed. But then they opened, clear and focused, not the eyes of someone just awakening but the eyes of someone who has lain awake for some time. Henry saw a book then, cracked open to its first or second page, on the bed beside Beatrice. Beatrice followed his eyes with her own and she closed the book without marking her page. Henry stood close to the door for a long time, unsure of what to do, until Beatrice removed her eyes from his and looked at the tray. 'Is that for me?' she said, and Henry said, 'Oh yeah. Yes, I mean. Yes, it's for you.' He jerked forward and spilled more coffee, and orange juice as well, and the two liquids swirled together like snakes. He was aware, as he set the tray down next to her book, as he pulled a chair close to her side of the bed, as she began to eat and he took a wet coffee cup into his hands and held it there, that the two of them were alone. No mother, no father, no Susan and John. Myra was downstairs, or Myra had returned to her trailer: it didn't matter, Myra wouldn't disturb them here. Here there were just four walls, himself, and Beatrice. The rest of the world was somewhere else, and again he had to fight the urge to run.

Beatrice ate slowly, and she ate one thing at a time. She picked up the large plate with the bacon and eggs, and she ate first her bacon and then her eggs, and then she set the plate back on the night table and picked up the small plate of toast and butter and jelly, and she spread the butter and jelly on her toast and ate it, and then she set that plate back on the table as well. Then her orange juice. Then her coffee. Henry looked at Beatrice's coffee, and her orange juice, and her toast and butter and jelly. Behind that sat Beatrice's body, reduced by illness and yet, for the same reason, made boundless by the unknown processes that were occurring within it. Behind Beatrice was a bare white wall the size of a movie screen, and in that wall were windows that showed only empty sky, and Henry remembered then a dog they'd bought for the kids when they lived in their first house. They'd kept the dog chained up in the fenceless back yard, and it had run endlessly on its chain, and over time its feet had cleared the earth completely of grass and worn a deep circle into the ground. In their second house the dog had run free in the fenced-in back yard, but it had run less, and Henry realized as he watched Beatrice eat her breakfast one piece of food at a time that when your choices are expanded infinitely you make fewer of them. You

become frightened by possibility; you become, somehow, satisfied with what didn't satisfy you before. He cleared his throat.
'You want anything?' He almost asked her if she wanted to
talk but his mouth refused to shape itself around the words
and he saw himself, mouth open like a fish gulping water, and
he shut his mouth quickly. Beatrice shook her head. She said,
'Thank Myra for me,' and her voice was cold. She didn't look
at him. 'Thank her for making me breakfast.'

Myra's cache of breakfast recipes was small, but familiar and
comforting. Every morning it was bacon and eggs, or ham
and eggs, or sausage and eggs. She neither ate nor cooked
lunch—neither did Henry, and neither did Beatrice—and Henry
had no idea what she did for dinner because by then she was
back in her trailer, having passed the day with Henry or with
Beatrice, though never with both of them. Henry was surprised
then, one morning when he woke up early, to find Myra sleeping on the couch; the sun wasn't up yet, and Myra slept in
yesterday's clothes. That didn't mean too much because Myra
often wore yesterday's clothes. But there were two pillows
under Myra's head, a sheet over the couch cushions, another
sheet between her and the blanket, and Henry suspected that
this wasn't the first night Myra had spent in their living room.
Still, he didn't wake her. He went instead to the kitchen and
started the coffee. For him, it was a graceless procedure. His
hands were still sore and stiff, and he dumped the grounds into
the pot, then added cold water, and as he looked at the grounds
floating in thin brown liquid he realized he'd messed up. He
was just emptying the pot into the sink when he heard a chuckle
behind him: it was Myra. Her hair had been roughly combed
into a ponytail but other than that she looked straight from
sleep, still blinking sand from her eyes. Myra's smile, Henry
thought, showed off the tiny wrinkles surrounding her eyes
and the larger ones framing her mouth, the loose line of skin
that was the beginning of a double chin, and looking at them
Henry was aware of his own wrinkles and his own double

178

chin, his own smile. Myra was sixty-three to his sixty, and he thought that it would be nice—it would be as nice as growing old could be—to grow old with her. 'Help?' she said. 'Thanks,' Henry said, and he stepped out of Myra's way.

He sat down then, and he must have dozed off because a small roar shook him roughly from sleep. 'What the hell—' he began, but by then the room was quiet again. 'Oh, sorry,' Myra said. 'The lady at the coffee store talked me into this.' She was holding an aluminum cylinder capped by a brown plastic cup. 'What the hell is it?' Henry said. 'Coffee grinder,' Myra said, 'for the beans. It's supposed to make a fresher pot of coffee.' 'Well, warn me next time,' Henry grumbled, but the kitchen was silent and the whine of the grinder just a memory in his ears, and after a moment he said, 'Sleep well?' 'I hope you don't mind,' Myra said. She looked out a window while she spoke, or at the coffee she was making, or at the cabinets as she pulled cups from them. 'I just thought it'd be easier for me to get an early start on breakfast.' 'Why should I mind?' Henry said. 'It's not like we're short on space here.' 'I know,' Myra said. 'I know. But it's your home, not mine.' 'I'm not so sure about that. I think this place is still pretty much its own master.' He waited a moment while Myra brought coffee and a tiny pitcher of milk to the table. When she was back at the counter he said, 'Wouldn't you be more comfortable in a bed? We could set up a room for you, no problem.' 'Oh, Hank, I just couldn't.' 'Myra,' Henry said. His hands were warm around the hot cup of coffee. 'Myra, that trailer can't be too comfortable for you, and it's probably full of awful memories. I could have a truck haul it out of here next week.' There was a sizzling on the stove that replaced Myra's voice for a moment, and then Myra put a lid on the pot and said, 'Hank, that trailer is my home.' Henry smelled sausage. He smelled coffee. He smelled his own body, still waiting to be washed. During his life he'd always found apologies difficult, and he didn't apologize now. A clock caught his eye. 'Hey,' he said, quietly, 'it's quarter of six. Isn't it a little early for breakfast?'

At the stove, Myra's back stiffened momentarily, but then she relaxed and her spatula stopped scraping the pan, and

179

then, with a click and a sputter, she turned off the flame. The room was silent until Myra sighed, grabbed the coffeepot and her cup, and came to the table. 'Hank,' she said immediately. 'Hank,' she said, 'when did Stan die?' Henry was startled. 'What?' 'When did Stan die, Hank? What day?' Henry thought for a moment. 'I don't know.' 'What month, Hank? Do you know what month Stan died?' Henry could only guess. 'June?' 'It was May, Hank, May twenty-second, in the afternoon. Five months ago.' Myra stopped then, bent her chin to her chest. The hair that wasn't caught in her rubber band fell over her forehead, reaching for but not quite touching her coffee. Henry apologized this time. 'I, um, I'm sorry, Myra.' He felt ashamed. 'I guess I forgot. There's no excuse for that.' 'Sure there's an excuse, Hank.' Myra looked up again, her cheeks red, puffy, her voice loud. 'Sure there's an excuse. No one really cared about Stan. In fact, Hank, no one gave a shit about Stan.' 'Oh, Myra—' ' "Oh, Myra" fuck. *Myra* didn't give a shit about Stan, Hank, that's what I'm trying to say.' Henry could only repeat himself: 'Oh, Myra,' he said, lamenting a tragedy which, with Stan's death, had become Myra's alone. 'We, we're relics, Hank,' Myra said then. 'We're the last generation to have long meaningless marriages. Wives waiting for their husbands to die, husbands waiting for their wives to die.'

Henry sat back suddenly, caught by the word 'we,' but Myra laughed. 'Now people don't give a shit about marriage or love. All they care about is prenuptial agreements.' Henry said the word. He said, ' "We"?' Myra blinked, and Henry said, ' "We," Myra? You and me we, or you and Stan we? Who's "we," Myra?' Myra looked down for a moment, then looked up, past Henry, to the ceiling. 'Oh, Hank,' she said, 'you're not trying to tell me you think you still love that woman, your wife, Bea, are you?' 'What's love, Myra?' Hank yelled suddenly. 'What is *love*?' 'Love,' Myra replied, and the haste with which she replied was revelatory, 'is when two people collapse into each other's arms,' and it was true: if Beatrice had been there, Henry knew, he would have collapsed into her arms. He would have caught her falling body in his own. 'Oh, Myra,' he said, 'she's *dying*.' And then he was crying. His lungs burned as he sucked

180

for air and his eyes blurred with tears. He tried to be quiet but soon he abandoned himself to his sobbing and put his head down on the table. His coffee cup fell to the floor, wet and splashing, hard and cracking, and he gripped the table's edges to keep from slipping out of his chair after it. Only when he had quieted a little did Myra whisper his name. 'Hank?' Compassion, love, confusion, empathy, her own sorrow, and not a little fear came out with the word, but hiding behind all those other emotions was awe: their kind of people didn't do this kind of thing, and especially not men. Henry opened his eyes. He looked along the surface of the table, saw scratches in the glass, irregularities, a short flat plain that seemed from this angle neither short nor flat. 'Forty years,' he said, 'forty years, Myra, forty years.' He brought his own hand into his line of vision. It seemed far away on the table. He looked at it out there, reaching for something, or waving, or just dangling limply from his wrist. 'Forty years,' he said, 'and all I ever wanted to do was *touch her*.' 'Oh, Hank—' Myra began, but Henry twisted in his chair and he grabbed her hand in his and pulled her close to him. 'Just stand here,' he said. 'Just stand here and don't say anything, please.' And then, because he felt he had to be honest, he said, 'Just let me pretend you're her,' and he laid his head against Myra's stomach and her rigid body and he cried, just like a baby.

The woman he cried for had spent two days and three nights in the hospital, like a cheap vacation package, while the doctors tried to figure out what was wrong. There was a history of poor diet, they said. There was a former history of alcohol abuse. There was a recent history of amphetamine and barbiturate abuse. The patient was elderly, they said, and then they showed the elderly patient's husband a new kind of photograph that wasn't an X ray and they pointed to the small dark spot which at first they had thought to be a tumor. Ulcer, they said, visibly proud, and Henry felt he understood their pride: they were cartographers, the photograph their map, and the dark

181

spot was a formerly unknown territory which had now been charted. The ulcer was small but contributing factors made its effects more pronounced. Diet, drinking, drugs. Age. Stress, they said, was often a co-factor in cases like these, and though they were nervous, they said, given the patient's history, they gave Beatrice a new prescription for Valium, and they renewed her prescription for anti-nausea medication, and they gave her another prescription that had something to do with her ulcer. Henry's understanding was that it wasn't going to make the ulcer go away—only surgery would do that—but it would keep it under control, and, given Beatrice's age, the doctors were leery about surgery.

After she came home it seemed he only saw her when he joined her sleeping body in bed and when he left it in the morning. Her medication seemed to be working. Color returned to her skin, her nausea disappeared, and she began to put weight back on. She refused to fill the prescription for the Valium, but even without it she slept all the time. She went to bed at eight, sometimes even seven, and she got up at nine or ten, and after she got up—Henry might pass her in the hallway, or see her walk past the doorway of whatever room he was in—she went straight to the kitchen and warmed up the coffee and food Myra had left for her, and after she'd eaten and washed the dishes, she bathed, and then she left the house for the day. She had insisted on a second car, and Henry had bought her a four-wheel-drive Audi, for the hills. For the first time in a long time he worried about money, but the Old Man had been a good provider: Henry knew that their cash, like their house, would last longer than they would. Each time Beatrice left the house Henry wondered if she was going to the hospital, or if she was going shopping, or if she was going sightseeing. He wondered if she was going to come back or if she might go gorging, as Ithacans referred to the college students who committed suicide by jumping off the cliffs around Taughannock Falls. He saw her: he was on the ground, she far above him; he'd never been to the cliffs or the falls, so in his mind they were all shadow and only Beatrice was distinct, bathed in sunlight, her arms outstretched, her legs bending then straightening suddenly and then she was in the air. She traveled up for just a moment and then she began to fall, and she fell endlessly, fell toward him where he waited to catch her, but she never reached him. He waited with his arms open but she never reached him, and they continued to share the same house but lead separate lives, share the same bed even, but keep, as much as possible, different sleeping hours.

But then one morning they woke at the same time, and suddenly she was there, and Henry caught her: he rolled himself out of sleep, he opened his eyes, he found himself looking right into Beatrice's eyes. He didn't think, he just reached a hand toward her hip, and when she didn't stop him he placed it there, and he was stung by this contact with her flesh, even buried under a nightgown and a sheet and a blanket and sixty-seven years. Beatrice sighed and closed her eyes and opened them, and she said, 'Don't say anything.' Henry wouldn't have dared. 'Please don't say anything,' she pleaded. 'Please,' she said, and Henry didn't, and he didn't move his hand and Beatrice didn't move her body. He went to sleep instead; it was the only thing he could do, and Beatrice did too, and he hoped that they would never awaken. But he did. An hour had passed, maybe two; his hand was prickly with pins and needles but it was still on Beatrice's hip; Beatrice was still sleeping. Henry slipped out of bed so that he wouldn't disturb her. The first thing he saw was a tray on his night table with two cups of coffee on it. He touched one; it was not quite cold, but touching it filled Henry's entire body with warmth, as though he were pressed against a giant coffee cup. Myra had been there, he realized, Myra had seen them. Henry started to take the coffee with him when he left the room, but then he left it there. He wanted Beatrice to see it when she awakened. He wanted her to see that Myra had been a witness to what had passed between them.

ξ

He came back in dreams first. Beatrice remembered his clumsy body rolling onto hers. His face had burrowed into the pillow beside her head, his fingers had clawed at her underwear, his penis had poked around inside her until it spasmed suddenly and slipped out of her body. On those nights pleasure had never been a question for either of them; for him it was something that the women's magazines told her was a 'release,' and for her it was mostly a matter of patience, and fear: she was afraid of what Henry might do if she didn't passively take his body on the rare occasions he rolled it atop her. When it happened she tried to think about something unpleasant but unrelated to the actual act, her burgeoning hangover, work, some bill collector she would call tomorrow to stave off another month, another week, another day. It was only when he pulled out and off of her that she felt cold and empty. Only then; never before, never after. Five minutes after he'd finished Henry would be snoring and Beatrice's mind would be focused on the unpleasant thoughts she had conjured up, and five minutes after that she would be asleep. Most mornings she couldn't remember if the night before had been one of those nights, or if the stains on the sheets had been there for years.

Now she woke early but stayed in bed late, and sometimes after she awakened she still remembered him, their cold bodies touching in the night. There was always in her mind the awareness that she had nothing to do, that, if she stayed in bed, the world wouldn't stop spinning. She felt better but she didn't feel well. She felt hungry but slightly repulsed by the thought of food; her stomach rumbled but threatened to pitch into nausea. She had pills for this but for some reason she could only take them with food, and just thinking about those terrible few moments when her ulcer would overwhelm her medicine and her stomach would burn as the acid ate at its lining, was enough to keep her in bed for another hour. Then, too, there was her lack of strength. It seemed like that to Beatrice: not a weakness exactly, but a lack, of strength, of energy, of will. Only when she was sure Henry and Myra had finished breakfast would she get up, and then, just to make sure, she showered, dressed, made the bed. Downstairs the kitchen would be a big room in which too many things were white or colorless or clear: all those white countertops and cabinets, the French windows, the glass table, the brushed steel of the appliances. It was a room which, despite its actual temperature, seemed as cold as the world outside, where the brown-leaved or naked limbs of trees poked at an overcast sky, and it seemed to wait for something to be pressed upon it, a picture, a coat of paint, a personality. Beatrice would crack a couple of eggs into a pan and reheat breakfast, warm coffee, refry bacon, look to see what Myra had left in the oven. When everything was ready she spread it out on the table, and sometimes just looking at it overwhelmed her with a sense of unearned plenty, and she felt full. But she ate anyway, took the first few bites out of a need not to waste food, and then the taste of butter and biscuits, maple syrup, bacon grease, would wake up her mouth and she would begin to eat in earnest. When she was full she reached for the newspaper. She looked past the stories about the coming war—she'd read them all, many times—for stories about the red deer. There were only a few now, and there were never pictures. She supposed it was better that way: illusions were neither created nor dispelled, only maintained. Hunters were coming from all over the country, she read, but they were keeping whatever they bagged to themselves, and there wasn't much in that for even a local newspaper to write about. She read the paper for only as long as it took her to drink a final cup of coffee, and then she cleaned the kitchen, wrapped up leftovers, made everything that had been white or clear or colorless before breakfast white or clear or colorless again.

It was the colorless kitchen that prodded her into action one day. She knew that somewhere in a box there was a bunch of pot holders and tea cozies and trivets that Susan had crocheted from colorful yarn, and Beatrice thought she could hang some on the walls, leave some on the table, just scatter them really, get some color into the room. As soon as she decided this she realized that she didn't know where their unpacked boxes were. The basement probably, or the attic, or maybe one of the extra rooms upstairs. It was a big house but there were a finite number of rooms in it and though she knew she could look in every one of them until she found the boxes, she decided to ask Henry. Not because she was afraid that walking all through the house would tire her, though she thought of that, but because she was making an effort. She was trying. Henry was in the living room. He had in front of him a box from which he was pulling marble chess pieces, and wiping them with a cloth. Beatrice watched him from the doorway for a moment, and then she knocked on the doorframe. Henry looked up. 'Oh,' he said, 'it's you.' 'I was just coming to ask you where the boxes are, the boxes with our stuff in them.' Henry blinked. 'The basement,' he said. 'The basement,' Beatrice said. 'Yeah.' 'Well, don't let me bother you,' Beatrice said then, and Henry, his eyes fixed on the piece he was wiping, said, 'You're not bothering me at all.' Beatrice heard his words, but couldn't think of a reply. Neither of them could, and, after a moment, she left him. She had tried enough for one day.

The basement was filled with boxes. The boxes had been divided into two stacks, based on which house they'd come from, and Beatrice could see scuff marks on the concrete floor, and she thought of the box of chess pieces Henry had with him upstairs. We're so close, she thought then, we're following one right behind the other. The boxes from the new house were sturdy, intact, and bare of markings—they were the boxes the movers had supplied—and the boxes from the old house were flimsy, many of them ripped or bulging, some of them barely held together by tape, and nearly all of them were beer or liquor cases. Beatrice went to that stack. She poked through them, surprised at how few were labeled. The labels that were there meant nothing to her: 'Gr. Rug.,' 'Ktn. Eqt.,' 'Gla. & Frm.' One of them said 'Copper,' and Beatrice tried to remember what they'd ever owned that had been made of copper. She started opening boxes; there were dozens of them, and because Beatrice couldn't imagine how they'd accumulated that much stuff she opened the boxes tentatively, wondering what she'd find. She found broken plates and creosote-coated pans, a collection of threadbare blankets, a lamp with a lightbulb still in it; the bulb wasn't broken but the lamp, she remembered, was. The pot holders were in that box but Beatrice set them aside and kept opening. She found her parents' white satin comforter, shiny like only acrylic shines and nibbled at by mice. One box held couch cushions to a couch that they'd left on the curb when they'd moved from their first house. The box marked 'Copper' clanked when she lifted it; it held six- and four- and two-inch lengths of copper pipe. There was a box of books from her time at college; she didn't recognize all of them, and it took her a moment to realize that some were Henry's. She found, finally, her father's old fedora, and after a puzzled moment she remembered that the post office had returned it to her the day after she'd sent it to Henry.

There were several boxes labeled 'John's Things,' boxes filled with toys that grew progressively larger and more expensive. Lincoln Logs, an Erector set, a rusted tricycle, the thin wheels of a ten-speed. In one box Beatrice found a few small toys, a wooden yo-yo, a portable radio that would have been spherical had it not been separated into two halves, a water pistol made from transparent amber plastic. She tested things: the yo-yo worked though she didn't work it very well, the catch that joined the two halves of the radio was broken, the water pistol, when she squeezed the trigger, hissed a short sigh of stale air. She dug deeper, pulled out several pieces of wadded newspaper, and then a few books, school texts mostly; on the inside cover of one she saw a note that read, 'Mrs. Reed's freshman English,' and underneath that John's name, and underneath that, his age: fourteen. At the bottom of the box was a portfolio. She'd felt like a snooping mom since the moment she opened the box, and there seemed an adolescent Do Not Open! quality about the triple-knotted string. But she hesitated only a moment and then, with fingers more nimble than she would have suspected, she pulled the knots apart and removed the top sheet of cardboard. A naked boy stared up at her. She didn't realize this immediately: what she saw was a tangle of thick lines which wavered on the paper like a visual stammer before gradually aligning themselves into a drawing, a drawing of a thin naked boy.

She stared at the picture for a long time. It seemed strange to her, incomplete, perhaps just not very good. There were three pairs of lines across the chest and abdomen that suggested protruding ribs, two smudges for nipples, a shadow for a navel. The boy's limbs were skewed and elongated, his joints knobby. His penis was just a limp stretched-out U, much too big for his body, Beatrice thought, but made useless by the fact that it was unattached to him, and his face was the most barren feature of all, just a small pout of a mouth unbroken by lips and two empty watching circles for eyes. No nose, no ears, no hair, above all, no expression, and Beatrice stared at the drawing for a while longer before she turned it over to look at the next one. On the back of the first drawing she saw two letters, an 'M' and an 'E,' and she wondered what that might mean for only a moment before looking at the next drawing. It was another nude, a grown man this time—she wasn't sure how she knew he was grown but she was sure he was. He looked a lot like the boy, thin, forlorn, half finished, though she suspected by now that the sketchiness of the drawings was deliberate. The man had no hair, she realized, and she flipped back to the boy and saw that he was hairless as well, and then she flipped to the next drawing—a woman—and saw that she was hairless too. Then she noticed three letters on the back of the second drawing, a 'D,' an 'A,' another 'D,' and she didn't need to turn the drawing of the woman over to know that it would have another three-letter palindrome on its back.

She looked at John's drawing of her: she looked particularly at the parts of her John would never have seen unless he'd been born with his eyes open. In his version her breasts were small, the lines that defined them shaky, as though he'd been unsure if they actually existed. The word 'dugs' came to her from somewhere. Wasn't 'dugs' another word for 'breasts'? If so, then these were dugs, holes rather than hills, dried out rather than filled up. Her abdomen was thin but puddly, her vagina a single pencil line that started virtually at her navel and disappeared between her legs. She stared at this drawing for a long time, though after a few moments she wasn't looking at it anymore, but focusing on the almost overpowering anger it produced in her. The image infuriated her—a body defined by sex yet somehow sexless, a body whose only function besides sex was to nurture but which was unable to fulfill that function as well. She wanted John in her hands right then so she could shake him, so she could point to this caricature and say, This isn't real! It isn't me! But then she looked at the face, and then she looked back at the face that was supposed to be Henry's, and the face that was supposed to be John's own, and she saw that they were all identical. Expressionless, virtually featureless, with sealed mouths that lacked both the power to eat and the power to speak, eyes without pupils or lids, which could neither close nor turn away. Even after she put the drawings away she felt those eyes on her.

There had been a fall. It was gone now: it was cold now and the wind was blowing, but sometimes it blew in traces of the last season. Beatrice would open her great big front door and the wind would swirl in a few leaves. Usually they were brown but sometimes they were not. Sometimes they were yellow, sometimes red; there were purples so deep they were almost black and there were black ones too, and there was a green one every once in a while, and once there was an azure blue one, and it was the blue leaf that finally made her remember the beauty she had just missed. She had been dazed by drugs and distracted by the battle of the house, she had been ill, and she realized now that she hadn't even noticed the famous New England fall. But she noticed, weeks later, the blue leaf. She looked at it for a long time where it lay, five fingers spread on her black and white tiled entryway. She was reminded of John's picture of her, not because of any similarity between the two images, but because of their difference. Though she could see herself in both drawing and leaf, it was the leaf that actually offered her something, and she picked it up and carried it with her tenderly and she looked through a few rooms until she found a book big enough to hold it—the leaf wasn't that big but the books in her house were that small—and when she found one she placed it flat between the inside front cover and the title page and placed the book in a drawer in her night table. She had an idea that she would open the drawer and

189

take out the book and look at the blue leaf sometimes, but she forgot about her scheme almost as soon as she turned her back on her night table. She came across the leaf then, every few months during the last year of her life, and each time she did she was surprised by it: surprised first by the simple fact of its existence, and surprised again, and again and again, by its beauty.

Leaves blew over the land like eddying pools of water, thick frothy rustling brown water that sometimes whirled up into the sky in little dust devils and fell back to the ground like dry raindrops. It was cold, and the cold was like a fact: it simply was. Even when the air was still, the sky clear, the sun bright, even then it was still cold. Beatrice saw it through a window one day, but because she knew she could resist it she smiled, and she grabbed the doorknob. 'Hey,' she heard behind her; the voice was Myra's. Beatrice let go of the doorknob reluctantly and turned. Myra wore faded blue corduroy pants, a colorless T-shirt, a maroon sweatshirt over the T-shirt. She held a dish towel in her hand. 'What're you up to?' Beatrice wasn't sure if Myra was drying her hands or merely wringing the towel. 'I was just going for a walk.' 'Have you seen the lake?' Myra said suddenly. 'The big lake. Lake Cayuga.' Beatrice could tell from Myra's tone that she was betraying ignorance of a major geographical fact. 'No,' she said, 'I didn't know about it.' 'Oh, you have to see it.' Her face brightened. 'I know, I'll take you there.' 'Wait, Myra—' Beatrice began, but Myra had run from the room. She came back with her coat. 'C'mon, it's a fifteen-minute drive. Ten. I'll have us there in ten minutes.'

It was only five minutes before the lake came into view: Myra piloted Beatrice's Audi around a long curve of highway and out of the corner of her eye Beatrice saw a gray strip that was the right lane of the road, and beyond that she saw a narrow slope of trees, and beyond that another gray strip which she first took to be a road below the one they were on. Then, when she realized it was water, she said, 'Oh.' She thought it was a river, and when she realized it was the lake she said, 'Oh,' again, and then she said, 'I had no idea.' 'There it is,'

Myra said. The lake was a long sliver cut into the earth, not very wide but stretching off to the north farther than Beatrice could see. 'The trick,' Myra said, 'isn't seeing it, it's getting to it. I *think* there's a road up here.' At some point Myra left the highway for a narrow two-lane tree-lined road that ran along the curve of the lake's shore. A line of houses had been built between the road and the lake, and as they drove mile after mile looking for a road that would grant them access to the lake Beatrice imagined the scene from the air: she saw the long narrow plain of dark water, the thin white line of the shore, the dots of houses stretched along the shore, the ribbon of highway girding them in. 'Myra,' she said then, 'this is ridiculous. We've driven twenty miles to go five feet. Can't we just pull off the road and walk down to the water?' Myra shook her head. 'Everything between the road and the lake is private property,' she said, 'and half these characters think it's legal to shoot trespassers.' Beatrice sighed; Myra drove on. Finally they reached a place where the houses stopped, and between the road and the lake there was a small cultivated park and a large parking lot. 'Here we are,' Myra said, and Beatrice sighed, 'At last.'

There wasn't much to see: just the water and the hill on the other shore, and a few houses on that hill. There were a couple of boats visible in the distance. There was a kayak, and a kayaker amusing himself: he paddled forward a few strokes, then backward; with a flip of his head and shoulders he turned himself over and submerged his upper body in the black water, and his exercise held Beatrice's attention for several moments. The wind whipped her hair across her eyes, she heard water lapping at the shore, and as she listened to the sound she remembered a sound that she or Henry used to make when they made love, way back when they still made love. With an intensity so shocking that she had to step back a few paces and sit on a picnic bench, Beatrice's entire body shivered in the cold wind and remembered sexual feeling. She heard a noise, shook her head to clear it. The noise was Myra's voice. 'Bea, honey? Bea, you okay?' Beatrice realized that Myra's hand was on her shoulder. 'Oh, I'm fine, Myra, I'm okay. I just had a hot flash.' Myra laughed lightly, but she put her hand on Beatrice's forehead, and Beatrice felt the chafed skin of Myra's knuckles against her head. 'You feel flushed, honey. We should get you back in the car.' 'Yes,' Beatrice said, 'sure. Let's go, let's get out of here.'

The sun had dropped lower in the sky since they'd left the house, and the light which shone through the trees was deeper, golden, it had a thick liquid quality to it. How was it, Beatrice wondered, that one thing could take up an entire day? As they drove she stared through the trees looking for glimpses of the lake. They'd been driving for a few minutes when the lake came fully into view, and Beatrice said loudly, 'Myra, stop the car.' 'Beatrice, I told you—' 'Stop the car, Myra. I don't care if you have to pull into the ditch, just stop the car.' 'All right, fine,' Myra said, slowing, stopping, parking. The car was half on the road, half in the ditch. 'But if we get hit—' 'Myra, what is that?' 'What's wha— Oh. Oh my. I don't know what that is.' It wasn't the lake that had caught Beatrice's eye, it was the large group of people standing on its opposite shore. Even from this distance Beatrice could see that most of them were fat, and she guessed from the number of white heads she saw that most of them were old as well, and they were all wearing swimsuits. There seemed to be a couple hundred of them, pale-skinned, dark-suited, and they waddled like a flock of penguins along the white beach and onto a black pier that ended, quite abruptly, in cold water. One by one they jumped in. 'What're they doing?' Beatrice asked. 'Well, they're jumping in,' Myra said, 'but don't ask me why.' 'They're swimming, Myra. Look, they're swimming.' 'Well, that's reassuring. I guess. At least they're not drowning.' Dozens of bodies were bobbing in the water: some just floated on their backs, others did a lazy breaststroke, others dove down and surfaced abruptly like small round whales. A few people waved at cameras, and flashbulbs clicked in the dim light. Beatrice rolled down her window and heard the faint sounds of laughter. One huge man climbed out of the water and belly-flopped back in. The sound of his splash came to Beatrice's ears a second after he hit the water. 'It must be freezing,' Myra said. 'I don't get it.' But

Beatrice didn't say anything. She didn't get it either but she couldn't stop watching as the bodies in the lake spread out from the dock. In the falling light heads floated atop the water like colorless balls. Then, in another minute, the light was gone, and Beatrice had to imagine the swimmers. She imagined that she was one of them, and felt the cold water surrounding her body. The only sign that the swimmers still existed was the sound of their laughter and calling voices: 'Over here.' 'No, over here.' 'Over here. Yes, over *here*.' Eventually Myra pushed the button that rolled up the windows, and in the silence Beatrice realized that she had been whispering the words with them: 'No,' she whispered, 'over here,' and then, aloud, she said, 'Myra, let's go home.'

All the lights were on: all the lights, and there were a lot of them. Beatrice could see the glow of the house a long time before she could see the house itself. The car seemed to crawl on the road toward its destination, and Beatrice had time to think a million thoughts as they drove the last stretch of highway, turned onto the driveway, parked, but she couldn't pin her mind down, couldn't focus on one thing. She felt that somewhere in her cluttered brain was the secret, the secret to everything, and all she had to do was unearth it, uncover it, remember it, and her troubles would be over. She remembered her illness, and she remembered the food Henry had brought her when she was well enough to eat. Her hands trembled as she got out of the car, she felt tired, exhausted: she would go in the house, she told herself, she would sleep. Still, she was hurrying, and she remembered the newspaper Henry left for her each morning, and the boxes each of them had poked through, and she was practically running up the freshly poured concrete of the sidewalk toward the front door, and her thoughts were running with her. One long horizontal white strip ending in a vertical white rectangle: the sidewalk said there was nowhere else to go but there. The door said nothing, but her mind said that there was nothing to do but walk through it. Her mind remembered John's pictures, and her mind remembered the blue leaf, and Beatrice glanced at a few windows but there were no shadows that indicated Henry's presence, and she remembered the sex, all the sex, that she'd ever had with him. She put her hand on the doorknob, and even as she turned her wrist to open it she remembered the swimmers and she realized that there wasn't any secret: there was no pivot on which their fortunes had turned. One thing had simply led to another. They had simply been put to a test, and failed. They had simply been human, and her frail, human wrist strained at her heavy door. Inside, Henry saw the doorknob twitch under her touch, he saw it turn first one way and then another. He saw the door move just a little bit as Beatrice pushed against it and then he heard a click and the door stopped; the latch was still stuck in the catch. He reached out then, grabbed the doorknob, turned it the rest of the way, and then, very slowly, he pulling, she pushing, the door started to open. Henry heard loud breathing, panting really, he realized he was holding his own breath. He continued to hold it. And then the door was open: the light flew out and the wind blew in, and so did Beatrice.

12

Hangdog

Her driving days were behind her. They just didn't have the money anymore. She only worked three days a week now, and as a result she spent almost all of her time at home. At home, and by herself: Hank worked every day, and his hours were getting longer and longer too. Bea wasn't sure how much longer because almost every night after he finished work he went drinking with the Old Man, and when she pressured him to ask for a raise, Hank said he had confidence that the Old Man would reward his faithfulness someday, and he refused to discuss the subject further. So she tried to fill her time by cleaning. It had been the one thing besides loving her husband that her mother had done well, and it was, Bea reflected, exactly one more virtue than her father had possessed. But there was no easy or effective way to clean a house as small as hers, especially in winter. If she scrubbed the linoleum which defined the kitchen area of the front room then she only brought out the stains and faded spots more clearly, and her soapy water caused the edges of the raggedy carpet which defined the living area of the room to disintegrate into a black oily scum; when she shifted her efforts to the carpet, vacuuming it with their wheezing old Electrolux, then she raised a cloud of dust which settled on the still-wet linoleum. They used the picnic table as a kitchen table now, and it gouged long gashes in the floor when she dragged it; a leg of the couch snapped off when she tried to move it, and she had to use her school books to prop it up. She washed clothes: sometimes she washed things which weren't dirty in order to fill the machine, and she ironed everything, even underwear, and folded and refolded and reorganized drawers in order to take up time. She made coffee, she drank whiskey with her coffee, or she drank whiskey with water, and she watched television while she drank her whiskey and coffee or whiskey and water. She experimented with the recipes that were on the backs of boxes, but everything tasted the same. She made a lot of things with red meat because Hank complained that the guys at work teased him for being so skinny, but all she succeeded in doing was giving them indigestion. Hank never commented on the food she made, even though it was usually overcooked or dried out by the time he ate it. This, Bea would've pointed out to Hank if he'd said something, was his fault, because he always came home later than he said he would. He usually came home after she was in bed and she'd hear him in the kitchen, and then she'd hear him in the living room, and then she'd hear him in the bathroom and when he came into the bedroom, undressed, and climbed into bed, she would pretend to be asleep and Hank, for his part, would pretend not to notice she was awake. Then they would race each other to fall asleep, and when Bea lost she often went into the living room rather than remain in bed, and these were the nights they ended up having sex.

'Still awake?' she would say as she returned to the room, or 'Can't sleep?' or 'How many sheep are you up to?' She'd asked that question only one time, and Hank had said, 'I count down. I count backwards.' 'Backwards?' Bea said. She'd been drinking whiskey, whiskey and water, water from the cooler. 'From a thousand,' Hank said, and Bea said, 'What were you up—I mean, down to?' 'Six,' Hank said, 'but I was on my third run-through.' 'Oh, honey,' Bea began, but Hank said, 'C'mere.' Fatigue overshadowed any sexiness he might have been attempting to inject into his words, and fatigue, and whiskey, removed any trace of sexiness Bea tried to put into her walk, as she shuffled to the bed. She thought that it really wasn't worth the effort any more, but it also wasn't worth the effort it would take to stop, and she sank onto the bed like a deflating hot-air balloon. Hank put a hand on her waist and she sighed: even then it went to the right place, even then it was where it

196

belonged. They kissed a few times with closed mouths; they closed their eyes and opened their mouths. Stale food, stale drink, secondhand cigarette smoke: Bea wasn't sure which tastes were hers and which his, but she put her hand on his waist and pulled his body close to hers. His penis was hard and poking through the fly of his boxer shorts, and Hank pushed her T-shirt just high enough so that it was out of the way and pulled her panties down a few inches, and then his hand disappeared for a moment. She took his penis in her hand, rubbed it around her vagina, and then his hand was back, knocking her hand out of the way. The K-Y was always a cold shock. There were some sins he never committed though, and he slid into her without hurting her. She didn't count his thrusts. One time she'd been surprised to find herself counting, and she'd been even more surprised when he finished at eight. Eight, and then he held it in her a moment, twitched a few times, and fell away. She tried not to take pleasure in it because more than once she'd just begun to enjoy the pace of his body moving into and out of hers and he had stopped, twitched, sighed maybe, fallen away. So she let him go until he came, and when he rolled off her she didn't stop him. In the half light she could see liquid drip from his mouth and his penis, which still poked through his wet underwear. She would retrieve only his hand, his right hand, which didn't have K-Y on it. She pulled it to her mouth and tasted the salt in the bit of sweat that she knew would be between his fingers, and then she put it on her breast and let go of it to see if it would stay and always, sooner or later, Hank pulled his hand from her chest to his.

His mother came by every once in a while, and the only thing that made her visits bearable was Bea's knowledge that eventually Candace would ask her to talk about her son's life. Candace would try to appear disinterested and fail, and as soon as Bea had told her something—'he works late,' 'he works every day,' 'he works all the time now,' 'he seems to be getting along good with what's his name, Kenny, the Old Man'—

Candace would gather her gloves and scarf and purse and she would announce, 'Well, I really should be going.' But one day, after Bea had provided yet another trivial piece of information, Candace didn't gather her gloves or scarf or purse. She looked at her watch and let her wrist drop, and she said, 'You see him about as often as I do, don't you?' 'What?' Bea said, and Candace said, 'We're just the same, you and me.' Bea sighed. 'Does this mean you want more coffee?' Candace laughed— Bea didn't—and as she got them more coffee she wished yet again that the kitchen had been separated from the living room, because she really wanted another shot in her coffee. Candace didn't say anything until Bea had come back to the couch, and she held her cup out weakly, absently, while Bea filled it. Some splashed on the coffee table while she poured. Bea wasn't sure if her shaking hand was responsible, or Candace's, but Candace said, 'Leave it. No one'll notice one more stain on that old thing.' Bea grabbed a towel anyway, tossed it on the spill. Candace sipped her coffee and finished a cigarette before she spoke, and Bea waited uncomfortably in silence.

Finally, Candace spoke. 'Bea,' she said, 'how many men have you known in your life?' 'Only Hank,' Bea protested, and Candace said, 'Jesus Christ, Bea, I don't mean in the biblical sense. I just mean how many men have you known, have you gotten to know well?' 'Why?' Bea said, but Candace just waved the question away with an unlit cigarette. Bea said, 'Well, my dad, of course,' and after a pause she said, 'My dad,' again, and then she said, 'There was this teacher at Suffolk, I was getting to know him, and, oh yeah, we had this neighbor who lived next to us forever. He used to let me pick flowers from his garden sometimes, but then he died. He was old, a widower, I think. And there were, you know, boys in school and stuff.' Candace had obviously heard enough. 'Good God, Bea, you had no business getting married.' Bea sat back. 'What?' 'Bea, can I talk candid here? Can I ask you how in the hell you thought you were going to take care of a man for the rest of his life without doing a little research first?' Bea was at a loss for words. 'I didn't know there was a manual. Getting married is just something you do.' 'That was your first mistake,'

Candace said, and she jabbed at Bea with her cigarette. 'Getting married is not something a woman just does. Getting married is done to her.' 'Please,' Bea said, 'this is the nineties.' Candace's laugh was short and unpleasant. 'This is *not* the nineties, Bea. This is Long Island. All you gotta do is drive down Sunrise Highway and look in the window of any car you pass that has a couple in it. I guarantee you that if they're under seventy-five he'll be driving.' Bea shrugged; she knew what Candace meant, but she didn't want to admit that she and Hank were just like everyone else on the island, so she tried to change the subject. 'Why do you hate him so much?' 'Bea,' Candace said, and her laugh was louder and more unpleasant. 'Are you really that naïve, or are you just stupid? Do you think I'd be over here right now if I hated him? Why *don't* I hate him is the question. Why don't *you* hate him?' 'He's my husband!' Bea said, and Candace sighed. 'There you go again. He's not your husband, he's another person. He's a man, for God's sake. And in case you haven't noticed, like most men he's also a selfish self-centered insecure little boy.' When Bea sipped at her coffee cup she discovered it was empty; she wished, suddenly, that she smoked. 'Look,' she said, and she could hear her voice tremble, 'what's your point? I mean, you already had your chance to raise him.' Candace let that line pass, but when she put her cigarette out she knocked ashes to the table and floor; Bea wasn't sure if nervousness or anger was responsible. 'Look at you,' Candace said, and she jabbed at Bea with a new cigarette. 'Your marriage is a mess, you're a mess. It's barely lunchtime and you're drunk.' 'I don't see where you get off giving anyone advice. You don't exactly have a model marriage.' 'Oh, don't mince words, Bea. I have a bad marriage. I have a marriage in name only. That's what make me an authority on the subject—so learn from my bad example.'

Candace waved her hand then, as if clearing the air of all the smoke she was generating, and then she leaned forward. 'This is what I came to say, Bea. I'm forty-four years old and I've spent all of those years around men. I've got a husband and I've got a son, I've got a brother and I had a father just like everyone else, so I expect I know what there is to know about men. And I'll tell you this: I've met a lot of whole women in my life, but I've never met a whole man. You meet a man, you look hard enough, eventually you'll see that there's at least one other man he uses to act out something he's not comfortable with, something inside himself. Something he's afraid of.' Bea looked at Candace blankly when she finished. 'What does that mean?' she said. 'What does it have to do with me?' 'It means,' Candace said, 'that the wife is always second fiddle. There's always someone one step ahead of you, and that someone is always another man.' It wasn't that Bea didn't believe Candace; it was just that she had feared that the person who had come between her and Hank was another woman. That was a threat she understood. But the idea of another man was something she hadn't considered before, and didn't know how to consider now. 'No one could ever come between Henry and me,' she insisted then, but she insisted quietly, and Candace moved closer to Bea. 'Bea,' she said, 'what do you want? What do you want, honey, what do you really and truly want?' Bea stood up as if Candace had struck her, and she walked as far from Candace's poking cigarette as the room would allow. 'What do I want?' 'I said it three times, Bea, I ain't saying it again.' It wasn't something Bea had thought about for a while—since she'd met Henry, since Henry had lived. And then, when she thought that, she said, 'I want things to be the way they were before.' Candace nodded her head slowly, but then she stopped, and then she shook it. 'Before when, Bea? Before they took your house, before you was married. Before—' 'Before Hank had his operation,' Bea said. 'Before he was cured.'

Bea said these words. She'd thought about them only as words, as sentences, as something to say, but the more she thought about them, the more she realized she was speaking the truth: what she said was indeed what she wanted, and what she wanted she could never have. She looked at Candace; she wondered if she was thinking these things as well. Candace didn't say anything for a long time. At last she started gathering her things. 'I don't know what to say to that, Bea. I don't know if you're full of shit, or if you've hit on something I don't want to think about. But I don't, Bea. I don't want to think about it.' 'Candace—' 'He's your husband, Bea. He's not mine anymore, not my son. He's made that clear. But you've got a piece of paper that says he's still your husband, so you do what you think best.' She was dressed by then, and on her way to the door, and Bea didn't want her to leave and leave her alone with all the thoughts she'd churned up. But she couldn't say anything to stop her. Candace kissed Bea on the cheek, something she hadn't done even at the wedding, and then she surprised Bea again. 'Take care of yourself,' she said. 'Save something for later.'

It wasn't a fair question to ask, Bea thought, as she'd thought every day since Candace had put it to her. What do I want? As though it could be gotten at so simply, as though it were a process as simple as boiling hard kernels of rice in a big pot of water until all the water was gone and the rice was soft and fluffy and edible, and you could say, That's what I want: rice. She was making dinner. Hank had said he would be home by nine, and it wasn't yet eight, and she was making chicken and potatoes and green beans. She was frying the chicken and baking the potatoes and boiling the green beans, and the front room was hot from the oven, and she thought, What do I want? I want to cool off. She grabbed a beer then, took it to the kitchen sink, opened the window over the sink, and stood there drinking her beer while cold air rushed in visibly in a stream of thick gray vapor. When her beer was empty and she was just starting to shiver she closed the window and went back to work. What do I want? she thought. I want my husband to walk through the door, right now, on time. I don't want him to kiss me. I don't want him to say, Hi, honey, how was your day? I don't want flowers. I just want him to be on time and sit down and wait for me to fill his plate, and I want him to eat the meal I cooked for him.

She set the table. Two of everything—cups, plates, forks, knives, spoons, napkins. The beans were done and she drained them; the chicken was done and she put it on a plate covered by a paper towel—a cake plate, a wedding gift—and put another paper towel over it to soak up some of the grease, and then she put the cover over the plate and watched steam coalesce inside it. She put potatoes on both plates, sliced them lengthwise, put butter into the slices. She served green beans to each of them, uncovered the chicken and served Hank a thigh and a leg, served herself a breast, and then she said, 'Fuck you,' out loud, and started eating. You said you would be home at nine and it's past nine now, it was nine o'clock nine minutes ago and nine minutes is all I'm willing to give you anymore, nine minutes is in fact about nine minutes more than I'm willing to give you right now, and nine minutes was about all it took her to eat dinner and nine minutes was about how long it took her to throw away Hank's dinner and wash the dishes. Eventually the kitchen was spotless, there was a beer in her hand and no sign of Hank, and she was hungry. She grabbed a piece of chicken from the fridge, sat at the table, picked at it, finished her beer, drank the last beer in the fridge. When that was gone she switched to whiskey and water.

At some point she noticed she was staring at the clock. The light from the fluorescent coil overhead reflected off the glass face of the clock and she couldn't read it, but she figured it must be time to start dinner. She peeled and boiled potatoes, she shook and baked pork chops, she set the timer for the pork chops, and then she stood at the stove and drank another whiskey and water and wondered why she was so tired; she looked at the clock on the stove to see how much time the potatoes had left and she was startled to see that it was nearly midnight. It was half past eleven. The pork chops would be done in ten minutes. Hank had been due at nine. Eight tiny potatoes rolled around in boiling water, and there were seven empty cans of beer lined up on the counter. Six pork chops sizzled in the oven and she watched the timer while away the time: five, she watched, four, three, two, one, zero, and before the timer had finished buzzing she had thrown the pork chops from the second dinner of the evening into the back yard. The potatoes followed, and the beer cans, and when she was finished her back yard was steaming like a geyser and the moonlight glittered off aluminum. What had she done wrong? What had she done to deserve this? She slammed the door on that thought. She went to bed. Just before she slept she saw Hank in her mind: he was on his hands and knees and he was naked like an animal. He gnashed pieces of meat in his mouth, swallowed mashed potatoes in white foamy mouthfuls. And then, while she slept, she was the one who ate.

Another night passed before she saw him. When she did see him the odor of beer on his breath was strong enough to overpower the odor of whiskey on hers. It was just past two in the morning; he was just coming in. 'Where were you?' she said, and Hank's head jerked up and he nearly fell over. The living room was dark and he clearly hadn't seen her. 'Bea,' he said, 'honey. You scared me.' 'Where were you?' she said again, and Hank put a hand on the old console television his parents had given them. 'Me and the guys went for a drink like we always do.' 'On Tuesday?' Bea said. With exaggerated nonchalance, Hank said, 'What? Are you saying you don't believe me?' 'I'd be a fool not to believe you,' Bea said. 'The evidence is on your breath. It's on your clothes for that matter.' 'What? Oh.' Hank pulled his T-shirt away from his body. It had a dark stain on the chest and stomach. 'That was Bud,' he said. 'He got really wasted.' He continued to hold his shirt out and look at it. Bea sighed. 'Has it been so long since you called me that you've forgotten our number?' 'Aw, Bea, don't be a ball-buster—' 'I'm gonna bust more than balls if you don't come up with a good excuse for not calling to tell me you were going out.' Hank inched his body onto the television until he was sitting. When his legs were off the floor his back slumped and his head hung low. He burped. Finally, he said, 'I forgot, I guess,' and Bea said, 'You forgot? That's funny, I didn't forget to make your dinner. Would you like something, Hank, would you like some toast? It was meat loaf about three hours ago but I'm afraid it got a little overcooked.' 'I'm not hungry—'

'Good, 'cause I threw it out!' Bea paused then; she sat up, slowly, to maintain her balance. 'Jesus Christ, Hank, sit up straight. Look at me when I talk to you.'

Hank pushed himself until his back was against the wall. The television was so wide that he couldn't bend his legs and they stuck out on either side of him. He still didn't say anything, and Bea decided to give up yelling for a minute. 'I'm just asking for a little courtesy, Hank. I just want a little respect.' She'd spoken softly; in the silence afterward she was aware of the pleading tone her words had possessed. Hank made a broad gesture with his arm. 'Respect is a two-way street,' he said, and Bea resumed yelling. 'How dare you say that to me! I keep this goddamn outhouse that you call a home spotless. I cook your goddamn meals for you even though I know you won't bother showing up to eat half of 'em, and I wash the fucking shit stains out of your underwear.' 'Now, don't exaggerate, Bea—' 'Shut up, Hank, just shut your trap. There's one thing I want to hear from you right now, and that ain't it.' Hank shut up without a struggle, leaving Bea faced with the prospect of maintaining the conversation on her own. 'Now look here, Hank. I'm just about at the end of my rope. I'm alone in this house every goddamned day of the week except when I work. I cook, I clean, I pay the bills, I run errands. I watch TV, I talk on the phone a little bit, I entertain your mother when she drops by. I, I've had it, Hank. I'm lonely. You don't come home till after I go to bed half the time, and when you do come home you ignore me, you eat your dinner and go to sleep.' 'Look, Bea, I work hard all day. A guy needs to relax with other guys sometimes, just like a girl has to hang out with her girlfriends sometimes.' He paused, then said, 'Why don't you make some friends, Bea? Maybe that'd help.' 'Because I'm not friendly!' Bea nearly shouted, and then she lowered her voice. 'You used to relax with me, in the bedroom.' 'Aw, Bea, that's a low blow.' 'It's not low enough, as far as I'm concerned.' Hank slid off the television, stood up. 'I'm going to bed,' he said. 'I'm going to the *bedroom*. I don't need to hear words like that from my wife's lips.' 'Bedroom,' Bea said—she had been waiting to say this—'is an anagram for boredom.' Hank stopped. He'd only gone a few steps. He looked at her blankly for a moment, and then he said, 'What's an ana—? Oh.' He stood there for a moment, and then made his way to a picnic bench and lowered himself to it.

'I want a kid, Hank,' Bea said then. 'I want a baby.' Hank didn't say anything, or move. He just sat there. 'Did you hear me, Hank? I want a baby. And don't tell me we can't afford it no more. We can't afford ourselves but we still find a way to get drunk every night, and we'll find a way for this. We'll—' 'Bea,' Hank cut in then. 'I don't want a kid. I'm ruining my own life, I'm ruining yours. I don't want to ruin a kid too.' 'I'll raise it, Hank. Me. Bea. I'll raise it.' This wasn't what she'd expected to say, but Hank hadn't said what she'd expected him to say. A year ago he'd wanted a baby, a year ago it was just a matter of money. 'I'll take care of it, Hank,' she said again, though she knew she was making a mistake. 'It'll be all mine,' she said, though she knew that wasn't true, and that it wasn't proper either. But she couldn't shut up. 'You'll come to love it, Hank, when you're ready it'll be there. And until then you'll hardly even notice it.' Hank sighed. He stood, wobbled his way to the couch. He was beside her on the couch, his hands were reaching for her body. She wondered if he was going to strike her, or caress her, or try to make love to her, but when she felt his hands on her arms she knew, and leaned into him. She didn't kiss him, though; she couldn't face him, and she wondered if Hank's mother had leaned into Hank's father this way. She'd dumped her pills out yesterday, put sugar pills in their place, just in case he checked, and she wondered, even as he laid her out, if her baby would grow to hate her as much as Hank hated his mother.

ξ

His tuna melt had congealed into a cheese-shrouded lump by the time Hank arrived at Sandy's house, and the beer, though not warm, had lost its edge; more than a few petals had fallen off a bouquet of flowers from his rather reckless driving. At work Sandy was Ann Heiser's replacement, and even a year after Ann Heiser had disappeared Sandy was still seen as a replacement, perhaps because Pauly was always saying, 'When my ex-bitch used to work here . . .' At work Sandy was quiet, almost mousy. She was short, five foot in bare feet, she said, and she also said that she was generously proportioned. She had hips, she had thighs, she had a heart-shaped ass, and she had big tits. If she were five-six, five-seven, she told Hank, they would be big breasts, but at her height they were just big tits. Breasts and breast size were important to Sandy. She liked to watch porn, and she liked to watch porn with Hank, but she didn't like women with unnaturally large breasts, and besides the tuna melt and beer and flowers Hank also had a video with him when he arrived at Sandy's house.

The lights weren't on inside, but the door was unlocked and Hank went in. Sandy lay on the couch covered only by a towel and a teddy. She threw the towel back like a flasher and called out, 'Stick it in, baby!' and Hank, pretending not to understand, said, 'The video?' Sandy sighed. 'Spoilsport.' She stood up, wrapped the towel around herself, and then, apparently thinking better of it, dropped it to the floor. She walked to Hank, who had gone to the VCR, and gave him a long kiss. 'Mmmm,' she said sarcastically, 'tuna. What other surprises have you got for me?' Hank gave her the flowers. 'Crushed chrysanthemums,' Sandy said. 'How thoughtful.' 'I got a John Holmes video like you wanted,' Hank said. 'It's got Seka in it too. I figured if you're gonna get your jollies I'd better get mine.' 'What makes you think I don't get my jollies from watching Seka, baby?' Sandy said, and then, when Hank looked shocked, she said, 'Don't you worry your pretty little head off. This is the only thing I get my jollies from.' Her hand was on his crotch, and when Hank felt it there he said, 'Oh, baby,' and kissed her nipple through translucent nylon. He started the video then, and they fumbled their way to the couch. 'Ugh,' Sandy said as Hank undressed, 'boxer shorts again. Baby,' she said, 'I'm gonna go to that adult boutique on Sunrise Highway and buy you something a little more slinky to wear.' Hank scoffed, 'They don't make lingerie for men,' and Sandy said, 'Boy, you need to enter the modern world. If

I wanted to I could buy this'—she fingered her teddy—'in your size.' Hank made a face. 'I don't *think* so.' 'I saw this one thing,' Sandy said, 'they call it the Pinocchio brief. It's got this little face, you know, right here, and when you tell me sweet little lies the nose starts to grow. They got this other thing, it's got, like, plastic pieces of fruit right here, apples, grapes, whatever, and you can guess what's the banana. They got one, it's like a regular little bikini except right here it's got a zipper and—' 'Sandy, if you don't stop that I'm not going to make it past the credits!' 'Now that would be a shame,' Sandy said, and then she started to do what Seka was doing to one of the ugliest men Hank had ever seen in his life. His eyes moved back and forth from Sandy's brown permed ringlets to Seka's platinum mass, and then he pushed Sandy's head off him.

'Holy shit!' he said. 'What is that thing?' 'What's what?' Sandy said, and turned to the video. 'Oh, that,' she said. 'That's John's dong. The biggest dick you'll ever see on a white man.' Hank didn't say anything. He stared at the image on the screen, a penis that looked to be at least a foot long. 'Wait a minute,' he said. 'You don't like big breasts, but you like this thing?' Sandy laughed. 'The way I see it, once a tit gets any bigger than a cantaloupe, say, a honeydew, there's not much you can do with it. But dicks are a different story. As far as I'm concerned, the bigger the better.' 'You, um, you haven't had anything *like that*, have you?' Sandy laughed again, and gave Hank's penis a little pull. 'Feeling insecure, babe? A little inadequate?' She laughed again. 'No, I've never had anything *like that*. But I have had a few respectable dicks in my bed, I will say that.' Hank was silent again. Sandy had once said she'd slept with at least one man for every year of her life, and when he asked how old she was she only said that she was on the sunny side of forty. He cleared his throat. 'Am I—' 'Hank,' Sandy said. She pulled him to the floor next to her and kissed him. 'You're fine,' she said. 'You're better than fine. You're real good.' She punched him on the shoulder like a Little League coach, and Hank laughed a little, nervously. 'Of course, at my age, any man whose face is less wrinkled than his balls qualifies as real good.' 'Sandy—' 'Hank, I'm just pulling your leg.' She pulled his dick, and then stared blankly at the television for a moment. 'Actually,' she said, 'you remind me a lot of my first boyfriend. Of course, that was probably a few years before you were born, but who's counting.' She smiled at herself. Almost inaudibly—but not inaudibly—she said, 'Twenty years later, who would've thought that the best sex of my life would've come from a black man? Biggest dick too.' 'What!' 'Oh, Hank,' Sandy said. 'You're the most easily shocked man I've ever had between my legs.' 'Sandy, don't talk like that.' 'I'll talk like however I want to talk, young man. I swear. You didn't think I was a *virgin* or something, did you?' 'It's not that,' Hank said, and Sandy said, 'Then what's the problem?' 'It's not, I don't know if it's a problem. It's, I guess I never thought of you doing it with . . .' 'With a black man? Hank, baby, we were engaged.' 'Now *that* is a bit much.' 'For who? For me or him? Or you?' 'Well—' He stopped suddenly. On the television John Holmes was fucking Seka doggy style, and Sandy was already turning onto her hands and knees. 'Oh, don't dig yourself in,' she said, and her voice seemed distant. 'Actually, I agree with you. Marrying LeRoy would've been too much, even for a feisty girl like me. It just wasn't fair, you know? His family didn't like me, and, shit, my family don't like anyone who ain't Italian. But it was thinking of kids that finally made my mind up. I didn't want no baby of mine called a nigger.'

Hours later: Sandy traced its shape with her finger. First one axis, then the other. She traced it as though it were two separate lines, and then she traced it as though it were two V's joined at their bases, and then she traced it like the X it was. 'Hey, Hank, what's this?' Hank looked up. He saw her abdomen first, the half dozen hairs leading to her navel, and then he saw the bottom of her breasts, the stretch marks on either side of them, the flat brown nipples still a little pink from when he'd nipped them moments ago. 'Hank?' When she'd spoken her breasts had wiggled. Her diaphragm had contracted just enough to send a small amount of air out her mouth to form her words, and the skin of her stomach had jiggled at this movement. 'Hank?' Wiggle, jiggle. 'Hank? Baby?' Hank remembered that he had been so twisted inside his mother's body—one leg in the birth canal, the other still in the womb—that a cesarean section had been needed to free him. He imagined her stomach slit open then, the way the back of his head had been, imagined the viscera underneath waiting to be scraped clean. He shook his head then, wiped his mouth. 'Sandy,' he said, placing himself, placing her. He put his face between her legs, kissed her for a while, and then he rolled over and laid the back of his head against her breasts. 'You taste so sweet,' he said. 'Oh, Hank,' Sandy said, 'it's a vagina, not an after-dinner mint.' Hank laughed then, but when he laughed he bent forward, and as he bent forward he felt Sandy's hand on the back of his head, sifting through his hair, finding his scar. 'So, what is this anyway?' 'Oh that,' Hank said. 'I've had that for as long as I've been alive.'

Sometimes, at work, he imagined the love they were going to make that evening; sometimes he even imagined the love they had made that morning. He remembered her smell, her taste, her touch, he remembered the words she had sighed into his ear, and the words he had sighed into hers. He looked at the clock sometimes, to see how long it would be before he could return to her, and if it was still early then he considered going into the bathroom to relieve himself. That was when he usually came back. He would look around guiltily, as though someone could see his erection, and he would see some snow on the cold cement floor, or he would see someone warming their hands by the stove in the shop. Then details would fall on him like an avalanche, a cold shiver run down his spine; eventually, he just bought a flask. It was cheap and tin and began to tarnish within a few days and it left an aftertaste in the whiskey he filled it with, Bea's whiskey, but the whiskey warmed him when he drank it, just enough so that he could tighten his grip on his pen and banish Beatrice from his mind, and return to work. One day he was just pulling it from his lips when the Old Man appeared in the doorway that led from the shop.

'Hey,' Hank said, 'I didn't think anyone was here but me and Sandy.' 'I just got back,' the Old Man said. He held out his hand for the flask, and Hank gave it to him as though he were giving a schoolteacher an illicit wad of gum. The Old Man took a pull, made a face. 'Shit, Hank,' he said. 'I'm an old man, can't be drinking this cheap shit.' He looked at his watch then, shrugged. 'It's late,' he said. 'Why don't we take this to the bar?'

Inside the bar it was early: there were only a dozen people, including the staff. 'What're you drinking these days?' the Old Man asked Hank. 'Coors, same as always.' The Old Man said to the bartender, 'Coors and Budweiser, both draft.' In a moment they had their beers, and they took a few swallows before speaking. Then the Old Man said, 'It's amazing we drink this shit when it's so fucking cold out. You'd think we'd drink fucking cham-o-mild tea like the ladies do.' Hank laughed. 'Yeah, I know what you mean. But after a couple of these you don't notice the temperature so much.' 'That's true,' the Old Man said. 'You about ready for another?' 'Shit,' Hank said, 'you're in a hurry tonight.' He drained his glass in a gulp, then said, 'Sure, hit me again.' When they had their refills, the Old Man said, 'It's weather like this makes me wonder why I ever went into goddamn plumbing.' 'I thought it was weather like this made you most of your money.' 'Shit, Hank, I don't give a shit about the money. I mean, you pay the bills, you take care of all that, everything else just makes money for the bank.' Hank nodded, then said, 'So, um, so why'd you go into plumbing in the first place?' 'Oh, hell, I don't know. I needed a trade and there it was, I guess. I was good at it.' The Old Man laughed. 'I got my start during summers off from school. Plumbing in the summer's a whole other ball game. You get to work outside, take your shirt off, get a tan, whistle at the girls when they walk by.' The Old Man paused long enough to order another round. 'What do you say, Hank, a shot of Jack to speed things up?' Hank said, 'I'm game, if you change that Jack to Jaegermeister.' The Old Man laughed. 'Well, we're gonna be good for shit tomorrow,' and Hank cracked, 'I thought that's what plumbers were good for: shit.'

210

The Old Man ordered their drinks, and Hank looked at the crowd that was trickling into the bar. It was almost exclusively men, just a couple of wives or girlfriends whose husbands or boyfriends held on to them by a belt loop. Everyone looked tired and cold; no one was shouting or laughing yet; it was still too early, people still too sober. The Old Man was talking again: 'Yeah, plumbing's a good thing to do when you're a kid on summer vacation. Look at the Miller boy, he couldn't wait to ride in a truck with his dad. Well, down the hatch.' He and Hank did their shots, and Hank took a swig of beer to wash the burn out of his throat. 'Sissy,' the Old Man said, but he grimaced against the Jaegermeister. Then he said, 'Course, then I went and ruined it all by opening my own shop.' 'Why d'you say that?' Hank heard his voice slur, tried not to think about it. 'It's the numbers, Hank, it's the goddamn numbers. Once you start seeing how much everything is, how much a pipe costs, how much a man costs for a day, it takes the fun out of everything.' Hank waited a minute, not sure he was following, and then he said, 'Well, why'd you do it?' ''Cause I loved plumbing, and 'cause I wanted to try and make a good living for my family.' 'Yeah?' Hank said. 'Yeah,' the Old Man said, loudly, as though Hank had challenged him. 'It probably sounds old-fashioned to someone your age, but I'm from the time when working hard, doing a good job, doing right by your family, meant something.' 'Why should that sound strange to me? To someone my age?' 'Shit,' the Old Man said, 'don't get me started, Hank. Don't get me started.' 'I won't,' Hank said. 'I won't get you started.' He felt a sloppy grin on his face, felt drunkenness pushing at him like a cresting wave, and, after a pause, a drink, another pause, and another long drink that finished his beer, Hank set his glass on the bar, and ordered another round.

'But *you*, Hank!' the Old Man said very loudly, very quickly, turning and pointing at Hank in big exaggerated gestures that spilled more beer, both his and Hank's, and prompted the man standing behind him to say, 'Hold on, old guy, this ain't the dance floor. Watch where you're going.' Hank said, 'Me?' '*You*, Hank,' the Old Man said. 'You a-a-and . . .' He stretched out the word like a game show host waiting for the door to slide open. 'Me and . . .' 'You and *Sandy*, Hank. You and Sandy.' Hank thought a long time about how to react to that. Finally he just took a drink. 'Me and Sandy,' he said. 'How about that?' he said, and he finished his beer. The Old Man looked at Hank's empty glass, looked at his own glass, which still contained an inch of liquid. 'I don't know about you, Hank, but beer ain't doing nothing for me now.' 'Nope,' Hank said, 'I feel sober as a newborn babe.' 'Take me up on that Jack now?' 'I think a shot of Jack would just about hit the spot,' Hank said. 'Matter of fact, make mine a double.' 'Two doubles,' the Old Man said. 'Tell you what, Hank, don't bother coming in tomorrow. I don't think you'll be no good to nobody.' 'Nope,' Hank said. 'I'm no good to nobody.' 'Well, here's to a good old-fashioned hangover,' the Old Man said. He handed Hank his drink and, after a moment's hesitation, they each tossed them back. 'Shit,' the Old Man said. 'Shit,' Hank said. 'Sandy,' the Old Man said. 'Shit,' Hank said, and then he said, 'Beer.' The Old Man nodded, and when they had their beers in their hands, he said, 'Sandy,' again. 'What about Sandy?' Hank said. 'Well, hell's bells, Hank, it wasn't six months ago you was telling the Miller boy and me and anybody else who'd listen how your wife was the fuckin' Queen of Sheba in bed, and now you're fucking some overweight underdressed receptionist who just happens to work in my front office.' Hank took a drink from his beer. He said, 'I guess I'd appreciate it if you didn't talk about my wife that way.' The Old Man started to say something but Hank cut him off. 'I don't care if you call me the fuckin' slimy piece of shit that I am, but Bea is a good woman, a respectable woman. And so is Sandy.' 'Hank—' 'And so is Sandy!' Hank said again, definitively, with a cutting gesture of his arm.

Eventually the Old Man said, 'Well, I apologize, Hank. I was outta line there, and you were right to call me on it. You have my apology, Hank.' Hank nodded. 'Six months?' he said. 'Maybe five,' the Old Man said, and Hank wailed then: 'I don't know what I did wrong!' He suddenly wanted to call the Old Man by his real name. 'I don't know what I did wrong, Uncle

212

Kenny. I, Uncle Kenny, I tried to love her. I loved her as best I could. But I did something wrong. I made a mistake, Uncle Kenny. I don't know what it was but I must've done something. She turned on me, Uncle Kenny, she just turned on me.' Hank attempted to snap his fingers but he was drunk and his hand was wet and the bar was loud: his fingers moved, but if they made a sound he didn't hear it. 'Like that, Uncle Kenny, she turned on me like that.' The Old Man had a fresh beer waiting for him. He said, 'Well, that's what women do,' and then, as if even he realized the inadequacy of such a statement, he said, 'Sometimes there's just nothing you can do, Hank. Sometimes it's out of your hands.' Hank looked at the glass. As he looked at it he forgot to hold on to it and it started to fall; he managed to tighten his grip before dropping it, but a good portion of his beer soaked into his pants. He wondered then how many he'd had that night, and he turned to look at the bar as though all of his empty glasses would be lined up there. But they weren't. Even his shot glass was gone, and a few damp arcs indicated the recent passage of a cloth. 'Hey, Hank, you okay?' Hank turned back to the Old Man, who said, 'Talk to me, buddy.' A smile spread itself on Hank's face like peanut butter on bread. 'Man, I'm wasted,' he said. The Old Man smiled back at Hank. 'You and me both,' he said, 'me and you both.' 'It feels good,' Hank said. 'Yeah, it feels good,' the Old Man said. 'What were we talking about?' Hank said. ''Cause I don't remember.' The Old Man said, 'That's good,' and Hank said, 'Let's have another beer.' 'Yeah, that's a good idea,' the Old Man said, and he held up two fingers.

Their beers approached from the end of the bar, and as they came closer Hank noticed for the first time that the bartender was a woman; he wasn't sure if she'd been a woman all night. She set their beers down on the counter, nodded at the Old Man, gathered up several mugs in each hand. Hank reached into his pocket quickly, dug out a grubby bill, pushed it down the front of her half-open blouse without looking to see how much money he was giving her. The bartender raised her eyebrows but didn't say anything, and Hank lost their staring match. 'Just showing my appreciation,' he said, dropping his eyes. 'That's fine,' the bartender said, 'but if you show me your appreciation again I'm gonna let my husband show you his.' She smiled at Hank and walked to the other end of the bar. Hank watched her ass move beneath her jeans. He considered saying something along the lines of 'can't live with 'em, can't live without 'em,' but instead he just asked the Old Man for another beer. 'You got a full one in your hand,' the Old Man said. 'Oh, right,' Hank said. 'Guess I'd better drink it.' And he did.

Sandy held Hank's head while he vomited. Sandy held Hank's head while he cried. Sandy held Hank's head while he screamed, 'Fuck you, cunt! Fuck your slimy hole!' but she walked from the room when he finished. 'Where are you going?' Hank screamed. Sandy stopped in the door, turned. 'Baby,' she said, 'you stink.' She made him get up in the morning and she dropped him around the corner from his house. She gave him some advice: 'Don't bother lying to her.' 'I'm sorry,' Hank said before he got out of the car. 'Don't be,' Sandy said. 'It was fun while it lasted.' She sat in her rabbit-pelt coat and didn't look at him, and she made him get out of the car then, and she drove away as quickly as her old Chevy would let her. As he walked toward his house Hank realized that at least he wasn't drunk anymore. That was the benefit of an early start: an early finish.

An image evolved while he slept that day, an image of himself and Bea. They would be clean, they would be sober, they would be well, or at least, neatly dressed. They would ride together in silence in the car. Bea would express surprise when she saw which restaurant Hank had picked out, the Fisherman's Club, right on the water. She would suggest that they couldn't afford it, but Hank would tell her that she was worth it and she would blush perhaps, or just fall silent. The restaurant would

214

be quiet, classy, dark. It would smell of cooked and raw fish, sea air, spicy fried foods, and into this atmosphere Hank would breathe his apology, his explanation, he would talk of the happiness they could still bring each other, the good life they could share, the children they would have. When he finally had his fantasy fixed in his mind it was dark. His eyes found the clock: it was just after eight. He slipped out of bed and went into the bathroom. He showered, he shaved, he brushed his teeth and gargled with Listerine. When he left the bathroom he saw Bea in the kitchen. She was making dinner. Hank thought of going to her as he was, wrapped only in a towel, still damp, smelling of soap. But he told himself that there would be time for that later, and he went into the bedroom to dress. It was Friday, there was the weekend to come. They would face the clocks to the wall as in the old days, leave the lights off; he wondered if they still had candles. While he was dressing he remembered that he would have to pick up his check and cash it because he was out of money, and he remembered also that the banks were closed. It was so complicated. He had his pants on and he almost took them off again, took them off and climbed back into bed. He had a headache. But he persisted, he dressed. He found the phone book in the living room, found the address of an Off-Track Betting establishment that also cashed checks. He grabbed his coat, his keys.

Bea spoke then. 'I'm making dinner,' she said, and Hank deliberated. Should he tell her to stop, tell her his plans? He just said, 'I'll be right back,' and Bea turned to him but didn't look directly at him. She had a greasy knife in her hand, and she said, more insistently, to a dent in the refrigerator, 'I'm making dinner. It will be ready in half an hour.' 'I have to cash my check before tonight,' Hank said, 'or we won't have any money this weekend.' He waited for Bea to say something— he waited for Bea to tell him they wouldn't need money for the weekend—and when she didn't he dashed through the door. He was gone for an hour and a half. Things happened during those ninety minutes, things which could be thought of in many terms, but to Hank everything was divided into two categories, success or failure, and he had failed. As soon as he pulled into the driveway he thought about backing out of it again. He thought about disappearing from Bea's life, just as he'd disappeared from his mother's, but he knew he couldn't do it. Running away, like anything else, was a task, and Hank didn't possess the skills for it, so, as he'd planned, he went inside and asked Bea to dinner. He found her on the couch. The television was on. The room was laced with smoke. 'Dinner?' Bea said absently. There was a glass in her hand and she waved it at the smoke. 'That's your dinner.' 'There was traffic,' Hank said, 'the check-cashing place was closed, the grocery store—'

This is what happened: he had picked up his check from the Old Man, and the Old Man had told him that Pauly had been arrested for the murder of Ann Heiser. He had left the shop quickly to make it to the check-cashing place, but the check-cashing place was closed. On the way to the King Kullen where Bea worked he heard on the radio that thousands of deer were being slaughtered in upstate New York in a quest for an elusive red deer pelt; so far, all of the pelts that had been produced were brown. At the King Kullen, he'd convinced an overtanned woman with a hairdo frosted like a zebra-striped torpedo to cash his check, and then, on his way out, he had passed three women. All of them were laughing, and one of them said, 'No, Joe's on his way to Florida. His grandpa's dying.' 'His grandpa's dying?' one of the others repeated; none of them stopped laughing. 'His grandpa's dying,' the first one said, 'he might even be dead already,' and that was it, they and their laughter passed out of earshot Henry had barely made it to his car before he broke into tears. He didn't know why he cried, or for whom: for Joe, or Joe's grandpa, or for the three girls who never stopped laughing. The red deer, and Ann Heiser, and Bea, and Sandy—who was Sandy? Hank wondered—seemed too distant to be part of his grief.

But before he could tell Bea any of this, she said, 'Did you stop for a quickie too?' 'What?' Hank said, and Bea said, 'Did you stop for a quick fuck too?' 'What?' he said again, and Bea said, 'It's funny. I only just figured it out. You'd think I'd've figured it out when you didn't come home last night but I just figured you'd fallen down drunk somewhere. Nope, I just got it, just'—she looked at her watch—'just thirty-eight minutes ago I realized you were fucking somebody besides me.' 'Bea—' 'You are a bastard, Hank. In every sense of the word you are a bastard.' And then, when Hank started to speak, she said, 'Nothing, Hank. I don't want to know nothing.' 'I love you, Bea,' he protested, and Bea said, 'I don't care.' Then Hank said, 'Bea, leave me,' in three heavy syllables. Years later Bea would tell Hank that she heard his words as 'Believe me,' and because she did believe him, and because she didn't know what to do about it, she stood unsteadily and walked toward the bedroom. She knew that the time had come for them to leave each other, but she knew too that they would not. Somehow, uncontrollably, they still loved each other, and their love would not let them free. With her realization that Hank was having an affair, she had felt herself on the brink of a great clarity. She had ridden her anger to the crest of a mountain, expecting that, like a skier, she would race away. But the new realization that they would never separate had simply knocked her down, and now she didn't want to realize anything else. She closed the bedroom door behind her, and as she lay down she heard a click, and then the loud continuous voice of the television filled the house.

13

Flush

She fell asleep to the sound of gunshots. They seemed to surround her, their explosions ripped the air apart, tore through her eardrums. There would be one blast, then another and then, after a pause, another. There would be two or three blasts fired at the same time, there would be a half dozen blasts fired consecutively, like a reveille or a salute. A shot would sound so close that she'd've sworn the hunter was in her back yard, and then, from a distance, another shot would come, like an answer or an echo. Some shots came from far away, but she heard the sound of the pellets clattering among the bare branches of the trees behind her house, a false harmless sound like grains of sand inside a shaken seashell. The shots seemed to go on all night, and even through her sleep Beatrice wondered how the hunters could see, and perhaps it was a memory, perhaps a premonition, but she saw the men with their guns, and on their heads were red hunting caps, and affixed to the bill of their caps were bright flashlights emitting a beam of light that cut the night just as their shotguns cut the silence. In her dream the deer hunters walked backwards through the forest, and their trails of light whipped along behind them like the tails of comets, and flashed off silvered leaves, and animals' eyes, and the barrels of their own guns.

In the morning, just after sunrise, Beatrice awoke. She woke slowly, and as she slipped from sleep she heard the sounds her body and Henry's body produced as they stirred on the bed. The rustle of limbs moving beneath a sheet and a blanket, the squeak of the box springs underneath the mattress, a long

218

exhalation of breath—she wasn't sure if it was hers or Henry's—and then Henry coughed in his sleep, and Beatrice, still dreaming, remembered something that happened a long time ago. She'd only been working for King Kullen for a few years then, when a little fad had circulated among the employees of the store like the chicken pox, or the flu, or a cold. For a few weeks that summer it was the rage to celebrate one's ten- or twenty- or thirty-thousandth day on earth. There had been other fads in the store, but the ten-thousand-day fad haunted Beatrice even to this morning, as she shifted around on the bed and unconsciously rubbed her stomach to quiet it, because she, along with Orchid and Flora, had been the only employees of the store who happened to be anywhere near the right age. In the case of each woman the response of the other employees had been the same: you're *that* old! Only Flora had seemed pleased by the distinction, because, although everyone knew she was well past retirement age, no one realized that her eighty-second birthday was only weeks away. In Orchid's case there was even more incredulity. Orchid had insisted she was fifty-four, but it wasn't until one of the checkout girls had lifted Orchid's wallet from her purse and examined the driver's license she found there that Orchid's claim was accepted. At the time, Beatrice had been twenty-seven, and less than a month from her ten-thousandth day; when it arrived, Violet presented her with a gift certificate good for a free fashion makeover at a beauty shop down the block and a cake impaled with a hundred candles, one for each hundred days of her life. Beatrice's nose wrinkled, remembering the smell of cheap paraffin, and she remembered that the first candles had nearly burned out by the time the last were aflame. She remembered too— she rubbed her stomach again, and rolled onto her back— that she had been forced to eat the cake by herself because the young pastel-covered checkout girls were watching their figures. It seemed that every time she put her fork in her mouth there was some Scarlett or Amber or Heather to exclaim in a thin voice issuing from thin lips, 'Oh, I just *can't* eat cake anymore, I blow up like a cow,' and by the end of that day

219

Beatrice had become so sick of chocolate and snide comments that, as soon as she'd arrived home, she forced herself to vomit.

Beatrice woke again with a start. The dream that had been washing over her was retreating with the same inexorable power with which it had arrived, and it left behind only her nausea and the strange weight of Henry's hand on her stomach. It was, she remembered distinctly, the second time in a week that she'd awakened with his hand on her body; it was also only the second time in almost forty years that she'd awakened that way. Beatrice heard Henry breathing heavily, snoring really, snoring quietly, and as she listened to him and wondered what she should do she put her hand on his, and Henry, conditioned after all these years to believe that the only time Beatrice would touch him in bed was when she wanted him to stop snoring, stopped snoring, and then he woke up. He lay on his left side with his right hand on Beatrice. She had looked at him when he stopped snoring, so when he opened his eyes she was looking into them, and she thought, Here's where it starts, here's where everything begins again.

Henry blinked a few times. Without moving his right hand he maneuvered his left hand up to his eyes and wiped the sleep away with his thumb and forefinger. When he was finished Beatrice saw him looking at her expectantly, but she hardly noticed because she was still caught by the expression that he'd wiped away. Not wiped away, but covered up, obscured, hidden: when Henry had opened his eyes, Beatrice would swear, he'd opened them fearfully, and his hand, caught between her hand and stomach, had trembled just slightly, and then this fear had blinked into sorrow, and the sorrow into tenderness, into—she allowed herself to admit it—into love, and then his hand had come and covered his eyes and when it was gone the eyes that looked at hers were virtually the same as they had been for the past forty years. They revealed nothing of himself to her, except one thing: he was waiting. He wanted her to do something. He turned his eyes from hers after a moment, looked somewhere down her body. It could have been at her breasts, or at his hand on her stomach, or at the bump of her feet under the blanket. She sighed then, and she opened her mouth to speak. She didn't know what she meant to say but it didn't matter because the words wouldn't come. Henry lifted his eyes when she sighed; he looked at her open mouth for a moment and then he looked into her eyes and then he looked down again, and he took up his waiting visibly, like another blanket. She almost lost it then, because she heard a bang downstairs, something unidentifiable but distinctly kitchen-sounding, and the first thing she remembered was those crazed red deer hunters, shooting up the sky all night long, and then she thought that Myra must be up and she thought that she should help her with breakfast, and she thought of what she was hungry for and what they had in the house, she thought of cooking and eating and washing dishes and wondered where Henry's video camera was, and if she knew how to run it. John had called last night; he had refused to give them his phone number and he had refused to visit them, but he had asked Beatrice to make him a videotape of the house. It occurred to her then that this tape would be a good thing to give Susan as well, and she wondered if that would bother John, he could be so touchy, and then she swallowed, and on her stomach Henry's hand squeezed once, and Beatrice said, 'Henry?'

He answered so quickly that it was clear he'd only been waiting for permission to speak. He said, 'My left hand hurts but my right hand doesn't.' He said, 'My arthritis, I mean. You know, cold makes my hands hurt and warm makes them stop hurting.' He said, 'My left hand is cold but my right hand is warm.' He waved his left hand in the air, squeezed her stomach with his right, as if to remind her which was which, and her stomach twitched under his touch. Beatrice knew what he wanted, and also wanted to vomit, but she made Henry say it, and hoped that he would say it, and do it, quickly. 'What do you want, Henry,' she said, 'what do you mean?' Henry hadn't been looking at her, but he looked at her now. 'I want to put my left hand on'—he stumbled for a moment and then he said it decisively—'on your body.' Beatrice didn't know what to say. She didn't know how to tell him that it was okay. She thought that she could say, 'You may,' but that sounded as formal and foreign to her as something a queen might say. She thought

221

she could say, 'Put your hand on my body,' but that sounded like something a whore might say. She thought about, 'C'mere, baby,' but then she would sound like his mother. What did a wife say? What did an old lady say? And then, too, there was her growing nausea; she was going to have to go to the bathroom soon, and finally she just said, 'Okay.'

Henry slid his hand under her body and encircled her waist with his arms and clasped his hands over her rumbling stomach. 'How did you sleep?' he said when he was still. Beatrice said, 'Those damn hunters kept waking me up.' 'Me too,' Henry said. 'Maybe I should post some no trespassing signs or something.' Beatrice said, 'Whoever heard of a hunter that could read?' Henry laughed a little and didn't say anything, and after that Beatrice just waited, for Henry's arm to fall asleep, for her nausea to recede, or for it to become overwhelming. It wasn't a long wait. It was a wait marked by the feeling of Henry's breath on the back of her neck, and the sounds and smells of Myra in the kitchen downstairs. She took in the room, saw objects she'd lived with for perhaps half her life, furniture, pictures, plants, in a space that was still strange to them and to her. None of them had any more meaning for her than pieces in a showroom; all of them could have disappeared and she wasn't sure that she would remember what was gone. Only this—only Henry's arms, and his breath on her neck—only this must remain. Still, she had to walk away from it. She got up slowly; she heard Henry speak to her but she didn't attempt to answer. She put her hand on her stomach, not just because it hurt, but so that Henry would see her gesture, and understand her. He was beside her then, quickly, and his hands were light on her body, but the support they offered was real, and he walked with her into the bathroom, sank with her to the floor in front of the toilet, stroked her hair while she vomited. She kept her eyes closed. She wanted to see neither herself nor what issued from her, and when she was done she looked up and Henry closed the lid of the toilet quickly. He handed her a tissue and as Beatrice wiped her lips he flushed. His face looked calm, and she felt the calmness in herself, the stillness in her body now that her stomach was empty and quiet. Henry put a hand on her face. 'You're flushed,' he said. Beatrice said, 'I'm old,' and Henry said, 'I'm old too.' Beatrice said, 'I'm dying,' and she saw Henry start to say that he was dying too, and then she saw him understand that she was speaking neither euphemistically nor philosophically. She was just telling the truth. He said, 'What do you need?' and Beatrice said, 'You. Only you.'

Among the scattered breakfast dishes on the table was a half pot of coffee; it was warm still, but not hot, and she set it back in the coffeemaker to heat up. She began taking dishes from the table to the counter by the sink. Under a towel, on a plate, she found a couple of pieces of toast. She bit into the crust of one and, finding that it wasn't stale, she sat down and spread a thin film of soft butter on it, and then a spoonful of strawberry jam. She'd almost finished it when she saw that her coffee was simmering, and she brought the pot to the table and refilled the cup she'd been using earlier. She'd just finished her toast when Henry walked into the room. 'Oh,' he said, and stopped short. 'Hi. I thought it was empty. The kitchen, I mean. I, um, I'll come back later.' He turned to go but Beatrice said, 'Don't be silly,' and Henry looked back at her. 'Sit down,' Beatrice said, 'have a cup of coffee.' Henry hesitated for a moment, then sat down, and Beatrice poured him some coffee. They'd been like that for only a moment when Myra burst into the kitchen. 'Shit,' she said, and Beatrice and Henry both jumped in their chairs. 'I thought I was alone here.' She looked at them briefly, and then she pushed a tangled dirty lock of hair out of her face and walked to the coffeemaker; she looked at it blankly, as if confused by the fact that there wasn't a pot in it. She turned to them. 'Have you seen—oh.' She took the coffeepot from the table and squinted at it—it was nearly empty—and then without speaking she went to the counter and began cleaning the coffeemaker. She hummed a little as she worked, and occasionally muttered something under her breath. 'Coffee,' she said eventually, audibly, and she went into

223

the pantry. Beatrice and Henry looked at each other, and Henry smiled, and shrugged his shoulders. Myra was in the pantry for a long time, first pushing things around noisily, and then, for several minutes, quite silent. Beatrice was just about to suggest that they go look for her when Myra emerged with a bag of coffee in her hand; there was a little smile on her face, her cheeks were red and her eyes bright. She turned to Beatrice and Henry for a moment and giggled, and then she went to the coffeemaker. When she had everything well under way, she turned to them and said, 'Well, I've got work to do. I'll see you later,' and then, in a gesture that made Beatrice sit back abruptly in her chair, Myra lifted her arms in the air as though she were holding a rifle, and she said, 'Boom! Boom, boom, boom!' and then she walked out of the kitchen.

Beatrice waited until she couldn't hear Myra's footsteps. 'Was she acting weird, or is it just me?' 'No weirder than usual, I guess,' Henry said. 'I guess the hunters was keeping her up too.' 'I guess,' Beatrice said, and then she said, 'Hey, help me with the dishes, okay?' 'Oh, sure,' Henry said. 'Let's do them, sure.' It was a mindless task: Beatrice thought she could've done it in her sleep—she thought she had, probably, many times—but there was something compelling about it too. It occurred to her that they had a dishwasher and they never used it. Washing dishes, she thought, was a definite task, a finite one: you washed the dishes until there weren't any more, and then you were finished. It was that simple, and not many things were that simple. The dirty pile shrank, the clean pile grew, soon all they would have left was putting the dishes away, and then they would separate. Beatrice cleared her throat; Henry hummed a 'Hmmm?' Beatrice said, 'I talked to John last night. He's moving back to New York City. He, um, he wants us to take pictures of the house. Videos if we feel like it.' Henry put a dish on the counter. 'He'd see it better if he came here.' 'Yeah, he would,' Beatrice said. She had a clean frying pan in her hand, and instead of putting it in the empty sink she waited for Henry to reach for it, and she didn't let go of it until he'd met her eyes. 'It would be nice if both our children visited us,' she said, 'but that's not going to happen.'

Henry took the frying pan from her and started to dry it before rinsing it off. He said, 'I never abandoned my parents.' He started to go on but Beatrice said, 'You didn't rinse the soap off that.' Henry stopped what he was doing, and did nothing for a moment, and then he ran the pan under hot water for a long time. Beatrice said, 'When's the last time you saw your father?' Henry said, 'That's different. My father wouldn't recognize me if I did go see him.' Beatrice started to wash something else. She couldn't see what it was under the soapy water, but she smelled bacon grease and felt small lumps breaking off a pan under her fingers, she felt metal growing smooth again; and she felt, she realized, not powerful, but competent, capable: she felt capable of ruining everything they'd achieved. 'I'm not saying it's the same thing,' she said. 'I'm just saying that you know as well as I do that our children aren't going to come and see us.' Henry stopped working now. He said, 'It's not right, Beatrice. You know it's not right. We never did nothing to them.' Beatrice saw that the pan she'd washed was the last dirty dish, and she rinsed it herself. 'No, Henry,' she said, 'we never did nothing to them.' She handed him the pan. 'We did it all to each other.' She handed him the towel, 'We just made them watch.'

She had been staring blankly at the camera, mute, when Myra walked into the room. 'Myra,' she said. 'Bea,' Myra said, and then she laughed. 'Bea, what the hell're you doing?' Beatrice pointed at the camera. 'I was getting ready to make John's Christmas present.' Myra laughed even louder. 'You're making him a video of *yourself* for Christmas? I mean, I know you don't like to be conventional and all, but couldn't he use a sweater or something?' Beatrice blushed. 'It was his idea, Myra. He asked for it.' Myra made her way to a chair, and Beatrice noticed that she was unsteady on her feet; when Myra spoke Beatrice smelled liquor on her breath. 'Let me get this straight,' Myra said, and then she laughed and turned to the camera. 'Oh, excuse me, John. Let me get this *right*. John asked you to make him a videotape of you for Christmas.' 'Me and Henry,' Beatrice said, 'that's right.' Myra shook her head. 'And you're just, like, you're just going to talk about yourself?' 'Well,' Beatrice said, 'Henry's going to take the camera around the house so John can see it. Show him our little slice of Heaven.' Myra snorted. 'It may be Heaven to you, but I just live here.' She stopped, then started again. 'Excuse me,' she said, 'I, um, I certainly wouldn't want to pry into the state of your financial affairs, but can't you afford to send him a plane ticket? I mean, wouldn't that be a more, um, direct way of doing what he wants to do?' Beatrice sighed. 'Look, Myra,' she said, 'you . . . I mean, I'm sure Henry must've mentioned that neither Susan nor John wants to come see us. I mean, they refuse to, they, um, they just won't do it.' 'Yeah, I guess I knew that. I guess I . . . yeah.'

Myra paused then. She looked very thoughtful, in the manner of a drunken philosopher. 'Bea,' she said. 'I seen you two. You and Hank, I mean.' Beatrice was wary. 'Yes?' 'What's going on, Beatrice? What's, I don't know, what's up? You seem awful lovey-dovey.' Beatrice thought for a moment. It was in front of her with perfect clarity, the events of the entire day, of all the days they'd spent in this house. She knew suddenly that she could explain it to Myra. She knew that all she had to say was that she loved him, that she had always loved him. But she knew, too, that she couldn't, that saying it would be wrong. Saying it would give a definite, and finite, meaning to something that was still undefined; saying it without Henry there, she realized, would make something that was both of theirs belong to her alone. Beatrice looked at Myra; she rocked slightly in her chair, as though to a song that played in her head. Her eyes were closed. 'Myra,' Beatrice said, and Myra opened her eyes dreamily. 'I don't know, Myra,' Beatrice said. 'Don't know what?' Myra said. 'I don't know how—'

'You know, Bea,' Myra cut her off. 'You know, I was just thinking. I was, um, I was just thinking.' She looked suddenly sheepish, and she focused her eyes on Beatrice's feet. Beatrice was confused and relieved. 'What, Myra, what were you thinking about?' 'There's another door in the pantry,' Myra said.

'You can't hardly see it, there's a shelving unit half blocking it, and someone's raincoat is hanging in front of it, but if you go through this door then you end up in another room that's shaped a little bit like this.' She moved her hands in the air; it seemed to Beatrice that she was drawing a triangle. 'At the other end of this room,' Myra said, 'is another door, and if you open that door then you're right behind that bookshelf.' Myra paused, pointed across the room, then went on. 'When I saw that, I just had the strangest feeling. You and Hank weren't in here, but I felt like a Peeping Tom anyway, and, um, and I realized that I've felt like a Peeping Tom since you moved up here.' 'Oh, Myra—' 'That's not what I'm getting at, Bea. That's not it. What I'm getting at, what I mean is, what I felt when I stood behind that door was, rules don't apply here. I mean, right here, the three of us, this house. And I felt like it was the three of us, I felt like it had something to do with me as much as with the two of you. I felt like, I don't know, I felt like one of us could kill the others and put 'em in the freezer or whatever, and no one would ever notice or get suspicious or anything. Or, hell, we could all climb into bed together. I'm sorry, Beatrice, I don't mean to be gross or anything, I, shit, I'm shocking myself even, but I just realized all the sudden that there's no one looking out for us or looking over our shoulder. We're all alone up here. No one's going to protect us, but no one's going to stop us from doing anything either.' Myra stopped for a moment. She looked up at Beatrice. 'That's all, I guess. That's it.' Beatrice said, 'Myra,' but she didn't say anything more, and Myra didn't seem to expect it. She sat next to Beatrice for a few minutes longer, and then she stood up and walked to the door. When she got there she paused, and slapped herself theatrically on the forehead and turned around. 'I almost forgot.' 'Forgot what?' 'Do you want to play cards?' 'Cards?' 'Me and Hank, we was thinking of a game of gin or something. Game of gin, glass of gin. You wanna join us?' 'No, Myra. I, um, I want to get this finished and then, I'm kind of tired, I think I'll go to bed.' 'Suit yourself,' Myra said. 'See you at breakfast.'

He wondered if they were going to have sex again. It was something he'd long wondered about for himself: would he ever have sex again? He supposed he could count up the number of years it had been since he'd last done it but he didn't want to. He remembered her name, though, which was Helen, and he remembered her home, which was a small clean apartment in a U-shaped complex in Lake Ronkonkoma. She'd worked for the Old Man's company, as had almost all the women with whom he'd had affairs. Most of them had been older than he, divorced once, like Sandy, or twice, like Helen, and when they started to be younger than he was Henry knew that he was going to have to quit soon, because he didn't want to turn into that. He let Helen be the last one because she was nice, and nice to him, and that pissed him off even as he appreciated it; there was always a discernible trace of pity for him, as though she were doing him a favor. The Old Man had given him the company long before then, and Henry had grown used to being treated by his mistresses as the boss, as the man who could give them a bracelet or a vacation or a raise, but Helen asked for none of those things, and in this way she reminded him more than anyone else of Sandy. She only listened to his rants about work, about his mother or his wife—Henry realized suddenly, guiltily, that he wasn't sure if his mother had been alive then, and then he realized that she had been dead for a long time—and she said, 'Oh, you poor thing,' and she took his cap off him and ran her fingers through his thin hair, and led him by his hand to her bedroom. She wasn't a passionate or even an energetic lover; she was tender and a little clumsy; she was, worst of all, sympathetic: she seemed to have sex with him only because she thought it would make him feel better, and for a while it did. But then it didn't, and so Henry ended their affair, and when Helen quit a few months later he gave her a nice severance package as he always did, and then he moved into the office that had belonged to the Old Man, who was dead by then, and he hired an old and ugly male account-

ant to work in the office between himself and the new receptionist.

Downstairs Myra was frying bacon. He'd only been awake
for a few minutes when he felt Beatrice stir next to him, heard
her breathing change; under the covers her fingers curled into
his and he flinched, just a little, because a few inches from their
entwined hands was his dick, and it was hard. 'You awake?'
he said quickly, and squeezed her hand. 'I'm awake,' Beatrice
said. He thought, very suddenly, about rolling over on top of
her. It wasn't an idea as much as it was a memory, and it was
so powerful that his right hand was in motion before he
was aware of it, lifting from the bed and traveling over his
body toward Beatrice's, towing the rest of him along like a
disabled vehicle. But when it passed before his eyes he saw its
pale skin, its wrinkles, its age spots and blue veins, and he
thought, I'm too old for this, and he brought his hand down
on his forehead, scratched, ran his hand over the thin stubble
that dotted the top of his head. 'I'd better go help Myra,'
Beatrice said then, and she seemed to wait for a response, and
when none came she said, 'You coming?' Henry pulled his
hand from behind his head and laid it on his lower stomach.
'I'll, um, I'll be down in a minute. You're still up for the falls,
aren't you?' 'Sure,' Beatrice said, 'I'm looking forward to it.'
He felt her pull her hand from his and he had to force himself
to let go. 'I'll see you downstairs,' she said, and when she was
gone he stood up and reached for his robe quickly—she'd left
the door open—and he knotted it over his erection. His robe
was flannel but not heavy, and his penis, which had found its
way through the fly of his pajama pants, poked against it
visibly. Henry looked down at it for a moment, and then he
laughed and made his way to the bathroom. He locked the
door behind him before he opened his robe. There it was;
the only question was, what should he do with it? He thought
about masturbating, and he gave it a couple of experimental
tugs with his arthritic fingers curled painfully around its shaft;
it had been months and months since he'd done even this. His
dick's only response was to go limp, and Henry looked at

himself in the mirror, shrugged, and then went down to breakfast.

He ate faster than the women—he always did—and he had time to go upstairs and dress before helping Myra with the dishes while Beatrice showered. She had been right: Myra was acting weird, and he'd meant to talk to her while they were washing dishes but she stifled all of his attempts at conversation. While they waited for Beatrice's hair to dry they sat at the table drinking coffee. Henry was too keyed up to speak, as was, apparently, Beatrice, and Myra just stared into her cup and said nothing. Eventually Henry and Beatrice took their leave. Myra just waved to them at first, but then a smile seemed to spring to her face and she called out, 'Don't fall in.' Her smile faded as quickly as it had come, and when Henry looked back at her one last time before going out he saw her sitting at the table, precariously twirling her cup of coffee on its base. Just before the door closed he thought he heard a crash, but he didn't look back.

The parking lot was almost full, and the long lawn that stretched in front of it was dotted with strolling people, most of them college-aged. Beyond the lawn Henry could see a thin body of water. He thought it was the lake, but then he realized it was the river that flowed from the waterfall. 'Where is it?' Beatrice said. 'I think it's about a mile upriver,' Henry said. 'You have to walk. There's supposed to be a path.' He turned to her. 'You feel up to it?' 'I'll be fine,' Beatrice said, and she pushed open her door. Henry got out, and when they'd both closed their doors he pressed the remote control button that locked the Jeep and activated the alarm. The lawn was snow-covered, the snow trampled flat and hard, and they walked across it in the same direction that everyone else was going and soon found themselves on a wide path that ran along the side of the river. The riverbed was wide and shallow and flat and most of it was empty of water; a thin stream wandered through it, and a lot of people were walking on the flat stone bottom of the bed. Beatrice and Henry walked slowly. He had his hands in his pockets because they hurt slightly and she'd looped her left arm through his right. The land rose around

230

them as they walked, though the path stayed flat. Soon they were in a chasm whose sides jutted steeply up from both sides of the river in visible layers of dirt and striated rock. Henry had a sense of walking into something, a mountain pass or an open-topped cave, or the primordial past. The air was windless where they were, and the sun shone through the naked branches of the trees. He heard voices sometimes, or laughter, that seemed to come from several places at once. 'It's an echo,' he said aloud when he'd figured it out. 'It's what?' Beatrice said, and then she said, 'What's what?' 'There's an echo,' Henry said. 'Listen the next time someone yells.' They walked along in silence; no one obliged them by yelling. 'Well, shit,' Henry said, and then he yelled it: 'Shit!' Shit, shit, shit, shit, shit, shit . . . 'Henry,' Beatrice teased him, and she squeezed his arm. 'You're acting like a teenager.' 'Oh, excuse me,' Henry said, and he laughed a little and yelled, 'Excuse me!' and his apology bounced around the rocks for a few seconds. They didn't say anything else until, suddenly, they saw the waterfall, and then Henry said, 'Wow,' and Beatrice said, 'Oh my,' and then she said, 'Henry, it's lovely. It's really beautiful.'

Taughannock Falls was a thin stream of water falling straight down for over two hundred feet before splashing in a cloud of mist into a perfectly round dark pool of water. The cliff from which the water fell was almost as spectacular. It was a U whose arms formed the chasm through which the river flowed. The cliff walls were as jagged and sharp as if they'd just been cut, but this jaggedness was covered with a smooth softening sheen of wet moss. 'Let's go down, Henry,' Beatrice said, and she led him to a small observation deck on the other side of the river. When Henry noticed that a lot of people had cameras, he said, 'Oh, shit, Beatrice, I forgot to bring the camera.' Beatrice looked around. 'Oh, well,' she said, 'John would've liked this, too.' Quietly, Henry said, 'I meant a regular camera. Pictures,' he added, and Beatrice put her arm back through his but didn't say anything. They stood at the stone railing and stared at the waterfall; a few people had climbed over the railing and walked onto the smooth gravel that surrounded the dark pool of water, and one couple had even clambered around to the very edge of the waterfall. They were so close they could stick their hands into the falling water. 'Goddamn,' Henry heard now. 'That's cold! Hey, Allan, c'mere, try this.' Henry realized as the boys switched places that the voices he was hearing belonged to them. 'Listen,' he nudged Beatrice, and Beatrice said, 'The echo, I know.' 'It's dope,' the boy said, 'go on, do it,' and the other boy said, 'I dunno, Byron,' and the boy called Byron said, 'Allan, come *on!*' 'They're talking in normal voices,' Beatrice said. 'It's the echo,' Henry said, and then he said, 'What's "dope"?' but before Beatrice answered him the boy called Allan stuck his hand in the water and yelled, 'Wow!' and the cliffs echoed it back, first wow, then ow: first excitement, then pain. 'Oh, wow!' he said again, and stood there, his light blue coat darkening with moisture, until Byron said, 'Okay, Allan, I've got a physics final I've got to get ready for,' and Allan said, 'Sure, Byron,' quietly, reluctantly, distinctly, and he pulled his hand from the water. He didn't shake the moisture from it but let it drip dry, and, fifty feet away, Henry could feel the cold on his hands, a cold so intense that, like the stream water Lucy had told him to dip his hand into, it was comforting.

'Henry?' Beatrice said. 'Beatrice, you're crazy. We'll break our necks.' 'Oh, come on, Henry. The ground's practically flat.' As she spoke, one of the boys—Henry had already forgotten their names—slipped and barely caught himself before falling into the pool. His 'Shit!' and then his laughter echoed through the cavern. 'Oh, come on, Henry. We drove all this way. Why should the kids get to have all the fun?' Henry didn't say anything. He just stepped over the wall and onto the rocks below. His hip hurt a little as his legs stretched, and he held up a hand to Beatrice with a grimace on his face. 'Oh, look like you're enjoying it, old man,' Beatrice said. They walked to the pool and stood there for a moment. Then Beatrice bent down and put a hand in the water. 'That's *cold*,' she said. 'We'd better not fall in.' Henry just nodded—he could tell the temperature from the mist on his head. He felt the water accumulate on his skin, bead, roll down his cheeks and the back of his neck. 'Well, let's do it before we catch a cold just standing here.' He led the way, holding Beatrice's hand at first and then letting go when the ground became slick and he needed his hands for balance. 'Hey, that's it, Grandpa, go for it,' he heard behind him. He was crouched low with his hands on rocks in front of him. Looking down, under his shoulder, he could see the boys looking at him. 'Fuck you,' he muttered, and the boys laughed and pointed. 'Henry,' Beatrice whispered, 'the echo.' 'The echo, Henry!' the boys called now, still laughing, still pointing. 'Hey, Hank, the echo!' Henry stopped short. 'Beatrice—' he said, but Beatrice put her finger to her lips. She was smiling, and she shooed him on with a gesture. 'Go, Beatrice!' the boys called, and Henry sighed and began climbing again. In a few paces the sound of the water was all he heard, and all of his exposed skin was soaking wet. His hands were throbbing with pain. And then, suddenly, he looked up and realized he was there, and in a moment he felt Beatrice's hand on his back, and she said breathily, 'You did it.' In the distance the boys were cheering, and Henry gave them a mocking smile and wave, and then he just stood there. 'Go on,' Beatrice called over the sound of the water, 'come on, stick your hand in.'

Henry did nothing. He didn't want to admit it, but he'd expected that making his way across the rocks to the waterfall would have produced something inside him: elation, if success; dejection, if failure. But instead all he felt was fatigue; it wasn't even an overpowering fatigue, it wasn't strong enough to offer a good excuse for his not feeling anything. He'd had a little fun and now he was tired; he'd walked across some rocks and now he was tired; in a moment he would put his hand into the falling water and it would be cold and his hand would ache, or it would be so cold that his hand would stop hurting, but even that wouldn't be a surprise, and that would be all: no revelations were going to drop into his hand with the water, no ghostly truth was writhing within the mist waiting for him to grab it. He looked down at the dark pool then. Beside him, a little below him, his old wife was looking up at him with a smile gone just slightly rigid, as when one waits too long for a picture to be taken, and in her full mouth with its straight white large teeth and her lips, crinolined, crenulated ever so slightly, and wet with the mist, he saw, suddenly, his mother's face, and even when he turned back to the pool of water he still saw her, remembered her, remembered her death. His mother had taken an overdose of painkillers. She died, not from the pills, but from the vomit she'd choked on but hadn't been able, or hadn't tried, to spit out. The name on the pill bottles had been his, and she had died clutching them in her hands. She had died with her face covered in a caul of vomit, and she had gone into the next world blind.

'Henry, don't you dare.' Henry stared at the black water a moment longer, and then he looked back at her, he looked back at Beatrice. 'Put your hand in the water, Henry,' Beatrice told him. He looked at her for a long time while his body shook a little and the rocks beneath his feet seemed to grow suddenly slippery, but when he opened his mouth to speak all he said was, 'I don't want to put my hand in the water.' 'Well, then don't,' Beatrice said. She said, 'Kiss me instead.' 'What?' 'Kiss me in front of those stupid boys.' 'Oh, Beatrice—' Henry began, but he stopped himself, and leaned down and did it. By then his lips and her lips were both wet and cold, and for the moment his mouth was pressed against them he felt and tasted nothing but water.

They heard the first shot while they were still sitting in the Jeep. They'd just driven up the driveway and the Jeep was off but still warm, and the air both in and outside of its cab had been quiet. It was dusk—driving around, shopping, a late afternoon meal—but not dark; it would be dark, it would be bedtime, soon. For a moment, as the sound of the shot faded from the air, Henry and Beatrice continued to keep their silence. Finally, Beatrice said, 'Was that a gun?' Henry laughed a little. He said, 'Do you mean, was that a gun, or do you mean, was that a gun on our property?' 'I meant,' Beatrice said, 'was that a gun in our back yard?' Henry laughed again. 'I think it was.' Beatrice sighed. 'Those fucking hunters,' she said, and then she added, 'or Myra?' Henry thought for a moment. 'Come to think of it, there was a gun in Myra's trailer.' 'But why would she shoot it?' 'Don't know,' Henry said. 'She doesn't seem to be shooting it now.' They sat together for a while longer. Finally, Henry said, 'It was a nice day,' and Beatrice said quickly, 'It was a beautiful day, Henry. It was really, truly lovely.' She seemed ready to go on but another shot cut her off, and after another long pause during which they just looked at each other—it had gone dark, Henry noticed, and Beatrice's eyes were invisible in the shadows—Beatrice said, 'I suppose we'd better go find out what's up.'

Before they'd rounded the back of the house they heard another shot. 'Okay, you guys, just drag your giggling asses out here.' Her voice was as loud as the shots had been; everything in this silence, in this darkness, was loud. 'It's not an execution, is it?' he called. 'Don't give me any ideas,' Myra called back. 'And don't waste my time.' 'Myra,' Beatrice called, and then they rounded the side of the house and Myra came into view. She looked as she always did, in old jeans, old coat, but she was holding a rifle in her hands, loosely, but not carelessly. 'Myra,' Beatrice said, 'whose gun is that?' Myra looked at it for a moment. 'Why, I guess it's mine,' she said to the gun, and then she looked up at them. 'I mean, no one's going to take it away from me, are they?' 'Beatrice was just wondering,' Henry said quickly, 'where it came from. Where you got it.' 'That's Bea for you,' Myra said. 'Bea always wants explanations. Bea always wants to know the reason why.' Neither Beatrice nor Henry said anything, and in a moment Myra said, 'It was Stan's.' 'Well, that's what Henry figured,' Beatrice said quickly. 'Henry told me that he thought Stan used to hunt.' Myra waited until Beatrice was finished and then she said, almost as an afterthought, 'Shut up.' 'Myra—' Henry said, but Myra cut him off with another 'Shut up.' She jerked her face toward his, and when her head turned her body swayed, and the gun moved, and Henry noticed that her finger still rested on the trigger. 'It's funny,' Myra said then, 'isn't it funny how when there's a gun in your hand people always do what you say?' 'That is kinda funny,' Henry said, and then he said, 'Isn't it

235

funny how when there's a gun in your hand all you can do is talk about it?'

'Myra,' Henry heard Beatrice say then, 'what were you shooting at?' 'I wasn't shooting at nothing,' she said. She jerked her head toward the sky, which held a few clouds, a few stars, a half-moon. 'I was shooting at the moon,' Myra said slowly, carefully, and then slowly, carefully, she raised the gun to her shoulder and pointed it high in the sky, and fired. Henry saw the gun recoil into her shoulder, and Myra took one unsteady step backward. A few seconds later he heard shotgun pellets clattering through the bare branches of trees near the stream. The barrel of the gun descended slowly after she fired, until finally it pointed at the ground. 'I was shooting at the moon,' Myra said again, 'because the sun was nowhere to be seen.' And then she looked up at them and said, 'But I can't seem to hit it.' No one said anything for a moment and then, with a skill and swiftness that startled Henry, Myra opened the shotgun and reloaded it. She turned, raised the shotgun to her shoulder, and fired two shots in quick succession. 'Jesus,' he said, 'that's loud.' 'What's "loud"?' Myra said. 'What's it matter, I mean, what's loud and what's quiet?' 'I only meant,' Henry said, 'that it hurt my ears.' 'If that's what you meant,' Myra said, and she fired another shot, 'then why didn't you say that in the first place?' 'Myra,' Beatrice said now, 'what's wrong? What's . . . honey, what's wrong?' 'Bea, you're so reassuring that way,' Myra said. 'You're so . . . predictable. As if you could ask me what's wrong and I could tell you, and then we could go look up the answer in Ann Landers and then everything would be okay. Bea,' Myra said, 'I don't know what the fuck is wrong, okay?' 'Myra—' Beatrice began, but Myra cut her off. 'I just wanted to shoot this gun, okay? I wanted to hear it. I wanted to make a loud noise.' Now Henry spoke. 'I don't understand, Myra.' 'Isn't that Bea's line, Hank?' 'No, Myra,' Hank said, a little annoyed with Myra's shenanigans now, 'it's my line. It's mine.'

Myra stood motionless in the dark for a moment, and then she smiled. She raised the gun to her shoulder and pointed it at Beatrice and Henry. Beatrice screamed; Henry did too, and he grabbed Beatrice and pulled her behind him, but by the time he'd done that Myra had turned toward the lawn and the mountain. When she fired, Beatrice, behind Henry, screamed again, and Henry screamed too, and with that first shot he went deaf. In the absence of sound all of his other senses were heightened. He could see every brown and gray and silver strand of Beatrice's hair and beyond it the bare and snow-covered patches of their furrowed back yard; he felt the fabric of clothing against his skin, and the chill of the air through it, and the pressure at various places where he touched Beatrice. Steam, like a plume of smoke, flew from his lips. Myra's tears made glowing trails down her cheeks. Her mouth formed words that didn't need to be heard, but when the gun fell from her shoulder sounds returned to his ears in steadily increasing volume. The thump of the gun on the ground was what he heard first, and then Myra's sobs. There was an occasional shot in the trees. He felt Beatrice turn in his arms to look at Myra, saw Myra take a few hesitant steps toward the mountain. He let go of Beatrice then and walked quickly to Myra and put his arms around her. She pulled against him once like a tree swaying against its tether, and then she stood still. Henry relaxed his arms on her body, let them hang loose around her stomach. It rose and fell under his hand, first rapidly, unevenly, then slowing until it moved with the steady regularity of a pump. He felt it contract when Myra spoke. 'It's just that I have nothing to do,' she said. 'I don't have nothing to do.' She paused a moment and then her stomach tensed again. She said, 'When he finally died I said to myself, What a relief, and I didn't mean it just for him. I meant it for me too. But now,' she said, and then she began crying in earnest, 'now I don't have no one, and I don't have nothing to do.' 'Oh, Myra,' Henry said, but he knew that she *was* alone. This light embrace was all he could offer her, and he realized finally, as he had never realized with Beatrice, that it wasn't enough. Behind him, Beatrice watched, and she felt, as acutely as Henry felt it, that there was nothing, really, that they could do for Myra. She realized then how greedy love is, how exclusive, and exclusionary. She realized that the best thing she could do for Myra

would be to go inside and it was only because she had faith
that Henry would join her later that she was able to, and she
did.

14

Manufactured Joy

The roads in Los Angeles are built to accommodate themselves and the cars they carry, but not the landscape. That was the difference, Bea thought late one night, between Long Island and Los Angeles. Eight, ten, twelve lanes of traffic, entering, exiting, merging, passing: Los Angeles roads create their own spectacle, and the distant skyline, the surrounding housing developments, the occasional glimpses or vistas of desert all seemed beside the point to Bea, who'd never been there, though she'd seen it on television or in the movies many times. But on Long Island, Robert Moses had different ideas. There had been an article in the Sunday *Newsday*, and Bea, who clung to the idea that she was keeping up her education, had read it carefully: Robert Moses, she'd learned, had wanted narrow roads. He wanted commercial and commuter traffic separated from each other, and he had low stone bridges built to ensure that big trucks would never rumble past little cars on his suburban parkways. Tall stands of trees line either side of his prettiest roads, the Northern, the Southern, the road named after him, and trees grew between the opposing branches of parkway as well, furthering the illusion that the road was a mountain pass, the only safe haven through a treacherous wilderness. Robert Moses' roads lay on the land's natural curves like a wet cloth over skin, or at least they pretend to, as they dip and rise in long gentle sweeps and, wherever possible, turn their backs on the polluted overcrowded mess they made possible. Their message is simple: over there it's dirty, but here it is clean; over there many obstacles block your path, but here nothing will

239

stop you. These were the roads Bea found herself driving again, the paths she preferred, especially at night after she'd pulled a late shift at King Kullen. That was another difference between Los Angeles and Long Island, Bea thought: Los Angeles roads seemed most real in the blazing light of day, whereas Long Island roads didn't come into their own until after dark. At night, sputtering engine noises were enough to drown out anything from outside, and Bea piloted her car in and out of the few other vehicles on the road in an insular cocoon of white noise. In the darkness, on these winding ribbons, the headlights of oncoming cars glinting through the trees in the median, it seemed to Bea that the cars moved as fish move, effortlessly, weightlessly, and as she drove Bea wished that the road could be as infinite as the ocean so that she could drive forever and never stop moving.

She defined her life in negative terms now, in a long list of things she'd never done, opportunities that had slipped past like exits off the highway: here MacArthur Airport, here Coney Island, here the Queens-Midtown Tunnel. I never flew in an airplane, she thought one night, never squeezed my hips down a narrow aisle or had coffee splashed on my lap by a bump in the air. I've never ridden a roller coaster, or a Ferris wheel, or had a plush purple elephant won for me at a shooting gallery. I've never been further underground than my basement, never in a tunnel, a cave, an abandoned tapped-out mine. And so on: she'd never held a thousand dollars in cash in her hands, and, after her great débâcle at work, she never would, at least not there. She never wore a fur coat, or a silk blouse, or a gold necklace, never owned a wig, never visited another country, neither India nor England nor Mexico nor even Canada; she'd never been more than five hundred miles from the hospital where she was born. She'd never been in darkness that wasn't somewhere illuminated by an electric light, never saw her face on television or heard her voice on the radio or read her name in a newspaper. Nobody ever made love to her outside, on dirt or grass or sand, and, at that point in time, nobody had ever made love to her besides Hank, and he never made love to her anymore. She'd never earned more than two hundred dollars a week in her life even though she worked extra shifts at King Kullen when they let her, which wasn't often. She knew every depressing number by heart: she averaged sixty hours a month; she felt lucky if she got twenty hours a week because they halved shift lengths so they could hire more high school girls and pay them less, and so, working only a couple days a week at minimum wage, taxes taken out, and with the kind of money she spent on booze—she allowed herself one bottle of whiskey each week, but she also bought Hank's beer for him, and they just deducted it from her check—her take-home pay added up to slightly less than nothing. She barely had enough left over to buy coffee and tampons and aspirin.

Her mother, she remembered during one late night drive, had never worn a pair of socks in her life. It was silk stockings or it was nothing, and every week when she'd have her manicure she'd have her feet done too. Bea remembered watching the process as a little girl. Her mother's feet emerged from shoes like fruit from its peels: they were small as dinner loaves and shaped like eggs, and in the beautician's hands they were sanded, polished, and painted until they resembled little jeweled boxes, and when Bea's mother stood around in her bare feet she appeared not just on the ground but attached to it, connected by ornately carved pediments. There seemed in these memories more possibilities, more life in her mother's feet than in all of the choices available to Bea. Bea herself wore socks, and they had holes in them. When she was bored at work she pushed her toes through the holes and then she used her toenails to scrape at the inside of her shoes, so that when she arrived home there would be a line of black leathery lint shoved beneath the nails, and after a while she got tired of scraping them clean with a butter knife or her house key, and the lint stayed there. Sometimes while she was watching television the distant image would blur, and her feet, one crossed over the other on top of the coffee table, would come into focus. They were yellow, pinched, dirty, like the feet of someone who was malnourished or too lazy—or too crazy—to take care of herself. And then Bea would admit to herself that she was lazy, and sometimes she'd pretend that she was crazy too. She had driven the length and breadth of Long Island pretending that she was escaping from this—the difference between her feet and her mother's—but if she'd really thought that she wouldn't have ended up right back where she'd started from, she would have been so terrified that she'd have crashed her car. That was the final difference between Long Island and Los Angeles: the roads in Los Angeles move millions of people from place to place, but on Long Island destinations are as illusory as the paths between them. You could drive forever on Long Island's roads and never get anywhere—and that, Bea realized, was the only real comfort they offered.

It was either very late one night or very early in the morning when a dirty boy walked into the store, where Bea was working her second shift of the day. She'd worked during the afternoon, gone home and fixed something for Hank and Susan and given the baby a bottle, managed to knock back a couple of whiskey-and-waters, and then she'd clocked back in for her extra shift, and as a result she was half asleep when the boy came in and she didn't notice him right away. She didn't see the beat-up tan leather of his work boots, or the faded, stained, and dirty denim of his jeans, or the reddish ripped cotton of his pocket T-shirt. The T-shirt was a little too short for him; it was wrinkled at the bottom as though it had been tucked in at some point but it had come untucked by the time he walked into Bea's life, and it rode a few inches above his waist, revealing a thin line of hair that traveled between his navel and the top button of his jeans. But the only thing Bea saw was the front of his backward baseball cap—he was a Mets fan—and she stared for several seconds at the spill of long curly brown hair hanging under its brim, and then she let herself glance briefly, appreciatively, at his broad shoulders and still-skinny waist, and at the curve of ass visible under the wrinkled hemline of his shirt, and then he turned a corner and disappeared.

After a moment Bea's eyes closed again and then her head dropped and she dozed listening to the other checkout girl—

242

her name was Heather, Bea thought, but she wasn't sure—chatter on the phone to her boyfriend. 'Excuse me,' she heard eventually, and then 'Excuse me,' again, and she thought Heather must be having an argument with her boyfriend, and then, 'Excuse me,' she heard a third time, and she realized the voice belonged to a man. 'Oh, Mr. Bolt—' she began, but she cut herself off when she saw that it wasn't her boss. 'Sorry to wake you,' the boy said. Bea blinked suddenly, and the boy's clear blue eyes and dirty cheeks and day-old stubble flashed in her mind. His lips were parted in a smile, and his teeth seemed very white in his dirty face. 'How can I help you?' The boy's smile widened. 'I'm looking for Shake 'n' Bake,' he said. 'And chicken. I could use a chicken too.' 'Right,' Bea said, thrown off by his smile and his question. People asked her how much things cost, not where they were. As she stood thinking the boy said, 'I'm going to my ma's for dinner tomorrow, and I promised her I'd pick up a couple-a things. I didn't think she'd hold me to it.' He laughed, and Bea laughed too, because he did. She fell silent after a moment and then she said, 'Hold on, will you?' and the boy said, 'I got all night,' and Bea said, 'Right,' and turned toward Heather. 'Hey,' she called, 'hey . . . Heather?' The girl looked up from the phone, her mouth pulled into a frown and a red crescent burned like a slap into her cheek where the receiver had pressed against it. 'Cover for me, okay?' Bea said, and Heather nodded and waved her hand at Bea, who turned back to the boy in the red shirt and blue jeans. She pulled her key from her register and said, 'I'll go with you.' As she stepped out of her station she said, 'You'd think I'd know where everything is by now, but they redecorated, um, redesigned, whatever they call it, and I still have to walk there.' 'Personal service,' the boy said. 'I can get into that.' Bea shot him a look. 'I've never known a man who couldn't,' she said, and then she made a business out of pinning her key to her smock just over her breast. 'Here we go,' she said, looking up, and the boy looked up slowly from her key. He grabbed a cart as they started and Bea's heart beat faster. This was going to take a while.

The store seemed completely empty. Bea didn't even see any

stockboys. The sound of their footsteps and the cart wheels squeaking and LITE-FM hanging over it all like a pall were the only things Bea could hear once they escaped the sound of Heather's voice. Bea found herself slightly ahead of the cart, and when she slowed down to talk the cart slowed as well. Oh, she thought to herself. She lifted her smock above her waist to reach into her back pockets as though she were looking for something, and then she pretended she couldn't find whatever it was she was looking for, and she shook her hair around her shoulders and let her smock fall over her ass again. The cart stayed behind her, which she took as a good sign. 'Now then,' she said, putting a hand on the cart to stop it, 'what kind were you looking for?' She turned to look at the boy who was looking not at the shelves but at her. 'What kind of what?' 'Shake 'n' Bake,' Bea said. 'Your mother's chicken, remember?' 'Oh, right,' the boy said, and then he paused, and it seemed to Bea that he somehow managed to shift his weight from his feet to his hips, which jutted out in front of him and pushed the cart against her stomach. 'There's, um, there are different kinds?' 'Well,' Bea said, holding steady against the pressure of the cart, 'I can't taste the difference between them myself.' She pointed at the shelves. 'There are yellow boxes, and blue boxes, and green boxes, and red boxes. The red boxes are original recipe. The others are, I don't know, nouvelle cuisine or something.' 'Oh, right,' the boy said. He turned from Bea to the shelves and pursed his lips, and then he grabbed several of the red boxes. 'My ma's pretty old-fashioned anyway. These'll be fine.' When he bent over to drop the boxes into the cart it pushed further into Bea's stomach, and she forced herself to stand firm. 'This way for chicken,' she said then, and turned, and the boy said, 'I'm right on your tail,' and then he laughed.

'I work road crew,' he offered as they walked. 'I'm on nights now, 'cause it pays better, but I think I'm gonna switch to days soon. I'm too old to stay up all night long.' 'Too old,' Bea laughed, and then she said, 'Let's change the subject before I embarrass myself.' 'Oh,' the boy said, 'I bet you don't embarrass easy. You don't, do you?' 'Do I?' Bea said. 'Not really. But it does happen.' The boy smiled. 'Tell me,' he said, 'tell me what embarrasses a pretty lady like you.' Against her will, Bea blushed. 'Chicken,' she said, too loudly, and the boy looked confused. 'Chicken?' 'Poultry,' Bea said, and pointed at the meat rack. 'Factory-farmed in New Jersey for your dining pleasure. How much do you need?' 'How much?' Bea smiled patiently, but she felt the blush cooling rapidly on her cheeks. 'How much, what kind? You don't have to get a whole bird.' 'Oh, right,' the boy said. 'I wasn't thinking. I mean, I wasn't thinking about how much. Chicken, I mean. How much chicken.' He stopped then, with a grin that was either shy or sly playing over his mouth. He lifted his cap up and ran his fingers through his hair; there was a half circle of dirt on his forehead from the opening above the cap's snap closure, and it looked to Bea like the upper half of a brown sun setting on a pale horizon. 'Um, how much is normal?' 'Well,' Bea said, speaking carefully, 'it depends on how many people you're feeding.' 'Right,' the boy said, 'it's me and Ma and Dad and . . . It's four,' he said. 'Four,' Bea said. The number, it seemed to her, had come out of nowhere, but not out of sequence. 'White meat?' she said as quickly and calmly as she could. 'Dark?' 'A little of both, I guess.' Bea sighed then. 'Well, here,' she said, and she grabbed a package of legs and thighs, another of breasts. 'This should be fine.' The man looked dubiously at the meat in his cart. 'Are you sure?' he said. 'That don't look like too much.' 'Trust me,' Bea said, her voice as cold as the meat she had dropped into his cart. 'Men always take too much and it always goes bad.'

The boy looked up at her for a long moment. Without his smile his cheeks were slack, and Bea imagined the jowls that would hang there before long. But he smiled quickly, tried again. 'You sound like you know what you're talking about,' he said. Bea found his eyes and held them. She said, 'This is more than enough chicken for four people,' and the boy's face froze for a moment and then he laughed nervously and said, 'Okay, you win.' 'I win what?' Bea said, and the boy said, 'No more chicken?' but Bea waved her hands in the air. 'That's it? That's all I win. No more chicken?' The boy laughed again, more nervously, and he blushed again, but Bea felt aggressive.

'Is that all you're having?' she said, 'just chicken?' The boy jumped as though she'd tickled him. 'Whoa!' he said, and Bea could hear in his voice how young he really was. He was, at any rate, much younger than her husband. The boy looked down at the near-empty cart, at the dry red boxes and the wet plastic-wrapped meat, and then he said, 'Oh.' He giggled. 'Ma didn't ask for nothing else.' 'Well, why don't you surprise her,' Bea said, giving the last word particular emphasis, 'and bring home something extra.' 'Well, I guess I could use a couple-a things myself,' the boy said. He was looking down when he spoke, and he looked up with an expression that Bea thought was supposed to be coy. He smiled. 'So, what do you recommend?'

Then time passed. Their whole lives passed, or at least his did. They filled up the first cart and then a second, but despite the fact that the boy kept reaching for more and more, Bea couldn't manage to make it any more than that: two carts full of groceries. The boy handled both of them, pulling one, pushing another, and the muscles in the forearm of his pushing arm stood out in thick lines whenever he steered the cart around a corner. Everything had a reason; everything he put into one of the carts had a history. Tomato sauce because he was Italian. Codfish filets because he was Catholic. A case of beer because he was an alcoholic; cheap beer because he was broke. *Sports Illustrated* and *TV Guide*: he'd played baseball as a kid, football in high school, and now he watched a lot of television and tried to shoot hoops once a week with his buddies. He fixed his own cars, but not his own meals; he'd met her in high school, 'on the rebound,' he said, from someone whose old man wouldn't let them get married. His head ached in the morning—Tylenol—and his back ached at night—Doan's. He had dreamed once, but not for very long, of going into sports medicine; when he flunked biology he dropped out of high school. His favorite nun had been called Sister Agnes, and he still thought about her sometimes. 'She always had high hopes for me,' he said, and then he repeated himself. 'She always had high hopes for me.' He'd never won the lottery, and now he limited himself to just one ticket a week. He didn't wear condoms. He had no children. He didn't buy anything specifically for his wife, tampons or Midol or hair spray. Bea watched his fingers pick up tartar-control toothpaste and registered for the first time the squashed pack of Marlboro's in the pocket of his T-shirt. He picked up razor blades and Aqua Velva, instant potatoes and gravy mix.

She waited for him to surprise her, at first expectantly and then desperately. She told herself that if he could surprise her even once then it would be enough, she would do it. She would do what Hank did. But with each new item he picked up one more facet of his day-to-day life was revealed to her, as vividly as if she looked into the small rooms of his small house through a closed-circuit camera. Everything added up, but too quickly, and not to very much, and after a while she wasn't even desperate anymore. She just didn't care. The dirt on his cheeks, which had seemed like the trophy of hard labor, now seemed like the sign of a boy too lazy to wash. His T-shirt was too small because he couldn't admit he was a grown-up, and so he bought clothes to fit the adolescent he wanted to remain. The Mets hadn't won in a long time. Finally, she said, 'Anything else?' and the boy looked down at first one cart and then the other. 'Toilet paper.' Bea just shook her head. She led him slowly back to paper products, dreading the ensuing conversation about what brand, what color, scented or unscented, quilted or squeezably soft, but for once the boy knew what he wanted. 'I like Scottissue,' he said, 'because they have that easy-start tab. I hate it when you have to shred the roll just to get it going.' He laughed and Bea didn't. She looked at him and saw him shitting, and she imagined the satisfaction he took in pulling his easy-start tab. She just said, 'Right,' and pulled him back to her register. As his bill rose higher and higher the boy's face fell lower and lower. He tried several times to start another conversation but each time Bea waved a box at him, ice cream, cupcakes, a TV dinner. When all his groceries had gone through and he'd given her the money for them, he made one final effort. 'My name's Joey,' he said, 'but my friends call me Screwdriver.' 'After the drink,' Bea said, 'or the tool?' The boy laughed. 'Hey, you're funny.' He paused. 'What's your

247

name?' Bea didn't bother pointing out that she was wearing a name tag. 'My name,' she said, dropping the last of his groceries into a paper bag, and putting the paper bag into a plastic sack, 'is Beatrice.' She pushed his groceries toward him. 'But the only people who call me that are dead.' The boy started to say something but Bea sighed loudly, and he stopped. She shook her head at him, not without regret; it wasn't the first time she'd seen a life collapse under the weight of accumulated details. She pointed at the door. 'Check-out time.'

ξ

Sometimes it hurt to breathe. The pain wasn't steady but pulsed, came in jagged spurts with each breath he took as though there were broken pieces of glass in his chest. He felt it in his heart and lungs and stomach, and at the back of his head too, and these were the only times when he let himself remember being sick. As he waited for the attack to pass he thought that this was it, that the miracle of his cure had finally run out on him and the early death he'd been promised was now upon him. But then, as always, the pain left as mysteriously as it had come, and all that remained was an ominous achey tingle in his fingers. The sound of his beating heart left his ears and the sound of the television—the bad jokes and canned laughter of an early-morning cable comedian—replaced them. With his right hand he clicked the television off and with his left he reached for his beer. It was empty. He sat for a moment, gathering his energy, and then a blurred bit of time passed and he was back on the couch, a cold can in his hand. He opened it, wincing against the ache in his fingers, and took a drink. He turned on the television. The children were sleeping. Bea wasn't home.

He wasn't sure what time her shift had ended though he was sure it had ended a while ago. But he wasn't waiting up for her. He'd been sleeping and the baby had awakened him; he'd tried to make him a bottle but hadn't been able to find any formula. Eventually he'd mixed the last few drops of milk with some water and warmed it on the stove and gave that to him.

The baby hadn't drunk it but finally he stopped crying anyway and fell back to sleep. Hank had put him back in his crib—the crib was in their room—and then he'd come out here. He kept the volume of the television low because occasionally he heard a short wet cry through the open door to the bedroom, but the baby didn't wake again. The only other sounds inside the house were the clink of his beer each time he set it on the coffee table, and the hum of the water cooler, and when, eventually, Hank started crying, he wasn't surprised. It had been happening ever since the baby was born, especially when he was alone, although sometimes it happened at work. He'd become skilled at doing it in absolute silence, and he sat quietly on the couch now, his stomach quivering inside his shirt, his breath ragged but quiet, and he waited for it to pass. He'd long since stopped wondering why he cried, although that evening he wondered if perhaps it was related to his pains, his trouble breathing. He even laughed at his tears a little, because they were so unreal, but the sound of his laughter was loud and strange, like the sound an old dog makes when it coughs, and Hank covered his mouth with his hand until both the laughter and the tears had passed.

When he thought he was finished crying he called his mother. He closed the door to the bedroom first, and he got a fresh beer, and he dragged the telephone to the end of its cord and sat on the couch—they'd had a cordless from their wedding but that had been broken in a fight years ago—and then he pressed the buttons slowly, carefully. He'd misdialed one time and the sleepy voice which answered had not been his mother's, had in fact demanded to know why he was calling his mother at this hour, and then called him a stupid piece of shit and hung up before Hank could answer. Sometimes Hank wished he could get that number again so he could explain, but he could never remember which was the wrong button or buttons he'd pressed, and so he just pushed in his mother's number, and waited for her to answer. No matter what time he called, she always answered.

'Hello?' 'Mom.' 'Henry.' She slipped sometimes and called him that. 'Hank,' she said then, 'how are you, Hank?' He waited before he answered, tried to think of something different to say, but finally he just said, 'Oh, I'm fine, Mom. I, um, you know, I don't complain.' He tried to keep his voice quiet because of the baby, but in his ears his voice sounded not quiet but muffled, distorted, the words oddly stretched out like a record played at the wrong speed. 'How're you?' 'Oh, it's all the same, Hank.' She laughed a moment. 'When you get to be my age your life doesn't really change. It kind of takes care of itself.' 'Oh, right,' Hank said, and tried to laugh. 'Right,' he said again. 'And Dad? How's Dad? 'Oh, your father hasn't changed since he started wearing big boy underpants. You can set your clock by your father.' 'Yeah,' Hank said, and then he said, 'I, um, I'm sorry to wake you. I, um, the baby woke me up and . . .' His voice trailed off. 'It's okay, Hank,' his mother said. 'How is my grandson?' 'Growing,' Hank said. 'He grows every day.' 'They do at that age.' 'Yeah, I guess they do. I guess Susan did. I guess—' His voice broke suddenly, and he clapped a hand over the receiver to conceal his sudden sob from his mother. She waited silently on her end of the line. Hank knew that she knew he was crying, but to actually cry out loud would be breaking the rules of the game, and he kept his hand over the mouthpiece until he was able to speak evenly. 'Bea's working late,' he said, and his mother said, 'She's been doing that a lot.' 'Yeah, she, um, she's had to cut down her day hours to, um, to take care of the baby.' 'Yes,' his mother said, but nothing else. Hank remained silent as well, staring at the distant muted television. There was a movie on now, or a rerun; people were sitting down to a meal, and Hank wiped at the tears on his cheeks with the back of a hand. 'Mom,' he said. 'Yes?' 'Mom, there's—' He stopped himself. He wasn't sure what he'd been going to say so he stopped himself until he could think of what it was. When he'd finally found what he was going to say, he said, 'Mom, I'm hungry.' That's not what he'd been going to say; he'd meant to say, There's no way out. He said, 'I think I'm gonna fix myself something to eat.' 'Okay,' his mother said. Hank couldn't tell if her voice was concerned, or bored, or merely tired. 'Call me in the morning if you want.'

'Okay,' Hank said. 'Sure, I'll—' but his mother had already hung up.

The bread of his uneaten sandwich—American cheese, lettuce, mayonnaise—was stale by the time Bea came home. It sat on a paper towel on the coffee table next to a row of beer cans, which made a faint metallic rattle when Bea closed the door heavily. 'Quiet,' Hank said, 'you'll wake the baby.' Bea didn't answer him; she dropped her purse on the television and then walked slowly into the kitchen. She came back with a glass in one hand and a bottle in another, and she put some water from the cooler in the glass; by that time they'd brought a chair and she sat down in it. When she still didn't speak Hank said, 'I can't believe you slam the door like that, especially at this hour.' Bea blinked. She looked into her glass, added a liberal dose of whiskey, and then she drained it. Hank opened his mouth to say something else but Bea suddenly looked at him and her eyes were so dead and cold that Hank forgot what it was he'd meant to say. 'I had a dream,' Bea said. 'I was driving around after work, and I dreamed that when I came home the house would be empty. No furniture, no dishes, no food.' She looked at him again, just long enough to say, 'No people,' and then she poured a shot into her glass and sipped at it. Her face twisted into a grimace against the liquor. 'It was just going to be me and these walls,' she said. 'The walls'—she looked up—'the ceiling'—she looked down—'and the floor.' She stamped her foot on it, as though affirming its solidity, but her shoe made almost no noise against the green carpet. She took another drink and grimaced, and then walked over to the cooler and ran a little water into her glass. She turned back to Hank with a flourish of her hand that spilled some of her drink on the carpet, and she said, 'I now know, for certain, for absolute certain, that even the most simple dreams do not come true.'

Hank stared at her while she drained her glass, ran more water into it, and returned to her chair to add whiskey to the water. When she was sitting down he said, 'You've flipped. You've finally flipped.' 'Oh no,' Bea said quickly. 'I haven't finally flipped. I flipped a long time ago. I flipped the day I said

251

I do. I flipped the day I met you.' Hank stood up then. 'You're drunk,' he said loudly. 'You've been driving that goddamn car drunk again. If you crash it, that's it. There isn't any money to get another one. There isn't—' He stopped when he heard the baby in the other room. Bea sighed, stood up. 'Asshole,' she said, and walked into the bedroom. While she was gone Hank got himself another beer. He was still standing in the middle of the kitchen when Bea came back into the living room with the baby. Though his wife and son were only a few feet away, they looked to Hank as though their features were distorted by distance. Bea held the baby in one hand and her glass in the other. She jiggled the baby unsteadily. Hank wasn't sure if she was attempting to rock him or preparing to throw him across the room, but the baby, at any rate, wasn't soothed. He screamed at the top of his lungs. 'Jesus Christ,' Hank said. 'The least you could do is put your fucking drink down. You're about to drop him.' Bea looked up from the baby vehemently. 'I will not drop my son!' she yelled. Hank could see her fingers digging into the skin of the boy's legs, making harsh white circles in his pink skin. He slammed his beer down on the table and walked quickly to her and pulled the baby from her arm. Bea's glass fell on the carpet, and something ripped when he pulled—the baby's pajamas, or Bea's shirt. He hoped it was just fabric. 'Bastard!' she screamed. She reached for the baby but Hank stepped back. In a voice that sounded like one rusty pipe being screwed into another, he cooed, 'There now, it's okay.' The baby wailed in his ear. To Bea, Hank said, 'Why don't you make yourself useful and fix him a bottle.' Bea stared at him from the center of the living room, and then she bent over slowly and picked up her glass and walked with it into the kitchen. When she was out of the living room Hank walked into it, and he paced back and forth. He could feel his hands trembling against the baby's skin, and his cries were making Hank's head hurt. He wanted to pick up his beer, but he couldn't get to it without passing Bea.

There was a noise behind him. He whirled quickly, hitting his hip on the corner of the television and almost losing his balance, and saw Bea at her chair, refilling her glass. The baby bottle wasn't in her hand, and he looked into the kitchen. An empty bottle stood on the counter. 'What?' Hank said. 'You're too good to feed your son now?' Bea went to the cooler and poured water into her whiskey. She took a drink, and then another, and she looked into her glass for a long time, and then she drained it. She looked at Hank when it was empty, and said, 'There isn't any.' Hank just looked at her. The room was silent except for the baby's cries and a few burps from the water cooler. 'What?' he said finally. 'What did you say?' Bea took another drink. 'I said there isn't any. No formula. No baby food. Payday tomorrow,' she said, 'I'll buy some then.' 'You get paid tomorrow,' Hank said. 'Where the hell is all my money?' Bea just looked at him for a moment and then she laughed. She stopped laughing to suck at her empty glass, and then she said, 'Here's your money, honey.' She held up her glass to Hank, and walked unsteadily to the coffee table. 'Here's your money,' she said, and with her glass she pushed Hank's beers over can by can, and each time a can fell to the floor she said, 'There's your money.' The last can she pushed over was still full, and thin yellow beer pulsed from the can's mouth like a flickering tongue, staining a dark circle on the carpet. Hank said. 'I do not believe we spent all our money on liquor.' 'All of it,' Bea said. 'Every last drop. I mean cent.' 'No,' Hank said again, louder. 'I don't believe it. I refuse to believe it!' 'Believe it,' Bea said. 'Liquor,' she said. 'Gas, electricity, water, mortgage, cable, pho—'

'Stop!' Hank's voice caused the baby to jerk in his arms and cry louder, but Bea just said, 'We don't have a penny to our names until I get paid tomorrow.' 'No!" Hank screamed. 'I don't believe it! I *won't* believe it!' 'Well, you'd better. You'd—' She stopped suddenly, her eyes fixed on some object behind him, and Hank looked at her sharply. 'What?' he said. 'Nothing,' Bea said. Hank shifted the screaming baby from one shoulder to another, and then he turned and looked where Bea was looking. There was nothing there except the water cooler. He looked at it for a long time, not understanding, until he realized that the inverted bottle of water which sat atop it was virtually full. 'No,' he said, without turning around. 'I don't believe it.' He looked back at her slowly. The baby screamed into his ear. Bea was staring into her lap. Hank said. 'Tell me you didn't buy a bottle of water when we were out of baby food.' Bea still didn't speak, and Hank said, 'Tell me, or I'll throw this kid right through the window.' 'It was you who bought the fucking cooler anyway!' Bea screamed. 'Fuck you, bastard, I forgot!' She leaped from her chair suddenly, spraying her drink over herself and the floor, and grabbed the baby from Hank's arms. 'Don't you ever threaten my baby again!'

Hank fell against the door when she hit him, and the door-knob jammed against his hip. 'You cunt!' he yelled. Bea was curled around the baby, her hair loose and hiding him from Hank, and it seemed her only reply was the baby's screams. 'I thought my mother was bad but you really take the cake. You're the sorriest excuse for a woman I've ever seen.' Bea looked up at him then. The baby was wedged tightly between her crossed legs as though it had been dropped there from a great height. After a pause she said, 'Let's keep this between you and me, okay? Leave your mother out of it.' 'I—' 'No,' Bea cut him off. '*Me*.' She paused, and then she said, 'I buy the food around here. The only money you spend out of your own pocket is on drinks for your buddies, and your goddamn whores.' 'They're not—' Hank started, but then he stopped himself and Bea said, 'I don't care who you stick your dick in, as long as it's not me.' Hank tried to push himself off the door but fell back against it. He closed his eyes again and tried to think, but the baby's cries broke apart his thoughts as soon as they entered his head. Maybe, he thought, maybe there was just nothing to think anymore. His head started to spin then, from the alcohol he told himself, and he felt as though he were falling backward off a cliff. Without realizing it, he sank to the floor, and he sat still for a long time, his eyes closed, his head throbbing. He was aware that he was sobbing again, and though he didn't will it his sobs made no noise. It was as though he could no longer make any noise at all, and he sat there silently, his eyes closed, invisible, until he heard a new sound, a creak from above. He opened his eyes suddenly and saw Susan standing at the top of the stairs. She stood crookedly as though she were recovering her balance, a hand pressed against the wall and her legs sticking out awkwardly from beneath an old T-shirt that had once belonged to him. 'Susan?' Hank said, not sure if anything would come out. 'Honey?' he said, louder, but she turned from him and ran through the door of her room and slammed it.

When Hank turned to Bea she was staring at him. Her face was streaked with tears and mascara, and the baby, still screaming, hung half-in and half-out of her lap. 'I just want you to know,' she said, 'that it's not just our lives we're ruining. I just want you to know that.' She looked down at the wailing thing lying on her legs and lifted it properly into her lap and ran heavy comfortless hands over it while it screamed louder and louder. Hank closed his eyes, but when he opened them his wife and child were still there, and the narrow walls of his house, and the liquor-stained carpet and broken-legged couch and cracked glass of the coffee table, and he was still there as well, and the images the television brought him of the outside world were still there, and they were no more comforting. He looked with his dead eyes across the room, and Bea was already looking at him, and when she spoke it was in a voice as flat as his soul. 'Oh, Hank,' she said. 'You should have just died.'

Years ago, she had gone to the auction. She had gone by herself; she didn't even tell Hank she was going. It was held at her old home, at the house that had belonged to her for just under a year and that had belonged to her parents for just over eighteen, and that for seven years after her mother's death and before her father's had belonged to no one, but had been occupied by herself and her father. There were notices on the mailbox, on the door, and there was even one fastened to a tree with coil upon coil of Scotch tape. They were all faded but they were all still legible, and they all announced to anyone who stopped to read one that she had failed to pay her father's bills, and as a result everything that she thought had belonged to her was being taken away.

She sat in her car and watched the other cars arrive. They were all big and they were all American, and they all looked a little beat up—there wasn't a new car in the bunch, or a red one for that matter, but there were lots of brown ones, and a faded yellow one, and one that was almost the color of the carpet that she and Hank hated, and they pulled up in the driveway and they drove onto the lawn and the ones who came late had to park all the way down the block. Some of the people who got out of the cars obviously knew each other. Big-bellied men in faded jeans and stretched-out T-shirts shook hands awkwardly, and women who cut their husbands' hair nodded hello to each other and pulled cigarette cases from vinyl purses, and lit cigarettes for themselves and for their husbands. It was afternoon and it was a weekend, so a few people had beers, and a few people made shows of turning down beers that were offered to them, and a few others made shows of accepting them, but most of them just drank unconsciously. The people were all strangers to Bea: she didn't know them and she didn't like them parking on her lawn and throwing their butts into her hedge; but they were all known to her too. They were unfamiliar, but not foreign. Her car was big and old and brown like theirs, and she carried a vinyl purse, and her radio was broken or she might have been listening to one of the radio stations they listened to. She cut Hank's hair—there was no need to pay somebody just to run the clippers over it. These people could have been her relatives; if they had been, she could get out of the car now, say hello, accept a beer, say no thank you to a cigarette, and the women would all remark on how hard it was for young people starting a family these days, and the men would put their arms lightly on her shoulder, they'd ask her how Hank's job was going, and those that could afford to would ask her if there was anything she wanted from the house, and they'd offer to buy it for her.

A man in an ill-fitting and ugly suit came from the back yard and said something, and then people made their way around the side of the house and Bea joined them quietly, nodded to those who nodded at her, and in the back yard she made her way to the front of the crowd. The pace was slow. Some of the bigger pieces of furniture were already outside and others were carried out by two young men who were the only people not shivering in the cold. It occurred to Bea at one point that no one there, not even the slow-witted auctioneer, knew who she was, and that, as in a movie, she could draw out someone around her and get that person to say something about the furniture, the house, and they would speak more candidly than they might otherwise, because they wouldn't know it was her house and her furniture, her life, they were commenting on. And then, surprising herself, she did it: she began speaking to a couple next to her, a man in his late forties, a woman in her early forties. He did most of the talking; his wife did most of the bidding, though in the end they bought very little: a floor lamp, the good china, which they said they were going to give to their daughter for her new house, her first house. 'They had good taste, these people,' the man said. 'Nice, solid furniture, a few antiques.' Her parents hadn't owned any antiques, and it took Bea a moment to realize that by 'antiques' he meant those pieces of furniture—the hutch, the little table that had been in the foyer—that imitated older styles of furniture. The man was still speaking: 'I don't think they had any children,' he said. Bea asked him how he could tell. 'Everything's white,' he said, and his wife said. 'You don't got no kids?' Bea shook her head. The man said, 'Well, you don't have white furniture, white carpets, a white bedspread especially, if you got kids.' Bea nodded her head, and then the man waved hello to someone. 'There's a group of us follows around the auctions. Not many people stay in it for more than a year or two, unless they're junk dealers.' Bea asked why not. 'Buy what you need after a while,' he said, and then he said, 'Me, I ain't got the stomach for much more.' He nudged his wife to go a little higher on the dining room hutch. 'If she's gonna have good dishes, she might as well have a hutch to show 'em off.' He paused for a minute and then he waved a hand at the furniture huddled against the back of the house. 'This is all a person's got to show for his life, after he's dead. You can't take it with you.'

Later in the afternoon the auctioneer picked up the pace,

and he managed to finish before the sun set. A few things didn't sell: the carpets they'd pulled from the floor, the mattresses. 'Funny thing about mattresses,' the man next to her said. 'People'll buy someone else's bed frame, but they don't like to sleep where someone else has slept.' Bea asked the auctioneer what was going to happen to the things that didn't sell. 'Don't know,' he told her. 'Don't handle that. Bank handles that.' She asked then if she could take anything. The auctioneer said no quickly, but then he looked her over from top to bottom, and he sighed and he said, 'I don't know why the people show up to watch their stuff being sold off, but they always do. When they're not in jail.' 'I just want the bedspread,' Bea said, and then she said, 'It was my parents',' and then she said, 'They're dead,' and then, finally, she said, 'It would be all I have to remember them by,' and she realized with a start that she wasn't lying. The man looked away when he told her yes, and she took it before he could change his mind, bundled it up in her arms like a sleeping child and stuffed it in the back seat of her car, and when she got home she left it there overnight, and then for two nights, then a week. Eventually she stuffed it into a box and put the box in the attic. It was the only thing up there—all of their other boxes were in the basement—and because of that it made her feel good. It meant that she and Hank actually had a little more than they needed, a little more than they could use, a little something in reserve. She liked the box up there, it was her little bit of luxury, though soon enough she forgot about it and it wasn't until years later, when Susan was seven and John was just born and they turned the attic into Susan's room, that she found it for the first time, dusty inside and out, and still stained with the loss of her and Hank's innocence.

15

The Last Frontier

The night before they were to look for the red deer, Beatrice and Henry sat up late with Myra in the living room. The television was on, muted, but the acting was so overdone that, like bad mime, the melodrama of its story was discernible even without sound. Occasionally they heard a gunshot. Myra had brought out a bottle; Henry had expressed reservations on Beatrice's behalf but Beatrice had shushed him and declared that she was feeling worlds better—she was—and so they sat up, drank, and talked until the television's blue light was the only illumination in the room. The light was given substance by the room's darkness and by Myra's cigarette smoke, and Beatrice often found her eyes returning to it: not the television but the television's thick concentrated glow, which cut across the room like a spotlight. It was focused on herself and on Henry where they sat across from the television on the couch, and excluded Myra, who sat on a chair beside them. Beatrice felt a little sad for Myra when she saw this, and she silently squeezed Henry's hand, and he squeezed back, but Myra seemed not to notice her solitary status. In fact, she held court, talking loudly, garrulously.

'When I met him he was the handsomest man I'd ever seen. He was head and shoulders taller than me, so I was always having to look up to see him, but it never failed that when I was looking up he was already looking down. We met at some party right after high school. It was the end of the summer, probably Memorial Day, and the people who were throwing the party had a pool, so most of the guys had a better-than-

259

usual excuse to take off their shirts, and most of us girls just had on our bathing suits and those little pool skirts we wore back then, when we still had a little modesty. Now, the difference between a real man and one of these guys'—she waved a hand dismissively at the television—'is that when one of these guys takes off their shirts all you see is how pretty he is, how pumped up, whatever they call it, which is what's supposed to happen when a *woman* takes off her shirt. But when a real man takes off his shirt you see how strong he is, and then you see how weak he is. Now, you take Stan. He, Stan, he used to think he was a bit too skinny when he was young, and so he wasn't always taking his shirt off like some of the other men he worked with, the Old Man's men'—here she nodded at Henry—'but that day at the pool party he had his shirt off, and I'll tell you, he was the man I noticed. You could tell right off that he wasn't no weakling. He was thin, sure, but not skinny. He looked like a man who took care of himself, you know, worked out, and you could tell that he worked for his money. He had the best shoulders on him then, and he had one of those really flat tummies that not many guys had back then. You know, not flat, but ripply with muscles. So, anyway, so that's what I mean when I say you can see how strong a man is when he takes off his shirt. But with a real man, you can see how weak he is too. Weak isn't the right word, it's something else, something, open, maybe, but that's not quite—'

'Vulnerable,' Beatrice said quietly. 'Yeah!' Myra said brightly. 'Vulnerable, yeah, that's it. Vulnerable.' She mulled the word silently in her mouth for a while, and then she said, 'What I mean is, what I mean by vulnerable is, when a man like Stan took his shirt off what you saw was all this baby-white skin that's normally covered up. You know, normally you just saw, like, tan forearms, a tan neck, but when Stan took his shirt off you could see the skin the way it used to be, all white and with, like, you know, little freckles and pimples and whatever, spots, and with Stan there was just a tiny bit of hair growing right here'—she put her hand between her breasts—'just a tiny bit, and you could tell he was kind of shy about it 'cause he held his beer can really high up to kind of keep it covered.

And the other guys would tease him about that, and pull his beer can down, and you know Stan, he was a good-natured guy, he'd just blush and let them do it, but you could tell those guys respected him and knew he wasn't no sissy 'cause they never pushed him too much.

'And now,' Myra said, 'I have to pause to take a breath.' She did, and leaned forward to refill her glass. 'How're you doing, Hank, Bea, you need any refreshment?' Henry held out his glass silently, and Beatrice held hers out as well but said, 'Just a little, thanks,' and Myra said, 'You want some water? I seem to remember you always used to take your whiskey with water.' 'No, thank you,' Beatrice said, and after a pause she added, 'That was a long time ago,' and this time Henry squeezed her hand, and she squeezed back, and he turned over his shoulder to look at her. Myra, still bent forward over the table, cast her upturned eyes from Henry to Beatrice and back again, and then she smiled. 'I saw that,' she said, and handed them their glasses. Henry smiled. He said, 'Go on with your story.' 'Well, I don't know that it's a story, really. I mean, it's just when me and Stan met, that's all.' And then she smiled shyly and repeated herself: 'That's all.' 'Myra,' Beatrice said then. 'Myra,' she began again, but it was no use: her words refused to do anything more than peep out from the shadows of her mind. Myra looked at Beatrice for a long time until finally Beatrice said, 'I'm sorry. I don't quite know how to say what it is I want to say.' She sighed. 'I'm sorry,' she said again. 'You'd think at my age I'd be a little better at speaking my mind. But it don't, it doesn't seem any easier than the day I met you.' She turned to Henry, and Henry said, 'Well, I always thought you had a way with words. I thought you expressed yourself just fine.' 'But I didn't, Henry, that's the point.' She turned back to Myra then. 'I mean, I think that's what I was trying to say to you. I was trying to say how hard it is to say something real, something beautiful, and how what you were saying was really very moving to me, and that you shouldn't sell yourself short, what you say, your life, you shouldn't sell it short. Because when you do, when you don't tell your old stories, don't believe in them, then they disappear, and you do too.' When she stopped she was out of breath and Myra was staring at her with, Beatrice wasn't sure, impatience or understanding, and then Myra smiled and turned to Henry. 'Boy, she does go on, don't she?' But she was clearly touched, and it was a moment before she went on with her story.

'Now, where was I?' she said finally. 'Oh, right, the party. Okay, so there's Stan, and he's like, hanging out with some of the other boys, and I was hanging out with my girlfriends. These were mostly kids we'd gone to school with, you know, and there was that sort of happy-sad feeling about it all 'cause some of the people that we'd considered our friends weren't there because they were already too busy with their jobs or their husbands or wives, or whatever. But mostly everybody was feelin' free and easy, and the party went on all day. Stan and I, we knew who each other was and all, but we didn't really know each other, and I don't think we said much more than Hi or Excuse me to each other all day long. *Although*'— and here Myra's face brightened, visible even in the dim light cast by the unwatched television—'although we did bump into each other once in the pool, and I mean hard. I was swimming under water with my eyes closed, and I heard this big splash and then crash! I was all tangled up with someone else and coughing and shit, and when I came up I was in his arms. I mean, he had his hands on my waist and my boobs were practically in his mouth and he was asking me if I was okay, and I was, so I told him so, and then he held on to me for just a bit more, you know, you can tell when somebody's touching you when they don't need to be, and then we both kind of laughed and swam away from each other. To this day—' Myra stopped herself, and then started again. 'I mean, I could never get him to admit that he did it on purpose, jumped on me, I mean. But I tell you, if I wasn't thinking about him before then I sure was after.'

She paused then, and looked into her glass, which she hadn't drunk from, and took a small sip from it. 'Well,' she said, 'eventually it got dark like it always does. It was a barbecue party, hamburgers and hot dogs and stuff, and I'm not quite sure how it happened but somehow I missed out on the first go at the food, and I ended up with this hamburger that was like a piece of charcoal, and when I sat down with it I was, like, you know, picking at it, and finally I just set it down and said Gross really loud, and that's when Stan, who must've been sitting right behind me, said, What's the matter? I remember I nearly jumped out of my skin. I think that's how you know you're in love with someone, when everything they say scares the shit out of you. Well, I told him about the hamburger, and he just said, C'mon, and then we got up and went over to the grill, and he found the ground beef and rolled out a few hamburgers, and then he put them on to cook. I remember I said to him, I'm perfectly capable of making myself a hamburger, but Stan just tried to look all macho and he said, Don't be silly, a barbecue's the only time it's okay for a man to cook for a woman. You know, Stan always was a little old-fashioned like that, what a man could do, what a woman could do, and later on that kind of shit just drove me outta my mind, but right then it seemed, I don't know, kind of sweet. The grill, it was a little ways away from where the other kids was eating, and we sat down on this bench and talked a little bit and watched the hamburgers cook. Eventually, I know this is the oldest line in the book, but eventually I remarked that it was getting a bit chilly and Stan, you know, that was the invitation he needed. He kind of put his arm around me and when I didn't go nowhere he moved over till he was sitting next to me, and his fingers played with my hair and all, and then he kind of ran them over the skin of my neck. I remember it tickled like crazy but I made myself sit still and take it 'cause if a man thinks he's being the suavest thing around and you say That tickles! then he's gonna get all self-conscious and run away.'

Here, Myra took another sip of her drink and lit a cigarette, and pulled on it slowly. Beatrice excused herself and hurried into the kitchen pantry, where she thought she remembered seeing some candles. While she was in the pantry she saw the other door, the door which opened behind the sitting room bookshelves, and she resisted the urge to sneak a look at that empty room. She found the candles, and a few white ceramic

263

candleholders, and brought them back into the living room. 'Oh, what a good idea,' Myra said when she saw them, and she lit them for Beatrice with her matches. Beatrice put a few on the coffee table and a few on top of the television, and then she stared at the television for a moment. The news had come on; tanks were moving through the desert. 'There's going to be a war,' she said. 'I can't believe there's going to be another war.' 'What was that?' Myra said. 'What'd you say?' 'Nothing,' Bea said, and she turned the television off. The room went suddenly dark, and Myra said, 'Oh!' The room grew gradually lighter as the candles gained their full flame, and Bea stood next to the television until the flickering light had stabilized, slightly dimmer than before but, Beatrice noticed contentedly, evenly distributed. She sat down then. 'I'm sorry,' she said, 'but the television was distracting me. This is much better.' Myra said, 'Yeah,' and after a long pause Henry said, 'Your burgers're about to burn on the grill.' Myra just said, 'Oh, yeah,' and then she said, 'Well, they didn't,' and then she stopped again and put out her cigarette, took another sip from her glass. 'It's not getting too late?' she said. 'Everybody's okay?' She looked at Beatrice and Henry and gestured with her drink, and Henry said, 'Yeah, sure,' and Beatrice said, 'Fine, thanks,' and then Myra sat back in her chair.

'Now, I know it's some kind of cliché or something, but that was the best goddamn burger I ever ate in my whole life.' She laughed, and Beatrice and Henry joined her, and she said, 'I mean, I remember every bite I took out of that burger. It was like biting and chewing and swallowing was whole new experiences, what with Stan's knee touching mine. We kind of rubbed knees a bit, but that's all, I was really hungry and I wanted that burger, but I wanted Stan too, and it was like with each bite of it I could taste him too, and I remember staring at him as I ate and he ate, and, you know, there was a little of this'—she stuck a finger into her mouth and licked it, a little lewdly—'but not too much. You know, I think you do that sort of stuff with someone you don't really care about, someone you're just going to fuck, and, ahem'—she giggled—'I'm not saying I was a virgin or anything like that, but that's neither here nor there. What I meant to say was, I don't think you need to get fresh with someone when, like, there's real emotion between you, even when it's too soon to really call it love. Well, we finished finally, finished eating, and Stan put our plates in the trash and got us fresh beers, I think just so he'd have the excuse of standing up and sitting back down next to me, and in a moment he put his arm around me and he said, How was that? and I said just what I said to you, It was the best burger I ate in my whole life. And then we started talking about what we was doing now that we was out of high school. Stan had gone straight to work for the Old Man, and even though the Old Man's company wasn't anything then to what it would become, it still seemed like a good thing, you know, a man with a job and a skill. I think I was still babysitting then or something like that, I don't think I had a job, I mean. Anyway, I think we was both so nervous and so relaxed at the same time that we could've sat there talking forever, but eventually we heard some of the guys making a lot of noise and we turned around to see what was up.'

Myra took a sip of her drink, and looked thoughtful for a minute. 'One of the guys,' she said then, 'one of the guys, and I cannot for the life of me remember his name, I've never been able to, not since the day it happened, but one of the guys was tottering toward the diving board, laughing and saying that he'd show them. The other guys was egging him on, and the girls, you know, they was being girls and clinging to each other or to their boyfriends, and saying Be careful and things like that. Well, I guess . . . I mean, what I found out later was that this guy said he could do a backward somersault off the diving board, and someone had said he couldn't, and someone else had dared him, you know, how boys like to do. And so this guy was stumbling toward the diving board, drunk as a skunk, and everyone was standing around and watching him like he was about to do an Olympic trick or something. More like a clown trick, I guess. And he, you know, he tripped going up the goddamn step to the diving board, but he caught himself and stood up and walked out to the edge of the board, and he put his arms out like an acrobat, and then he said, I swear to

Christ, Ladies and gentlemen, the death-defying feat you are about to witness is the feat of a lifetime.'

Myra stopped. She reached for her glass and took a long drink from it, and then she set it back on the coffee table. 'I just want to tell you something,' she said. 'I don't remember what that boy's name was and I don't remember what he looked like really, but I remember that he was pretty, like a girl is pretty, the kind of pretty that you want to take care of, and I remember I wondered why the hell someone didn't get up and stop him and I thought, Because guys don't take care of other guys, and girls only take care of the guys they're married to. But no one takes care of a pretty boy except his mother. What he needed right then and there on that diving board was his mother, and she wasn't there.' Myra stopped again, drank again. Beatrice thought she saw water in the corner of her eyes. 'Well, he started to bounce, and he nearly wobbled over and fell in, and everyone laughed at him, but he caught himself and stood up straight again. You know how it is when you're drunk but then suddenly you think you're not, but you still are? Well, he got that look on his face, real serious and concentrated, and then he put out his arms again, and jumped, and bounced again, and then he jumped again, and then he bounced again, and then he was in the air and if you blinked you'd've missed it, he flipped a backwards somersault right over the end of the board, and when he came down there was this awful whap!'—Myra clapped her hands together, and Beatrice and Henry both jumped—'and then he just kind of sloshed into the water.'

'My God, what happened?' Beatrice said. 'Well, that's what we all wanted to know, of course. Everyone was up and running around, and some dumb little girl was screaming her head off. Guys were diving in left and right, and hell, they was all drunk too, and crashing into each other and the side of the pool, it was a mess, one of them broke his wrist somehow and had to be fished out himself. And it was all no use, 'cause he was already dead.' 'Myra, please,' Henry said, 'what happened?' 'Well, I suppose it's obvious,' Myra said. 'That whap! we all heard was his head hitting the diving board, and what

266

with him going down and the diving board going up, his poor skull just split right open.' She put her hand on the back of her head, and Henry put his hand on the back of his head, and Beatrice put her hand over Henry's. She felt his fingers as they traced the faded X, and then she pushed them out of the way and rubbed it herself. Maybe it was because of the scar, or because of the way Myra had told the story, or because of what had happened a few nights ago with Myra and the gun, or maybe it had to do with everything, or just the whiskey, but the death of the boy, nameless and faceless but beautiful, seemed very real to Beatrice, and sad, and it was obviously the same for Henry and Myra as well. They all sat in silence together, as though in mourning, and then gradually they picked up their drinks and finished them, and Myra smoked part of another cigarette. Then she put it out and started speaking again.

'Stan was one of them that dove in the pool. I don't know if he was less drunk than everyone else or if he was just lucky, or unlucky, whatever, but he was the one who actually dragged the boy out of the pool. He dragged the boy onto the cement around the pool and then he just came back over to me, and we stood there waiting for the ambulance. He started shivering because it was dark and cold, and I found him a towel and put it around his shoulders, and then I put my arm around him, but he didn't stop shaking. It seemed like forever before it was all over, the ambulance, the police, everybody's parents and all that, and then people were kind of picking up their things and he came over to me and asked me how I was getting home. I said I imagined I'd call my dad, and he said could he drive me home and I said sure. So then he drove me home and we didn't say much, just directions, and then we were there and he parked on the street instead of in the driveway so we wouldn't wake my folks with the lights. He wasn't shivering no more, but his hair was still wet and you could tell he was really bothered, so I said, That was really brave of you, pulling him out like that, and he said, It wasn't brave, it wasn't no different from hauling a big fish out of the water. I said, Still, I don't think I could've touched a dead body, and he said,

Well, I didn't know he was dead, and then we got quiet again. But finally he said, I wonder, I just wonder if he'd known that he was going to die, would he still have done it? I said, Of course not, but he said, I don't mean if he knew he was going to hit his head, I just mean if he knew he was going to die in general. I mean, if he was just, like, aware that he had to die sometime, that he could die anytime, then would he ever have got up there on that diving board? Well, I didn't understand him, and I said so, and that's when he got, not teary-eyed, Stan never cried, but he got teary-voiced, and he said, It's just that when I touched him I knew right away he was dead, just dead, nothing else, he wasn't even himself any more. He was just dead. And then Stan said, I realized that there but for the grace of God go I, it could've been me being fished out of that pool as easy as it was him. He said, We waste so much time, I remember him saying that. We waste so much goddamn time. He said, If we lived every day knowing, I mean really knowing that we were gonna die, would we still do all the stupid shit we do? And I had no answer for that. I still don't, not really. Because, I mean, I know what the answer is supposed to be, but I think that if we really lived our lives that way then we'd all go crazy. You need time, you need, I don't know, you need illusions. Stan never took a risk in his life, never wasted time, never minced words. He asked me to marry him that night. But I don't think he was ever not scared again, right until the very end.'

She stood up then, but Beatrice said, 'Myra, wait.' Myra stood there, waiting, and Beatrice could see that there were tears in her eyes. 'Myra,' Beatrice said, 'honey, what's the matter?' 'Oh, it ain't nothing, Beatrice. It's, you know, it's only been a few months, you know. That's all.' 'Oh, Myra.' Beatrice said quietly. Next to her, Henry started to shift uncomfortably, still a man, even now, afraid of tears, especially a woman's tears. Beatrice started to say something but Myra, staring off into space, spoke before him. 'We spent our whole lives together. Our whole lives. We didn't even like each other most of the time but, you know, we made do, we did okay for each other, and for Lucy. She didn't turn out too bad.' 'She's a good kid. We both got good kids,' Henry said, and Myra laughed and said, 'You know, sometimes I wonder. I mean, a girl her age, no husband, no boyfriend even, and she knows her way around under the hood of a car better than Stan did. Sometimes I wonder if she's, you know, like your John. But,' she said suddenly, loudly, 'but I don't know, and I don't know about Stan either.' 'Don't know about what, Myra?' Beatrice said. 'Nothing,' Myra said, 'I don't know nothing.' She looked then at Beatrice, at Henry, at them together. She said, 'You spend your whole life with another person, and if you're lucky then the one thing you realize is that you never really know what makes them tick, what's going on in their head. You never really know them.' Beatrice caught her breath at Myra's words and at the bitterness in her voice, and she turned suddenly to Henry. He looked back at her, a puzzled expression on his face that melted slowly into a smile when he saw her own smile. 'What?' he said, and Beatrice just said, 'What a relief, that's all. What a relief.' There was a long silence between them and then Beatrice heard Myra clear her throat. 'I, um, I'm gonna go back to my trailer now. You're gonna have to get up early if you want to see anything.' She started toward the door then, a woman neither short nor tall, from the back neither young nor old, nor fat nor skinny, not one thing, not another. She seemed to Beatrice compact and magnificent, a woman whose worth would never quite be realized until she, like Stan, was gone. 'Wait, Myra,' she called, reluctant to let her go. Myra stopped at the door. 'Um, how, I mean, um, what did you say?' Myra looked confused. She yawned, put her hand on the doorknob. 'To who?' 'To Stan.' 'Oh,' Myra said. She smiled. 'I'm a lot of things,' she said, 'but I'm nobody's fool. I said no.'

In her bedroom Beatrice was old and tired again, dry-skinned, wrinkled, not really drunk but thick-headed. Her stomach lagged a pace behind her as she walked between the bed and the bathroom. Some habits hadn't changed: she changed in the privacy of the bathroom, and then Henry did, but as they walked past each other he put his hand out and touched her lightly on the stomach. 'Ouch,' she said, stopping and placing

269

her hand over his. 'I think you were right.' 'About what?' 'About the whiskey,' Beatrice said, and Henry's face grew concerned. 'Are you okay?' 'I'm fine,' Beatrice said, 'just, I don't know, pre-hangovery, that's all.' 'Well, go get in bed, and I'll be there in a minute. You want anything?' Beatrice smiled. 'Warm milk?' she said, and Henry laughed. 'Oh, honey, you are old. We're both old. Warm milk would be wonderful right now.' She was alone for a few minutes then. She lay down and Henry changed, and then he shuffled off in his bare feet toward the kitchen. He minced when he walked, said 'ow' each time he put a foot down on the cold floor, and Beatrice heard him depart like a train in a trail of decreasing noise. 'Ow, ow, ow, ow, ow, ow, ow, ow, ow, ow,' and then he was gone, and the house fell under the eerie spell of country quiet. In the silence even the thoughts in her head seemed loud. Myra's story had left her strangely sad, subdued, and she wondered at that until she realized that it had been a long time since she'd been able to feel merely sad, to be moved by a plight other than her own. The sadness she felt was small, simple, isolated, one emotion floating in a sea of other emotions, of, she had to admit, even though it embarrassed her for some reason, of happiness. She was happy. Wasn't that something? Her story had a happy ending. But that thought stopped her. With each fresh memory she unearthed she found it more and more difficult to believe that the person she was now was the same person she'd been so long ago. That other woman, that Bea, felt like a distant relative, a cousin, a young niece who had occasionally shared stories with this Beatrice. No, she thought, this wasn't a happy ending to that story: it was a fresh start to another. The story would be shorter this time, there was no way around that, but it would be different too. It had started differently and it would progress differently, and eventually, sooner or later, well, sooner probably, it would end differently. But not yet. Not tonight.

Then Henry was back, his 'ows' preceding his arrival, a tray in his hands, steaming cups on the tray, a little bit of spilled milk sluicing back and forth like the tide. 'Are you going to drink that,' Beatrice said as Henry settled in beside her, 'or are you just going to warm your hands?' 'Yes,' Henry said, 'and

270

yes.' Then they were in bed together, and after a moment they each made the long journey toward the bed's center, until they were shoulder to shoulder and hip to hip. Beatrice felt Henry's cold feet next to hers, and she rubbed at them. 'Maybe you should sleep in socks,' she said, and Henry said, 'I'm old enough to drink warm milk, but I'm not old enough to sleep in socks.' 'Suit yourself,' Beatrice said, amazed at the simplicity of even this little exchange. She drank some of the milk. 'Mmmm,' she said, 'is that cinnamon?' 'Yeah,' Henry said. 'It's nice,' Beatrice said, and Henry said, 'Yeah,' again, and then he said, 'My mother used to do it for me sometimes, when I was sick. When I was a kid, I mean.' 'Oh,' Beatrice said, and she rubbed Henry's thigh through the blanket. After a moment she stopped, but she let her hand rest on Henry's leg, and then he put a hand on top of hers. 'Oh, Henry,' Beatrice said quietly. 'What?' 'Oh, nothing. I feel silly, that's all.' 'What? Why?' 'I don't know. I feel like a kid again, like a little girl, a teenager.' 'Well, that's good, isn't it?' 'Yeah, that's good,' she said, though it wasn't really. 'Well, then, don't feel silly.' 'Yeah, sure,' Beatrice said, but she still felt silly. She finished her milk, put her cup on the bedside table. Henry drank his cup in a long swallow, then put it on his table. Then they were back in the center of the bed again, Beatrice's hand found its place on Henry's thigh and Henry's hand found its place on Beatrice's hand. They sat without speaking until Beatrice lifted Henry's hand and kissed the back of it. Long slightly brittle gray hairs tickled her lips. When she'd replaced their hands on his leg Henry said, 'That was nice.' 'Yeah,' Beatrice said. He took his hand from hers and ran it along her forearm slowly, and then he lifted her hand to his mouth and kissed it. His lips were warm and wet from the milk, but Beatrice knew that they would be cold and dry otherwise. When he brought their hands down he put them on her leg. All the layers of cotton between his hand and her thigh couldn't keep it, her thigh, from trembling. 'Are you cold?' Henry said. 'Oh, no,' Beatrice said. 'No, I'm not cold. Your feet are, though,' she said, pushing at them with her own. In a moment their ankles were crossed over each other. 'How do you feel?' Henry said. 'Good enough,' Beatrice said, and she felt Henry start a little and say, 'You mean—' and she stopped him quickly. 'No,' she said, and then, flustered, she said, 'I mean yes. I mean, I don't mean no. I mean, I just feel good enough. As good as can be expected, I mean. Better than can be expected. I feel good. I feel really good even. Good enough, even.' Henry was silent for a moment. Then: 'You mean. . . .' He let his voice go, and when it was gone Beatrice said, 'Yes.'

He used a finger to turn her face toward his: the finger was on her chin, and even her chin could tell that it was an old finger, could feel the wizened skin and the pointed calcified nail. Then she was facing him and he her, and they examined each other with the unblinking not-quite-impartial gazes of mirrors. Here is Beatrice's husband as she saw him for the last time: his head was egg-shaped, the thin side down, the fat side up, the dome of it bald save for the thin and thinning white fringe that wreathed it like a laurel crown, the naked skin a white glazed in pink, the pink dotted with brown spots and the spots, if Beatrice squinted, dotted within themselves with flecks of white. There were all the old, usual features, the mouth, the nose, the eyes, though they'd faded with the years, lost some of their color and their shape. The mouth was a simple oval now, slightly pierced in the center by the part of Henry's lips, and the eyes paralleled its shape; mouth and eyes were nestled in wrinkles, the mouth with a faint white film at its edges from the milk and the eyes slightly rheumy with mucus. The nose, as noses on old men do, seemed to have grown larger, and jutted out of Henry's receding face. The bone that formed its bridge was pronounced and sharp, and the nostrils exuded a generous mop head of bristles. The skin over his cheekbones was flat, though not taut, and the skin hung off the bone like curtains and gathered in loose jowly folds at the bottoms of his cheeks, and a fold of skin stretched from his chin to his throat like a cockscomb. Beatrice looked at the different parts of Henry's face for so long that they became discrete entities in her eyes, not the parts of a single face, but merely a mouth, a nose, an eye, another eye, a fluted veined translucent ear. She saw age in each of these details but not

272

just age. She saw something more: she saw ears, eyes, nose, mouth, she saw his face, in each of its ages, as it had been and as it was now; she saw history. She saw time.

She reached a hand out then and put it on the back of his head, felt the scar that she'd felt only an hour ago. In the blackest of those black years it had burned like a white beacon, the one part of him she could never bring herself to loathe. Now, under her fingers, it was new to her yet again, that scar, the miracle of Henry's life. It was always new to her and Beatrice wanted everything she experienced from then until the day she died to be as new and as shocking as her experience of that scar. She wanted everything to be as if for the first time: every cup of coffee, every car ride, every kiss should surprise her. She wanted to be surprised when Henry took his clothes off and when she took her clothes off, she wanted to be shocked when their bodies finally folded into each other. You know a few things when you walk into a room filled with strangers. You know that they probably won't throw something at you, a knife, a book, a drink, you know that they won't switch languages when they talk to you or to each other, you know that they probably won't flee. But for exactly the same reason you know that they won't grab you, embrace you, tell you that they love you, and if there is any comfort at all to be found in strangers, it's in the fact that they're strangers, unknown to you and you unknown to them. This man, her husband, this man whose head she was pulling slowly toward hers, this man had been that stranger, that roomful of strangers, and he was still a stranger. Freed, finally, of the burden of knowing him, of finishing him like a book or a journey is finished, she loved him, and she made love to him.

What is sex but a catalogue of physical acts that have as their only similarity the contact—anticipated, consummated, separated, and joined together again—of one body with another? It is nothing more. Everything else, everything important, is inevitable but not inherent, is brought to it as narrative is brought to language. Do you want that catalogue? Which parts of which body came into contact with which parts of the other body, and when, and for how long? Where was there

273

comfort and where pain, what actions produced gasps and what produced sighs, what were tried once and abandoned, what repeated over and over again? I break off from Beatrice now, finally. I could imagine her behavior, could invent it as I have invented so many other things—indeed, I have imagined it, I couldn't stop myself—but I won't write them down. Feel free to put their bodies under the blanket, or on top of it, or a few feet up in the air if you want; I will say only this: the body is the last frontier. The world has been discovered, and there is nothing left to uncover but ourselves. In the past few days they had shared things which one had thought of and the other had not. 'Brush your teeth with warm water,' Henry had told Beatrice, when she'd told him how brushing her teeth hurt her every morning and evening. 'Clip your toenails after a long bath,' Beatrice had told Henry when she saw him struggling with the hardened yellow caps of his toes. 'The hot water softens them up.' Sex was just one more thing for them to share. When I return to them they are clothed again and sleeping. They are old, and beneath the blankets. Henry's left foot sticks out into the cool room; when he wakes up it will hurt, but it will be the only part of him that hurts. Still, he will not feel young again. He will feel like he has rejoined the earth.

ξ

Beatrice was wet with sweat when Henry woke up. She moved in her sleep, slowly, jerkily, moaning occasionally; it was this moaning which had awakened him. He looked at her for a moment, wondering if she were having a bad dream or if she was in pain, but his eyes and Beatrice's skin told him nothing. Gently, he put a hand on her shoulder; his hand was cold but Beatrice's shoulder was hot, even through her nightgown. Henry shook. It didn't take much, and then Beatrice was awake. 'Ow!' she said, a long diphthong of sound. 'I'm sorry,' Henry whispered. Beatrice was quiet, her eyes still closed, and then she said, 'Not you. My head.' Henry leaned forward and kissed her forehead; it was wet, hot, tasted, as it had tasted during the night, of salt. Eyes still closed, Beatrice smiled, and

274

then she said, 'Ow' again, and frowned. 'What can I get you?' Henry said. Beatrice opened her eyes, looked into Henry's. She sighed. 'Ibuprofen. Coffee. Another kiss.' Henry gave her the kiss first, then the ibuprofen and a glass of water from the bathroom. He was about to go to the kitchen and make coffee when Beatrice called him back. He limped to her. 'Yes?' he said. Beatrice smiled weakly. 'Put socks on, okay?' Henry put socks on.

The kitchen was empty, the coffee came quickly, and toast as well, butter and jelly on the side if she wanted it. When he came back he placed the bed-tray over Beatrice's lap and then he climbed in bed beside her. 'I don't think I can go out today,' Beatrice said, reluctantly, very quietly. 'That's okay,' Henry said, 'that's fine, that's all right. We'll go another day.' 'No,' Beatrice said. She said, 'You go. We can try to go together sometime, but you go today, alone. Take your camera.' 'Bea—' 'Henry,' Beatrice said firmly. 'There aren't going to be any left before too much longer, and, I don't know, and . . . ' When her voice trailed off—Henry resisted thinking that it had died—he took her hand. 'Do you want me to call the doctor?' 'No!' She lowered her voice. 'No.'

Then he was dressed to leave, and Myra was there to watch Beatrice. His camera was a weighty pendant hanging from his neck, his old hunting cap a red beacon on top of his head. 'Go,' Beatrice said when he lingered, 'before you catch cold, go.' Then he was moving across the back yard: it had snowed several times that winter, just a bit each time, and he felt his boots push through layers of crust and soft snow with each step. He worried that his hands were going to hurt but so far they felt fine, warm in sheepskin gloves Beatrice had bought for him; only his foot hurt, his left foot. Then he worried about the stream, but he'd crossed its frozen snow-covered surface before he realized it; the only sign that it existed was a slight dip in the land and a thinning of the trees. Then there was the mountain. 'Oh God,' he said aloud, remembering the torture of it in the summer. 'Oh shit.' But the trail was visible through the trees and as he headed toward it he saw animal tracks going in the same direction, birds, squirrels, raccoons, something bigger, foxes or dogs maybe, and deer. And men: the hunters had been this close to the house. He remembered the sound of their shots, and he remembered the sound of their bullets rattling through the branches, and he wondered how much land he would have to enclose in a fence to protect his family, how high the fence would have to be, how thick.

He walked slowly, his body warm in his clothes, his eyes keen for any signs of movement. The only things he saw were birds, a small flock of cardinals flitting around, the brilliant red of the males and the rose-tinted brown of the females. That was it, he thought, the muted red of the females, that was the color the deer would be. He heard the woodpecker before he saw it, black-bodied, red-headed, then gone. He stopped when he thought he was getting too warm, leaned against a wide trunk and played with his camera. 'Oh no,' he said aloud, and a flock of good-sized brown birds, grouse maybe, or quail, took to the air behind him. He opened the back of the camera: it was empty. He'd forgotten film. He looked back, looked for his house—his house, Beatrice's house, the stilled violence of their fusion—and he saw it, or pieces of it, through the vertical bars of leafless trees. It was too far to turn back. He pulled the camera off his neck, straining his arms against his coat's pull as he stretched the neckband around his cap, and he hung it from a knob on the trunk he'd been leaning against, and then he started up again. It seemed too soon when he reached the top, the end of the trees, the narrow stone stairway, the plateau beyond it. He could remember every step of his walk up, and that didn't gel with his memory of his last ascent. It troubled him for some reason, and he wanted something to tell him why this climb had been so much easier than the last. He poised on the plateau's threshold, thinking, until it occurred to him that the first time you do something is always the hardest, the most amazing and the most memorable, and every subsequent time is easier but also a bit anticlimactic. And then he thought, It was probably just the sex, and he stepped out onto the plateau.

From the plateau there was the view of the world that had convinced him to move here. This was the winter version; if anything it was even more conventionally pastoral than in summer, with the snow ameliorating or obliterating many of the signs of human encroachment. Roads weren't asphalt slurs on the ground, but rutted trails. Fields weren't cultivated and rigidly ordered, but smooth and white as a powdered cheek, broken only occasionally by sheared stubble. Houses lost their hard shapes under snow blankets, and threads of smoke from chimneys indicated the warmth inside. For a long time the smoke seemed to Henry to be the only thing moving. He saw no cars on the road, no birds in the air, no evidence besides the strewn cigarette butts and spent shell casings of the hunters who'd obviously spent some time here. The casings were red and yellow and green, and the way they were partially submerged in the snow made Henry remember the nights of exploding gunshots, and he imagined the residual heat in the casing's metal caps melting them into the snow. He realized then that these were shotgun casings: someone had been hunting birds up here, not just deer, and as he remembered the sound of pellets falling through the trees behind his house he thought again that he would build a fence to protect Beatrice and himself, and Myra. He would build a high whitewashed stone wall inside which they would live their last days in safety. Then a moving piece of red caught his eye and he turned quickly. But it was just a car, cutting noiselessly through the distance. He thought that it was a good thing he hadn't brought his gun, else he'd probably have fired at the car. He heard the shot before he felt it hit. It sounded like a gunshot but felt like a baseball bat crashing into the back of his head. Even as he fell he knew: 'The fucking cap!' he shouted. 'You shot my fucking cap!'

10

A long time later he opened his eyes. There was only sky above him, clear cold blue sky. He thought about getting up but he was warm and comfortable on his back—only his foot still bothered him, and only a little. He thought, Why bother? He turned his head: blood-stained snow was all he saw. No, he thought. Snow-stained blood. He thought of Beatrice. 'You dumb woman,' he growled. 'It was your idea that I wear the cap.'

9

Footsteps. His killer bent over him, drab, dressed in brown, distraught. 'Jesus, buddy,' he said. 'Oh, Jesus. I mean, *Jesus Christ*.' He wrung his hands. 'Why the fuck did you wear *red*?' The hunter was young and Henry pitied him: he would live with this for a long time. 'My wife,' Henry laughed. 'You know how it is.' His voice hardened. He couldn't move his outstretched arms so he grabbed the hunter with his eyes. 'You must get my wife!'

8

This time he thought he was blind but it was only his eyes, still closed. He left them closed. He felt it pulling him down. It pulled him down. He let it pull him down. When Beatrice came, she would pull him up.

7

O her crashing footsteps and O her gasps for breath. O her
screams and her wails, O for the wretched figure for whom he
opened his eyes. Her wild mane O, and O for the death mask
that was her face. O for the clothes which hid her from him
like so much excess skin, O Beatrice, old age Beatrice, age old
Beatrice, my Beatrice, O.

6

He said, 'You should've stayed in bed.' She crashed to her knees beside him. '*You* should've stayed in bed!' It hurt to turn his head. 'Would you?' he said. 'Could you?' he said. 'Behind me.' In her hands his head felt painless, weightless; if she'd let go it would have floated away, but she set it down gently in the lap of her dress and craned her head over his. Her water— tears, sweat, saliva—dripped onto his face. He closed his eyes and felt her rain.

5

Her voice brought him back. 'He's waiting for the paramedics. He'll bring them here.' Henry opened his eyes. 'That,' he said, 'is an unnecessary detail.' He laughed. 'He shot me like I was a red deer,' he said. 'Like *I* was a red deer.' Beatrice's face was upside down. Slowly, it righted itself in his eyes. 'Beatrice,' he said then, and closed his eyes. He had waited a long time to say these words: 'I'm dead.'

4

It pulled him down; he felt her pull him back up. Tired, irritated, he opened his eyes. 'Beatrice,' he said, 'let me go.' She shook her head. 'Henry,' she said. 'Oh, Henry.' 'You're sick,' he said. 'Go home.' He smiled. 'You'll catch your death of cold.' 'I won't leave you,' Beatrice said. 'Beatrice,' he said, 'it's better this way.' 'Better?' It seemed she knew to lean close. 'We'd've just fucked it up again,' Henry said. 'This way,' he said, 'we're saved.' And then he said, 'Count for me.' He said, 'Count down.' 'Count?' Beatrice said. 'Down,' Henry said. 'Count down.'

3

Ten, Henry heard her call out, and felt her voice roll over the land. *Nine*, she said, and the trees shook. *Eight*, she said, and the ground rumbled. *Seven*, she said, and Henry said, 'Yes,' and closed his eyes. *Six*, she sobbed, *five, four, three*. Her words were a hurricane, blowing his life across the world. *Two*. His limbs had been straight but now his body curled into a blood ball between her splayed legs. *One*, she whispered, and Henry's eyes snapped open.

2

Now the deer. From all directions, the deer. Vermilion, crimson, scarlet: the red deer. Leaping, bounding, hurtling through the air, the red deer, Henry's blood on the ground and in the sky and in Beatrice's eyes the red deer.

1

And now it stops. Henry's words came but his lips didn't move: now, at last, it stops. The canopy of flying bodies crashed to the ground around them. Hooves shredded the snow but none touched them. Henry's eyes were open but they didn't see Beatrice. His last words were his last breaths: oh Beatrice, oh Beatrice, he breathed. There's God.

Also available in Vintage

Dale Peck

FUCKING MARTIN

'In his daring debut novel, Dale Peck has written an unflinchingly honest, dark coming-of-age story about a young gay hustler who goes from Kansas to New York and back again to nurse his dying lover...By breaking the story line and blurring the identity of his characters and the hard boundaries between the stories, Dale Peck succeeds in exploring the experience of being gay with remarkable complexity and depth of feeling'

Catherine Texier,
New York Times Book Review

'*Fucking Martin* is a rare first novel, with a rare title to match. Dale Peck's most wounding tale is written in response to a pained and violent childhood. This is fiction as exploration, therapy, exorcism. And fiction is most definitely the word: not autobiography dressed up and thrown down on the page, but a life's raw material rigorously and thrillingly transformed'

Laurence O'Toole, *New Statesman*

'Peck writes with passionate intensity...a fascinating first novel'
Times Literary Supplement

VINTAGE

Also available in Vintage

Harold Brodkey

PROFANE FRIENDSHIP

Growing up in Venice of the 1930s, Niles O'Hara, the son of an expatriate writer, befriends a Venetian boy, Giangia-como Gallieni. After the war Niles returns, only to become involved with his childhood friend, who is now an adoles-cent with a wartime history of sexual trespass. Searching, comic, romantic and ironic, *Profane Friendship* is a remark-able study of a strange, provocative, powerful relationship conducted in the triumphant beautiful setting of the world's most alluring city.

'Brodkey's prose is unlike any other writer's. It is intensely personal...and shockingly obsessive'
James Wood, *Guardian*

'*Profane Friendship* resolves itself into something quite simple in the mind. What it imprints on the memory is not just the extraordinary sentences, but the impression of one bright idea, like a single movement'
Philip Hensher, *Guardian*

'I was knocked sideways by the breathtaking ambition of the novel and the range of Brodkey's emotional and cultural intelligence'
Michael Ratcliffe, *Observer*

VINTAGE

Jamaica Kincaid

THE AUTOBIOGRAPHY OF MY MOTHER

The Autobiography of My Mother is narrated by a seventy-year-old West Indian woman looking back on her life and evoking the relationships that have given it meaning. Her themes are sex, human relations, and the interplay of power and powerlessness, and how easy it is to fall from one into the other. Her story, which begins at the height of imperialism and ends in the twilight of colonialism, abounds in the vivid characters, strong situations, and pyrotechnic writing that make Jamaica Kincaid one of our most compelling novelists.

'Writing in precise, lyrical prose that uses the repetition of images and words to build a musical rhythm, Jamaica Kincaid conjures up the world in Dominica in all its beauty and casual cruelty, a world in which the magical coexists with the mundane, a world in which the ghosts of colonialism still haunt the relationships between men and women. In doing so she has written a powerful and disturbing book'
New York Times

'The most beautiful prose we are likely to find in contemporary fiction...brilliant'
New York Times Book Review

VINTAGE

Also available in Vintage

Alan Isler

THE PRINCE OF WEST END AVENUE

In the Emma Lazarus retirement home in uptown Manhattan, the Jewish inmates embark on a chaotic, bitchy production of *Hamlet*.

'Hilariously funny...a wonderful achievement. Not since Malamud have comedy and tragedy, pathos and romance come together so effortlessly'
Gabriel Josipovici, *Jewish Quarterly*

'Masterly, imaginative and provocatively disturbing in its effortless transitions between the comic and the tragic'
Geoffrey Elborn, *Guardian*

'An exceptionally and enviably good first read'
Rachel Cusk, *The Times*

'Poignant and delightfully clever'
Observer

'A masterpiece'
Hugo Barnacle, *Independent*

VINTAGE

Also available in Vintage

Nicholson Baker

THE FERMATA

Arno Strine, a modest temporary typist, has perfected the knack of stopping time in its tracks and taking women's clothes off. He is hard at work on his autobiography, *The Fermata*, which proves in the telling to be a provocative, very funny and altogether morally confused piece of work.

'The book is bursting with sex and beauty, wound together profoundly and pornographically. It is bountifully Rabelaisian and intensely refined...I have never read anything quite like it...*The Fermata* should be celebrated'
Mary Gaitskill

'Lots of nakedness, quite a few surprises...His novels have the brazen, daring timidity of love letters you know you'll never post'
Sunday Times

'Witty, dry and thought-provoking, a great addition to Baker's unique observatory of contemporary life'
Vogue

'The funniest book about sex ever written'
Kate Saunders, *Literary Review*

VINTAGE

Also available in Vintage

John Cheever

THE STORIES OF
JOHN CHEEVER

These outstanding stories from the American award-winning novelist show the power and range of one of the finest short story writers of the century.

'He lies, in American writing, somewhere between Scott Fitzgerald and John Updike...these are stories of love and squalor, set in a world in which momentary glimpses of brightness – sea, clouds, light, the East River, a wife in a torn slip at the dressing table – contend with time, social change, and the chaos of history'
Malcolm Bradbury, *New Statesman*

'One of the finest storytellers writing in English today'
The Times

'The Cheever corpus is magical – a mood, a vision, a tingle, all quite unexplainably achieved'
Newsweek

VINTAGE

Also available in Vintage

Philip Roth

SABBATH'S THEATER

'Sabbath explodes like some mad genie out of his
bottle…[*Sabbath's Theater*] has more firestorming prose
than any other novel I have read this year'
Anthony Quinn, *Observer*

'A work of near-heroic vitality and cunning'
Justin Cartwright, *Sunday Telegraph*

'Soaring above all other novels I read this year…A postwar
American masterpiece'
James Walton, Books of the Year,
Daily Telegraph

'I finished *Sabbath's Theater* with my heart and blood
pumping and thumping, the pulse racing to the last savage
lines, the pay-off'
Linda Grant, *Literary Review*

'In time this will be seen as Roth's best novel so far'
James Wood, *Guardian*

V

VINTAGE

A SELECTED LIST OF CONTEMPORARY AMERICAN FICTION
AVAILABLE IN VINTAGE

☐ THE FERMATA	Nicholson Baker	£5.99
☐ THE RUNAWAY SOUL	Harold Brodkey	£7.99
☐ PROFANE FRIENDSHIP	Harold Brodkey	£6.99
☐ THE STORIES OF JOHN CHEEVER	John Cheever	£9.99
☐ FALCONER	John Cheever	£5.99
☐ MAO II	Don DeLillo	£6.99
☐ RATNER'S STAR	Don DeLillo	£6.99
☐ DEMOCRACY	Joan Didion	£5.99
☐ ARC D'X	Steve Erickson	£5.99
☐ CATCH-22	Joseph Heller	£6.99
☐ SOMETHING HAPPENED	Joseph Heller	£5.99
☐ THE PRINCE OF WEST END AVENUE	Alan Isler	£5.99
☐ KRAVEN IMAGES	Alan Isler	£5.99
☐ THE AUTOBIOGRAPHY OF MY MOTHER	Jamaica Kincaid	£8.99
☐ FUCKING MARTIN	Dale Peck	£5.99
☐ GRAVITY'S RAINBOW	Thomas Pynchon	£6.99
☐ THE CRYING OF LOT 49	Thomas Pynchon	£5.99
☐ PORTNOY'S COMPLAINT	Philip Roth	£5.99
☐ SABBATH'S THEATER	Philip Roth	£6.99
☐ CIVILWARLAND IN BAD DECLINE	George Saunders	£5.99
☐ THE VOLCANO LOVER	Susan Sontag	£5.99
☐ SLAUGHTERHOUSE 5	Kurt Vonnegut	£5.99

- All Vintage books are available through mail order or from your local bookshop.
- Please send cheque/eurocheque/postal order (sterling only), Access, Visa or Mastercard:

☐☐☐☐☐☐☐☐☐☐☐☐☐☐☐☐

Expiry Date:_____Signature:_____

Please allow 75 pence per book for post and packing U.K.
Overseas customers please allow £1.00 per copy for post and packing.

ALL ORDERS TO:

Vintage Books, Book Service by Post, P.O.Box 29, Douglas, Isle of Man, IM99 1BQ.
Tel: 01624 675137 • Fax: 01624 670923

NAME:_____

ADDRESS:_____
_____
_____

Please allow 28 days for delivery. Please tick box if you do not
wish to receive any additional information   ☐

Prices and availability subject to change without notice.